the Crumrin

VOLUME ONE

Chronicles

The Charmed & the Cursed

AN ONI PRESS PUBLICATION

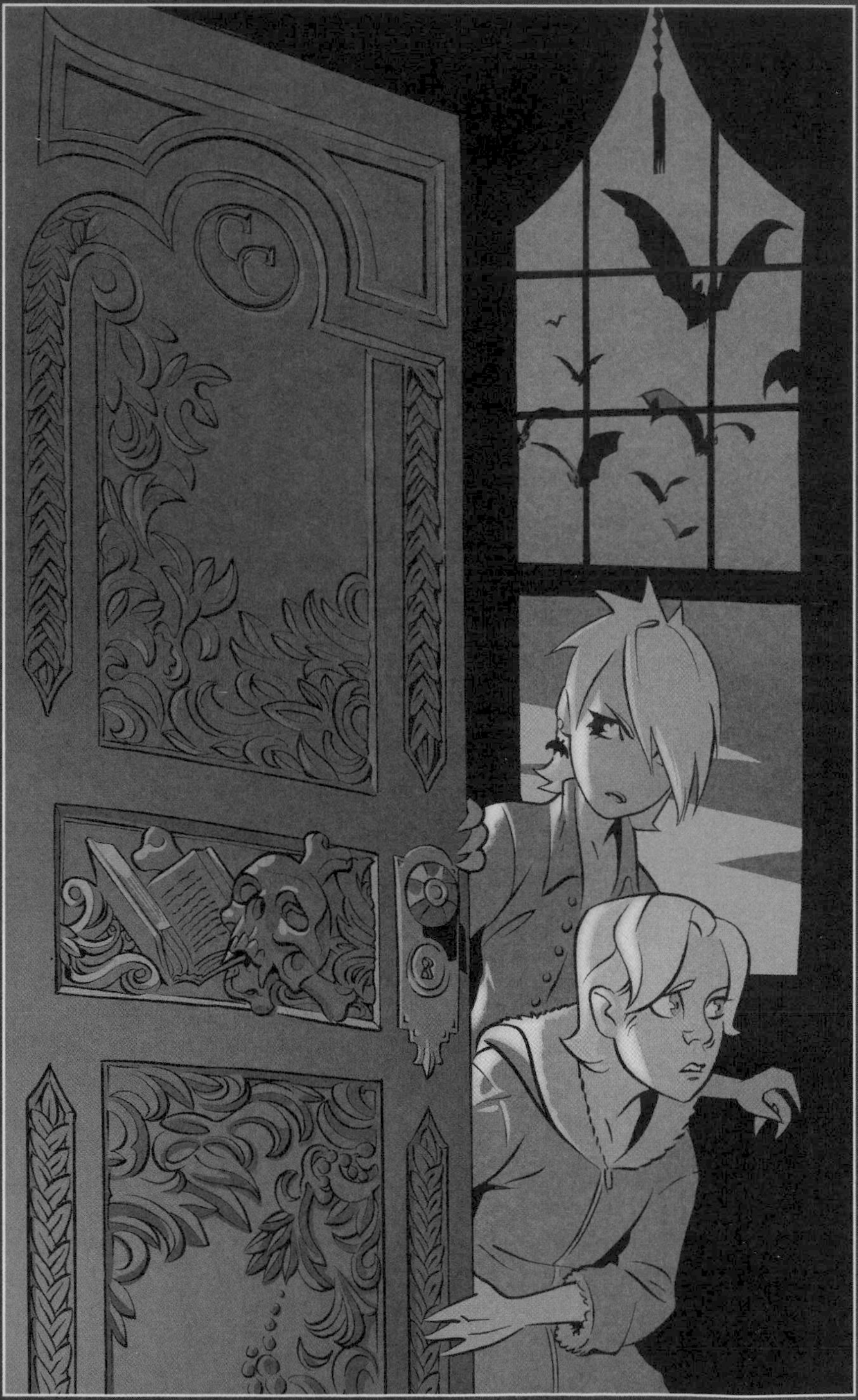

the Crumrin

VOLUME ONE

Chronicles

The Charmed & the Cursed

Written & Illustrated by

— ❖ TED NAIFEH ❖ —

Colored by

WARREN WUCINICH

Original Series edited by
JILL BEATON

Collection edited by
SHAWNA GORE

Original Series Design by
KEITH WOOD & ANGIE KNOWLES

Logo & Design by
SONJA SYNAK

·✧· ALCHEMY, MAGIC & LOVE ·✧·

> "The meeting of two personalities is like the
> contact of two chemical substances: if there
> is any reaction, both are transformed."
>
> —*Carl Gustav Jung*

BEFORE WE HAD SCIENCE, THERE WAS ALCHEMY. THE GOAL OF ALCHEMY WAS TRANSFORMATION —usually of metals, but sometimes of people. Ancient alchemists believed that by combining the right ingredients and performing the right rituals, you could purify and perfect one thing into a different, better thing. Lead could be purified into gold, for instance. And people could be perfected, body and soul, into immortality.

That idea of transformation, of reaching perfection, has been with humans a very long time. In a way, it's at the heart of what we think of as magic. Someone ordinary can be transformed into someone special with a spell or a talisman. The common, the everyday, can be elevated to something wondrous with the right words or the right ingredients. Eye of newt and toe of frog. Abracadabra! It's a beguiling thought. Who doesn't want a little extra charm? A little glamour? But remember, that extra shine only transforms you from a window into a mirror no one can see through. Magic always comes at a cost.

For alchemists, the philosopher's stone represented that transformative ideal. It could be used to change lesser metals into gold and produce the elixir of eternal life, if only they could figure out the right recipe. The wrong recipe—and they were all wrong recipes— could kill, and sometimes did. The passion for transformation took its toll.

In stories, magic often transforms with sacrifices—long hair, an eye, a voice, a life. If you are lucky, the last of the three wishes is the one you use to undo the damage caused by the first two. Maybe you made the wrong sacrifice once. But perhaps it's not too late to take the hand that's offered and walk into that twilight kingdom forever, saving three lives instead of one. And perhaps it's not too late to leave the magic behind and go home.

Eventually, alchemy developed into the modern science we know as chemistry. But it traveled a twisted path to get there. In Renaissance Europe, alchemy became conflated with magic and the occult, and it's easy to see why. Alchemists produced powerful acids, discovered zinc, and figured out how to make porcelain. They wrote in arcane symbols and used terms freighted with power and mystery. They called potassium nitrate the "cold dragon," while "burning spirit of Saturn" is known today as acetone—nail polish remover.

Many alchemists were charlatans who used sleight of hand to "create" gold and were imprisoned as frauds. Some accidentally poisoned themselves or their clients with alchemical potions intended to cure disease. Some were executed for practicing the black arts. Like magic in fantasy stories, alchemy could backfire against those who practiced it. Death is a transformation, too. Sometimes you don't get the transformation you intended.

Love is a form of alchemy, capable of transforming. When you love someone, they are transformed in your eyes. They become special to you. You are also transformed—you want to help your loved one, you want to see them safe and happy. You no longer put yourself first. Love transforms by the sacrifice of self-interest.

Martin Luther King Jr. said, "Love is the only force capable of transforming an enemy into a friend." This force only works if you transform yourself first and become capable of loving your enemy.

Love often demands the sacrifice of aspects of ourselves. Sometimes, love drives us to sacrifice everything. Like alchemy, like magic, you can't always predict the result of transformative love. Sometimes you get gold. Sometimes you get poison. But you won't know unless you make that sacrifice and transform into the purest version of yourself.

I tell my son that there are three ways to make a family:

By blood.
By marriage.
And by love.

Love has the power to transform strangers into family. It can bind you to others in ways you can't foresee. The energy of that transformation can create whole new worlds.

If that's not alchemy—if that's not magic—I'm not sure what is.

Kelly Crumrin usually writes about health, medicine, and chronic conditions. She lives in Northern California with her son, her partner, and cats Halloween Kitty and Lobby. She really likes trees.

In 2002, her partner at the time named a comic-book character after her. They are still best friends.

Published by Oni-Lion Forge Publishing Group, LLC

president & publisher, James Lucas Jones

editor in chief, Sarah Gaydos

e.v.p. of creative & business development, Charlie Chu

director of operations, Brad Rooks

special projects manager, Amber O'Neill

director of marketing & sales, Margot Wood

sales & marketing manager, Devin Funches

marketing manager, Katie Sainz

publicist, Tara Lehmann

director of design & production, Troy Look

senior graphic designer, Kate Z. Stone

graphic designer, Sonja Synak

graphic designer, Hilary Thompson

graphic designer, Sarah Rockwell

digital prepress lead, Angie Knowles

digital prepress technician, Vincent Kukua

senior editor, Jasmine Amiri

senior editor, Shawna Gore

senior editor, Amanda Meadows

senior editor, licensing, Robert Meyers

editor, Grace Scheipeter

editor, Desiree Rodriguez

editor, Zack Soto

editorial coordinator, Chris Cerasi

vice president of games, Steve Ellis

game developer, Ben Eisner

executive assistant, Michelle Nguyen

logistics coordinator, Jung Lee

publisher emeritus, Joe Nozemack

onipress.com lionforge.com
tednaifeh.com /tednaifeh

First Edition: July 2021

ISBN 978-1-62010-930-4
eISBN 978-1-62010-943-4

1 3 5 7 9 10 8 6 4 2

Library of Congress Control Number: 2020947312

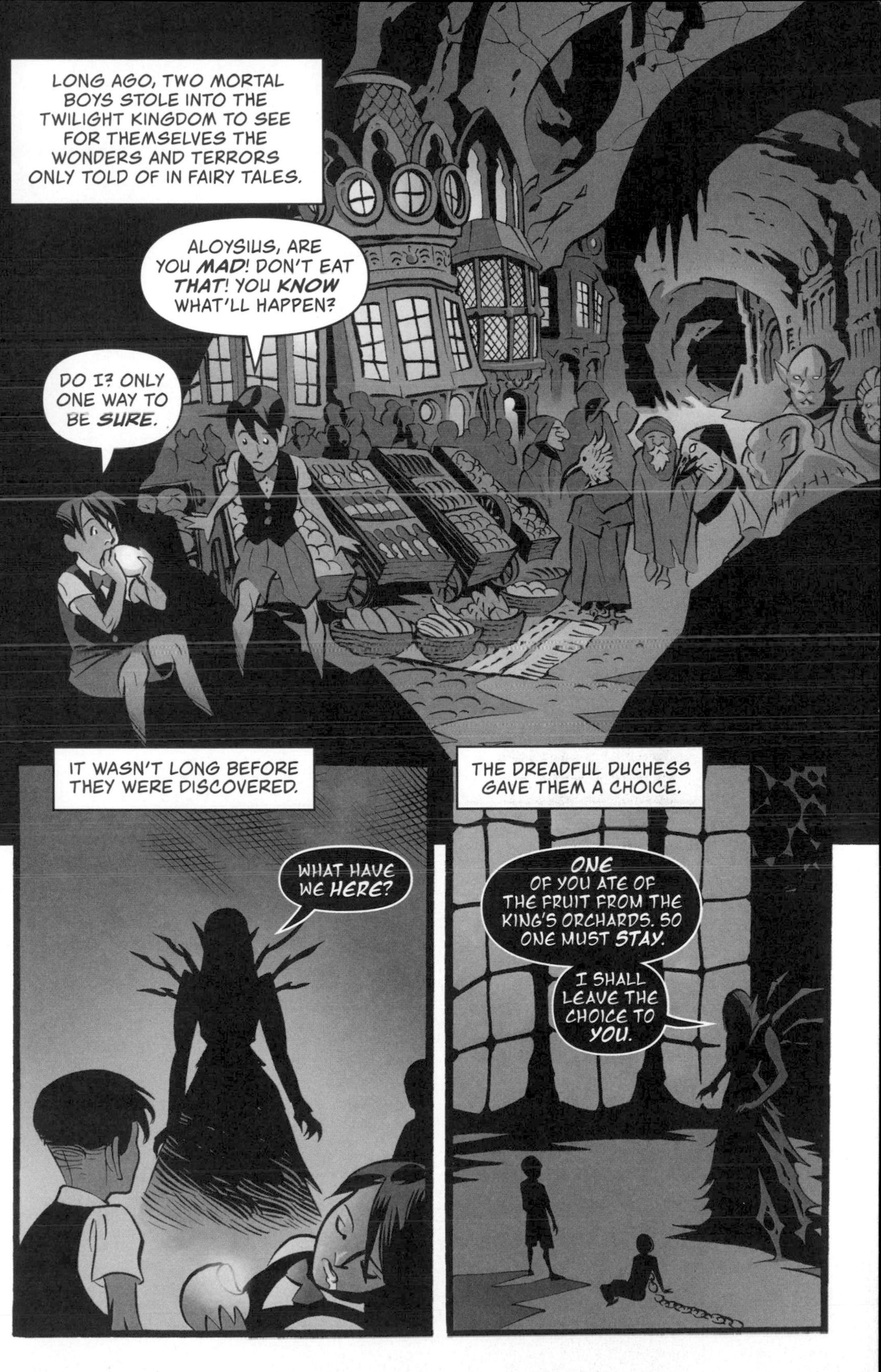
LONG AGO, TWO MORTAL BOYS STOLE INTO THE TWILIGHT KINGDOM TO SEE FOR THEMSELVES THE WONDERS AND TERRORS ONLY TOLD OF IN FAIRY TALES.
ALOYSIUS, ARE YOU MAD! DON'T EAT THAT! YOU KNOW WHAT'LL HAPPEN?
DO I? ONLY ONE WAY TO BE SURE.
IT WASN'T LONG BEFORE THEY WERE DISCOVERED.
WHAT HAVE WE HERE?
THE DREADFUL DUCHESS GAVE THEM A CHOICE.
ONE OF YOU ATE OF THE FRUIT FROM THE KING'S ORCHARDS. SO ONE MUST STAY.
I SHALL LEAVE THE CHOICE TO YOU.

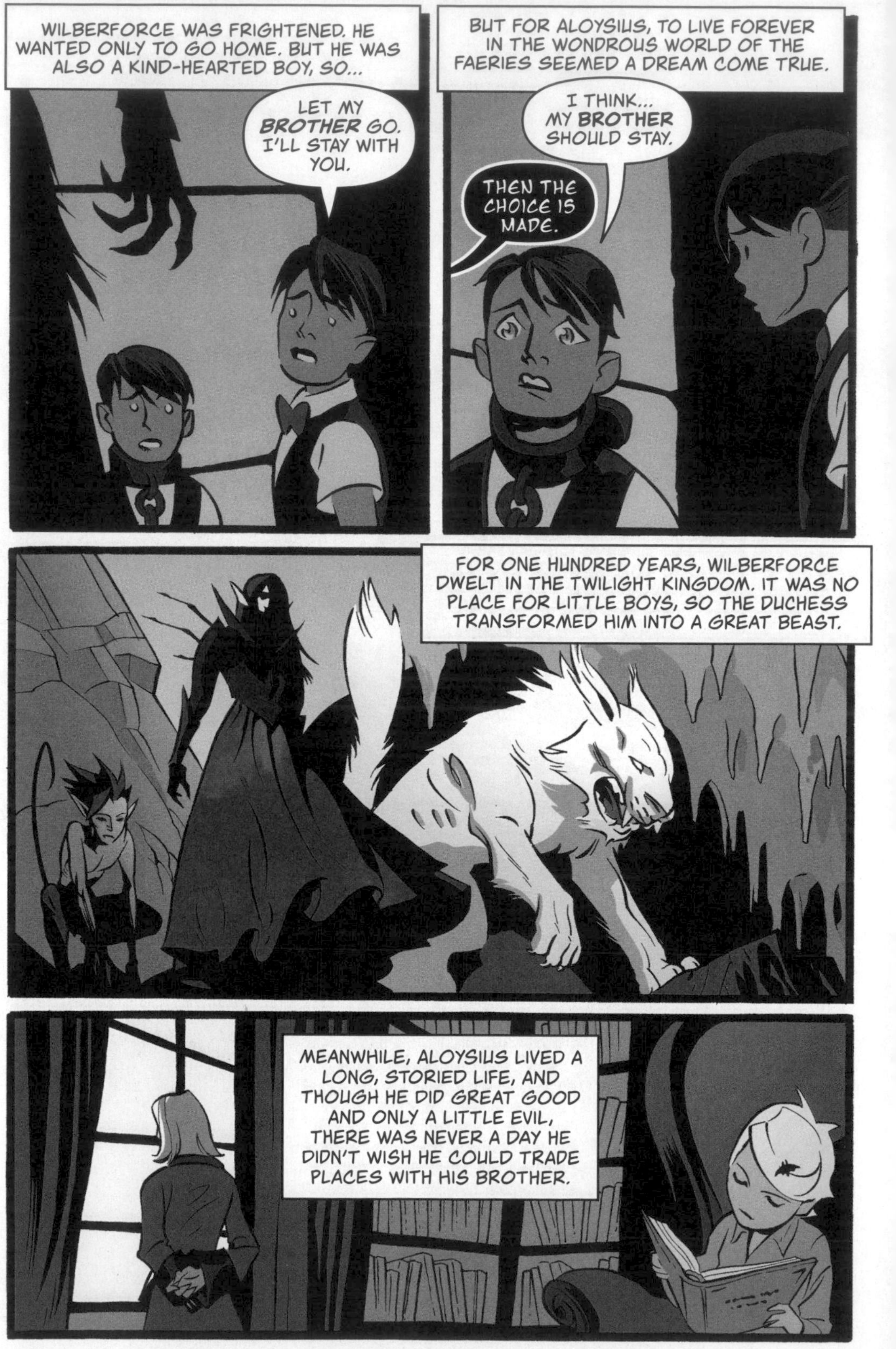
WILBERFORCE WAS FRIGHTENED. HE WANTED ONLY TO GO HOME. BUT HE WAS ALSO A KIND-HEARTED BOY, SO...
LET MY **BROTHER** GO. I'LL STAY WITH YOU.
BUT FOR ALOYSIUS, TO LIVE FOREVER IN THE WONDROUS WORLD OF THE FAERIES SEEMED A DREAM COME TRUE.
I THINK... MY **BROTHER** SHOULD STAY.
THEN THE CHOICE IS MADE.
FOR ONE HUNDRED YEARS, WILBERFORCE DWELT IN THE TWILIGHT KINGDOM. IT WAS NO PLACE FOR LITTLE BOYS, SO THE DUCHESS TRANSFORMED HIM INTO A GREAT BEAST.
MEANWHILE, ALOYSIUS LIVED A LONG, STORIED LIFE, AND THOUGH HE DID GREAT GOOD AND ONLY A LITTLE EVIL, THERE WAS NEVER A DAY HE DIDN'T WISH HE COULD TRADE PLACES WITH HIS BROTHER.

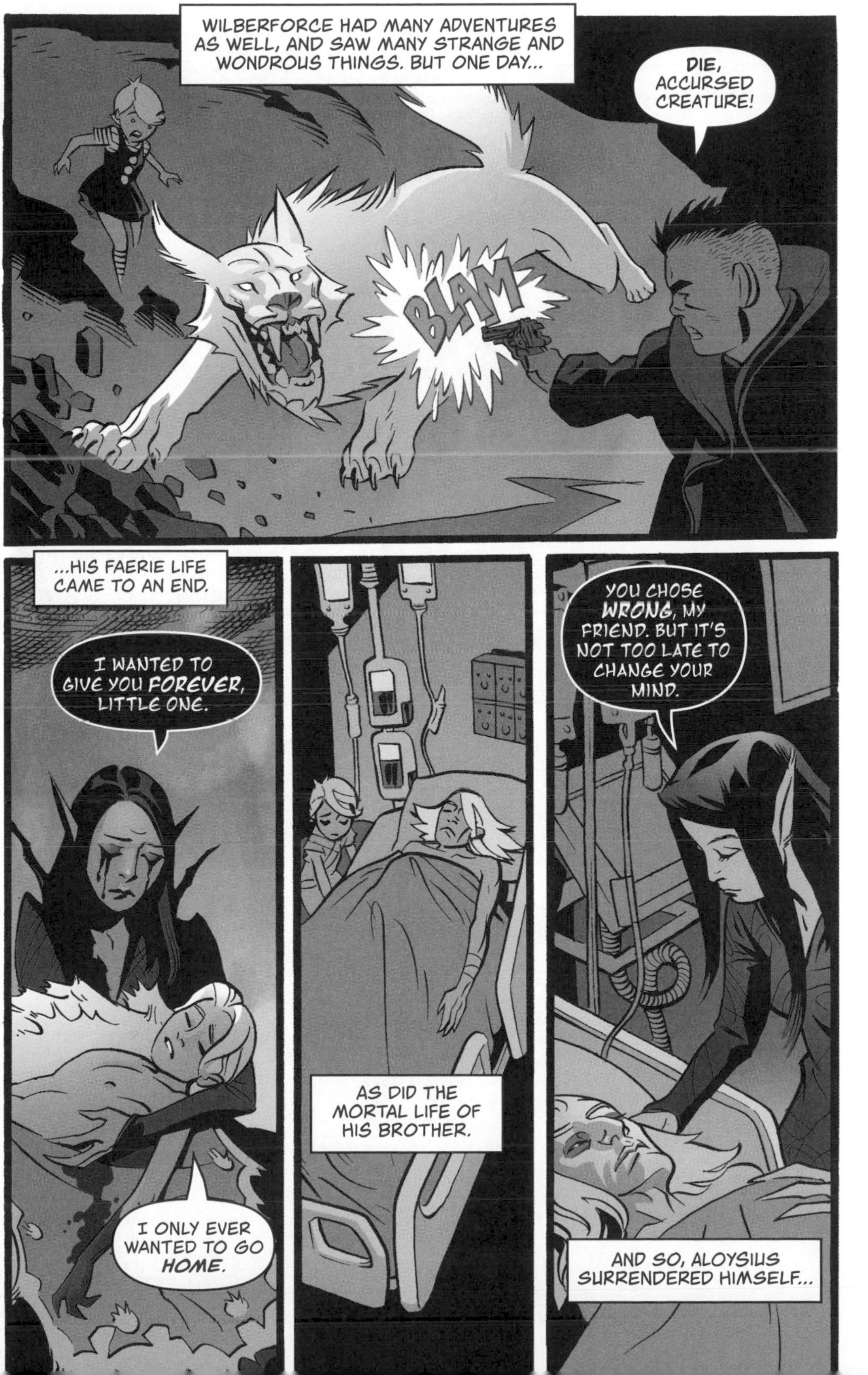
WILBERFORCE HAD MANY ADVENTURES AS WELL, AND SAW MANY STRANGE AND WONDROUS THINGS. BUT ONE DAY...
DIE, ACCURSED CREATURE!
BLAM
...HIS FAERIE LIFE CAME TO AN END.
I WANTED TO GIVE YOU FOREVER, LITTLE ONE.
I ONLY EVER WANTED TO GO HOME.
AS DID THE MORTAL LIFE OF HIS BROTHER.
YOU CHOSE WRONG, MY FRIEND. BUT IT'S NOT TOO LATE TO CHANGE YOUR MIND.
AND SO, ALOYSIUS SURRENDERED HIMSELF...

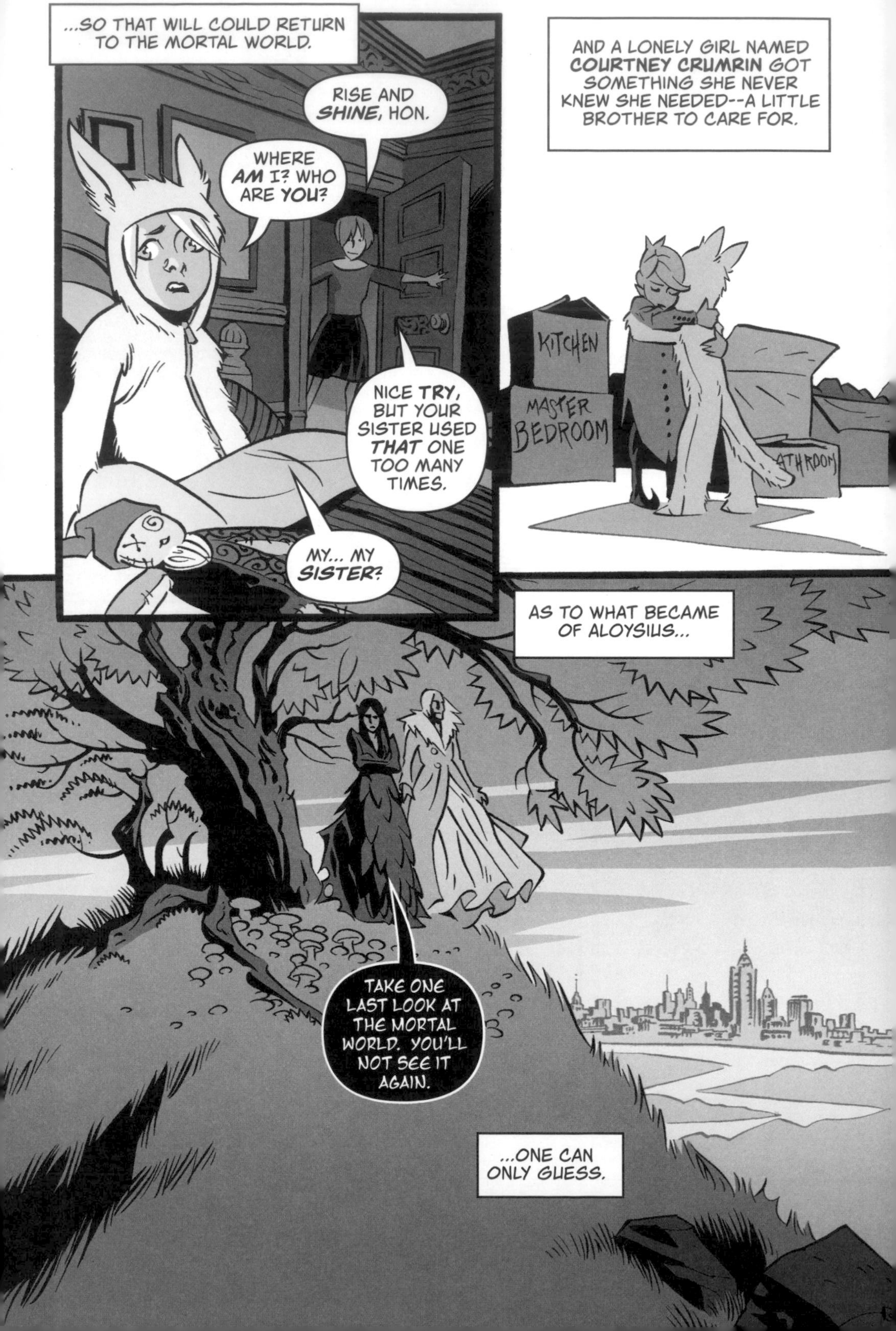
...SO THAT WILL COULD RETURN TO THE MORTAL WORLD.
RISE AND SHINE, HON.
WHERE AM I? WHO ARE YOU?
NICE TRY, BUT YOUR SISTER USED THAT ONE TOO MANY TIMES.
MY... MY SISTER?
AND A LONELY GIRL NAMED COURTNEY CRUMRIN GOT SOMETHING SHE NEVER KNEW SHE NEEDED--A LITTLE BROTHER TO CARE FOR.
KITCHEN
MASTER BEDROOM
ATHROOM
AS TO WHAT BECAME OF ALOYSIUS...
TAKE ONE LAST LOOK AT THE MORTAL WORLD. YOU'LL NOT SEE IT AGAIN.
...ONE CAN ONLY GUESS.

BUT AFTER A LIFETIME OF WONDERS, CAN ONE TRULY EVER CALL THE ORDINARY WORLD HOME?

MUST I GO?

THEY'RE JUST REGULAR *KIDS.* YOU'VE FACED *MUCH* SCARIER THINGS.

I *SUPPOSE,* BUT...

THEY DON'T SEEM TO LIKE ME. THEY CAN *SEE* I'M...

WELL, *YOU* KNOW...

...DIFFERENT.

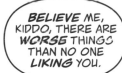

BELIEVE ME, KIDDO, THERE ARE *WORSE* THINGS THAN NO ONE *LIKING* YOU.

OKAY. I SHOULDN'T *DO* THIS, BUT...

HERE. IT'S NOT SUPER *POWERFUL*...

...BUT IF YOU EVER GET TOO *LONELY,* JUST PUT IT ON.

AND DON'T *FORGET*...

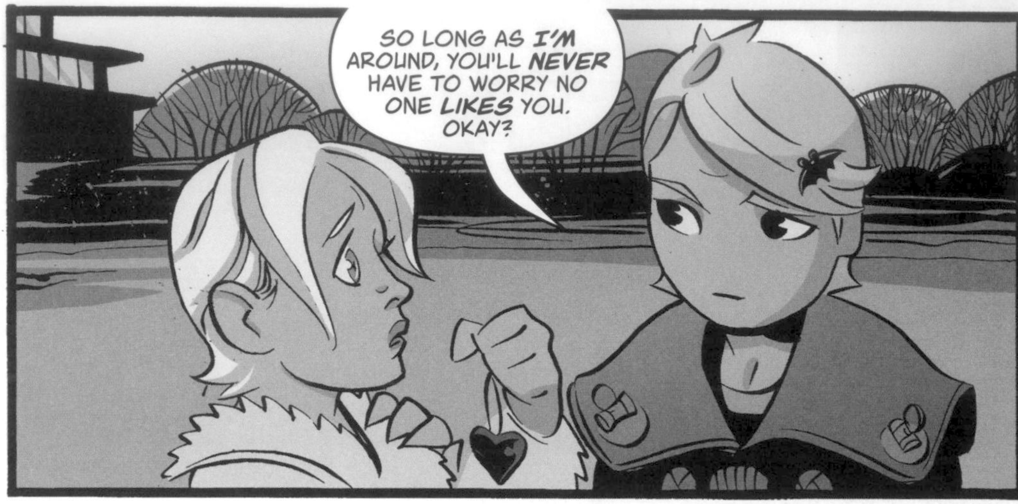
SO LONG AS I'M AROUND, YOU'LL NEVER HAVE TO WORRY NO ONE LIKES YOU. OKAY?

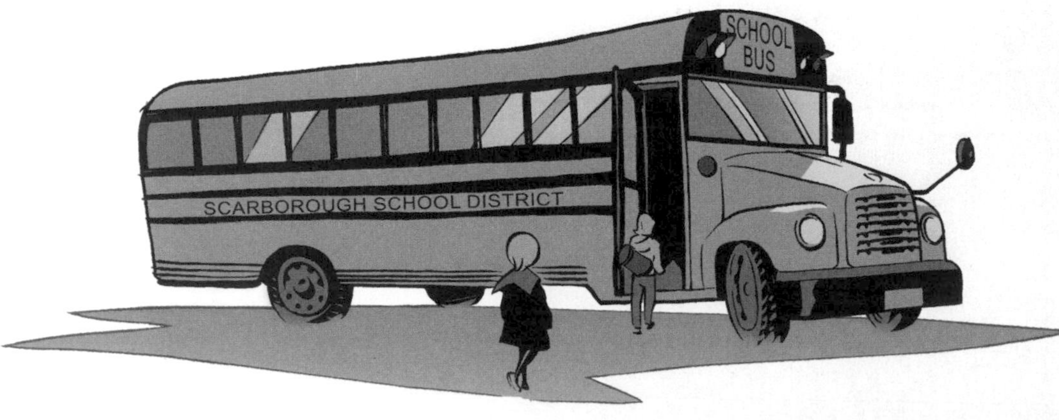
SCHOOL BUS
SCARBOROUGH SCHOOL DISTRICT

Chapter 1
Charmed

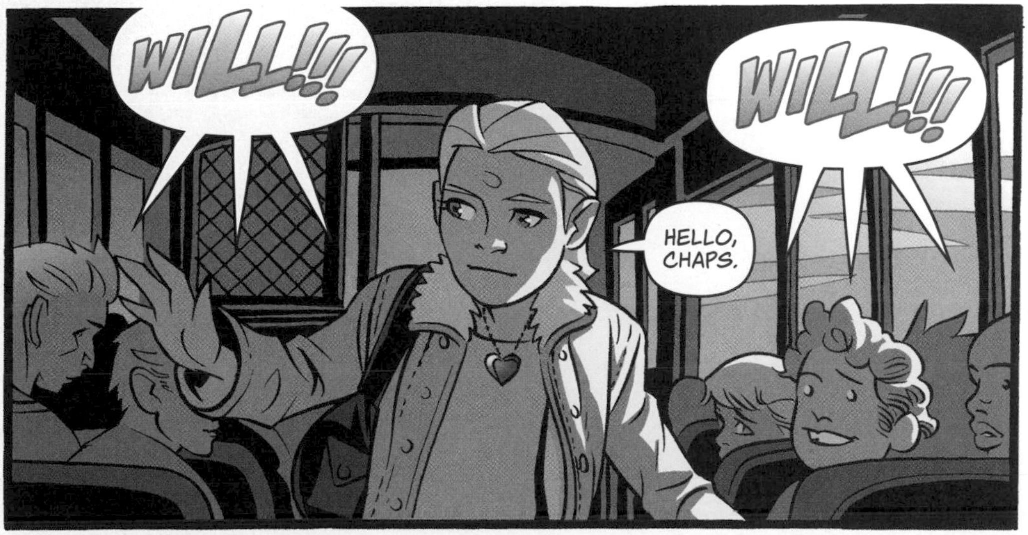
WILL!!!
HELLO, CHAPS.
WILL!!!

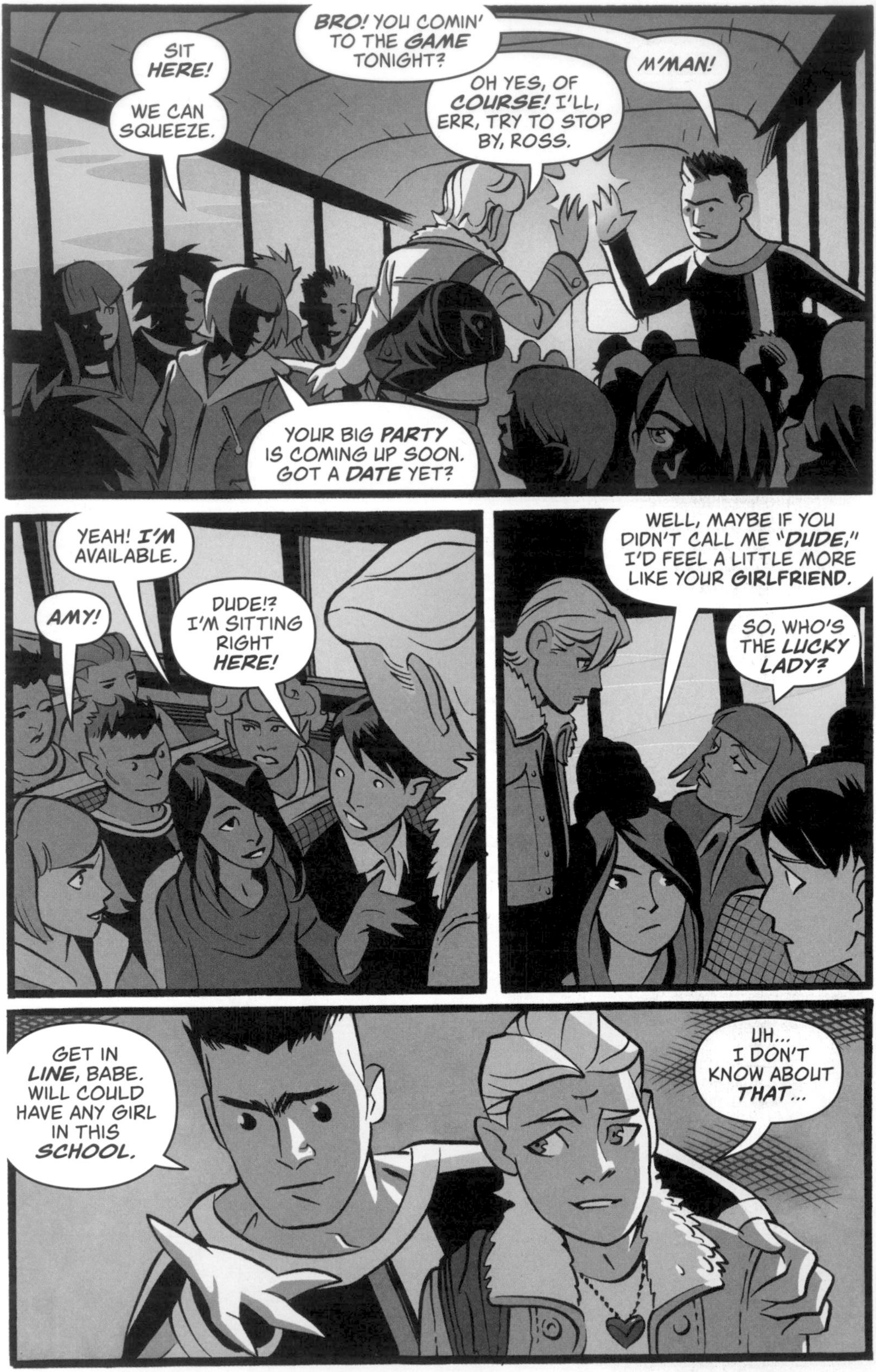
SIT HERE!
WE CAN SQUEEZE.
BRO! YOU COMIN' TO THE GAME TONIGHT?
M'MAN!
OH YES, OF COURSE! I'LL, ERR, TRY TO STOP BY, ROSS.
YOUR BIG PARTY IS COMING UP SOON. GOT A DATE YET?
YEAH! I'M AVAILABLE.
AMY!
DUDE!? I'M SITTING RIGHT HERE!
WELL, MAYBE IF YOU DIDN'T CALL ME "DUDE," I'D FEEL A LITTLE MORE LIKE YOUR GIRLFRIEND.
SO, WHO'S THE LUCKY LADY?
GET IN LINE, BABE. WILL COULD HAVE ANY GIRL IN THIS SCHOOL.
UH... I DON'T KNOW ABOUT THAT...

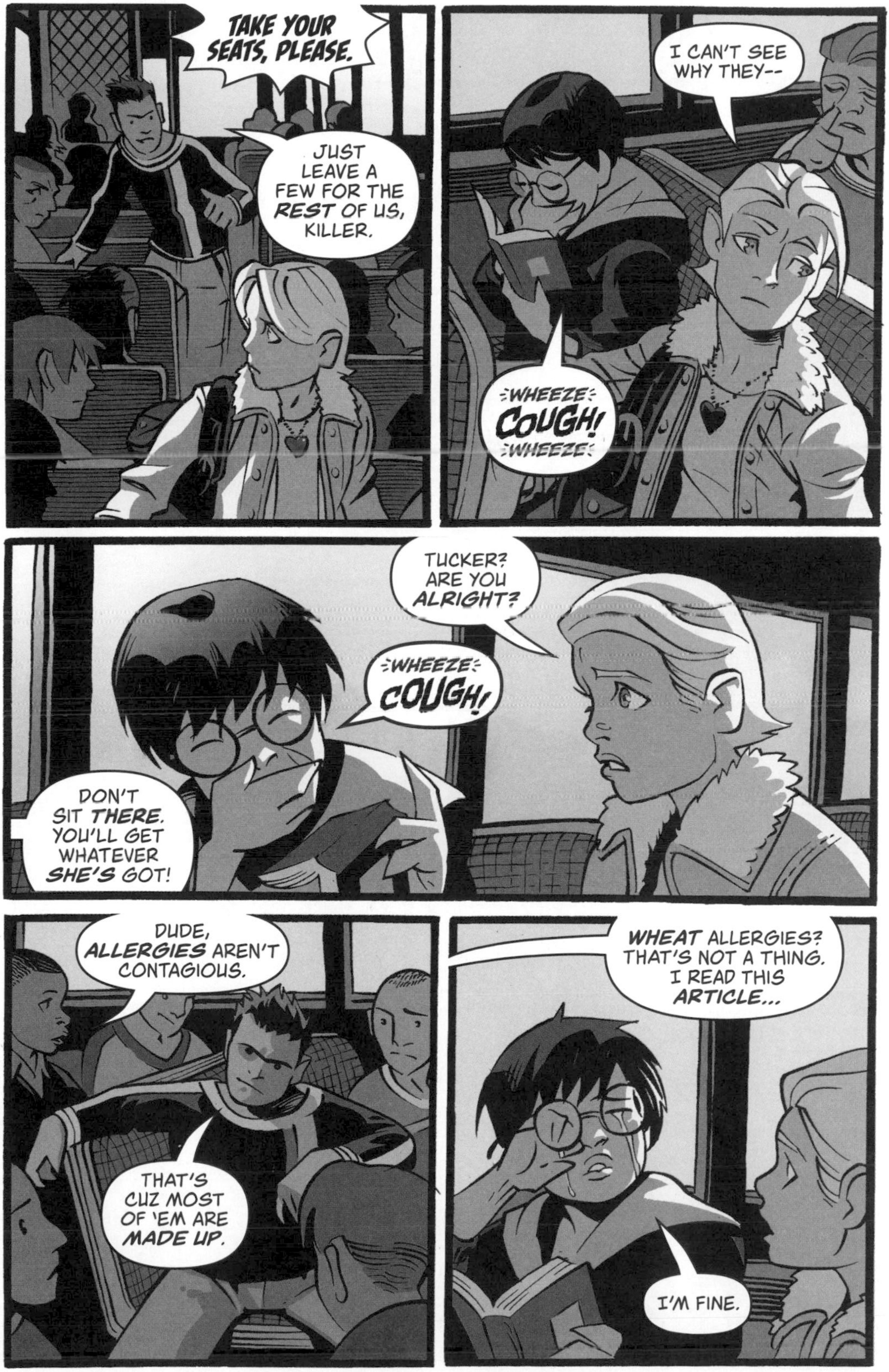
TAKE YOUR SEATS, PLEASE.
JUST LEAVE A FEW FOR THE REST OF US, KILLER.
I CAN'T SEE WHY THEY--
WHEEZE COUGH! WHEEZE
TUCKER? ARE YOU ALRIGHT?
WHEEZE COUGH!
DON'T SIT THERE. YOU'LL GET WHATEVER SHE'S GOT!
DUDE, ALLERGIES AREN'T CONTAGIOUS.
THAT'S CUZ MOST OF 'EM ARE MADE UP.
WHEAT ALLERGIES? THAT'S NOT A THING. I READ THIS ARTICLE...
I'M FINE.

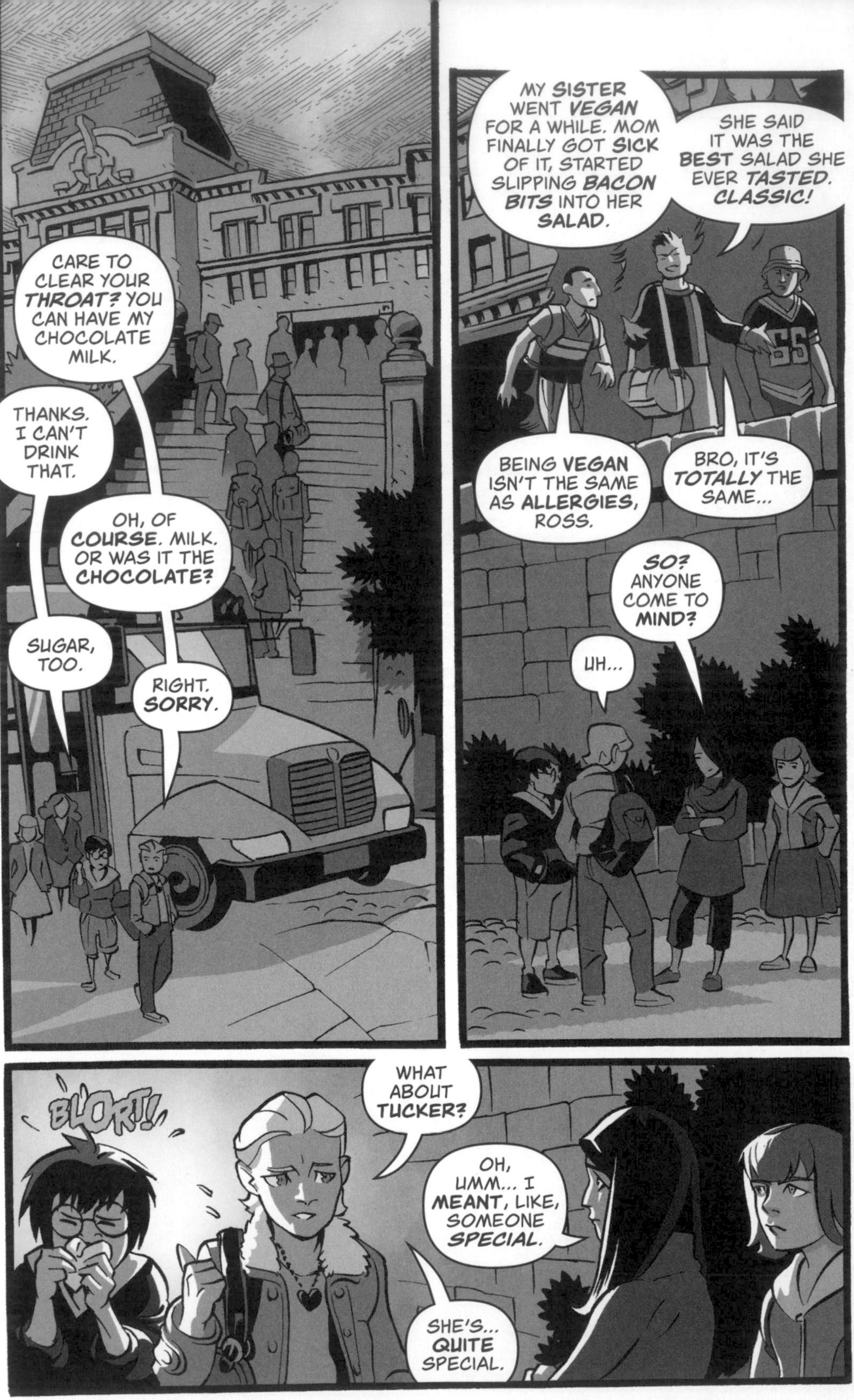
CARE TO CLEAR YOUR THROAT? YOU CAN HAVE MY CHOCOLATE MILK.
THANKS. I CAN'T DRINK THAT.
OH, OF COURSE. MILK. OR WAS IT THE CHOCOLATE?
SUGAR, TOO.
RIGHT. SORRY.
MY SISTER WENT VEGAN FOR A WHILE. MOM FINALLY GOT SICK OF IT, STARTED SLIPPING BACON BITS INTO HER SALAD.
SHE SAID IT WAS THE BEST SALAD SHE EVER TASTED. CLASSIC!
BEING VEGAN ISN'T THE SAME AS ALLERGIES, ROSS.
BRO, IT'S TOTALLY THE SAME...
SO? ANYONE COME TO MIND?
UH...
BLORT!
WHAT ABOUT TUCKER?
OH, UMM... I MEANT, LIKE, SOMEONE SPECIAL.
SHE'S... QUITE SPECIAL.

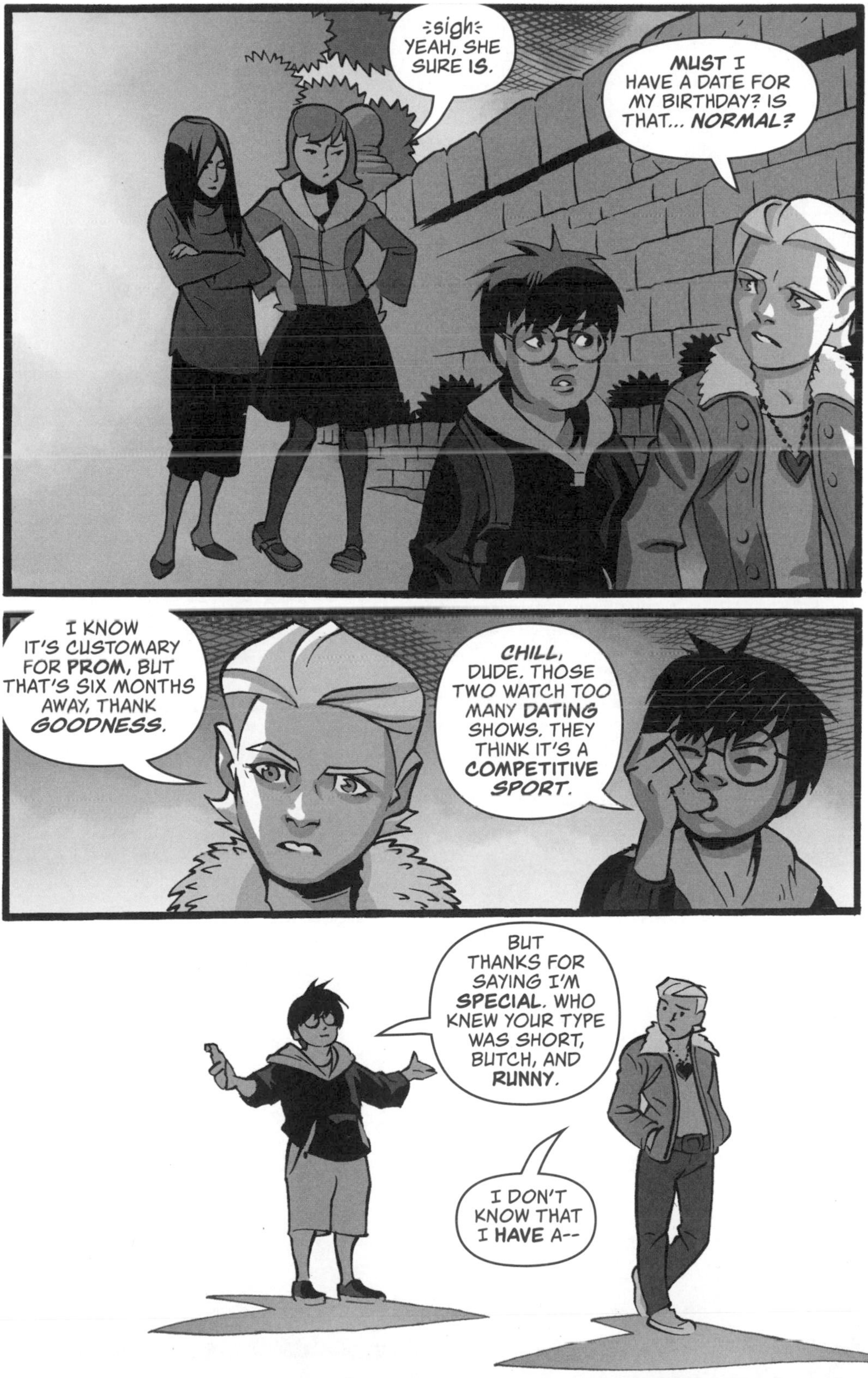

:sigh: YEAH, SHE SURE IS.
MUST I HAVE A DATE FOR MY BIRTHDAY? IS THAT... NORMAL?
I KNOW IT'S CUSTOMARY FOR PROM, BUT THAT'S SIX MONTHS AWAY, THANK GOODNESS.
CHILL, DUDE. THOSE TWO WATCH TOO MANY DATING SHOWS. THEY THINK IT'S A COMPETITIVE SPORT.
BUT THANKS FOR SAYING I'M SPECIAL. WHO KNEW YOUR TYPE WAS SHORT, BUTCH, AND RUNNY.
I DON'T KNOW THAT I HAVE A--

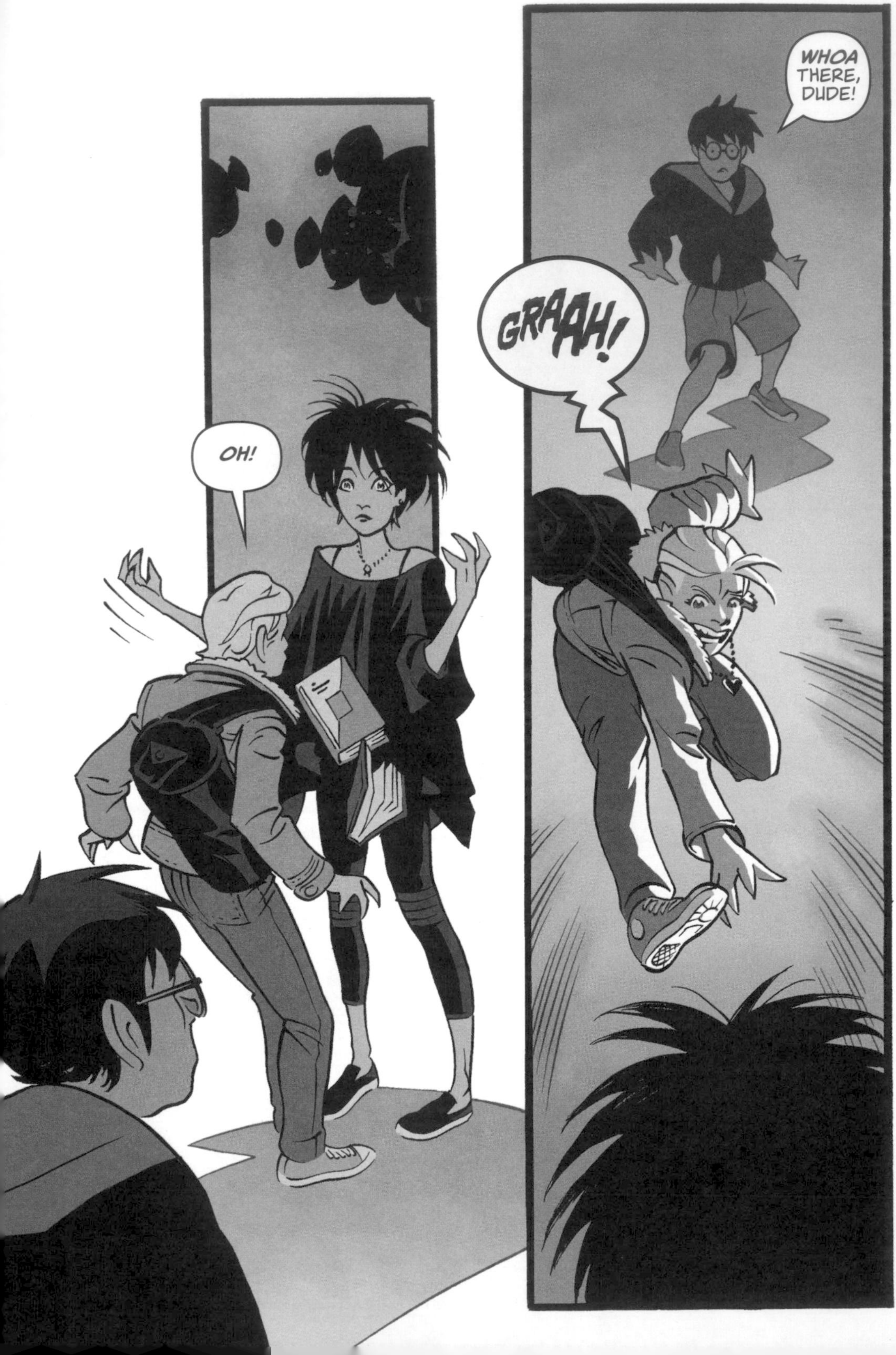
OH!
WHOA THERE, DUDE!
GRAAAH!

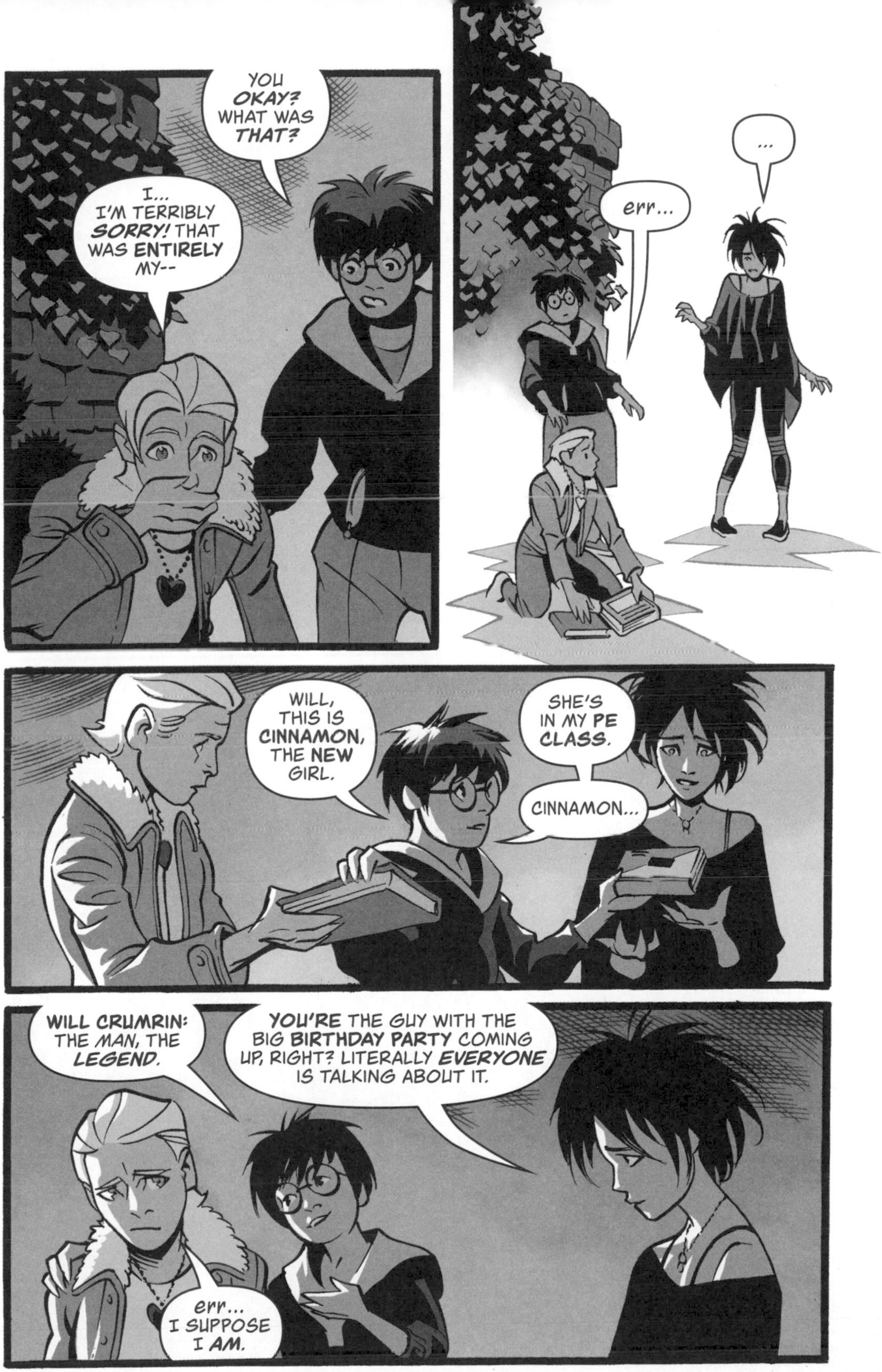
YOU OKAY? WHAT WAS THAT?
I... I'M TERRIBLY SORRY! THAT WAS ENTIRELY MY--
...
err...
WILL, THIS IS CINNAMON, THE NEW GIRL.
SHE'S IN MY PE CLASS.
CINNAMON...
WILL CRUMRIN: THE MAN, THE LEGEND.
YOU'RE THE GUY WITH THE BIG BIRTHDAY PARTY COMING UP, RIGHT? LITERALLY EVERYONE IS TALKING ABOUT IT.
err... I SUPPOSE I AM.

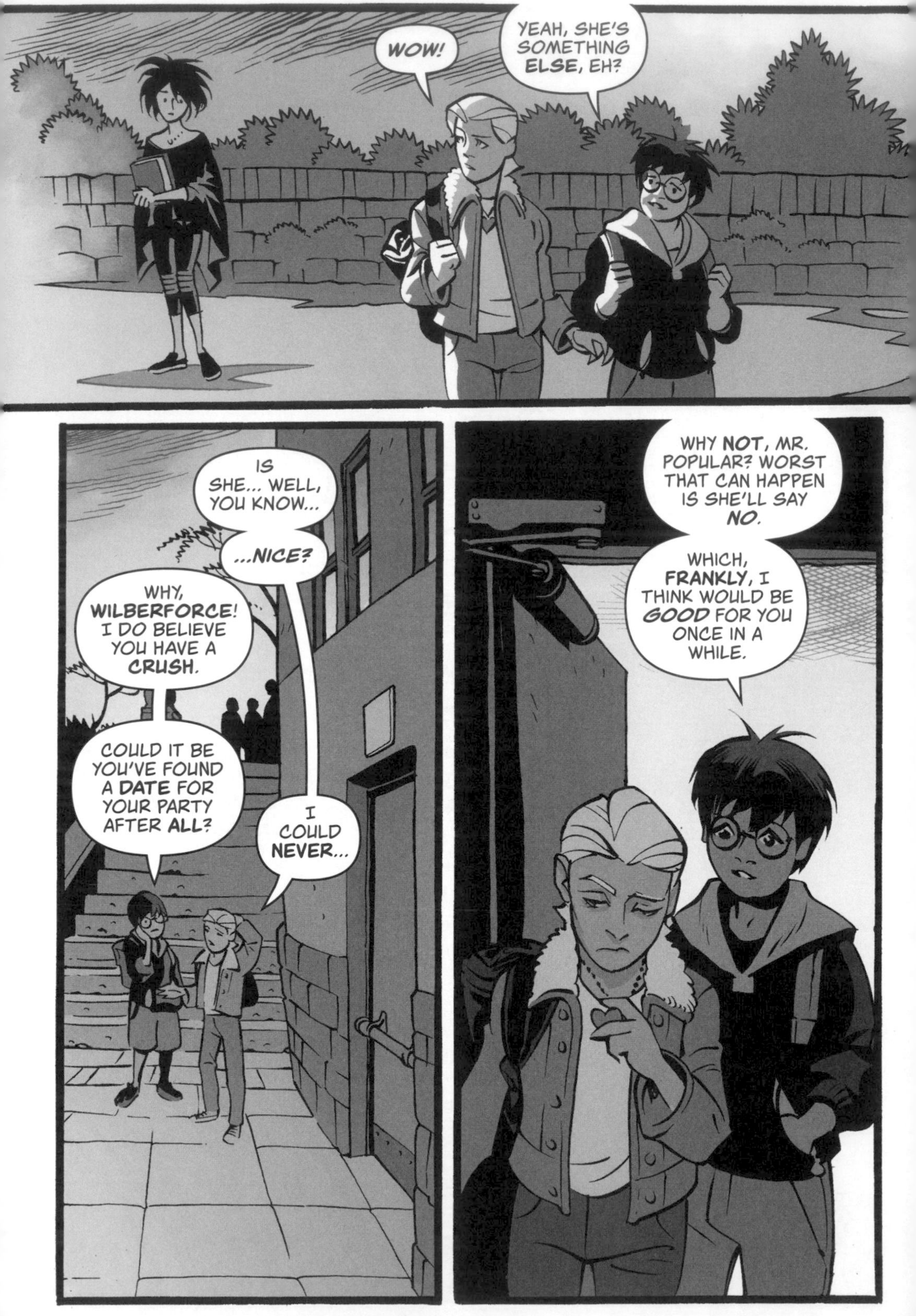
WOW!
YEAH, SHE'S SOMETHING ELSE, EH?
IS SHE... WELL, YOU KNOW...
...NICE?
WHY, WILBERFORCE! I DO BELIEVE YOU HAVE A CRUSH.
COULD IT BE YOU'VE FOUND A DATE FOR YOUR PARTY AFTER ALL?
I COULD NEVER...
WHY NOT, MR. POPULAR? WORST THAT CAN HAPPEN IS SHE'LL SAY NO.
WHICH, FRANKLY, I THINK WOULD BE GOOD FOR YOU ONCE IN A WHILE.

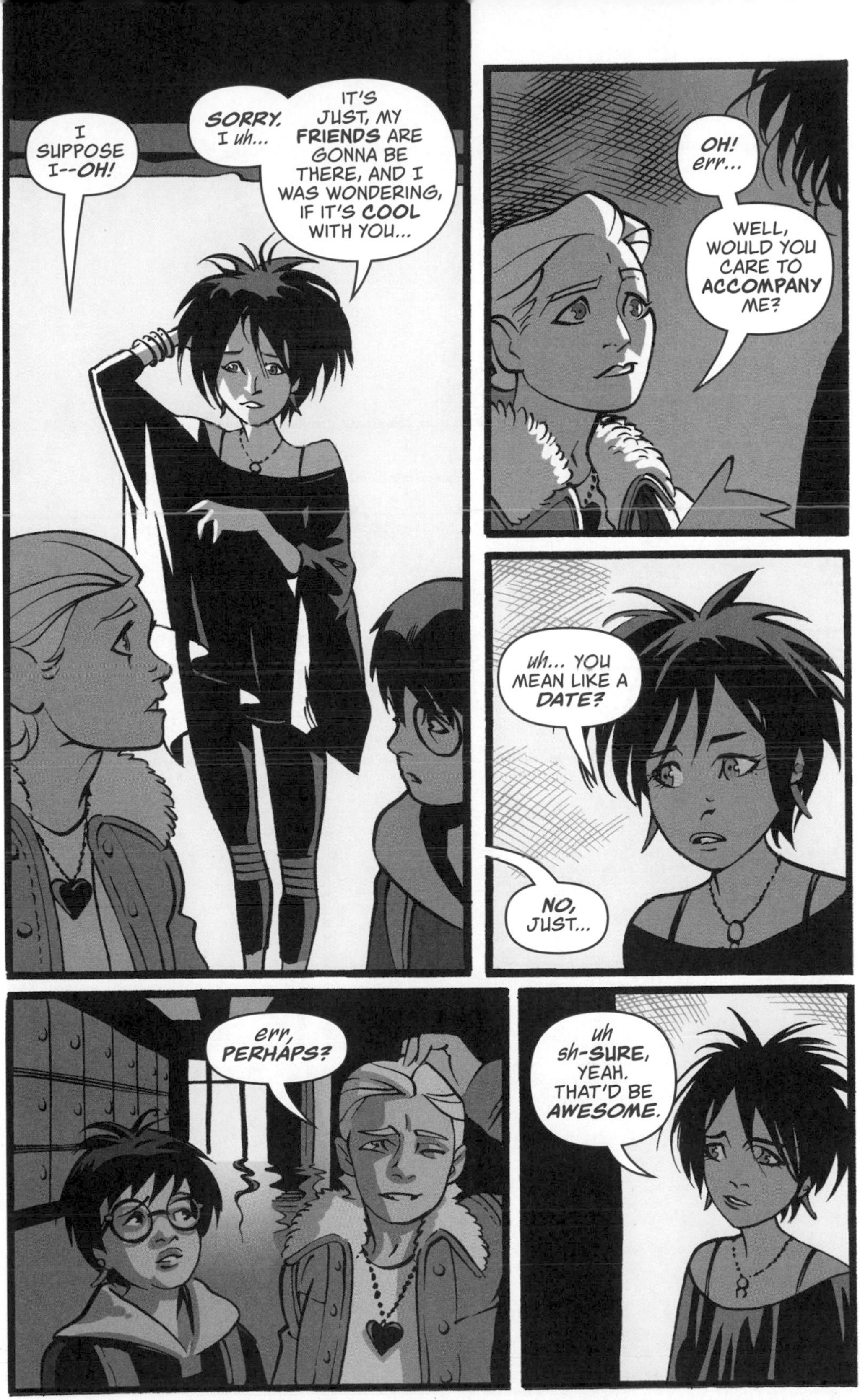
I SUPPOSE I--OH!
SORRY. I uh...
IT'S JUST, MY FRIENDS ARE GONNA BE THERE, AND I WAS WONDERING, IF IT'S COOL WITH YOU...
OH! err...
WELL, WOULD YOU CARE TO ACCOMPANY ME?
uh... YOU MEAN LIKE A DATE?
NO, JUST...
err, PERHAPS?
uh sh-SURE, YEAH. THAT'D BE AWESOME.

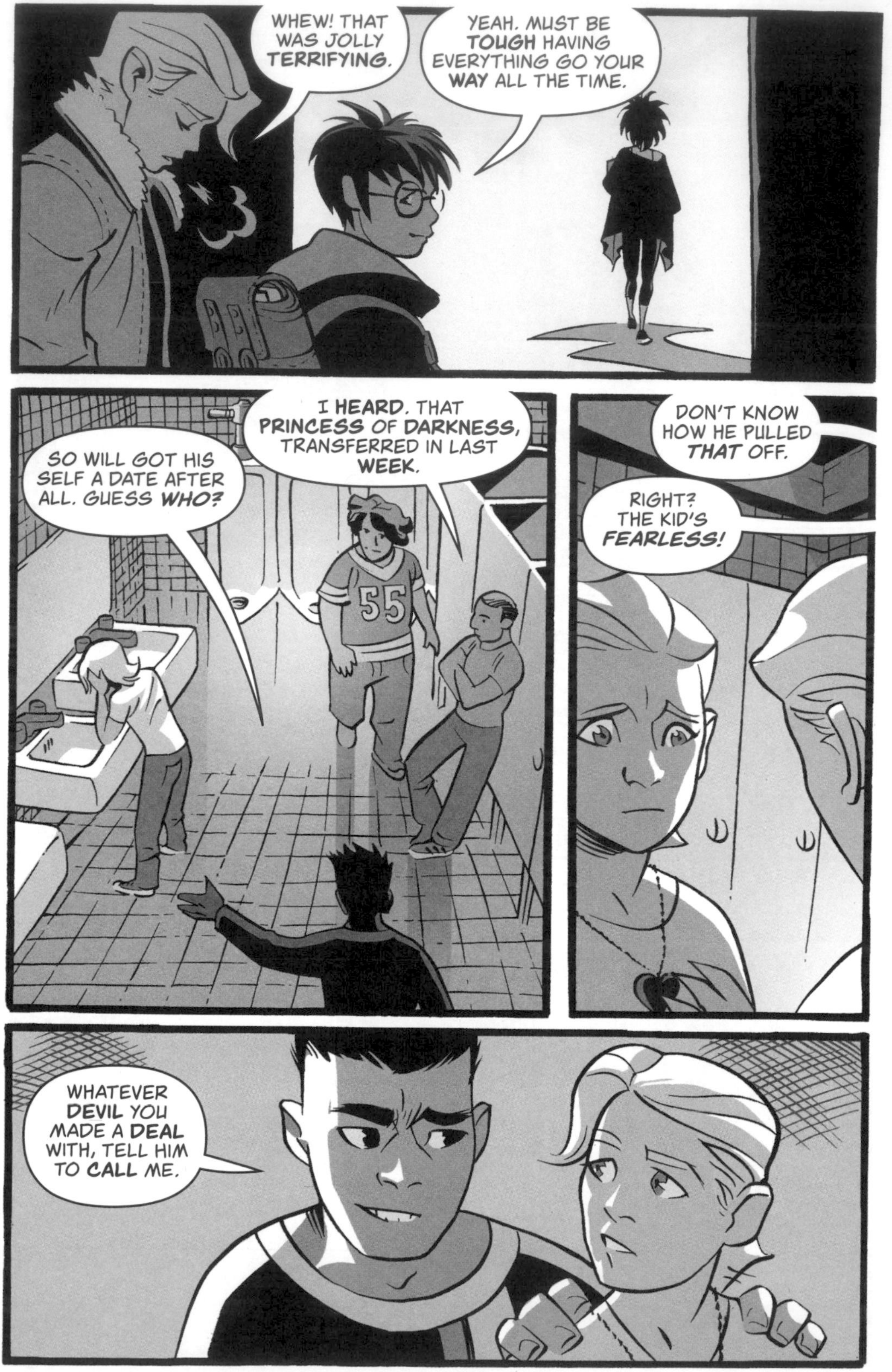
WHEW! THAT WAS JOLLY TERRIFYING.
YEAH. MUST BE TOUGH HAVING EVERYTHING GO YOUR WAY ALL THE TIME.
SO WILL GOT HIS SELF A DATE AFTER ALL. GUESS WHO?
I HEARD. THAT PRINCESS OF DARKNESS, TRANSFERRED IN LAST WEEK.
DON'T KNOW HOW HE PULLED THAT OFF.
RIGHT? THE KID'S FEARLESS!
WHATEVER DEVIL YOU MADE A DEAL WITH, TELL HIM TO CALL ME.

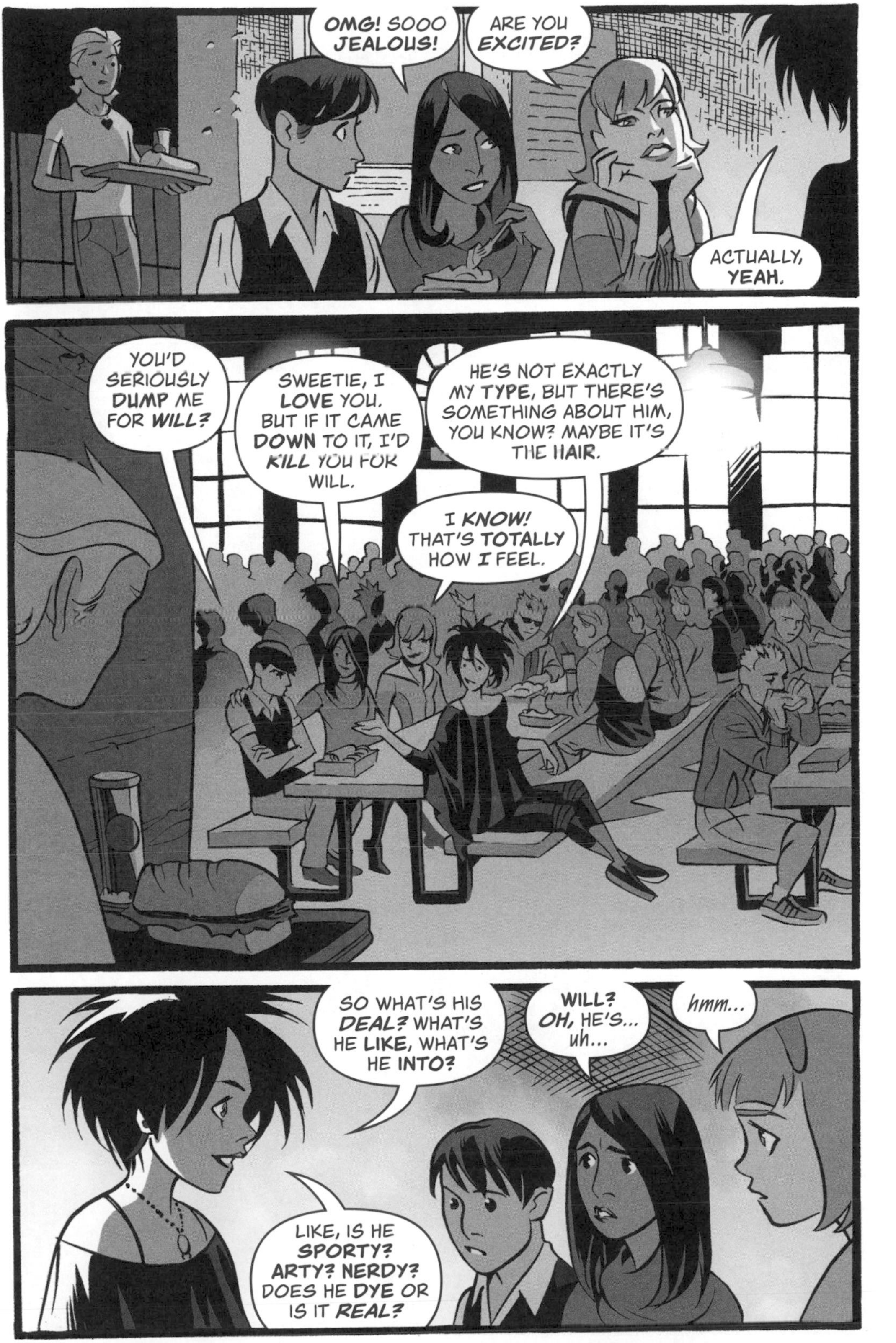
OMG! SOOO JEALOUS!
ARE YOU EXCITED?
ACTUALLY, YEAH.
YOU'D SERIOUSLY DUMP ME FOR WILL?
SWEETIE, I LOVE YOU. BUT IF IT CAME DOWN TO IT, I'D KILL YOU FOR WILL.
HE'S NOT EXACTLY MY TYPE, BUT THERE'S SOMETHING ABOUT HIM, YOU KNOW? MAYBE IT'S THE HAIR.
I KNOW! THAT'S TOTALLY HOW I FEEL.
SO WHAT'S HIS DEAL? WHAT'S HE LIKE, WHAT'S HE INTO?
WILL? OH, HE'S... uh...
hmm...
LIKE, IS HE SPORTY? ARTY? NERDY? DOES HE DYE OR IS IT REAL?

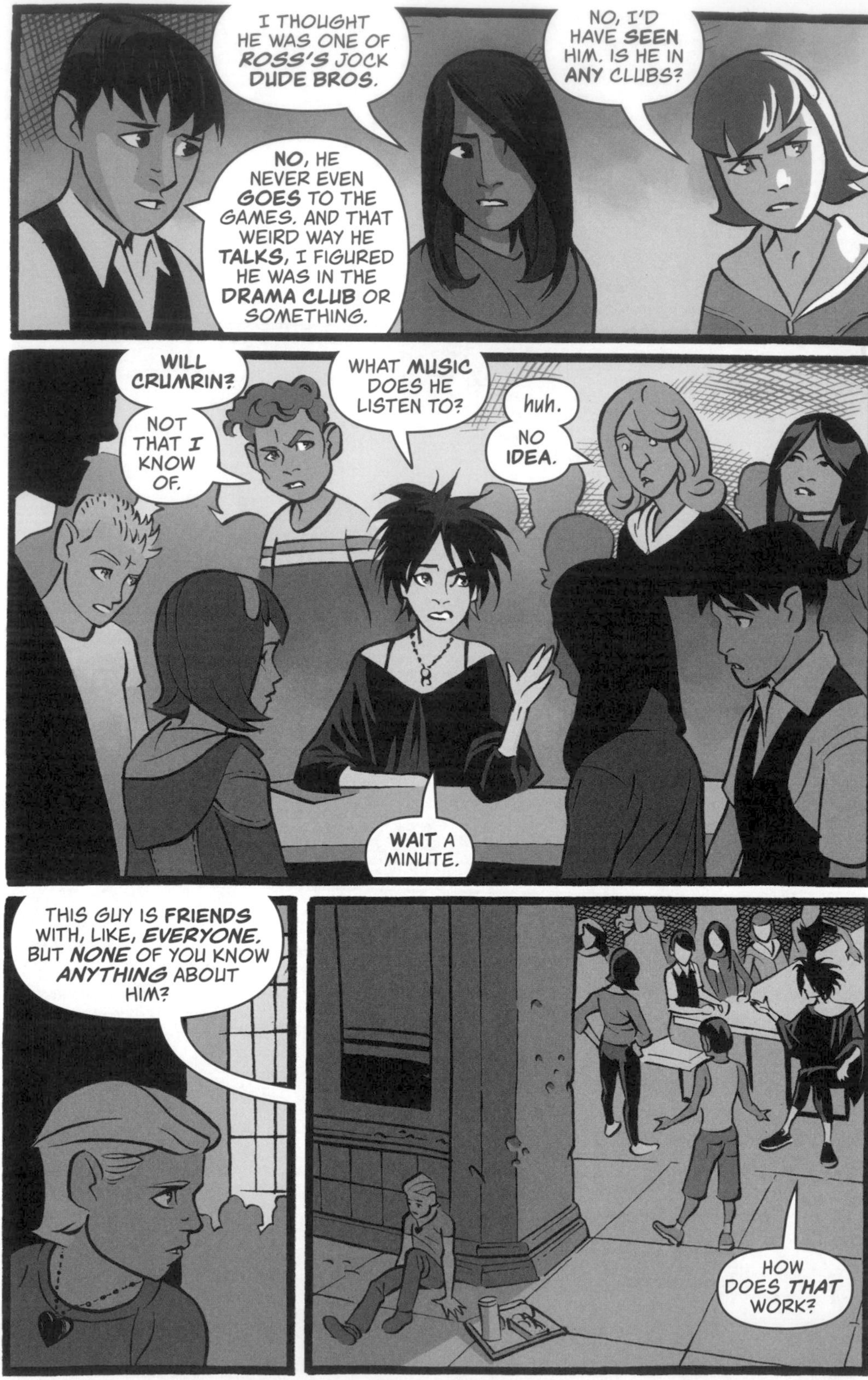

I THOUGHT HE WAS ONE OF ROSS'S JOCK DUDE BROS.
NO, HE NEVER EVEN GOES TO THE GAMES. AND THAT WEIRD WAY HE TALKS, I FIGURED HE WAS IN THE DRAMA CLUB OR SOMETHING.
NO, I'D HAVE SEEN HIM. IS HE IN ANY CLUBS?
WILL CRUMRIN?
NOT THAT I KNOW OF.
WHAT MUSIC DOES HE LISTEN TO?
huh.
NO IDEA.
WAIT A MINUTE.
THIS GUY IS FRIENDS WITH, LIKE, EVERYONE. BUT NONE OF YOU KNOW ANYTHING ABOUT HIM?
HOW DOES THAT WORK?

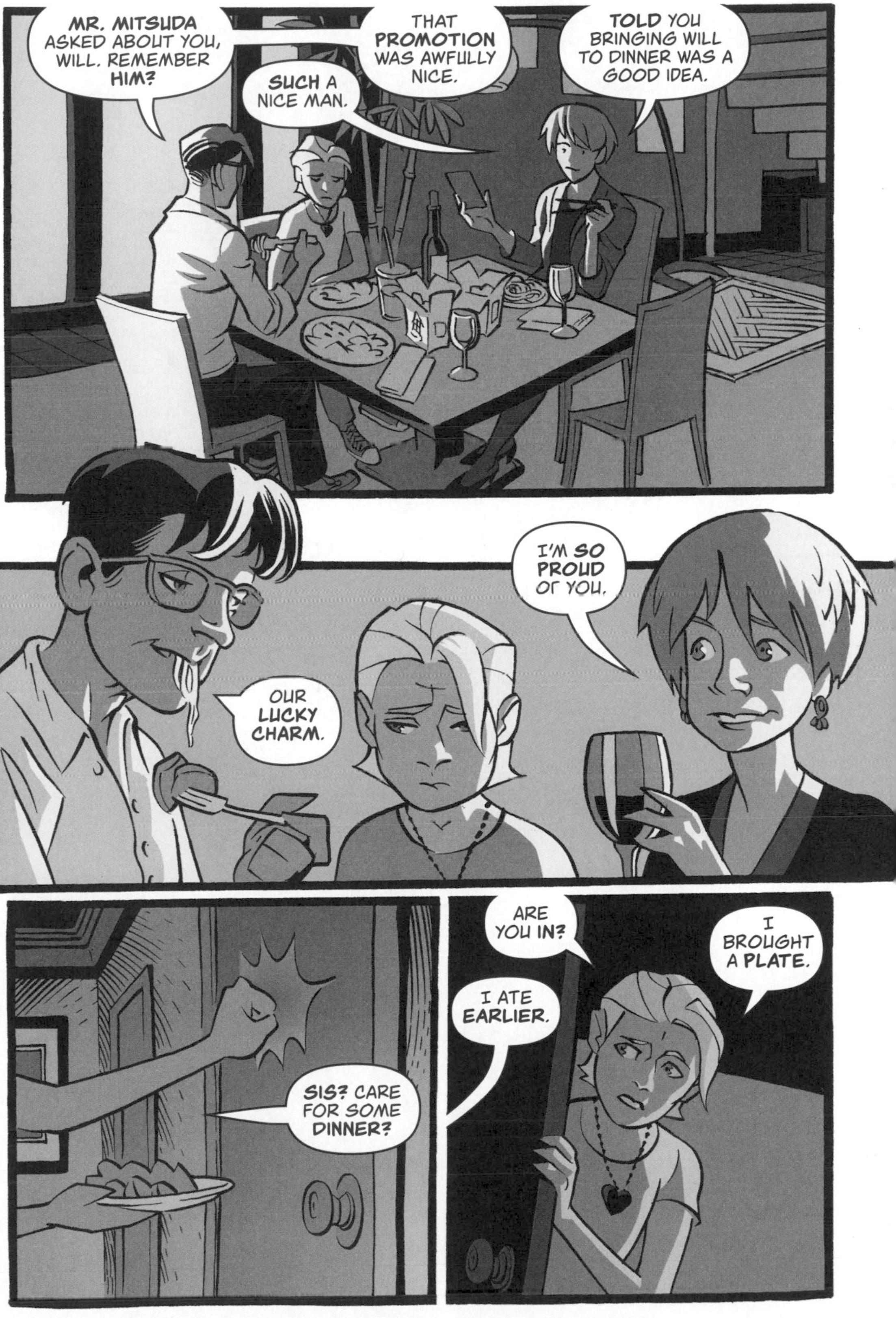
MR. MITSUDA ASKED ABOUT YOU, WILL. REMEMBER HIM?
SUCH A NICE MAN.
THAT PROMOTION WAS AWFULLY NICE.
TOLD YOU BRINGING WILL TO DINNER WAS A GOOD IDEA.
I'M SO PROUD OF YOU.
OUR LUCKY CHARM.
SIS? CARE FOR SOME DINNER?
ARE YOU IN?
I BROUGHT A PLATE.
I ATE EARLIER.

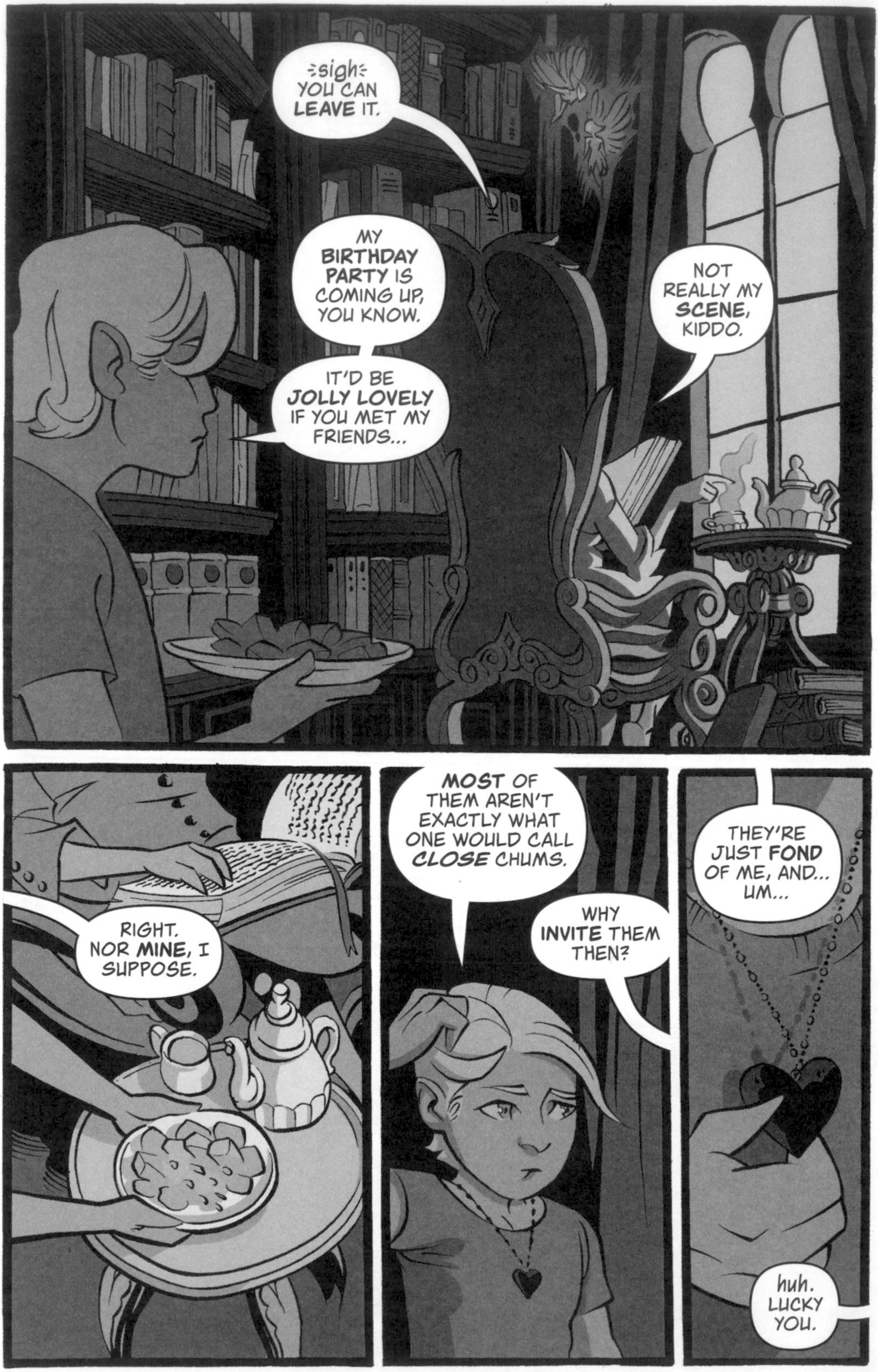

=sigh= YOU CAN **LEAVE** IT.
MY **BIRTHDAY PARTY** IS COMING UP, YOU KNOW.
IT'D BE **JOLLY LOVELY** IF YOU MET MY FRIENDS...
NOT REALLY MY **SCENE**, KIDDO.
RIGHT. NOR **MINE**, I SUPPOSE.
MOST OF THEM AREN'T EXACTLY WHAT ONE WOULD CALL ***CLOSE*** CHUMS.
WHY **INVITE** THEM THEN?
THEY'RE JUST **FOND** OF ME, AND... UM...
huh. LUCKY YOU.

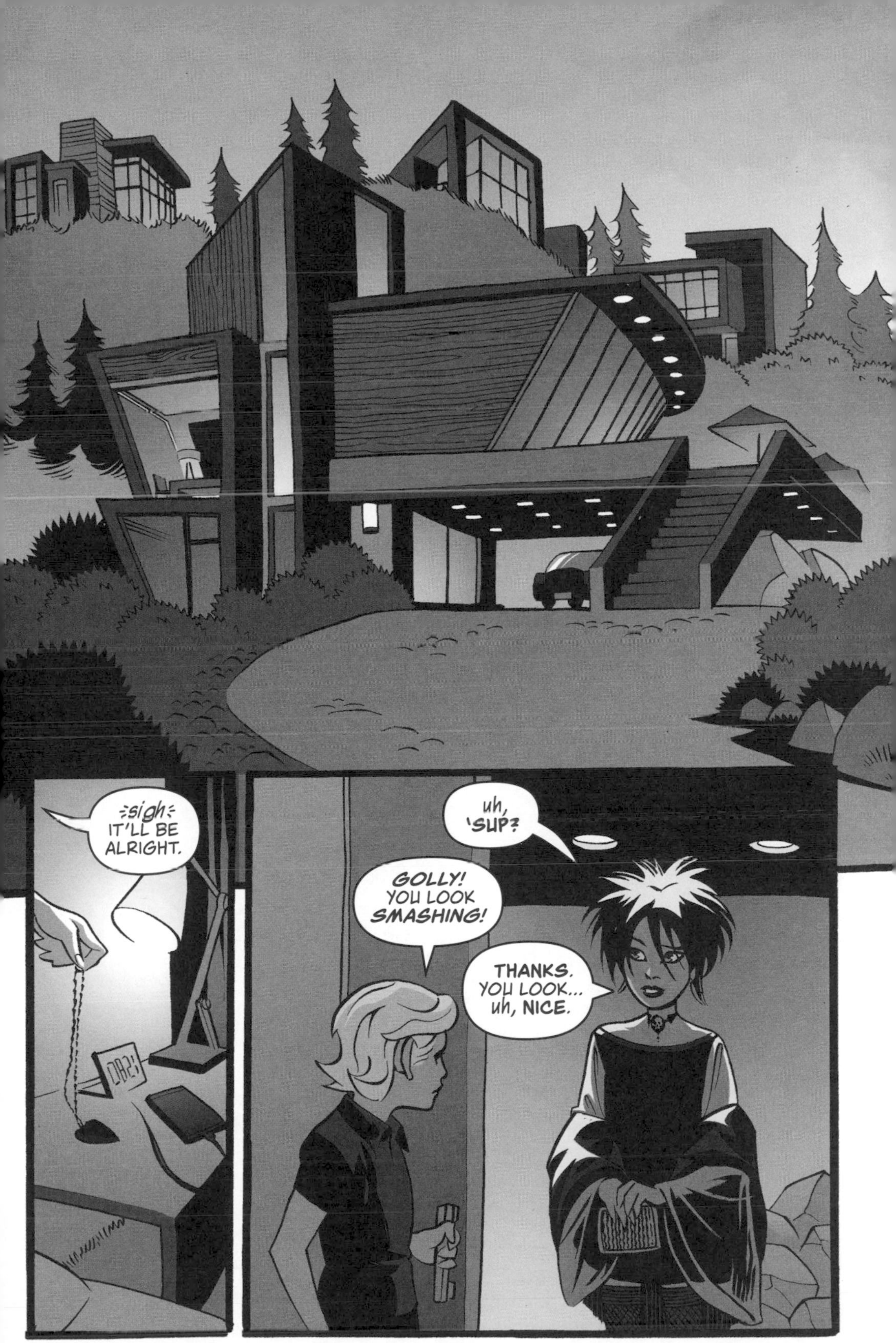

=sigh= IT'LL BE ALRIGHT.
uh, 'SUP?
GOLLY! YOU LOOK SMASHING!
THANKS. YOU LOOK... uh, NICE.

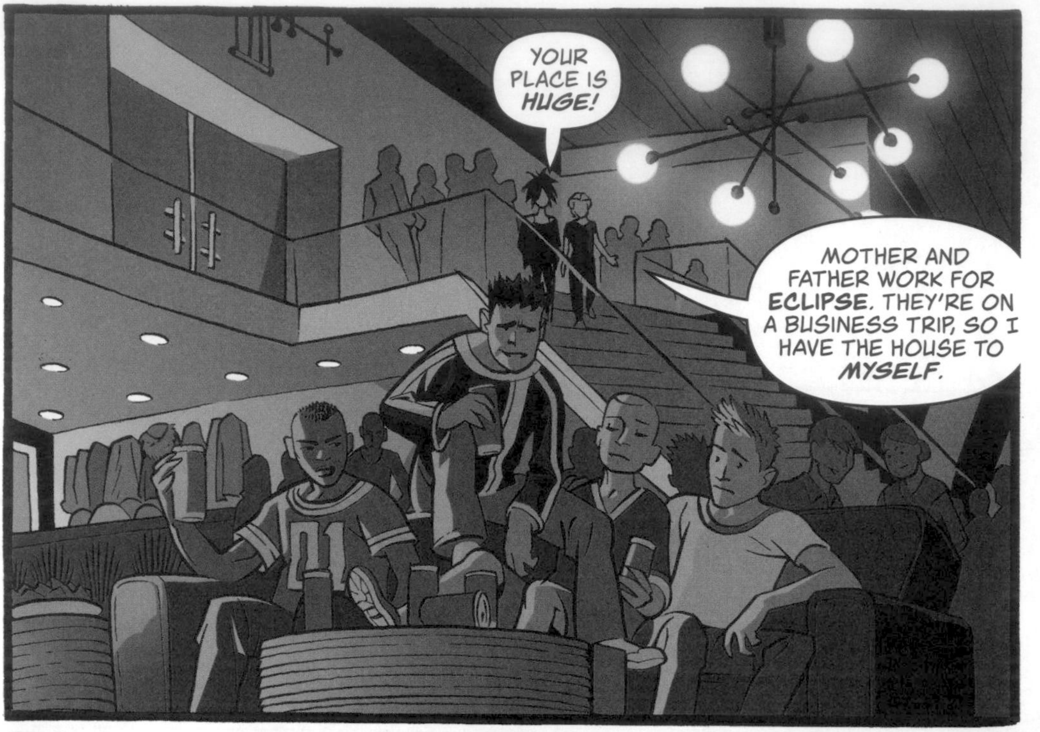
YOUR PLACE IS HUGE!
MOTHER AND FATHER WORK FOR ECLIPSE. THEY'RE ON A BUSINESS TRIP, SO I HAVE THE HOUSE TO MYSELF.

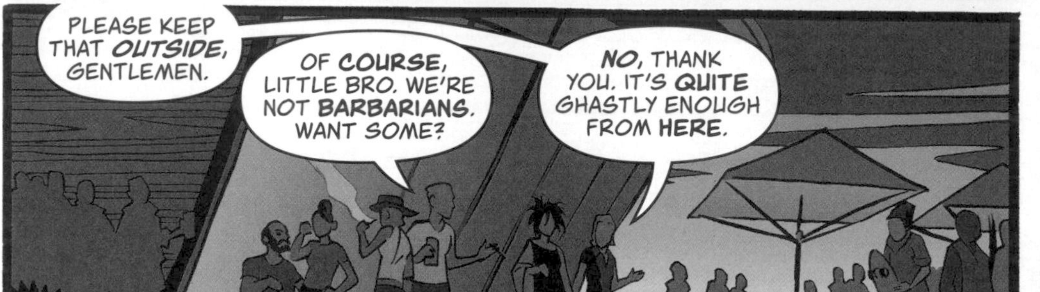
PLEASE KEEP THAT OUTSIDE, GENTLEMEN.
OF COURSE, LITTLE BRO. WE'RE NOT BARBARIANS. WANT SOME?
NO, THANK YOU. IT'S QUITE GHASTLY ENOUGH FROM HERE.

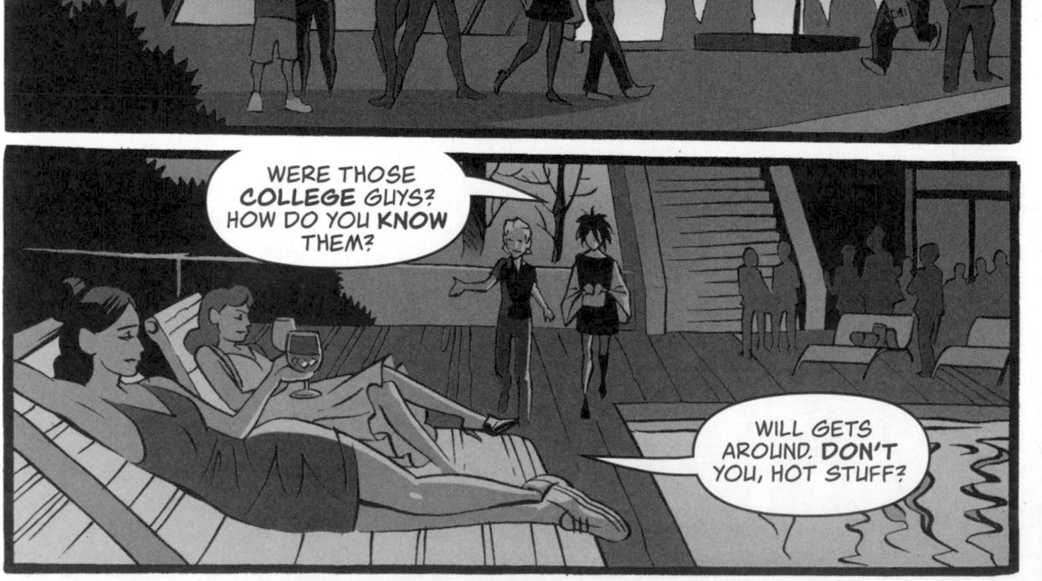
WERE THOSE COLLEGE GUYS? HOW DO YOU KNOW THEM?
WILL GETS AROUND. DON'T YOU, HOT STUFF?

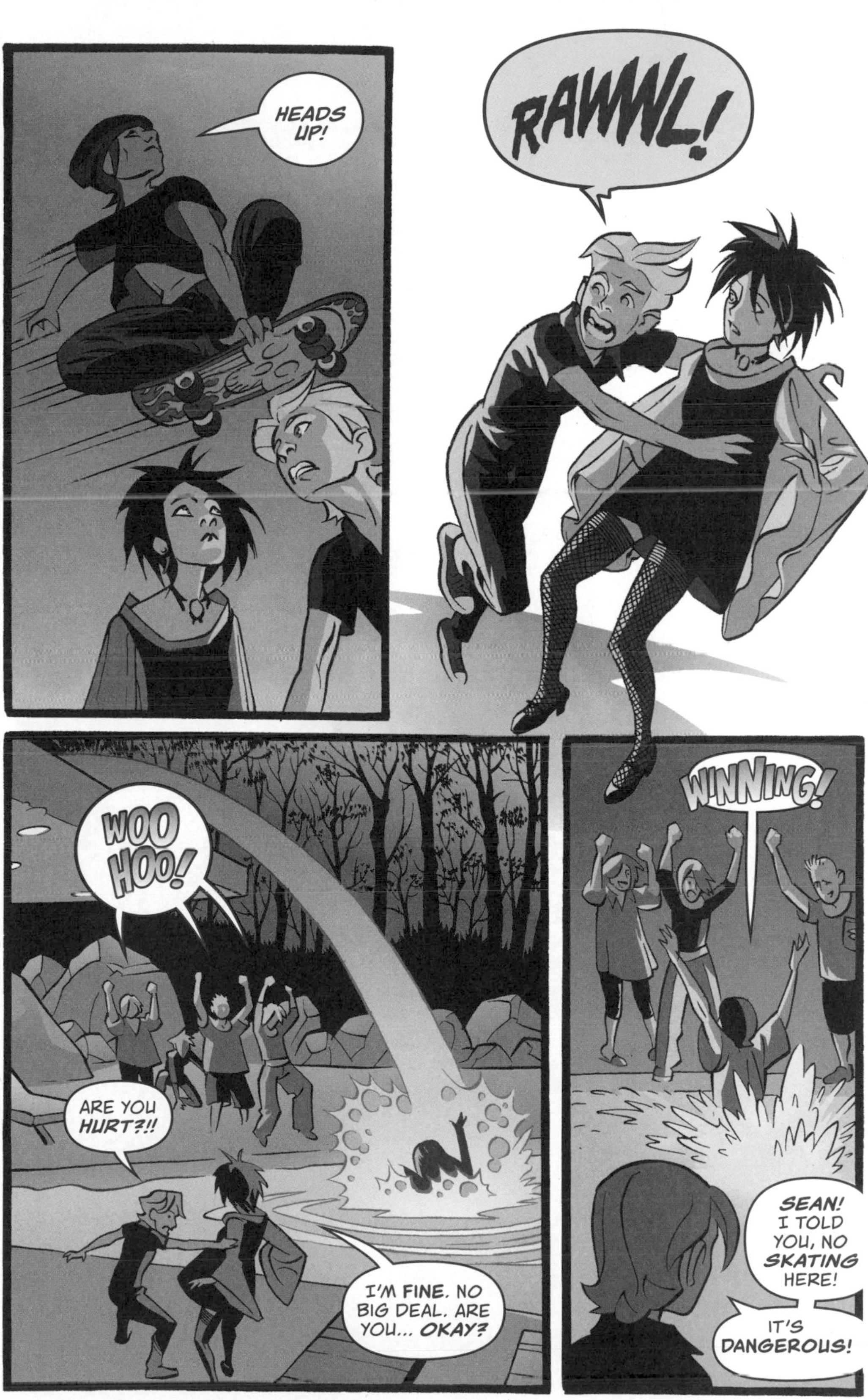
HEADS UP!
RAWWL!
WOO HOO!
ARE YOU HURT?!!
I'M FINE. NO BIG DEAL. ARE YOU... OKAY?
WINNING!
SEAN! I TOLD YOU, NO SKATING HERE!
IT'S DANGEROUS!

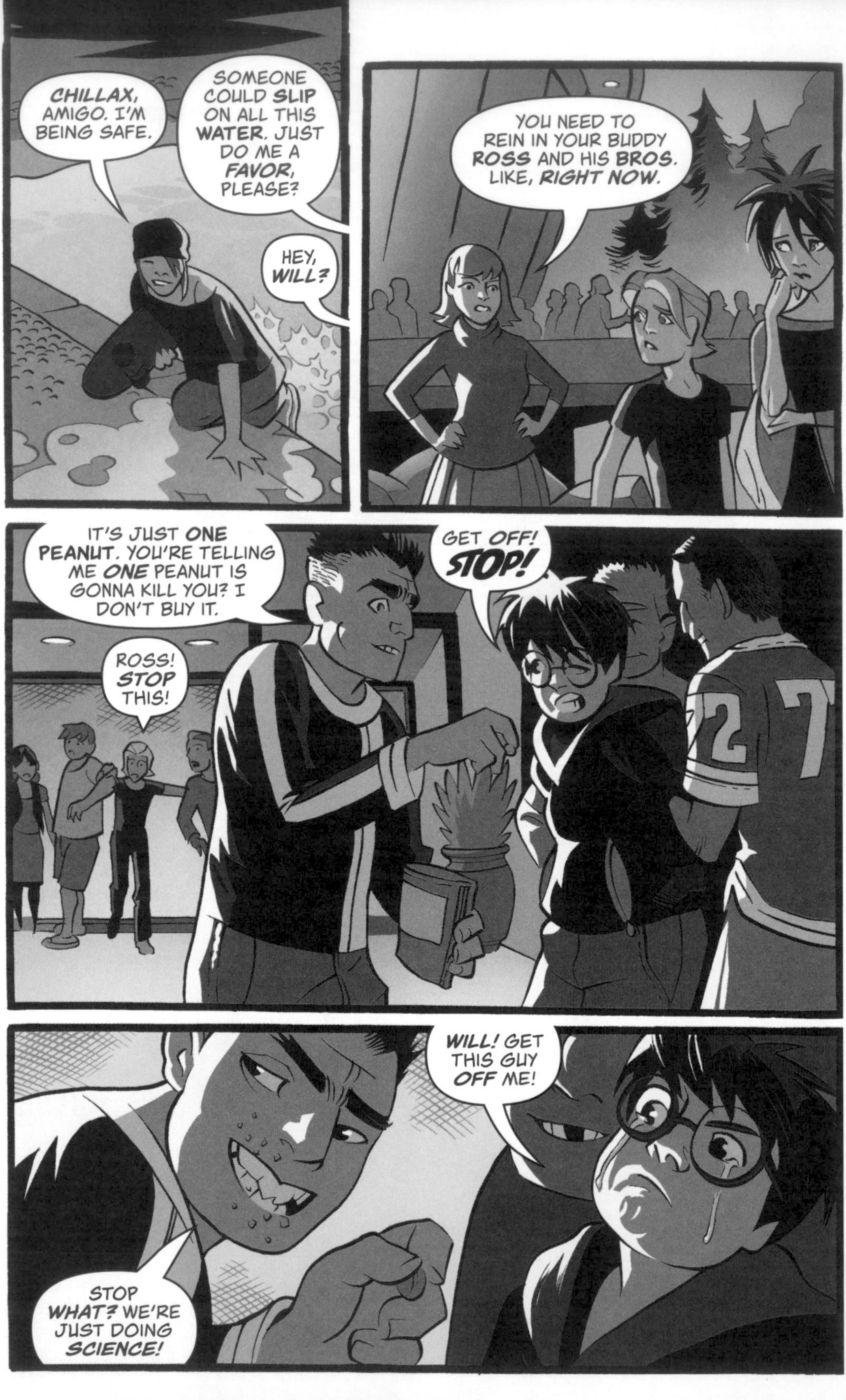

SOMEONE COULD SLIP ON ALL THIS WATER. JUST DO ME A FAVOR, PLEASE?
CHILLAX, AMIGO. I'M BEING SAFE.
HEY, WILL?
YOU NEED TO REIN IN YOUR BUDDY ROSS AND HIS BROS. LIKE, RIGHT NOW.
IT'S JUST ONE PEANUT. YOU'RE TELLING ME ONE PEANUT IS GONNA KILL YOU? I DON'T BUY IT.
GET OFF! STOP!
ROSS! STOP THIS!
72
WILL! GET THIS GUY OFF ME!
STOP WHAT? WE'RE JUST DOING SCIENCE!

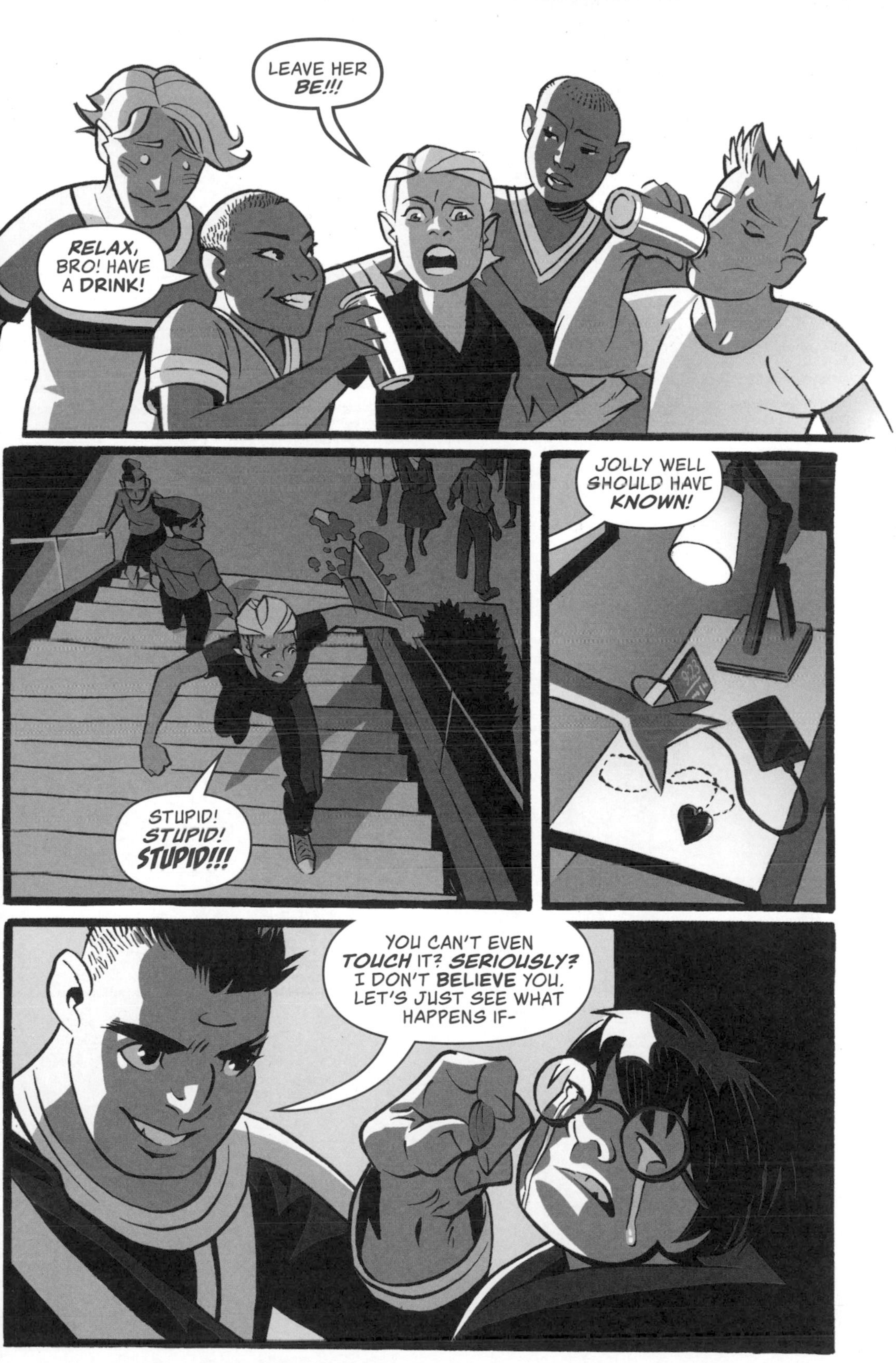
LEAVE HER BE!!!
RELAX, BRO! HAVE A DRINK!
JOLLY WELL SHOULD HAVE KNOWN!
STUPID! STUPID! STUPID!!!
YOU CAN'T EVEN TOUCH IT? SERIOUSLY? I DON'T BELIEVE YOU. LET'S JUST SEE WHAT HAPPENS IF-

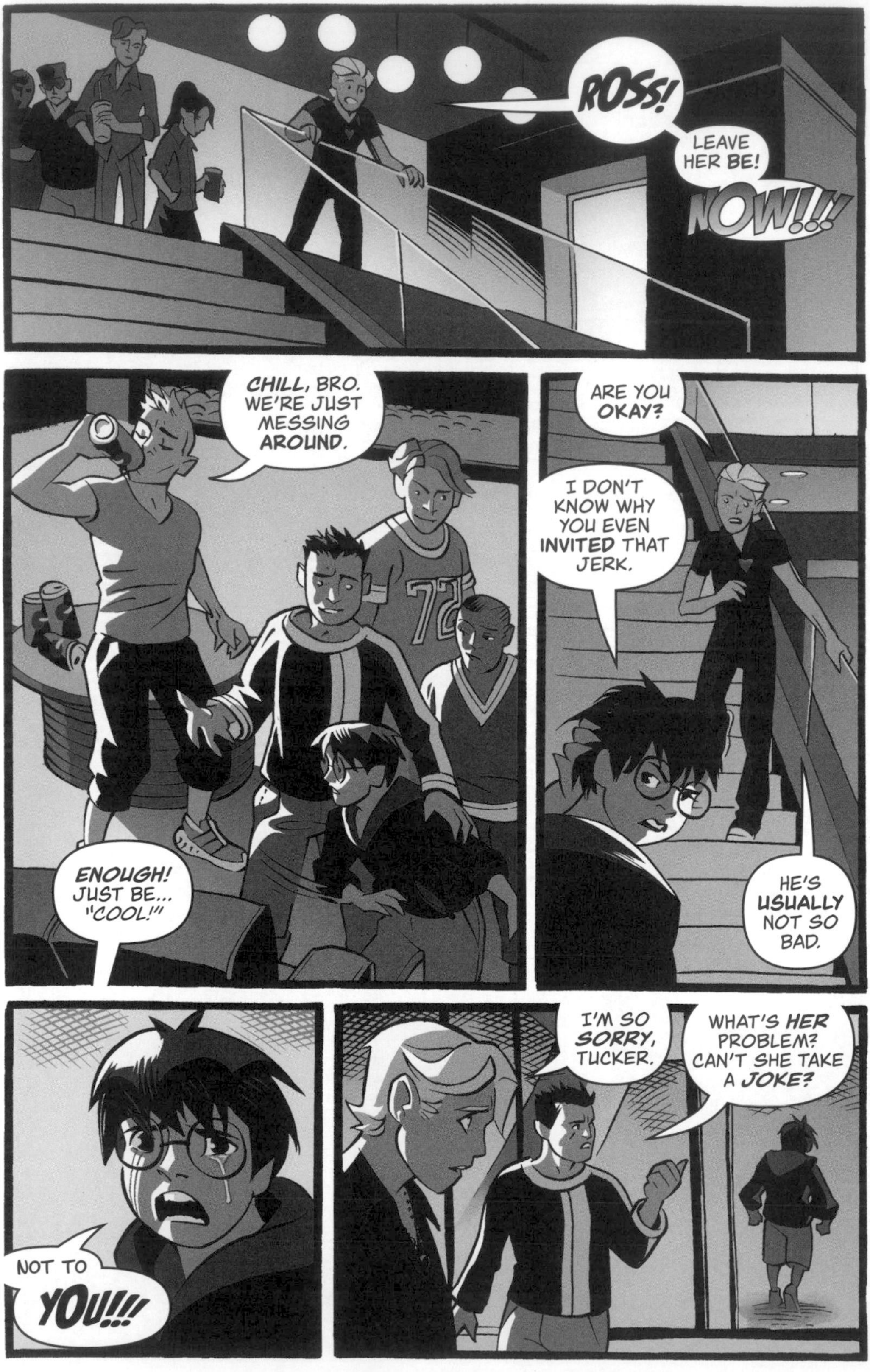
ROSS!
LEAVE HER BE!
NOW!!!
CHILL, BRO. WE'RE JUST MESSING AROUND.
ENOUGH! JUST BE... "COOL!"
ARE YOU OKAY?
I DON'T KNOW WHY YOU EVEN INVITED THAT JERK.
HE'S USUALLY NOT SO BAD.
NOT TO YOU!!!
I'M SO SORRY, TUCKER.
WHAT'S HER PROBLEM? CAN'T SHE TAKE A JOKE?
72

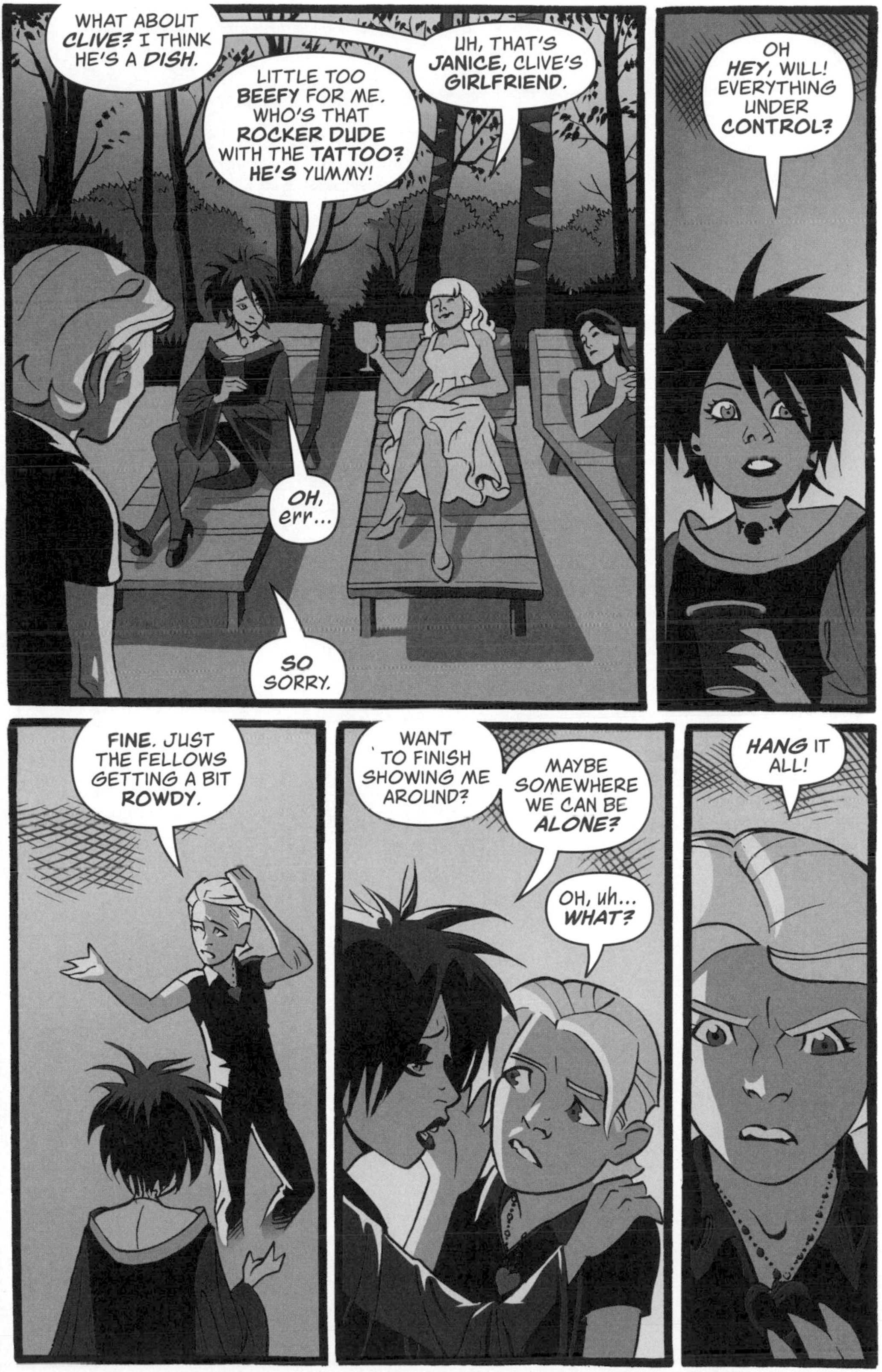
WHAT ABOUT CLIVE? I THINK HE'S A DISH.
LITTLE TOO BEEFY FOR ME. WHO'S THAT ROCKER DUDE WITH THE TATTOO? HE'S YUMMY!
UH, THAT'S JANICE, CLIVE'S GIRLFRIEND.
OH, err...
SO SORRY.
OH HEY, WILL! EVERYTHING UNDER CONTROL?
FINE. JUST THE FELLOWS GETTING A BIT ROWDY.
WANT TO FINISH SHOWING ME AROUND?
MAYBE SOMEWHERE WE CAN BE ALONE?
OH, uh... WHAT?
HANG IT ALL!

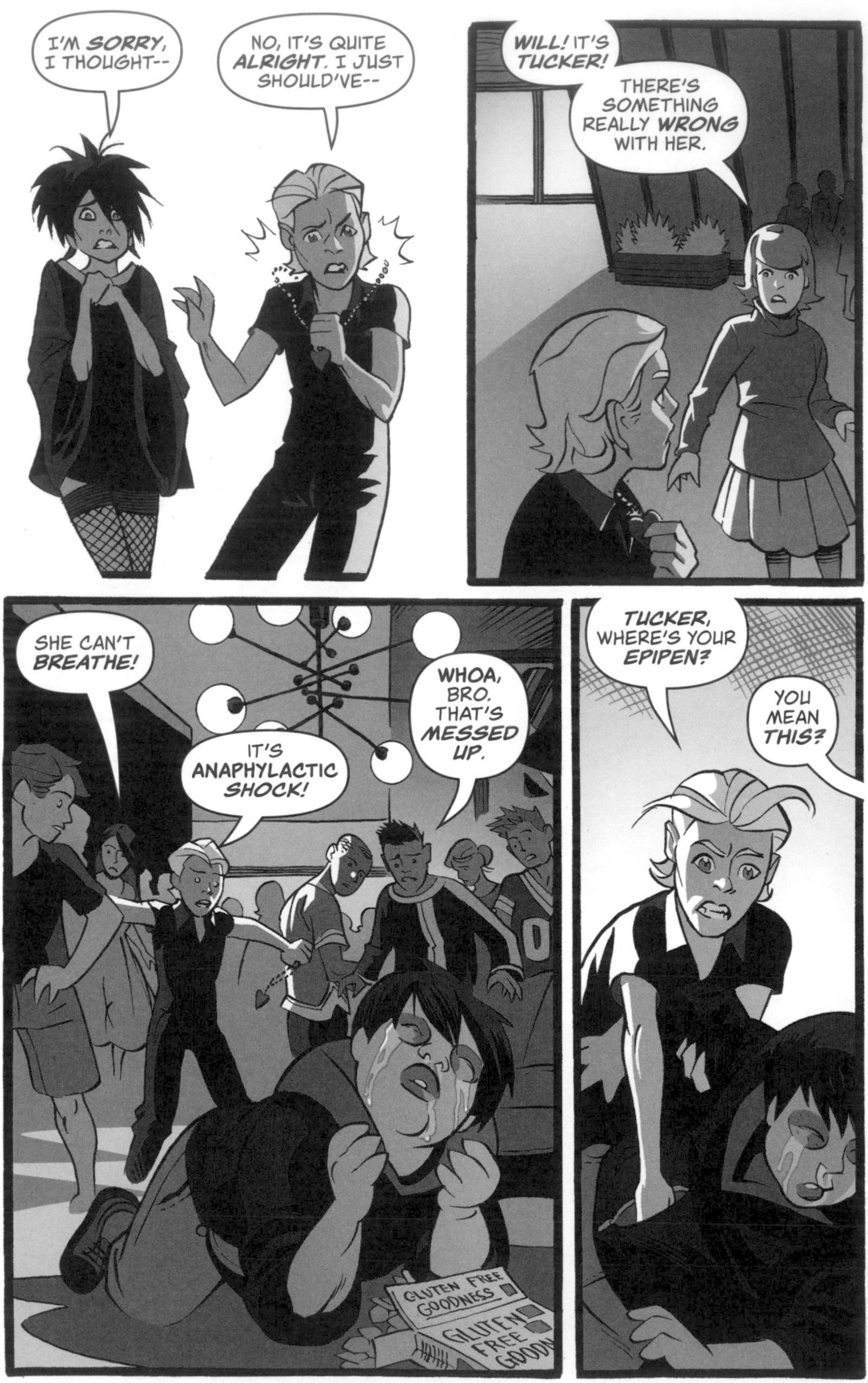
I'M SORRY, I THOUGHT--
NO, IT'S QUITE ALRIGHT. I JUST SHOULD'VE--
WILL! IT'S TUCKER!
THERE'S SOMETHING REALLY WRONG WITH HER.
SHE CAN'T BREATHE!
IT'S ANAPHYLACTIC SHOCK!
WHOA, BRO. THAT'S MESSED UP.
GLUTEN FREE GOODNESS
GLUTEN FREE GOODN
TUCKER, WHERE'S YOUR EPIPEN?
YOU MEAN THIS?

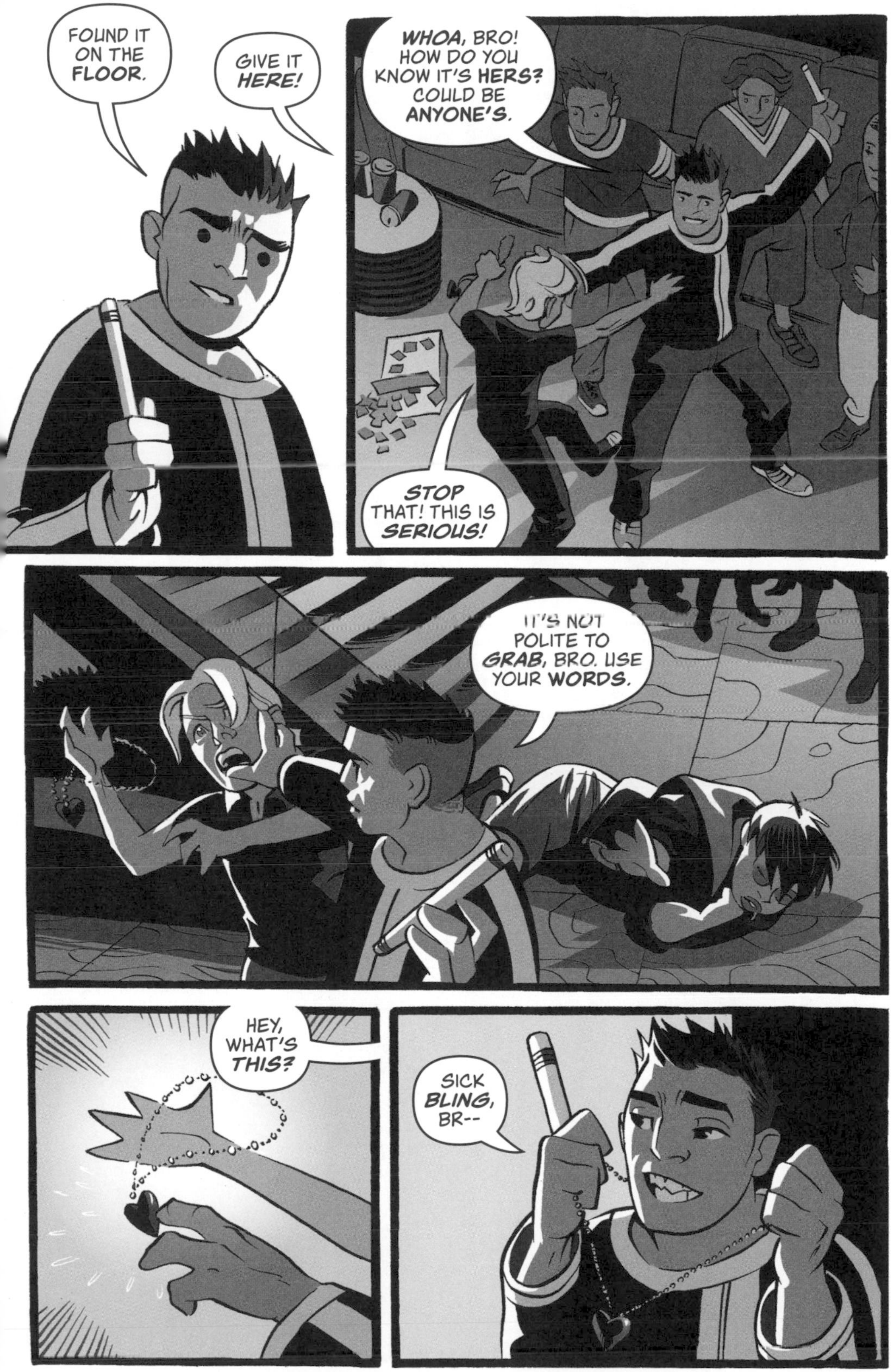
FOUND IT ON THE FLOOR.
GIVE IT HERE!
WHOA, BRO! HOW DO YOU KNOW IT'S HERS? COULD BE ANYONE'S.
STOP THAT! THIS IS SERIOUS!
IT'S NOT POLITE TO GRAB, BRO. USE YOUR WORDS.
HEY, WHAT'S THIS?
SICK BLING, BR--

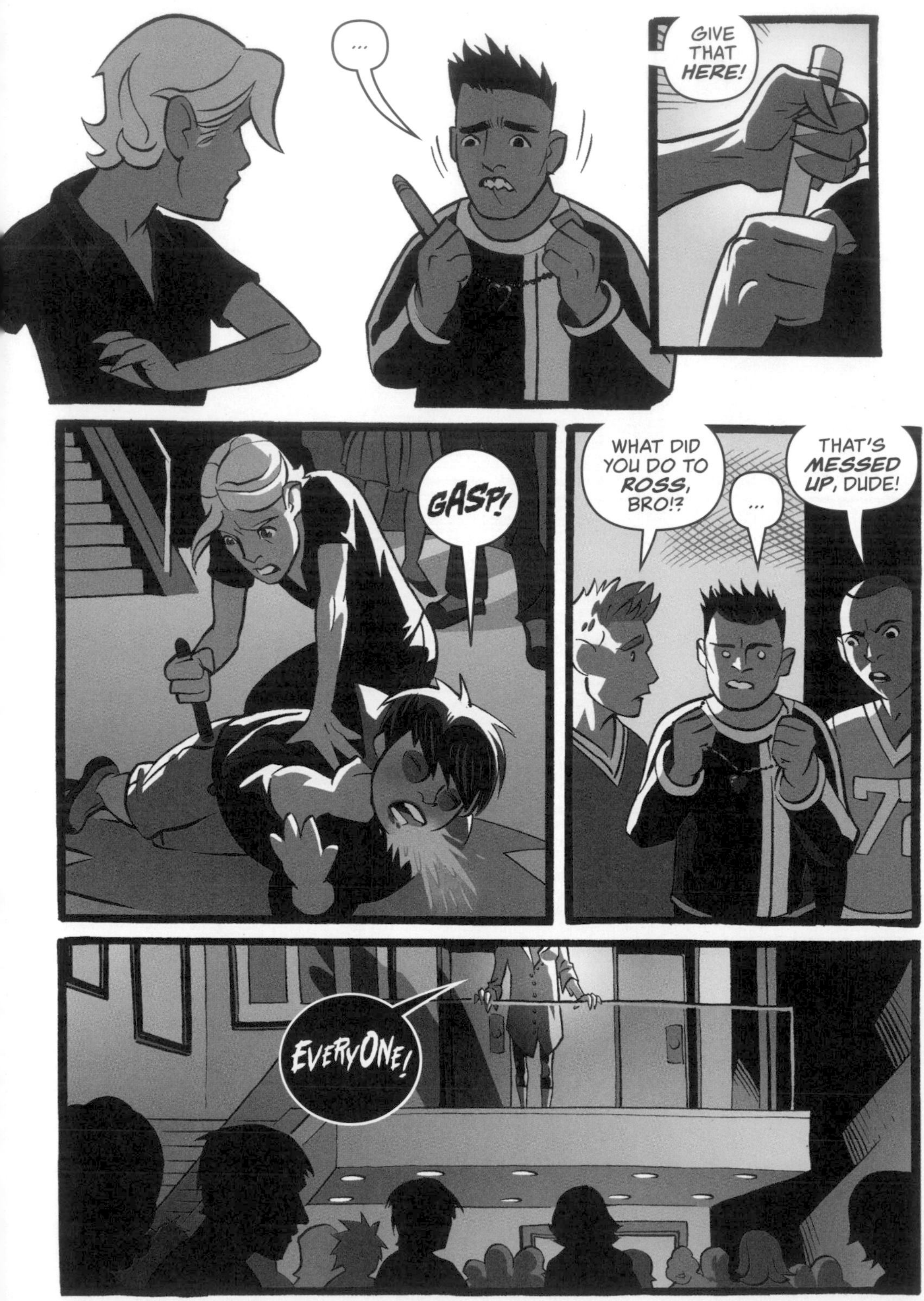
...
GIVE THAT HERE!
GASP!
WHAT DID YOU DO TO ROSS, BRO!?
...
THAT'S MESSED UP, DUDE!
EVERYONE!

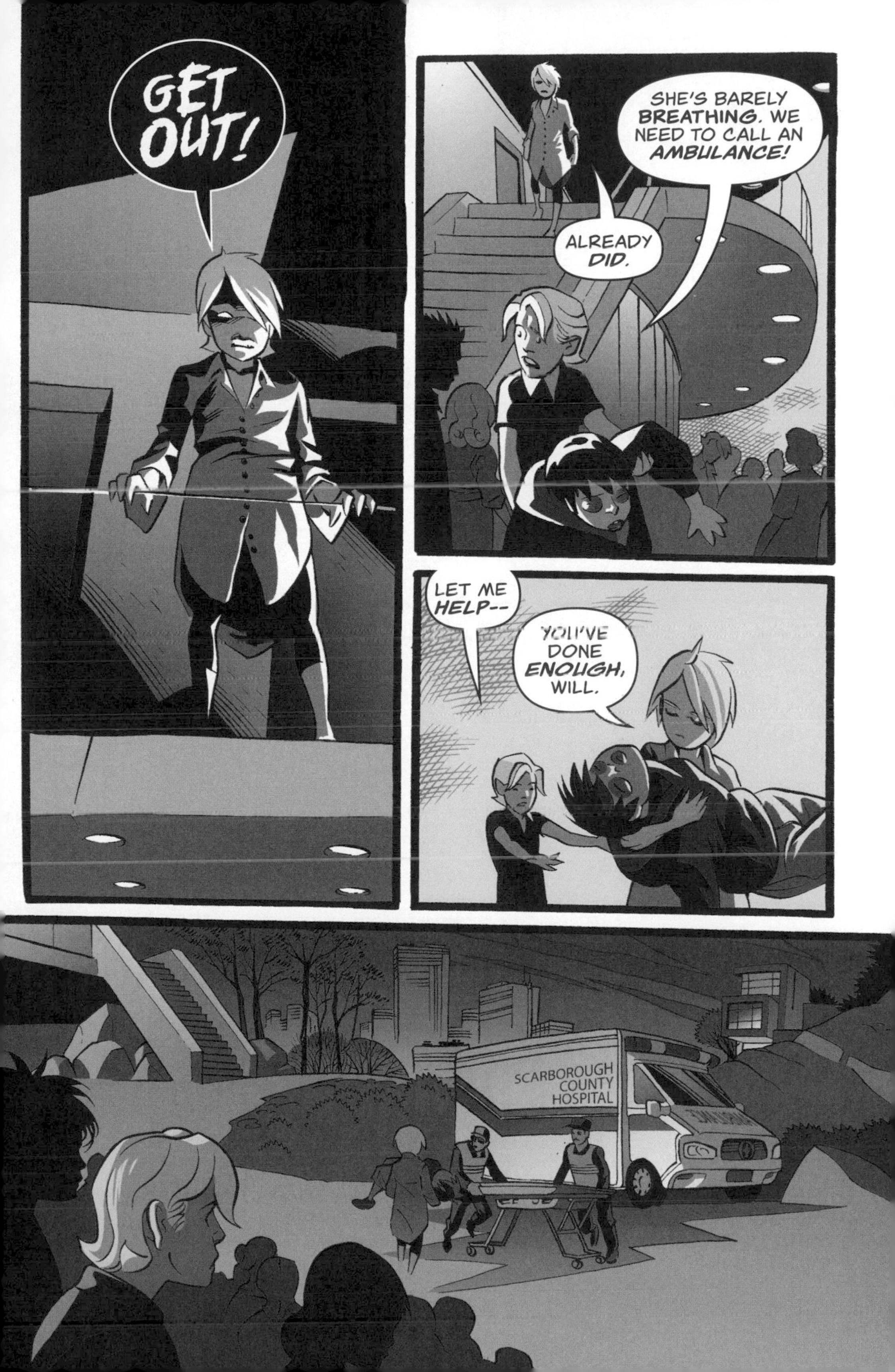
GET OUT!
SHE'S BARELY BREATHING. WE NEED TO CALL AN AMBULANCE!
ALREADY DID.
LET ME HELP--
YOU'VE DONE ENOUGH, WILL.
SCARBOROUGH COUNTY HOSPITAL

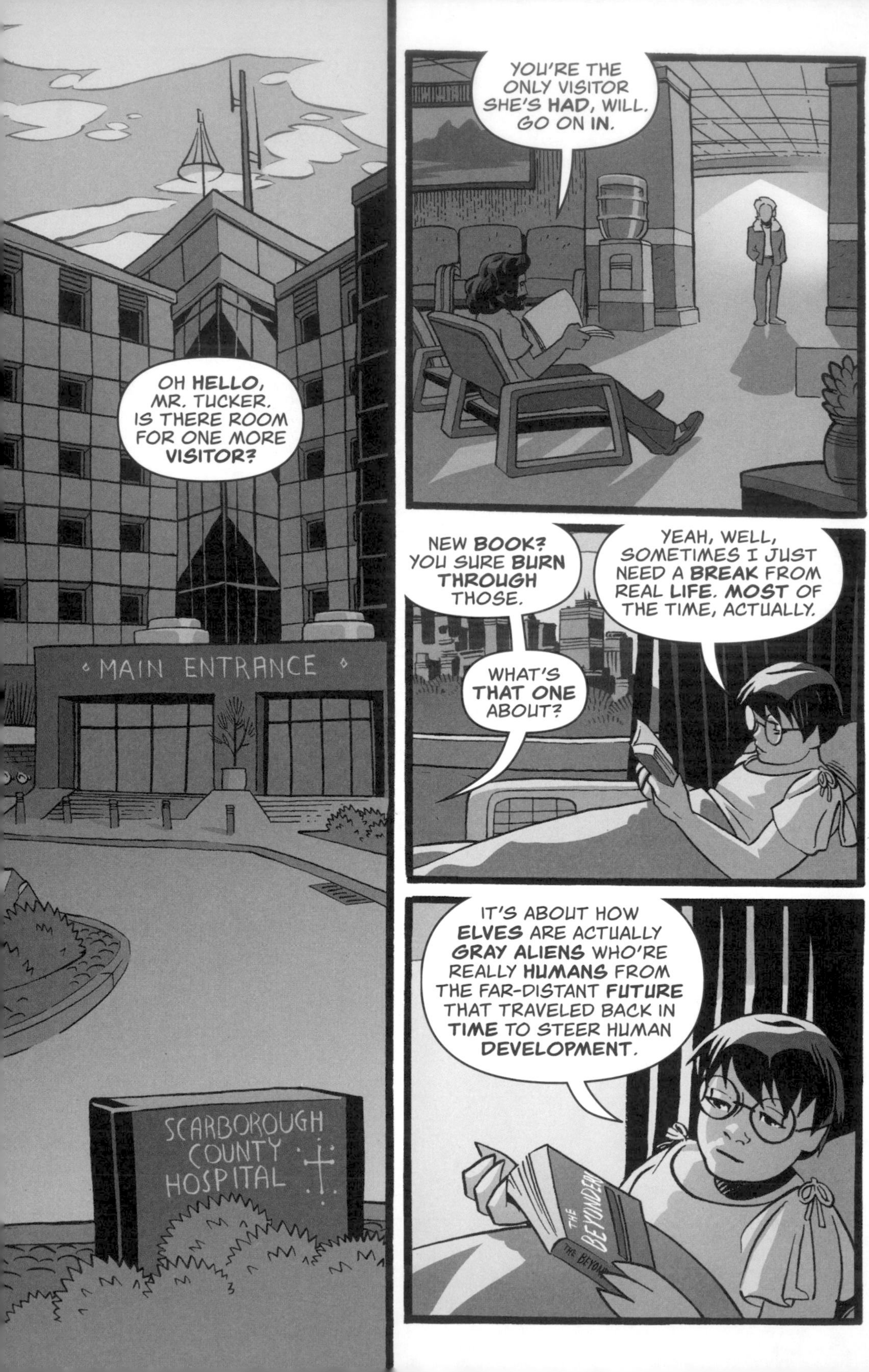
OH HELLO, MR. TUCKER. IS THERE ROOM FOR ONE MORE VISITOR?
MAIN ENTRANCE
SCARBOROUGH COUNTY HOSPITAL
YOU'RE THE ONLY VISITOR SHE'S HAD, WILL. GO ON IN.
NEW BOOK? YOU SURE BURN THROUGH THOSE.
YEAH, WELL, SOMETIMES I JUST NEED A BREAK FROM REAL LIFE. MOST OF THE TIME, ACTUALLY.
WHAT'S THAT ONE ABOUT?
IT'S ABOUT HOW ELVES ARE ACTUALLY GRAY ALIENS WHO'RE REALLY HUMANS FROM THE FAR-DISTANT FUTURE THAT TRAVELED BACK IN TIME TO STEER HUMAN DEVELOPMENT.
THE BEYONDER

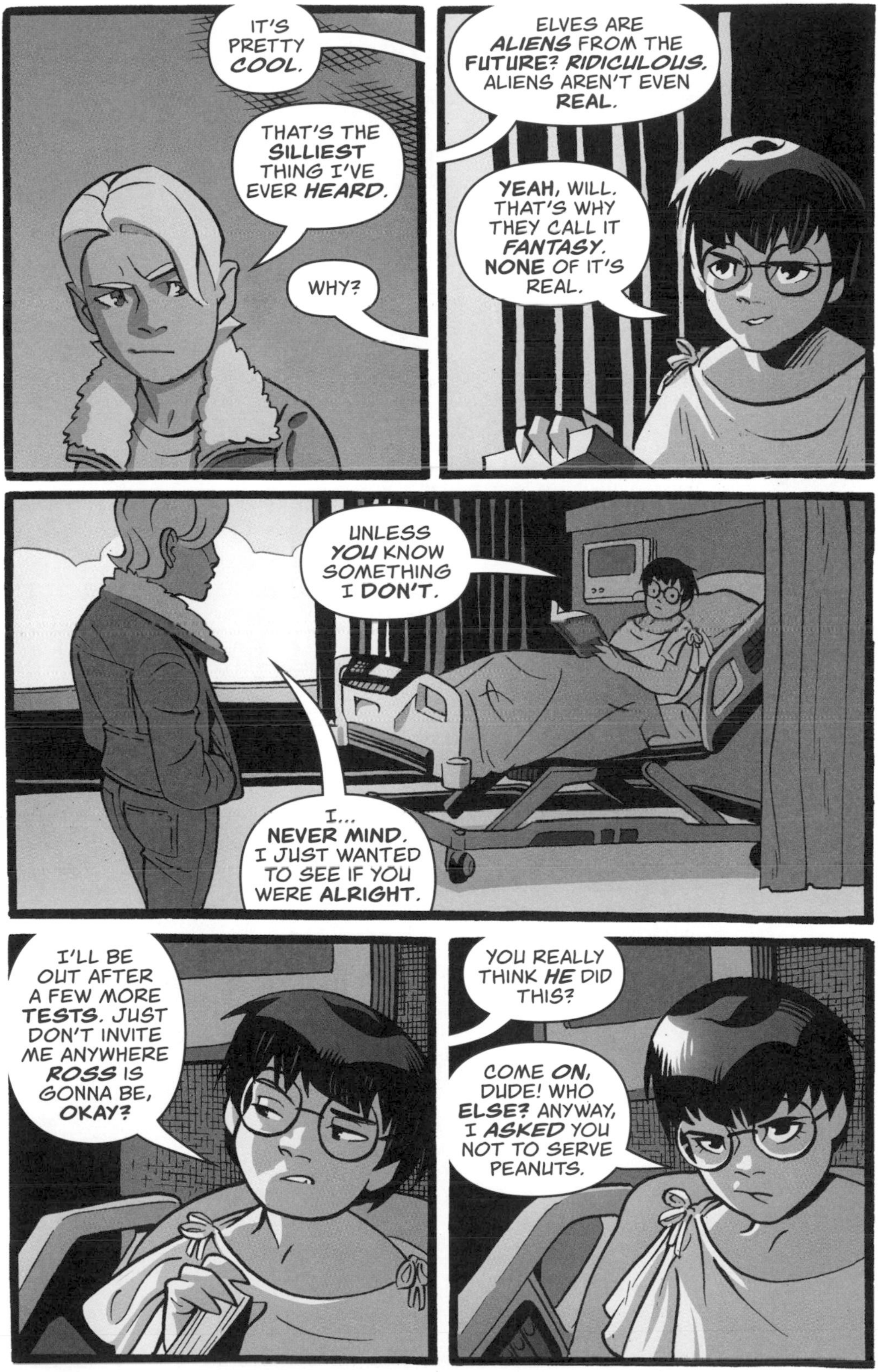
IT'S PRETTY COOL.
ELVES ARE ALIENS FROM THE FUTURE? RIDICULOUS. ALIENS AREN'T EVEN REAL.
THAT'S THE SILLIEST THING I'VE EVER HEARD.
WHY?
YEAH, WILL. THAT'S WHY THEY CALL IT FANTASY. NONE OF IT'S REAL.
UNLESS YOU KNOW SOMETHING I DON'T.
I... NEVER MIND. I JUST WANTED TO SEE IF YOU WERE ALRIGHT.
I'LL BE OUT AFTER A FEW MORE TESTS. JUST DON'T INVITE ME ANYWHERE ROSS IS GONNA BE, OKAY?
YOU REALLY THINK HE DID THIS?
COME ON, DUDE! WHO ELSE? ANYWAY, I ASKED YOU NOT TO SERVE PEANUTS.

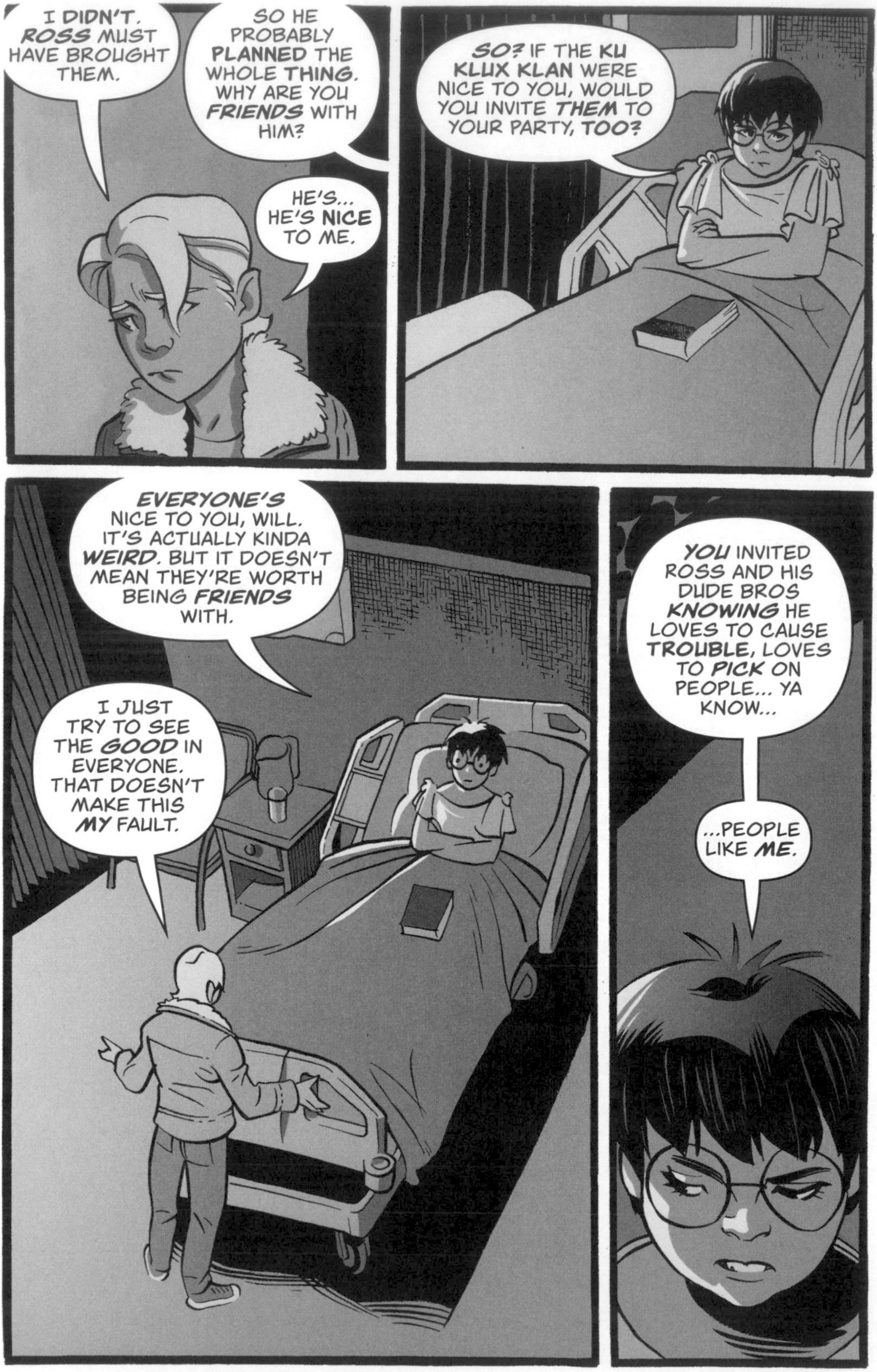
I DIDN'T. ROSS MUST HAVE BROUGHT THEM.
SO HE PROBABLY PLANNED THE WHOLE THING. WHY ARE YOU FRIENDS WITH HIM?
HE'S... HE'S NICE TO ME.
SO? IF THE KU KLUX KLAN WERE NICE TO YOU, WOULD YOU INVITE THEM TO YOUR PARTY, TOO?
EVERYONE'S NICE TO YOU, WILL. IT'S ACTUALLY KINDA WEIRD. BUT IT DOESN'T MEAN THEY'RE WORTH BEING FRIENDS WITH.
I JUST TRY TO SEE THE GOOD IN EVERYONE. THAT DOESN'T MAKE THIS MY FAULT.
YOU INVITED ROSS AND HIS DUDE BROS KNOWING HE LOVES TO CAUSE TROUBLE, LOVES TO PICK ON PEOPLE... YA KNOW...
...PEOPLE LIKE ME.

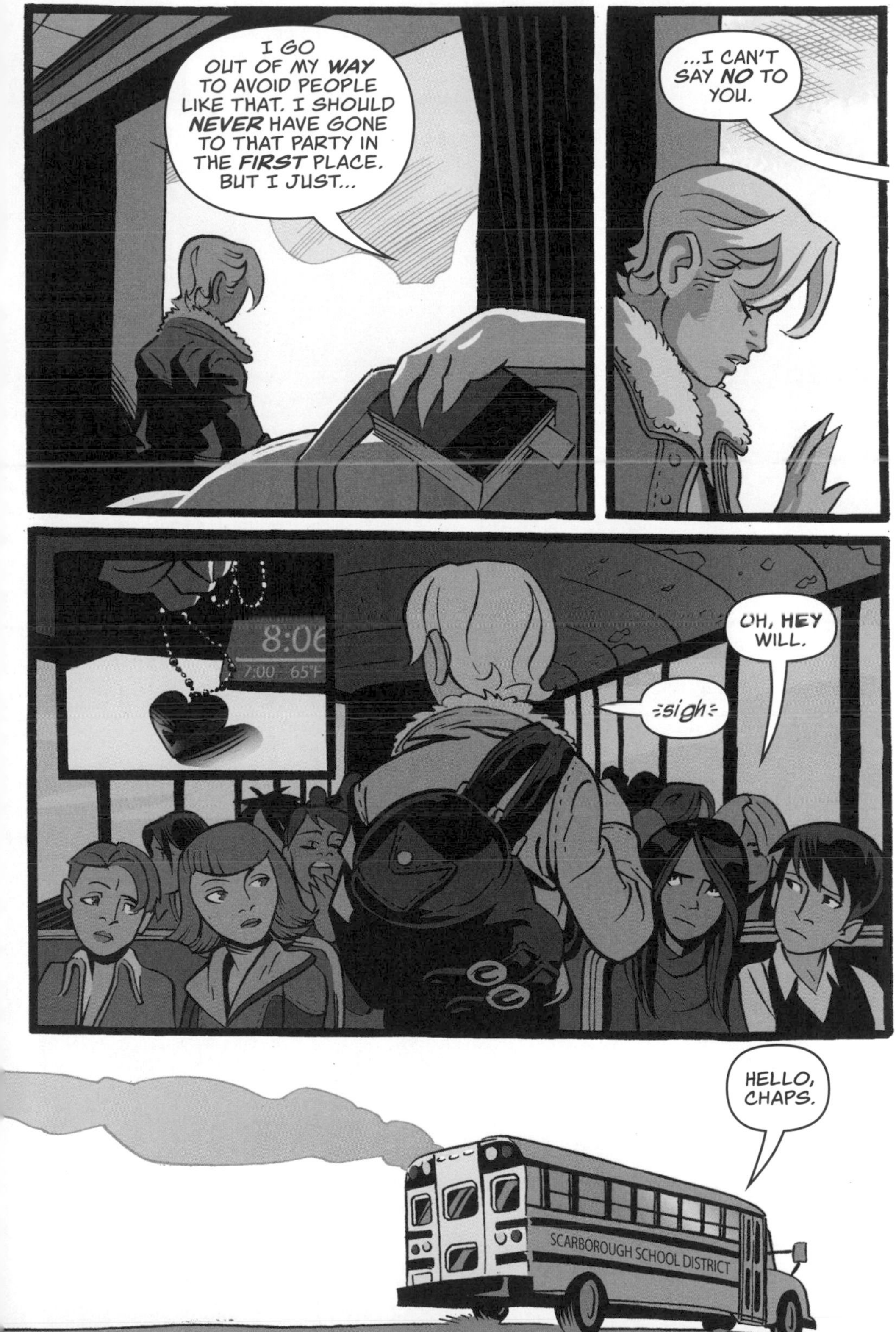
I GO OUT OF MY WAY TO AVOID PEOPLE LIKE THAT. I SHOULD NEVER HAVE GONE TO THAT PARTY IN THE FIRST PLACE. BUT I JUST...
...I CAN'T SAY NO TO YOU.
8:06
7:00 65°F
OH, HEY WILL.
sigh
HELLO, CHAPS.
SCARBOROUGH SCHOOL DISTRICT

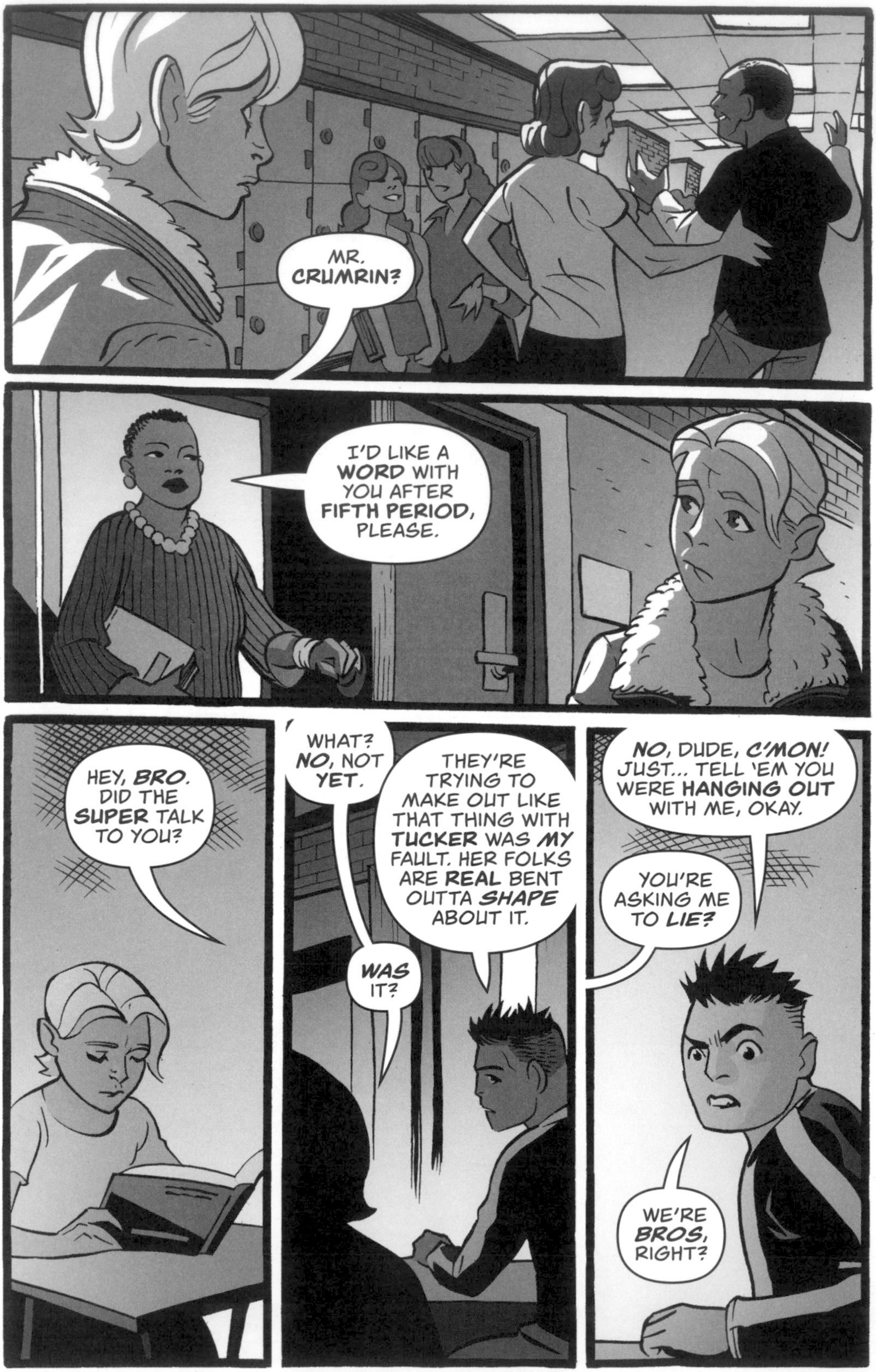
MR. CRUMRIN?
I'D LIKE A WORD WITH YOU AFTER FIFTH PERIOD, PLEASE.
HEY, BRO. DID THE SUPER TALK TO YOU?
WHAT? NO, NOT YET.
THEY'RE TRYING TO MAKE OUT LIKE THAT THING WITH TUCKER WAS MY FAULT. HER FOLKS ARE REAL BENT OUTTA SHAPE ABOUT IT.
WAS IT?
NO, DUDE, C'MON! JUST... TELL 'EM YOU WERE HANGING OUT WITH ME, OKAY.
YOU'RE ASKING ME TO LIE?
WE'RE BROS, RIGHT?

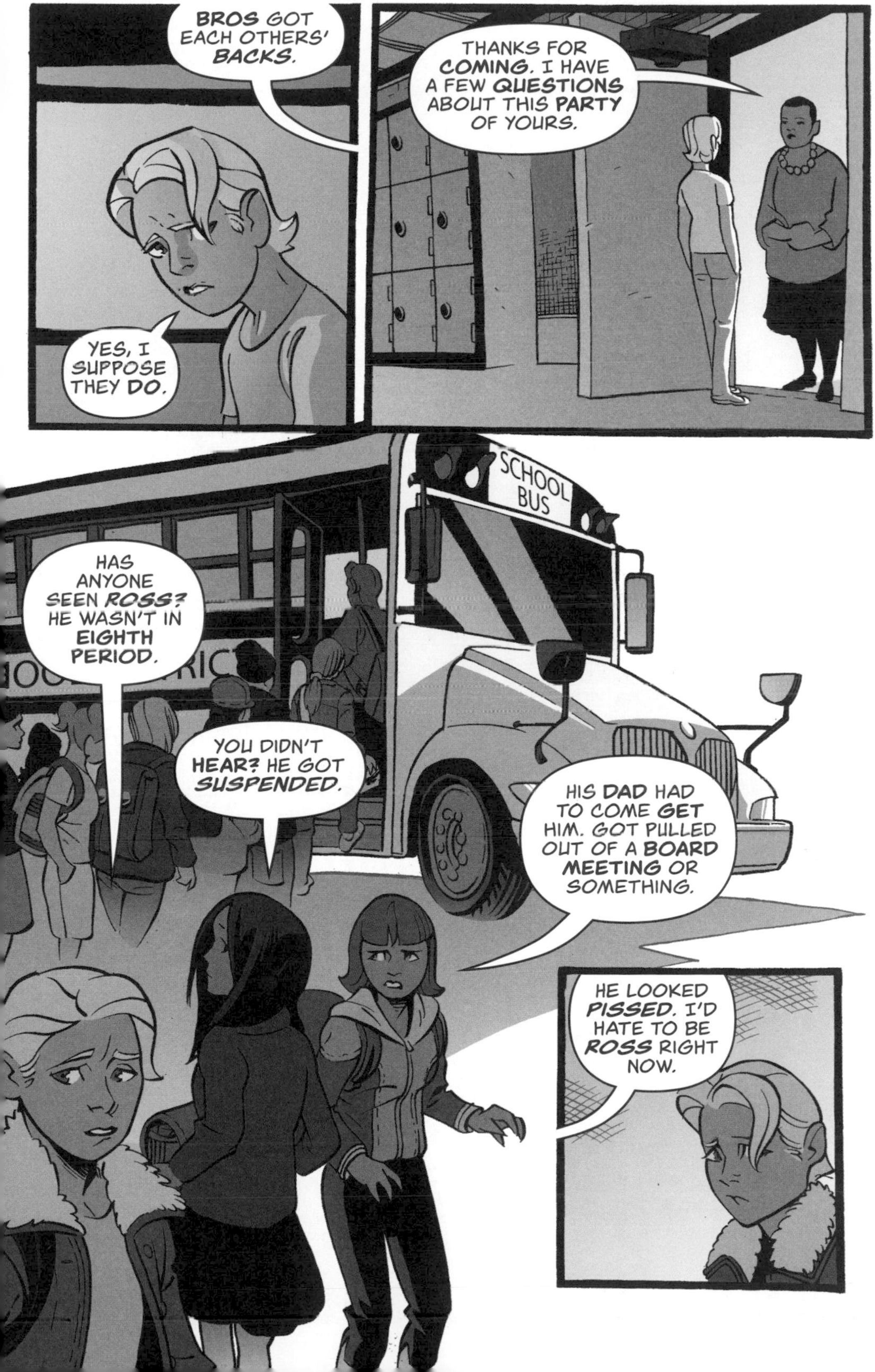
BROS GOT EACH OTHERS' BACKS.
YES, I SUPPOSE THEY DO.
THANKS FOR COMING. I HAVE A FEW QUESTIONS ABOUT THIS PARTY OF YOURS.
SCHOOL BUS
HAS ANYONE SEEN ROSS? HE WASN'T IN EIGHTH PERIOD.
YOU DIDN'T HEAR? HE GOT SUSPENDED.
HIS DAD HAD TO COME GET HIM. GOT PULLED OUT OF A BOARD MEETING OR SOMETHING.
HE LOOKED PISSED. I'D HATE TO BE ROSS RIGHT NOW.

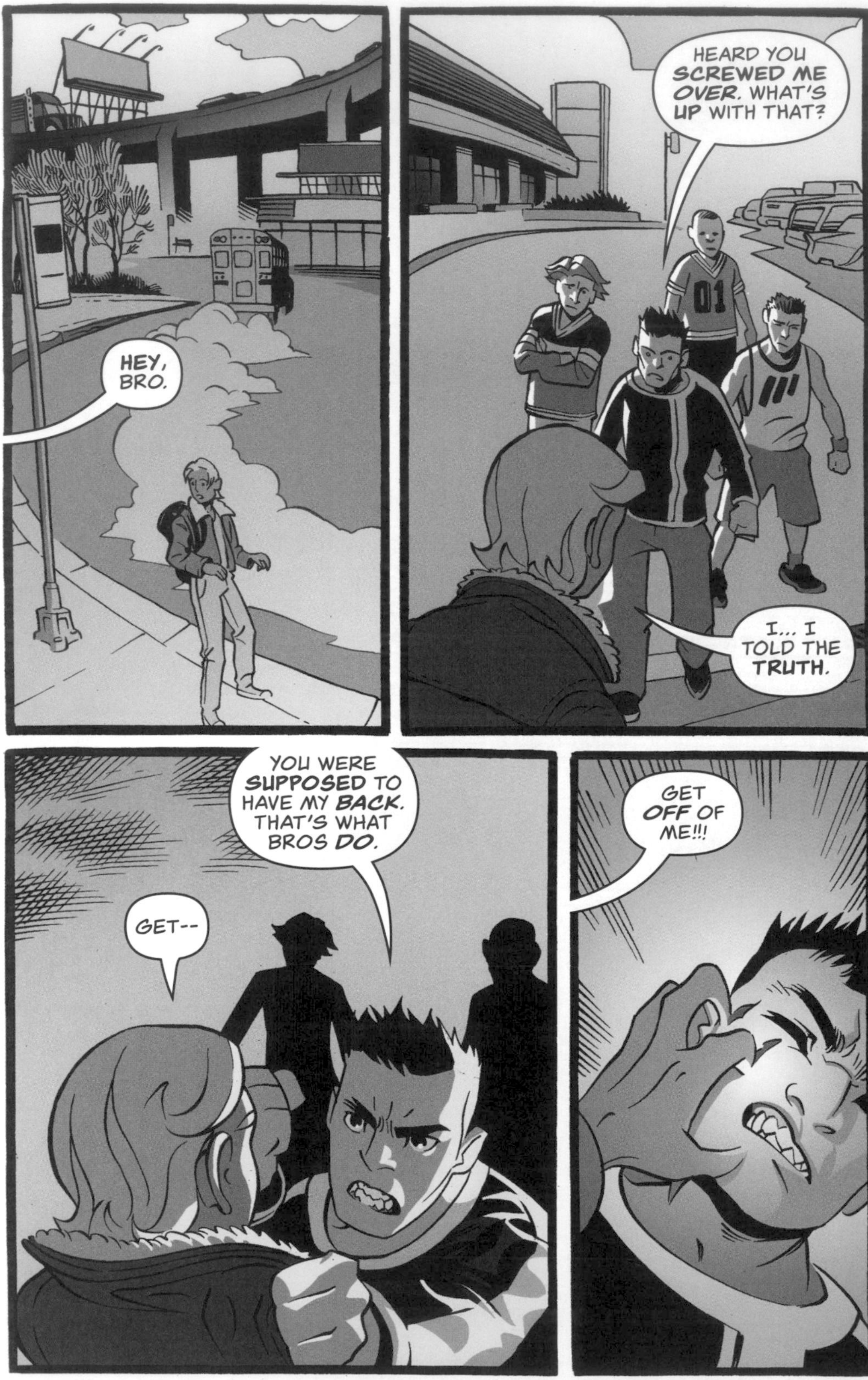
HEY, BRO.
HEARD YOU SCREWED ME OVER. WHAT'S UP WITH THAT?
I... I TOLD THE TRUTH.
YOU WERE SUPPOSED TO HAVE MY BACK. THAT'S WHAT BROS DO.
GET--
GET OFF OF ME!!!

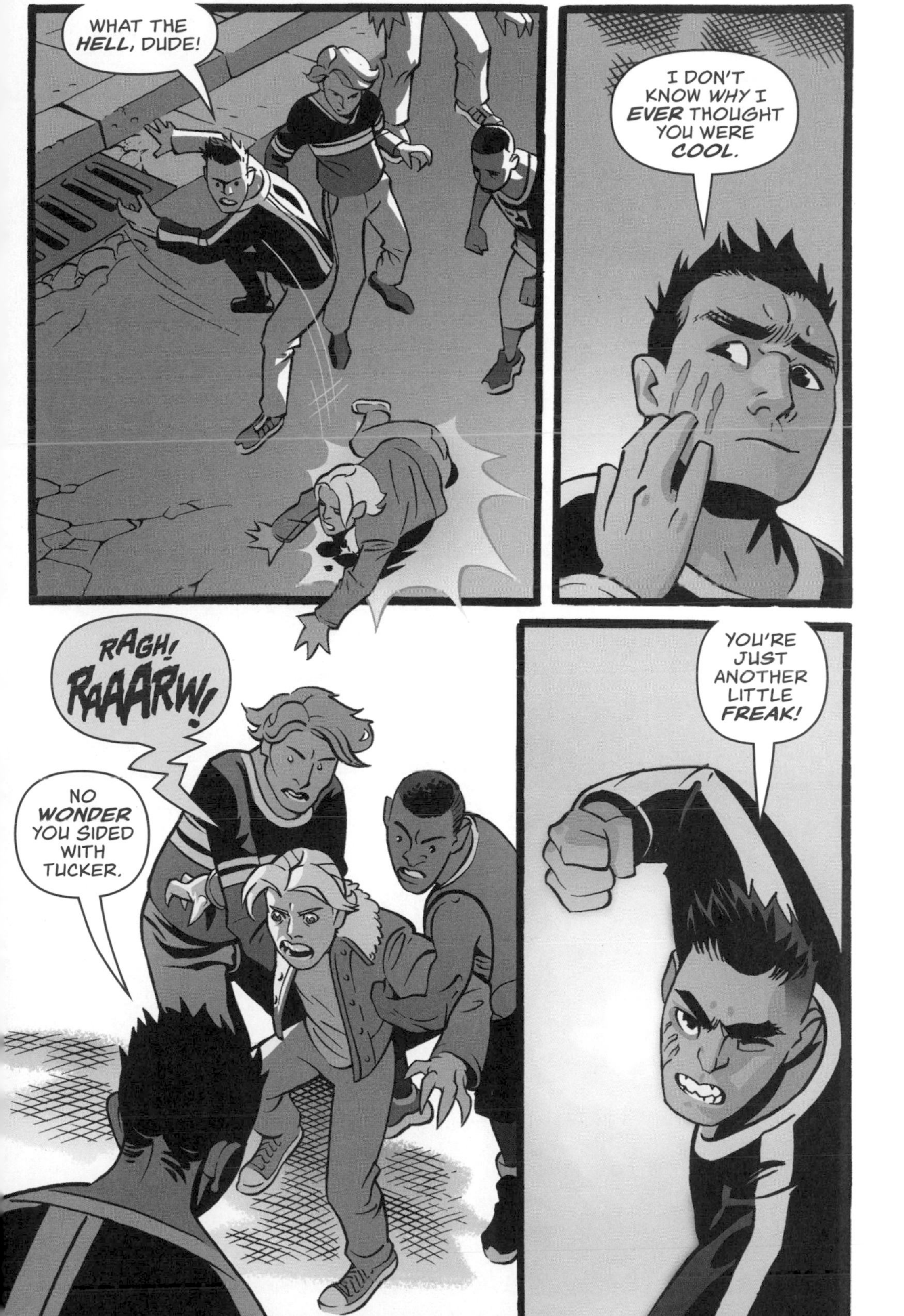
WHAT THE HELL, DUDE!
I DON'T KNOW WHY I EVER THOUGHT YOU WERE COOL.
RAGH! RAAARW!
NO WONDER YOU SIDED WITH TUCKER.
YOU'RE JUST ANOTHER LITTLE FREAK!

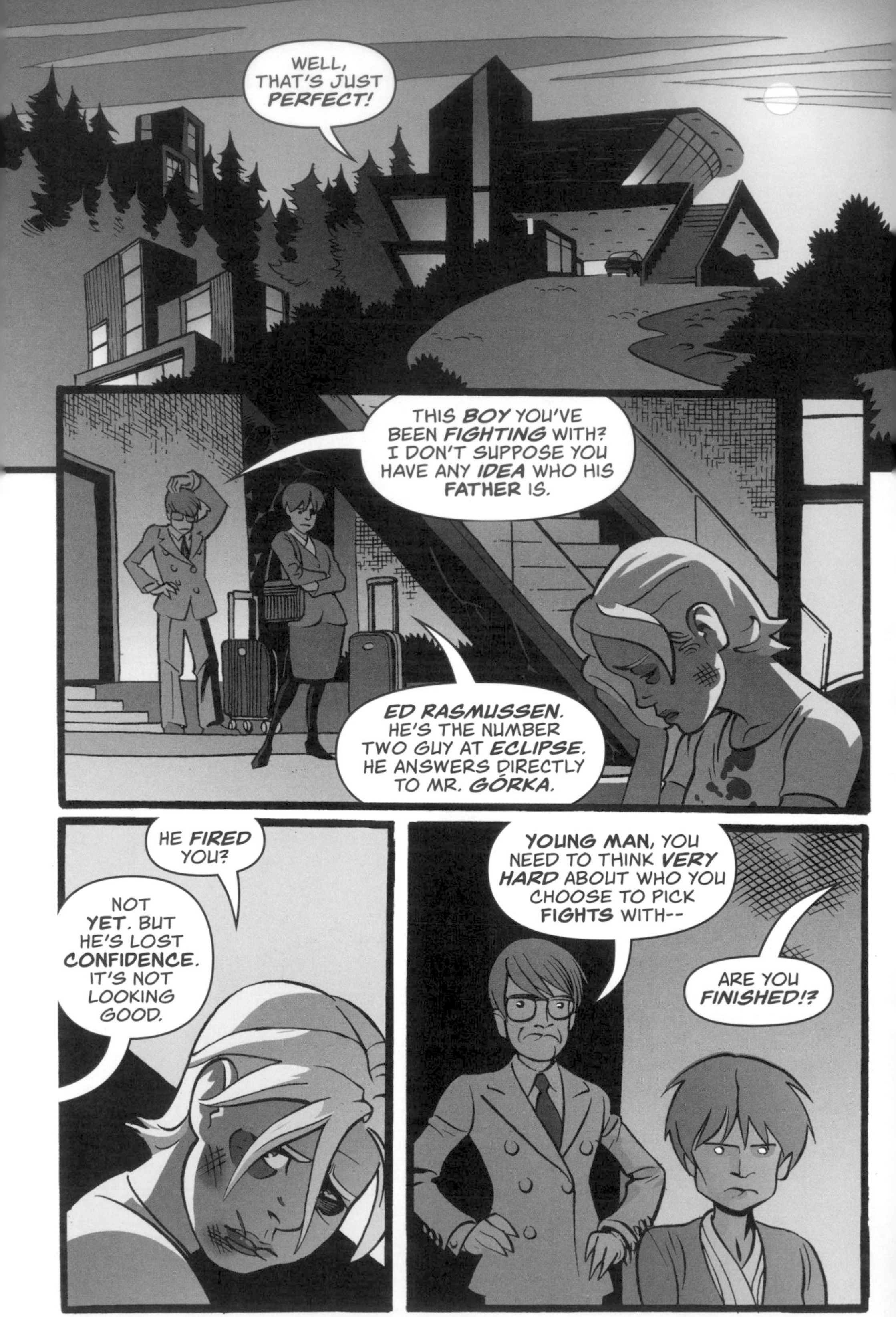
WELL, THAT'S JUST PERFECT!
THIS BOY YOU'VE BEEN FIGHTING WITH? I DON'T SUPPOSE YOU HAVE ANY IDEA WHO HIS FATHER IS.
ED RASMUSSEN. HE'S THE NUMBER TWO GUY AT ECLIPSE. HE ANSWERS DIRECTLY TO MR. GÓRKA.
HE FIRED YOU?
NOT YET. BUT HE'S LOST CONFIDENCE. IT'S NOT LOOKING GOOD.
YOUNG MAN, YOU NEED TO THINK VERY HARD ABOUT WHO YOU CHOOSE TO PICK FIGHTS WITH--
ARE YOU FINISHED!?

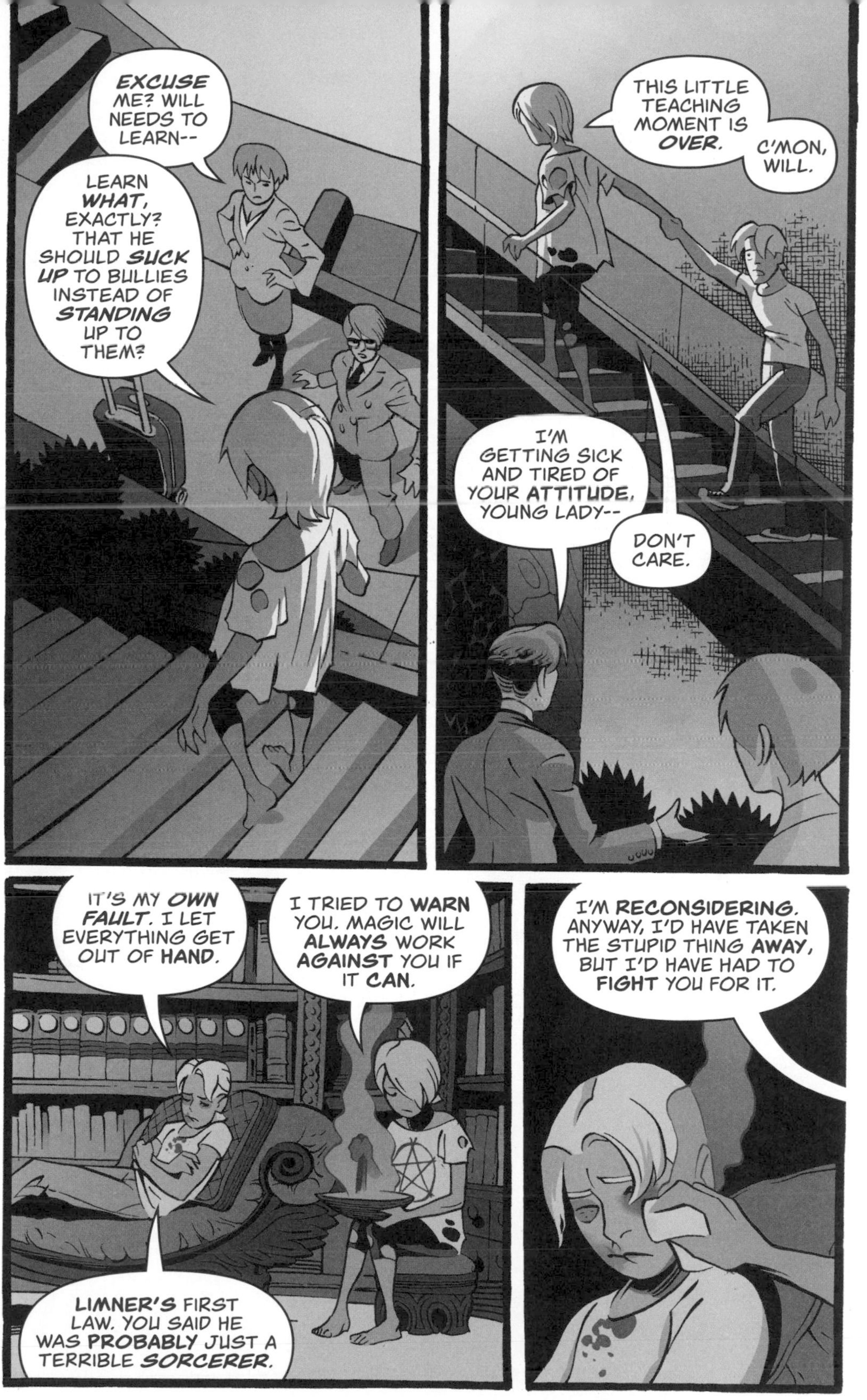
EXCUSE ME? WILL NEEDS TO LEARN--
LEARN WHAT, EXACTLY? THAT HE SHOULD SUCK UP TO BULLIES INSTEAD OF STANDING UP TO THEM?
THIS LITTLE TEACHING MOMENT IS OVER.
C'MON, WILL.
I'M GETTING SICK AND TIRED OF YOUR ATTITUDE, YOUNG LADY--
DON'T CARE.
IT'S MY OWN FAULT. I LET EVERYTHING GET OUT OF HAND.
I TRIED TO WARN YOU. MAGIC WILL ALWAYS WORK AGAINST YOU IF IT CAN.
LIMNER'S FIRST LAW. YOU SAID HE WAS PROBABLY JUST A TERRIBLE SORCERER.
I'M RECONSIDERING. ANYWAY, I'D HAVE TAKEN THE STUPID THING AWAY, BUT I'D HAVE HAD TO FIGHT YOU FOR IT.

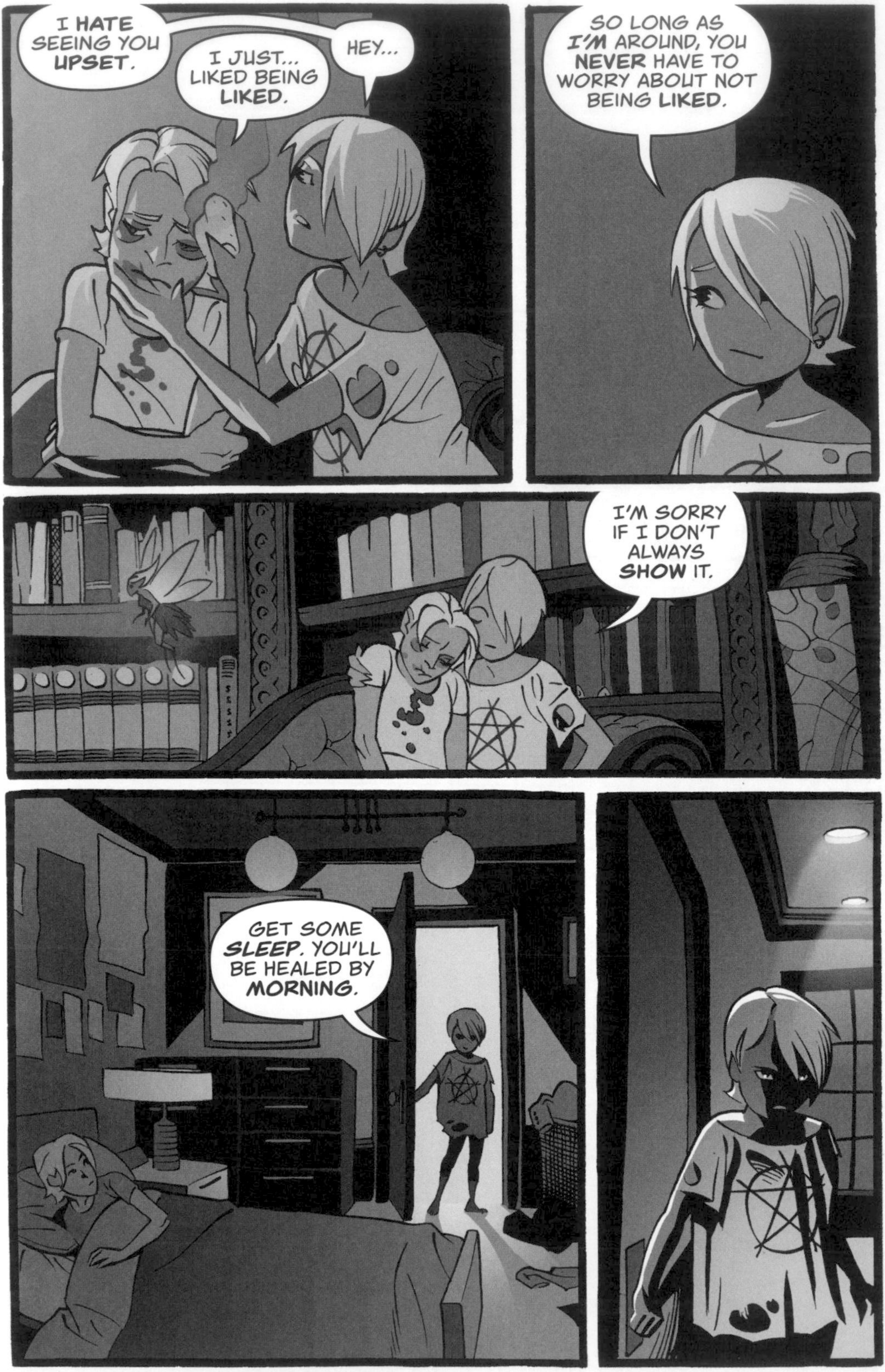
I HATE SEEING YOU UPSET.
I JUST... LIKED BEING LIKED.
HEY...
SO LONG AS I'M AROUND, YOU NEVER HAVE TO WORRY ABOUT NOT BEING LIKED.
I'M SORRY IF I DON'T ALWAYS SHOW IT.
GET SOME SLEEP. YOU'LL BE HEALED BY MORNING.

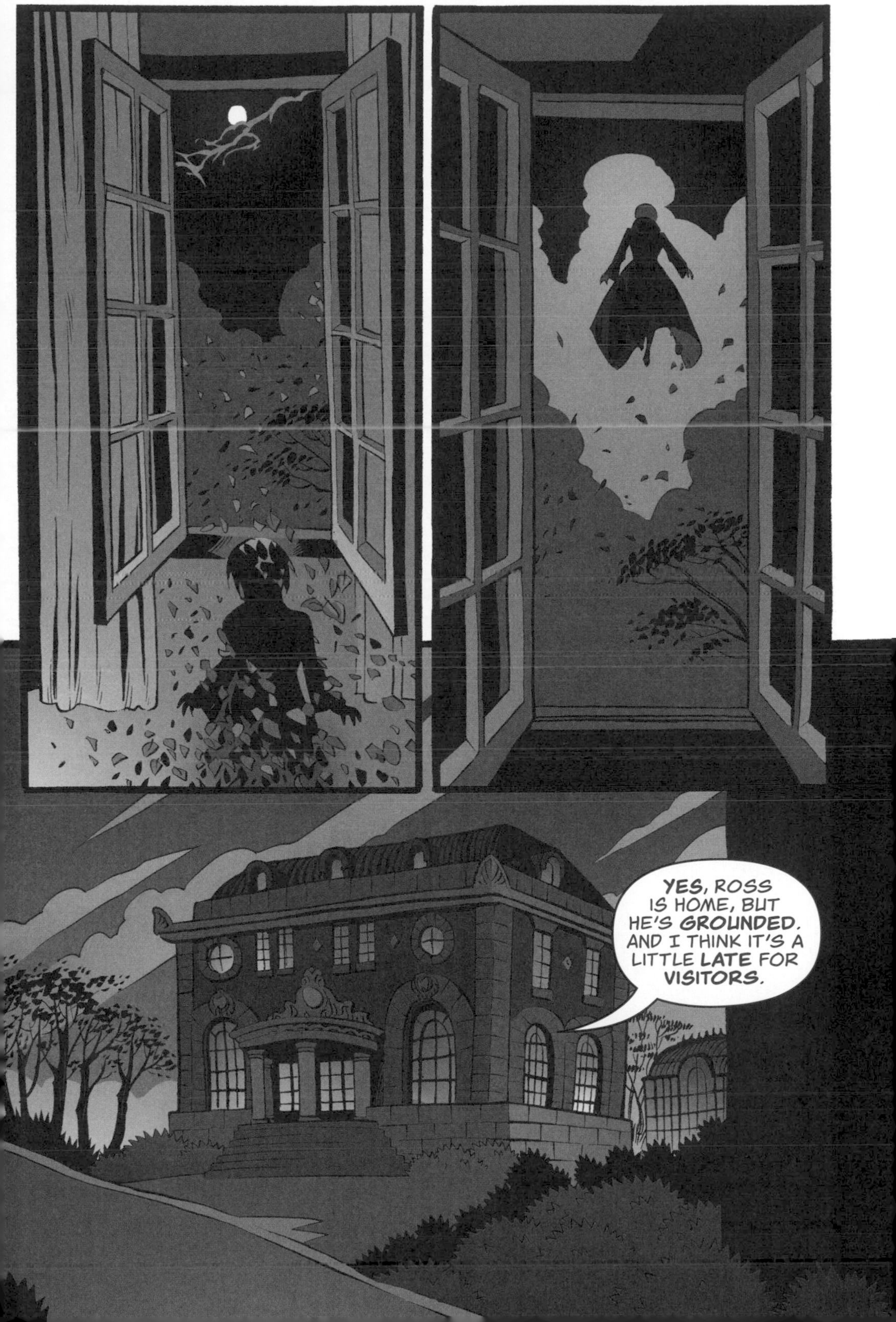
YES, ROSS IS HOME, BUT HE'S GROUNDED. AND I THINK IT'S A LITTLE LATE FOR VISITORS.

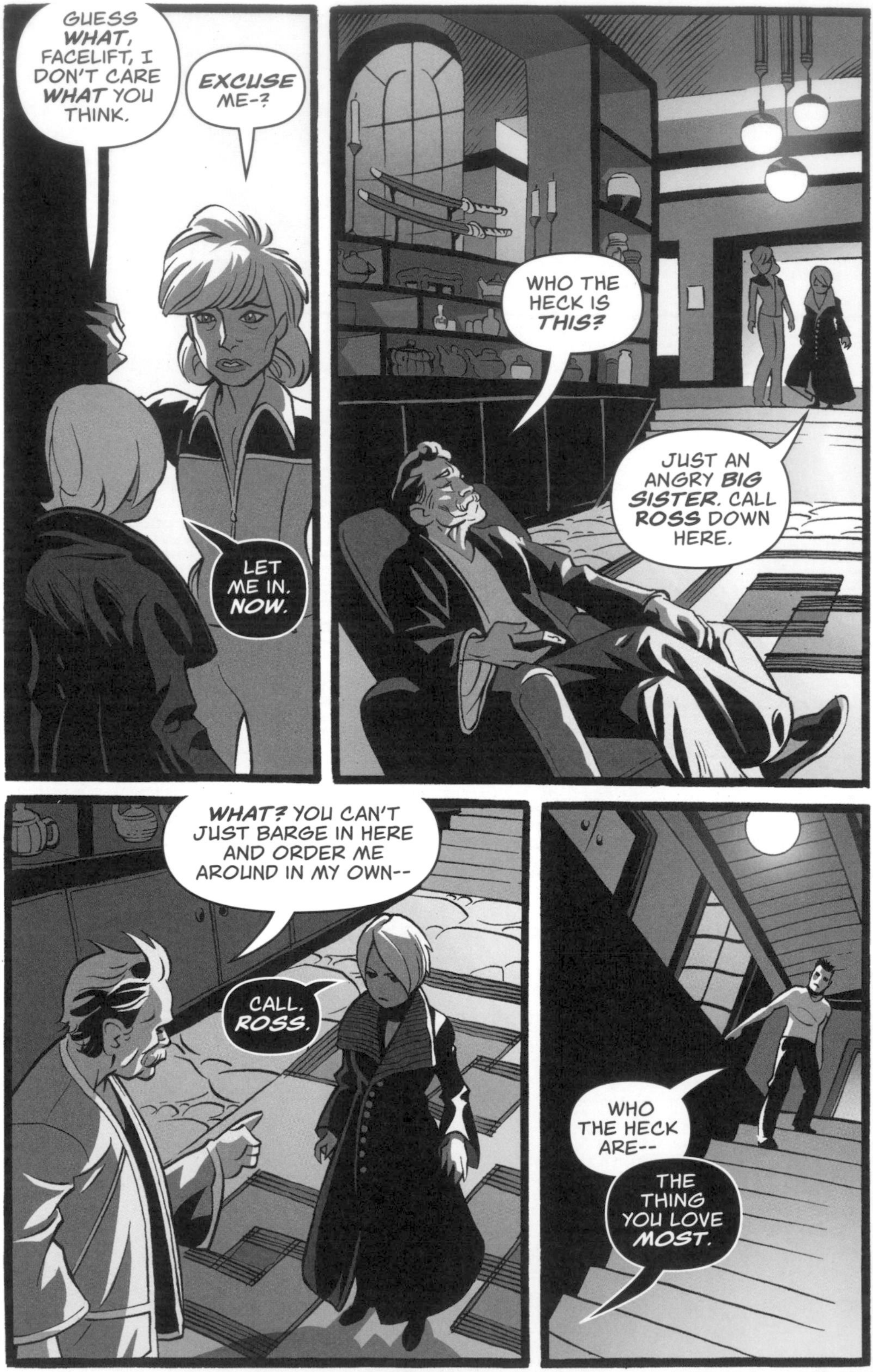
GUESS WHAT, FACELIFT, I DON'T CARE WHAT YOU THINK.
EXCUSE ME-?
LET ME IN. NOW.
WHO THE HECK IS THIS?
JUST AN ANGRY BIG SISTER. CALL ROSS DOWN HERE.
WHAT? YOU CAN'T JUST BARGE IN HERE AND ORDER ME AROUND IN MY OWN--
CALL. ROSS.
WHO THE HECK ARE--
THE THING YOU LOVE MOST.

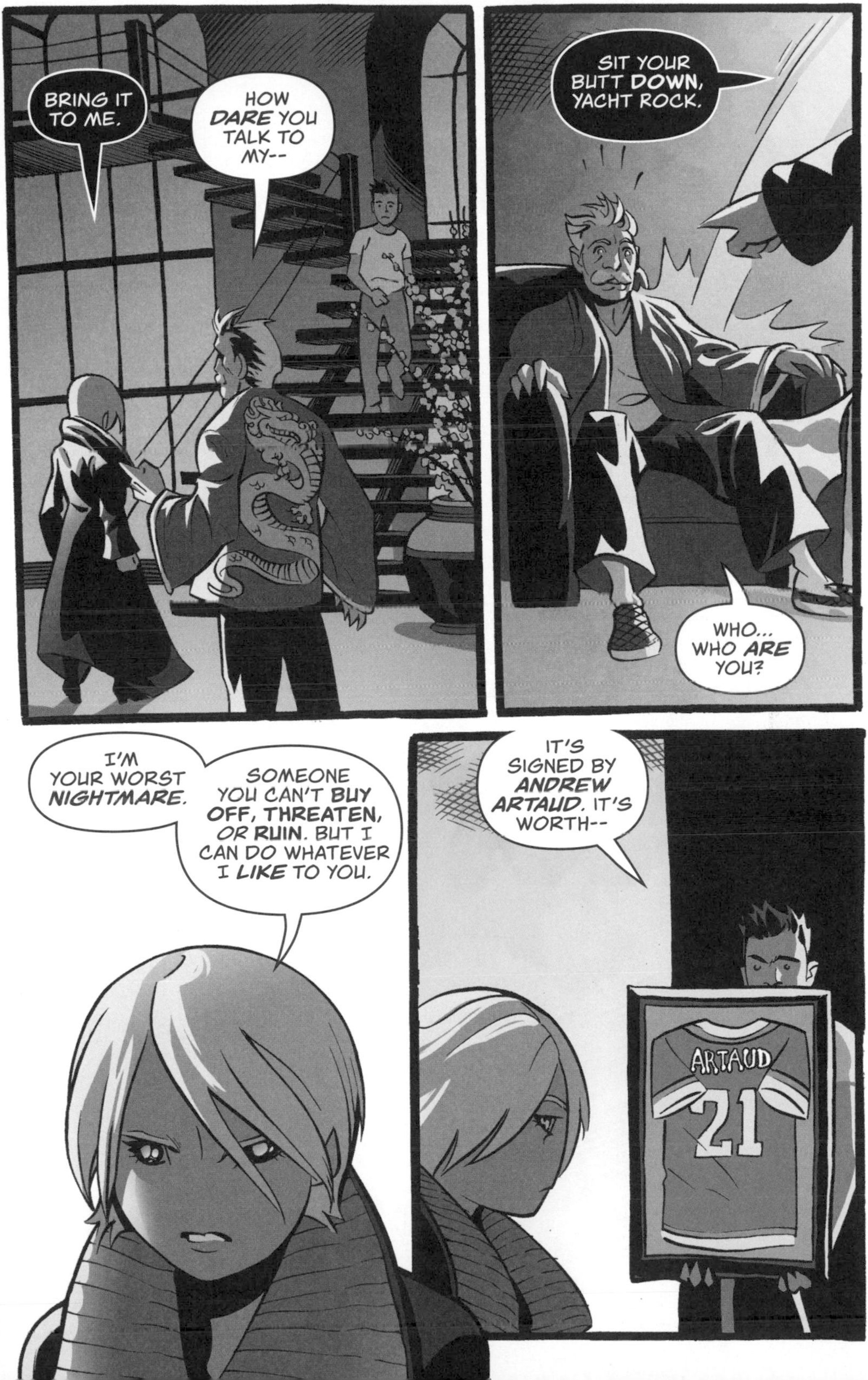
BRING IT TO ME.
HOW DARE YOU TALK TO MY--
SIT YOUR BUTT DOWN, YACHT ROCK.
WHO... WHO ARE YOU?
I'M YOUR WORST NIGHTMARE.
SOMEONE YOU CAN'T BUY OFF, THREATEN, OR RUIN. BUT I CAN DO WHATEVER I LIKE TO YOU.
IT'S SIGNED BY ANDREW ARTAUD. IT'S WORTH--
ARTAUD
21

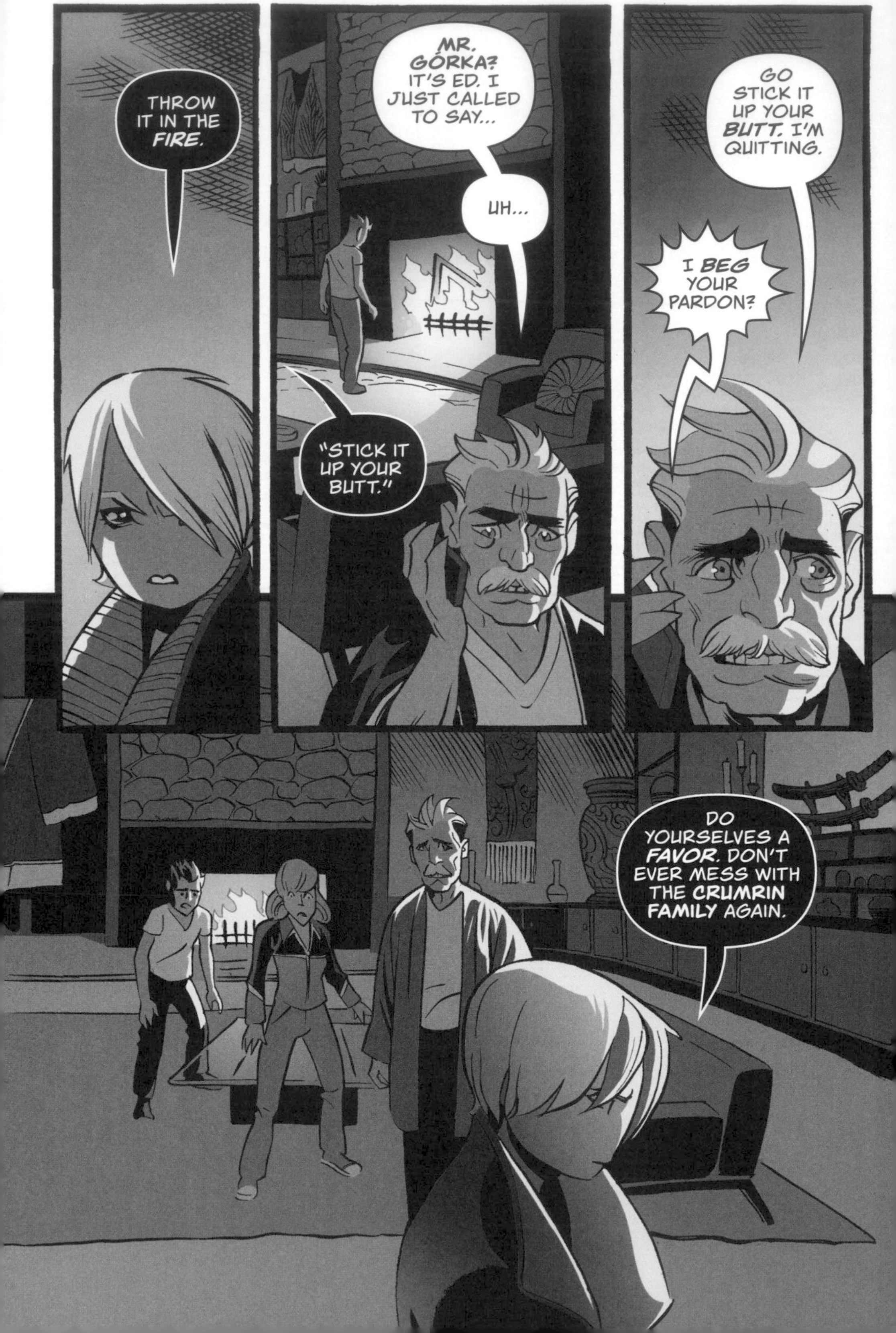
THROW IT IN THE FIRE.
MR. GÓRKA? IT'S ED. I JUST CALLED TO SAY...
UH...
"STICK IT UP YOUR BUTT."
GO STICK IT UP YOUR BUTT. I'M QUITTING.
I BEG YOUR PARDON?
DO YOURSELVES A FAVOR. DON'T EVER MESS WITH THE CRUMRIN FAMILY AGAIN.

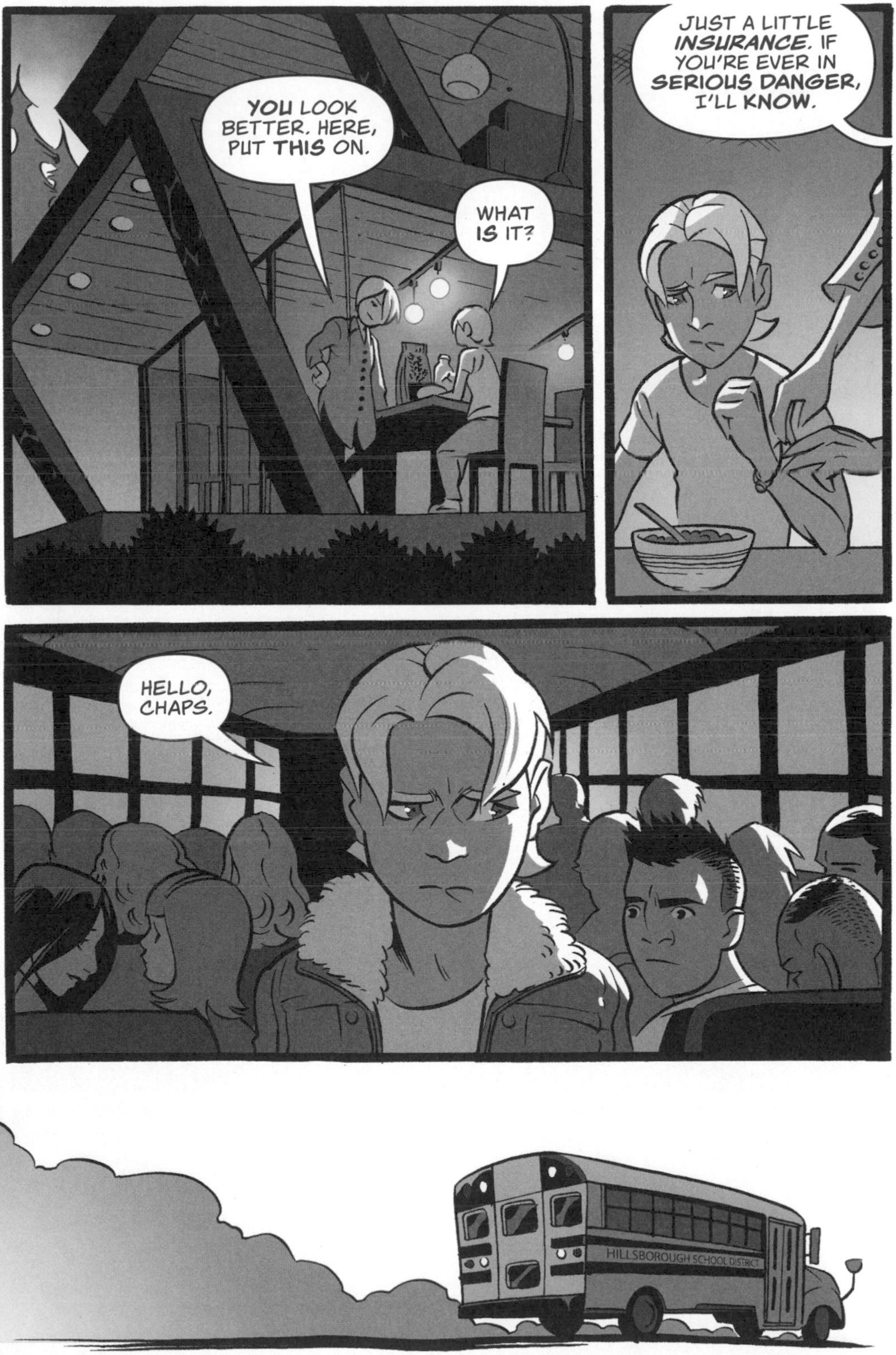
YOU LOOK BETTER. HERE, PUT THIS ON.
WHAT IS IT?
JUST A LITTLE INSURANCE. IF YOU'RE EVER IN SERIOUS DANGER, I'LL KNOW.
HELLO, CHAPS.
HILLSBOROUGH SCHOOL DISTRICT

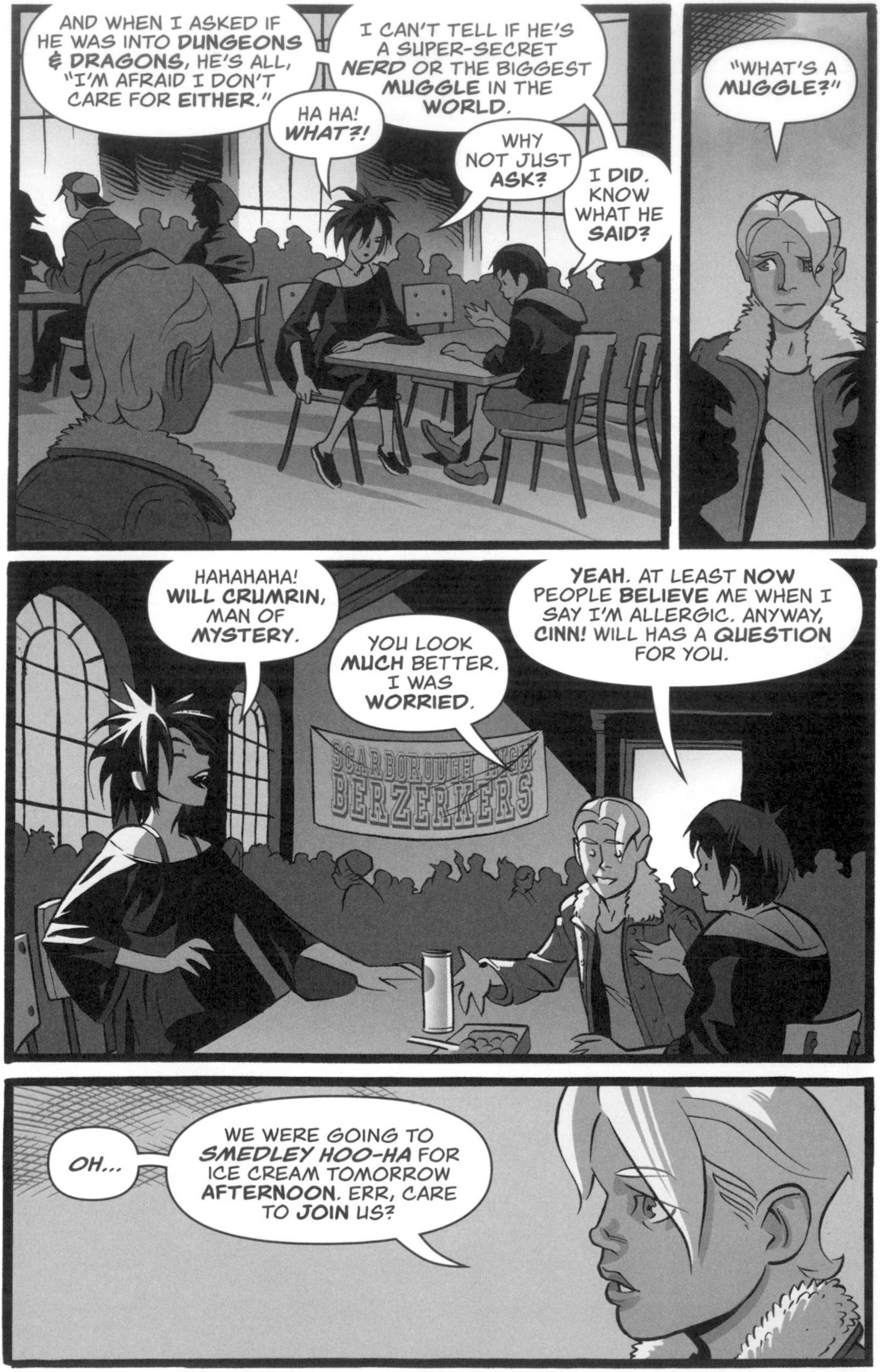
AND WHEN I ASKED IF HE WAS INTO DUNGEONS & DRAGONS, HE'S ALL, "I'M AFRAID I DON'T CARE FOR EITHER."
HA HA! WHAT?!
I CAN'T TELL IF HE'S A SUPER-SECRET NERD OR THE BIGGEST MUGGLE IN THE WORLD.
WHY NOT JUST ASK?
I DID. KNOW WHAT HE SAID?
"WHAT'S A MUGGLE?"
HAHAHAHA! WILL CRUMRIN, MAN OF MYSTERY.
YOU LOOK MUCH BETTER. I WAS WORRIED.
YEAH. AT LEAST NOW PEOPLE BELIEVE ME WHEN I SAY I'M ALLERGIC. ANYWAY, CINN! WILL HAS A QUESTION FOR YOU.
SCARBOROUGH HIGH BERZERKERS
OH...
WE WERE GOING TO SMEDLEY HOO-HA FOR ICE CREAM TOMORROW AFTERNOON. ERR, CARE TO JOIN US?

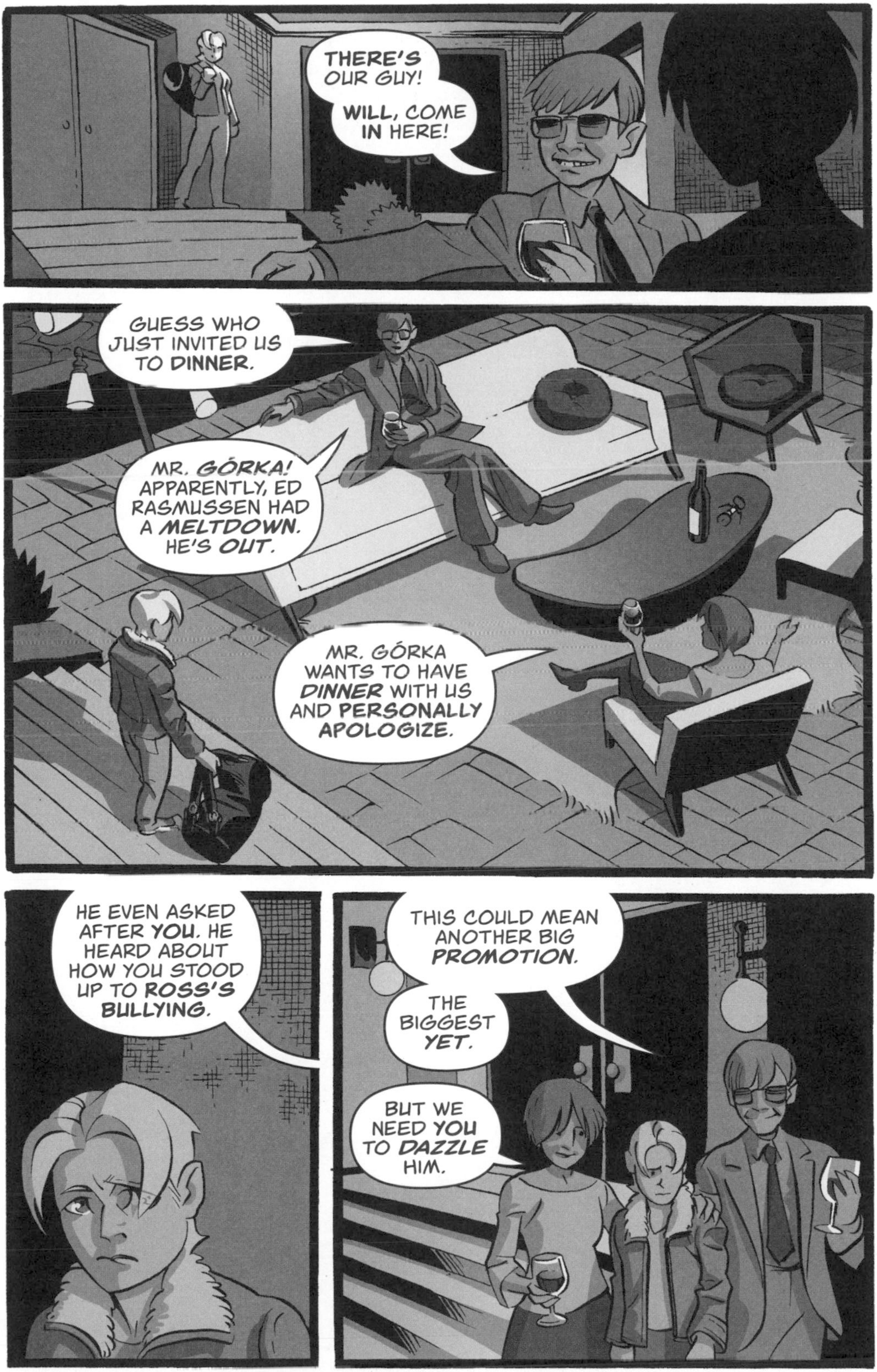
THERE'S OUR GUY!
WILL, COME IN HERE!
GUESS WHO JUST INVITED US TO DINNER.
MR. GÓRKA! APPARENTLY, ED RASMUSSEN HAD A MELTDOWN. HE'S OUT.
MR. GÓRKA WANTS TO HAVE DINNER WITH US AND PERSONALLY APOLOGIZE.
HE EVEN ASKED AFTER YOU. HE HEARD ABOUT HOW YOU STOOD UP TO ROSS'S BULLYING.
THIS COULD MEAN ANOTHER BIG PROMOTION.
THE BIGGEST YET.
BUT WE NEED YOU TO DAZZLE HIM.

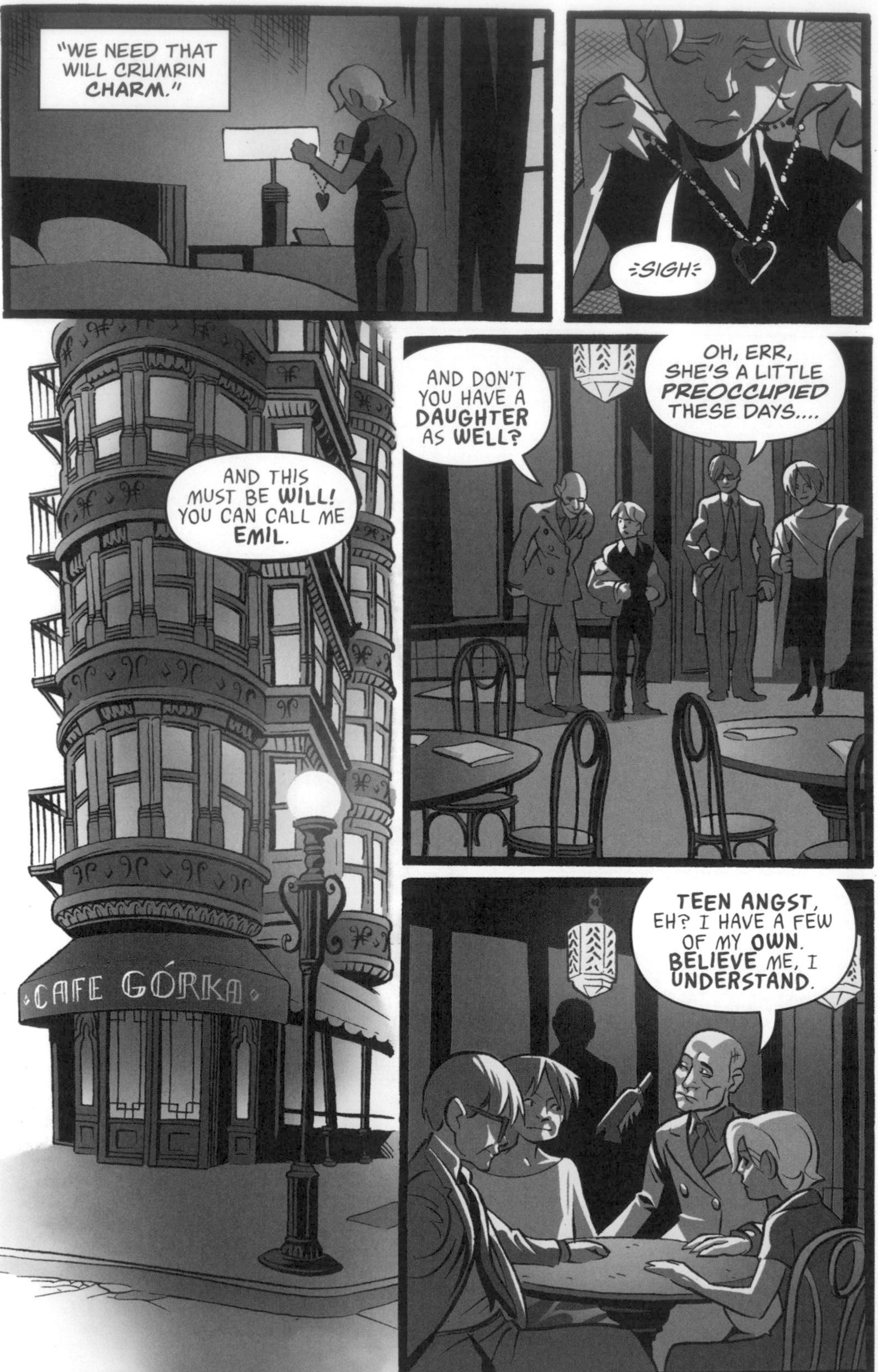
"WE NEED THAT WILL CRUMRIN CHARM."
SIGH
AND THIS MUST BE WILL! YOU CAN CALL ME EMIL.
CAFE GÓRKA
AND DON'T YOU HAVE A DAUGHTER AS WELL?
OH, ERR, SHE'S A LITTLE PREOCCUPIED THESE DAYS....
TEEN ANGST, EH? I HAVE A FEW OF MY OWN. BELIEVE ME, I UNDERSTAND.

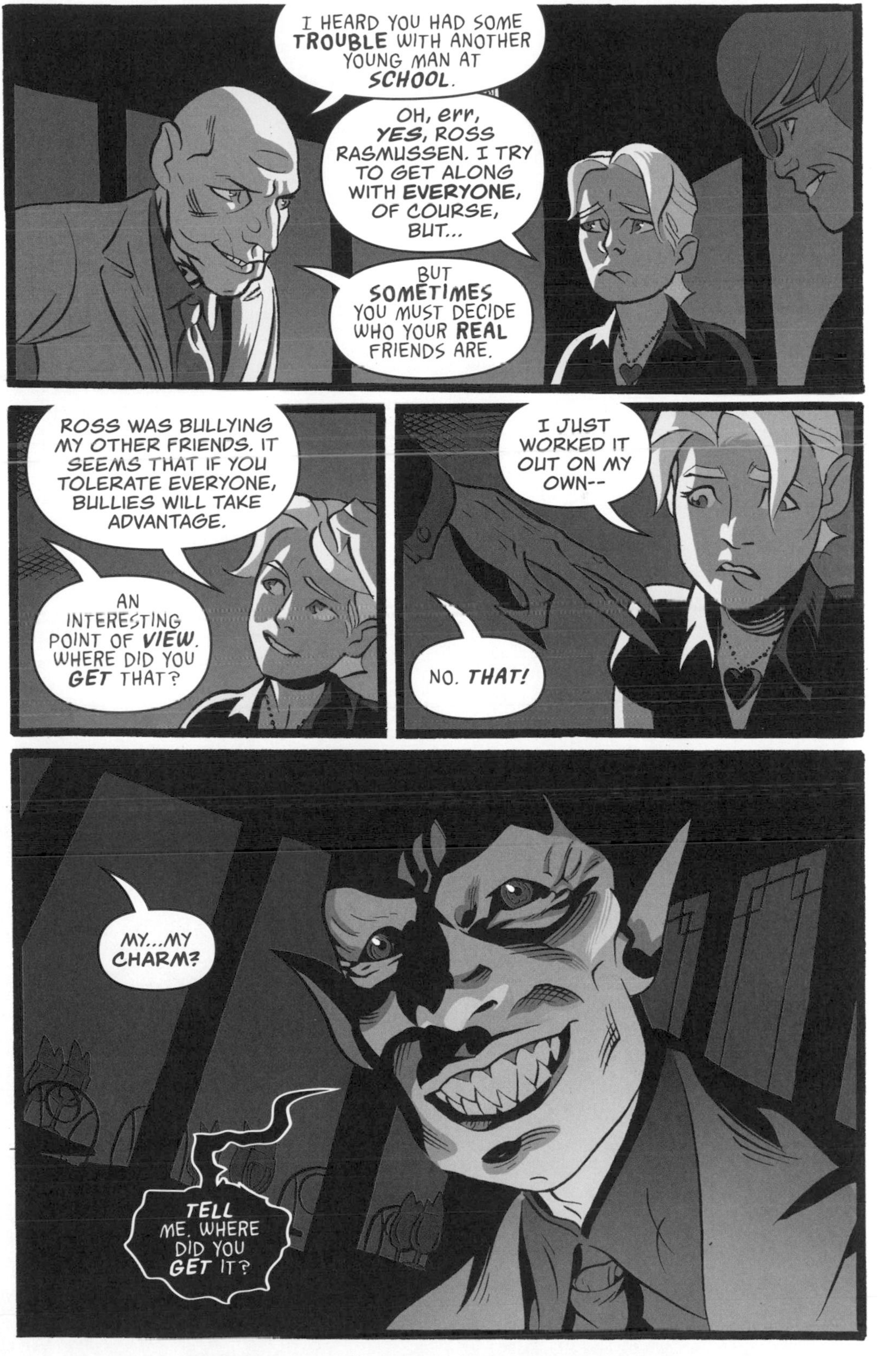
I HEARD YOU HAD SOME TROUBLE WITH ANOTHER YOUNG MAN AT SCHOOL.
OH, err, YES, ROSS RASMUSSEN. I TRY TO GET ALONG WITH EVERYONE, OF COURSE, BUT...
BUT SOMETIMES YOU MUST DECIDE WHO YOUR REAL FRIENDS ARE.
ROSS WAS BULLYING MY OTHER FRIENDS. IT SEEMS THAT IF YOU TOLERATE EVERYONE, BULLIES WILL TAKE ADVANTAGE.
AN INTERESTING POINT OF VIEW. WHERE DID YOU GET THAT?
I JUST WORKED IT OUT ON MY OWN--
NO. THAT!
MY...MY CHARM?
TELL ME. WHERE DID YOU GET IT?

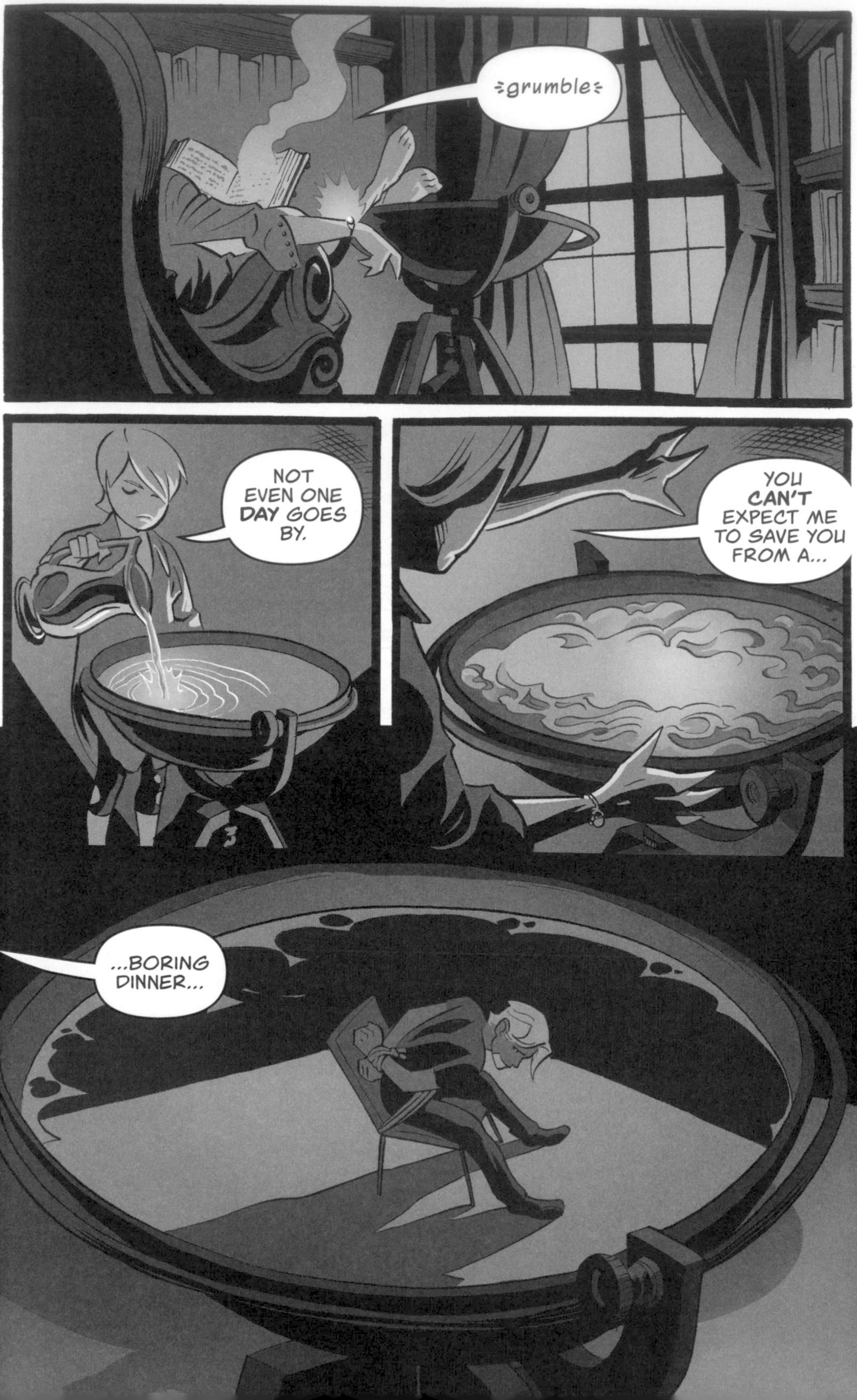
grumble
NOT EVEN ONE DAY GOES BY.
YOU CAN'T EXPECT ME TO SAVE YOU FROM A...
...BORING DINNER...

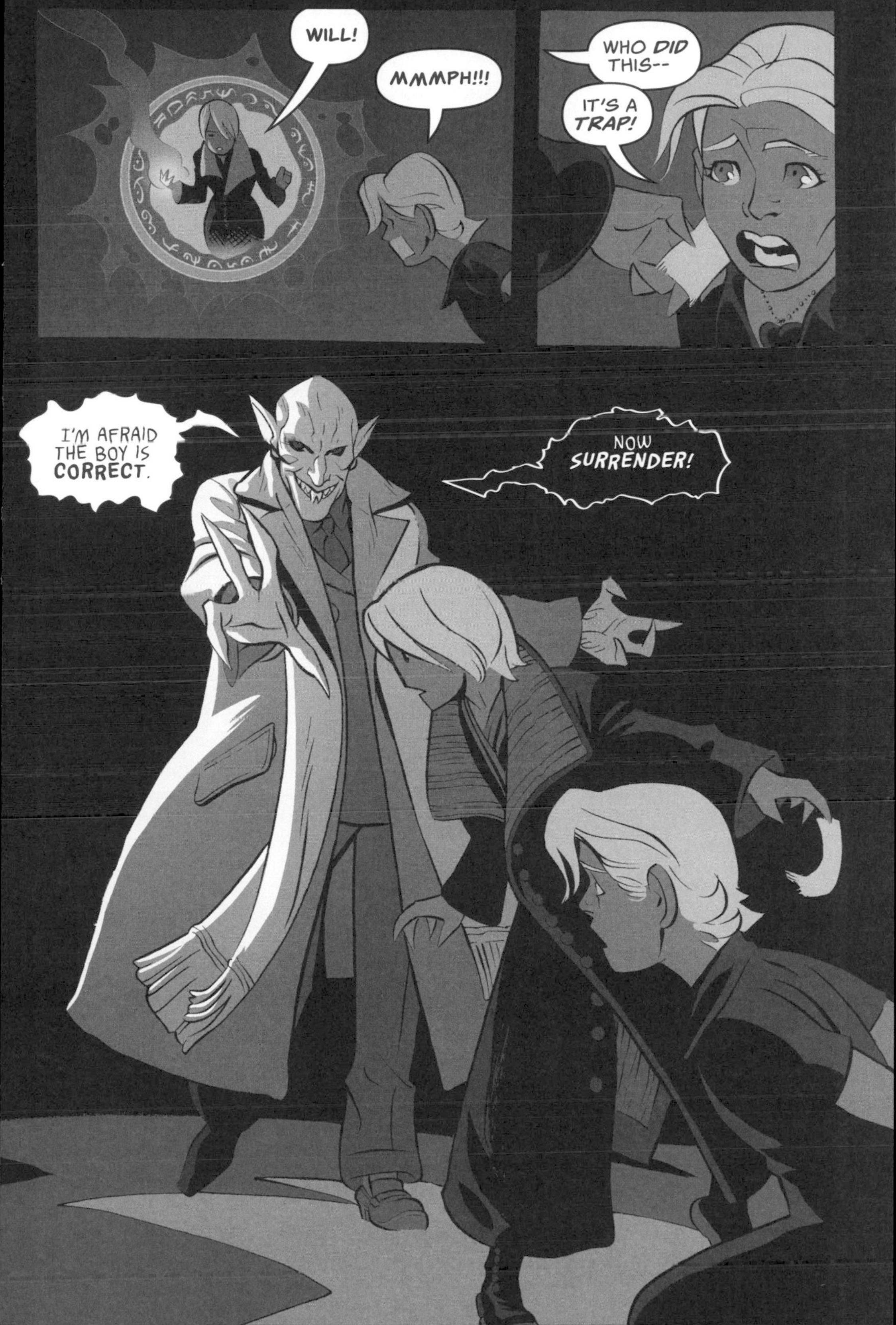
WILL!
MMMPH!!!
WHO DID THIS--
IT'S A TRAP!
I'M AFRAID THE BOY IS CORRECT.
NOW SURRENDER!

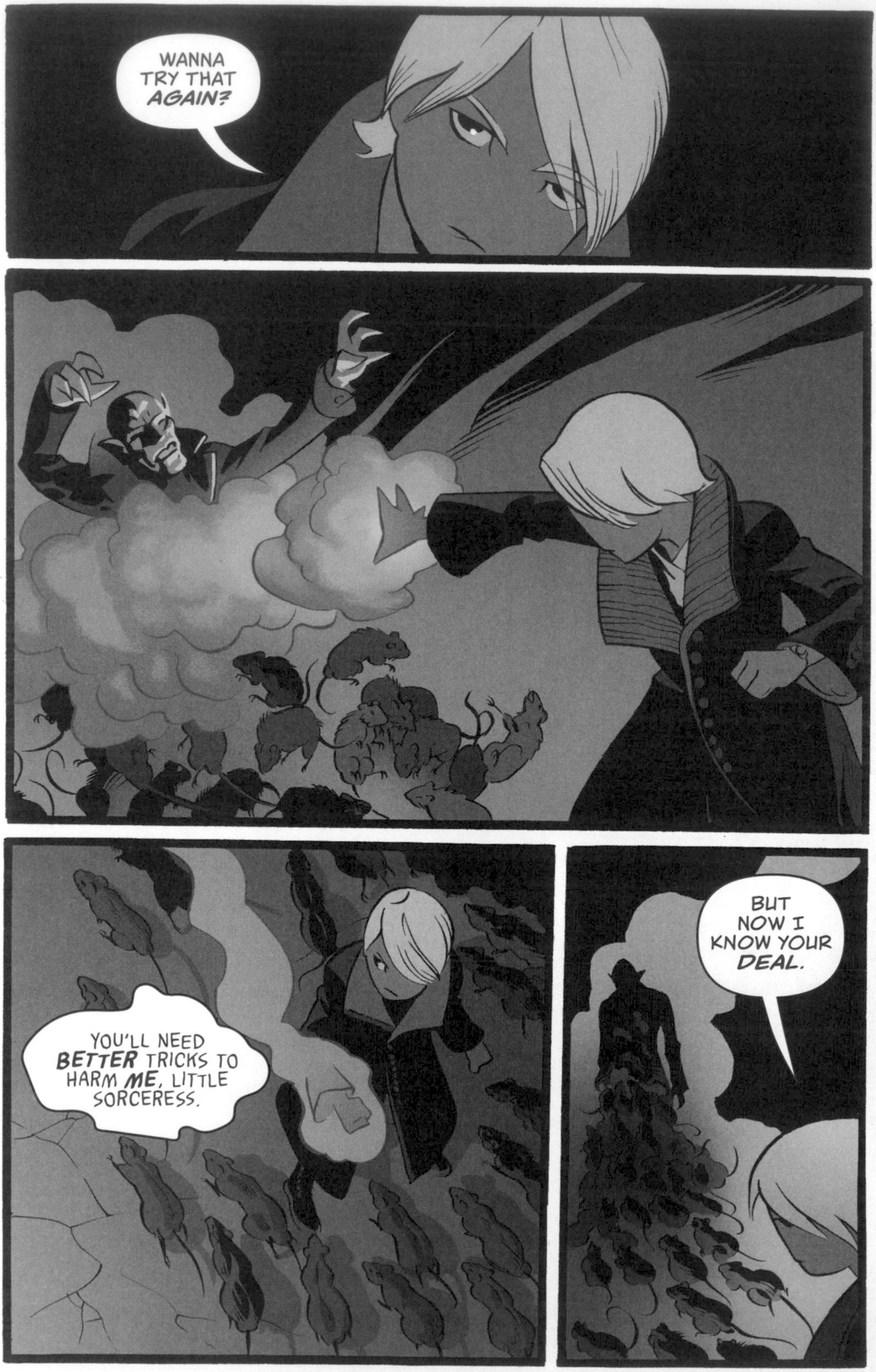
WANNA TRY THAT AGAIN?
YOU'LL NEED BETTER TRICKS TO HARM ME, LITTLE SORCERESS.
BUT NOW I KNOW YOUR DEAL.

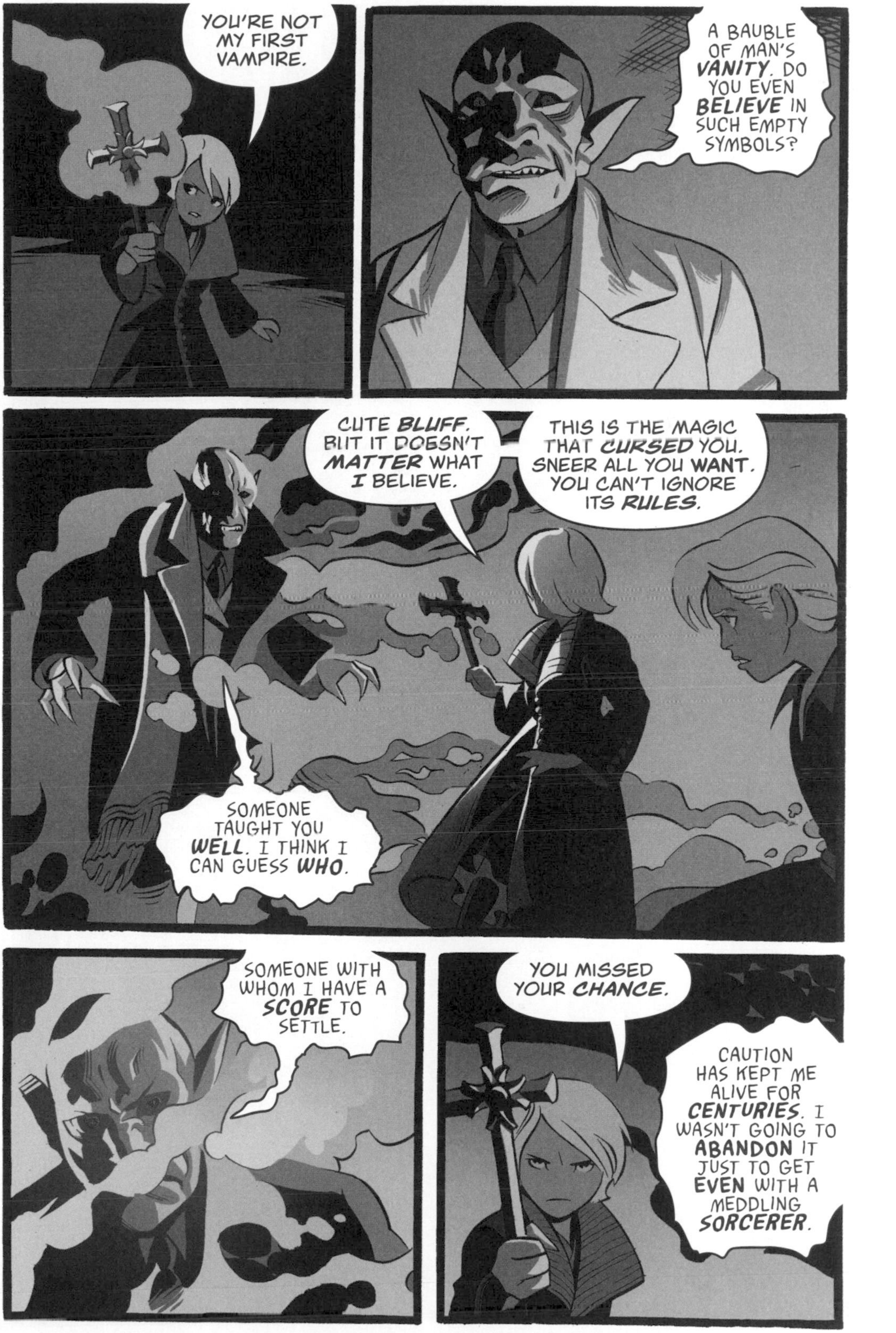
YOU'RE NOT MY FIRST VAMPIRE.
A BAUBLE OF MAN'S VANITY. DO YOU EVEN BELIEVE IN SUCH EMPTY SYMBOLS?
CUTE BLUFF. BUT IT DOESN'T MATTER WHAT I BELIEVE.
THIS IS THE MAGIC THAT CURSED YOU. SNEER ALL YOU WANT. YOU CAN'T IGNORE ITS RULES.
SOMEONE TAUGHT YOU WELL. I THINK I CAN GUESS WHO.
SOMEONE WITH WHOM I HAVE A SCORE TO SETTLE.
YOU MISSED YOUR CHANCE.
CAUTION HAS KEPT ME ALIVE FOR CENTURIES. I WASN'T GOING TO ABANDON IT JUST TO GET EVEN WITH A MEDDLING SORCERER.

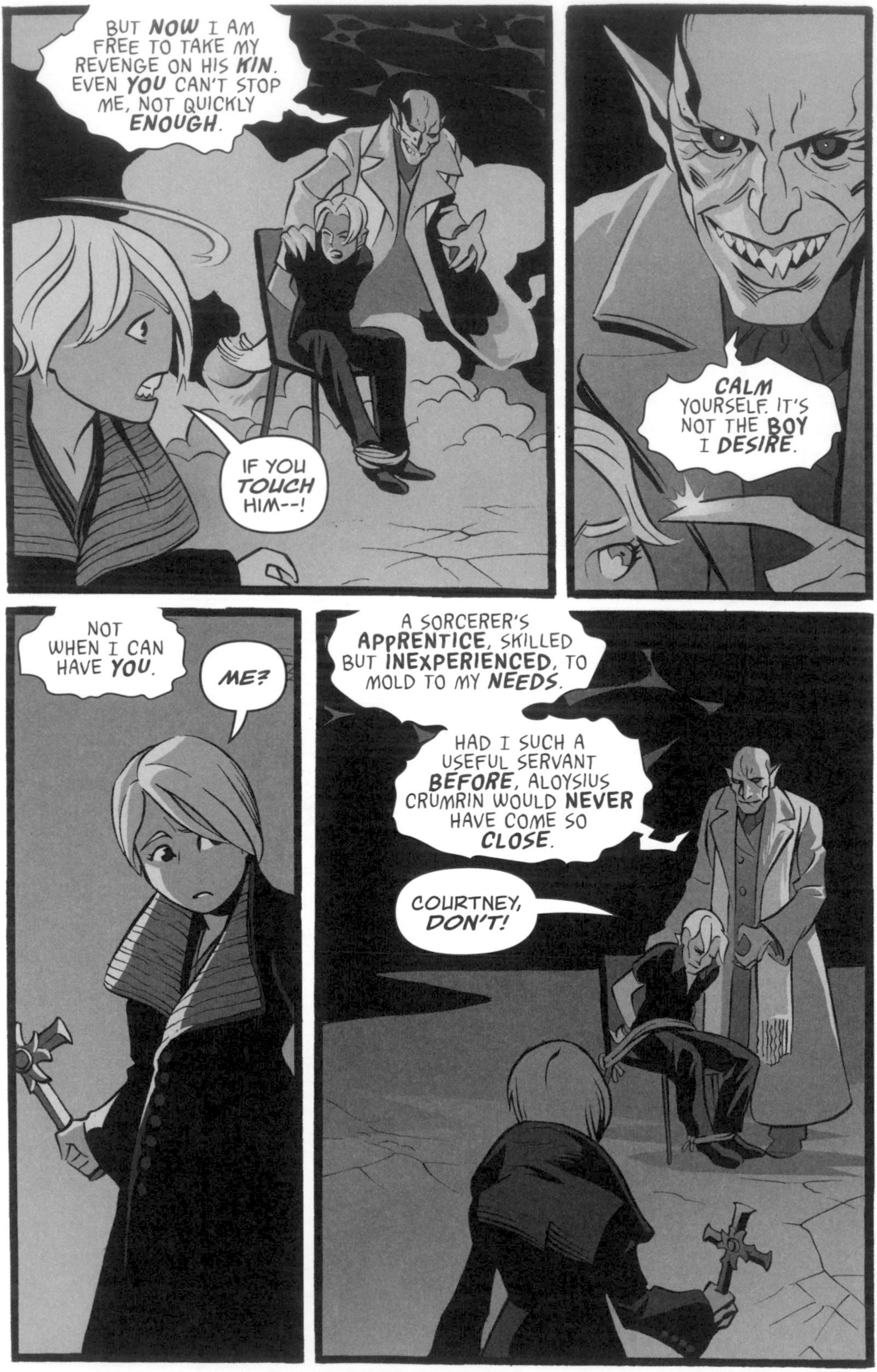
BUT NOW I AM FREE TO TAKE MY REVENGE ON HIS KIN. EVEN YOU CAN'T STOP ME, NOT QUICKLY ENOUGH.
IF YOU TOUCH HIM--!
CALM YOURSELF. IT'S NOT THE BOY I DESIRE.
NOT WHEN I CAN HAVE YOU.
ME?
A SORCERER'S APPRENTICE, SKILLED BUT INEXPERIENCED, TO MOLD TO MY NEEDS.
HAD I SUCH A USEFUL SERVANT BEFORE, ALOYSIUS CRUMRIN WOULD NEVER HAVE COME SO CLOSE.
COURTNEY, DON'T!

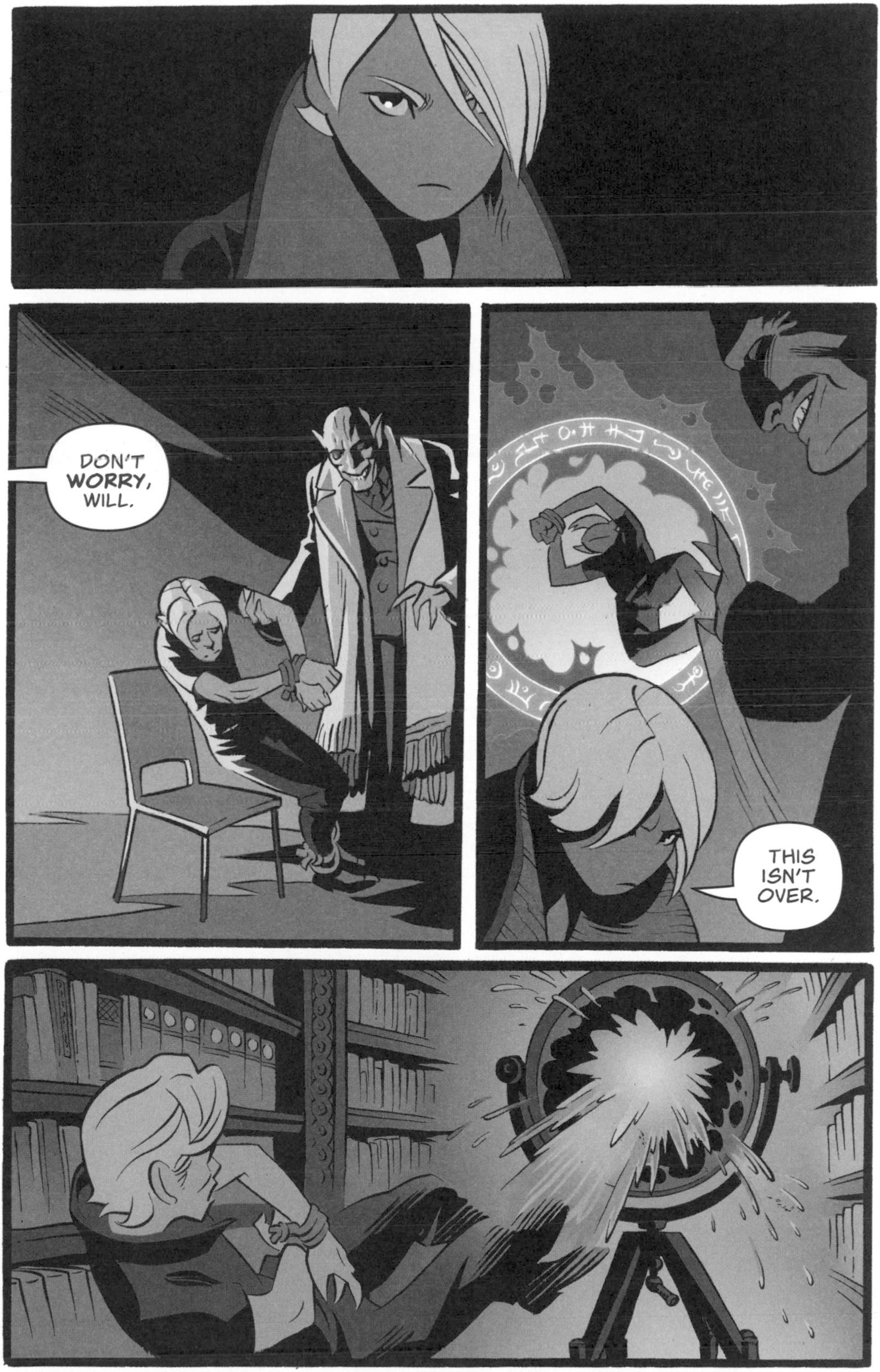
DON'T WORRY, WILL.
THIS ISN'T OVER.

Chapter 2
Cursed

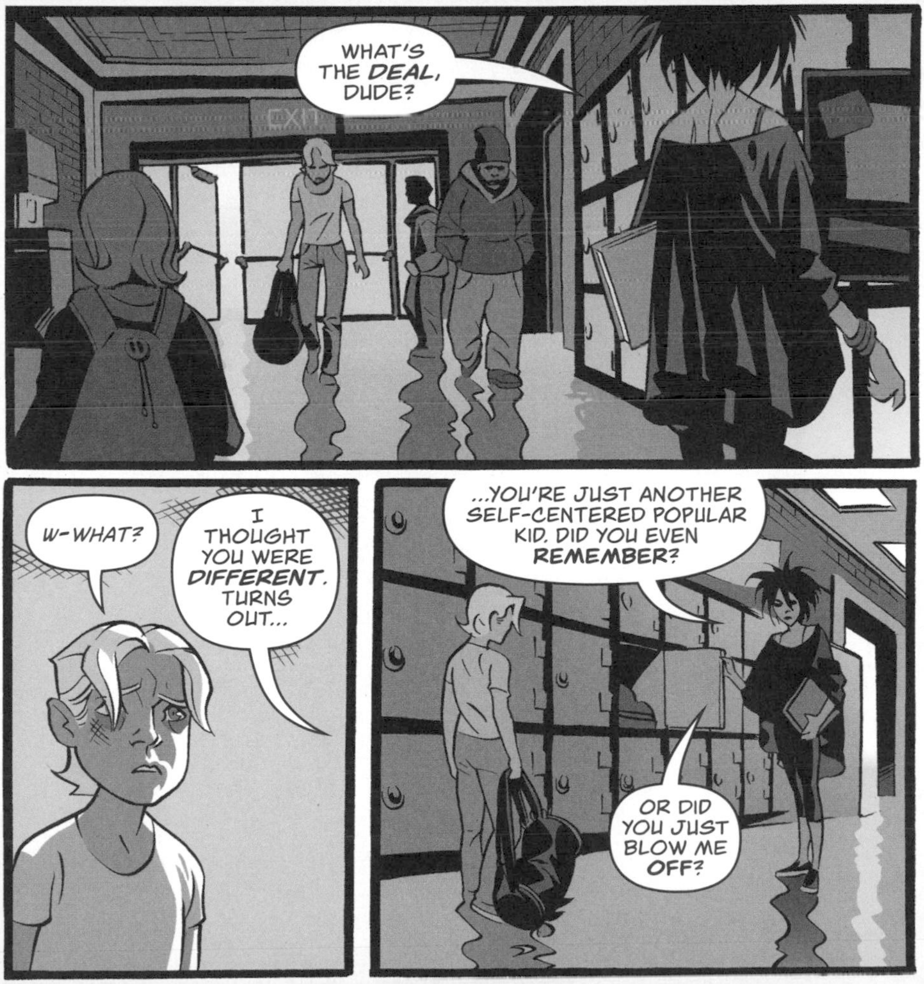
WHAT'S THE DEAL, DUDE?
EXIT
W-WHAT?
I THOUGHT YOU WERE DIFFERENT. TURNS OUT...
...YOU'RE JUST ANOTHER SELF-CENTERED POPULAR KID. DID YOU EVEN REMEMBER?
OR DID YOU JUST BLOW ME OFF?

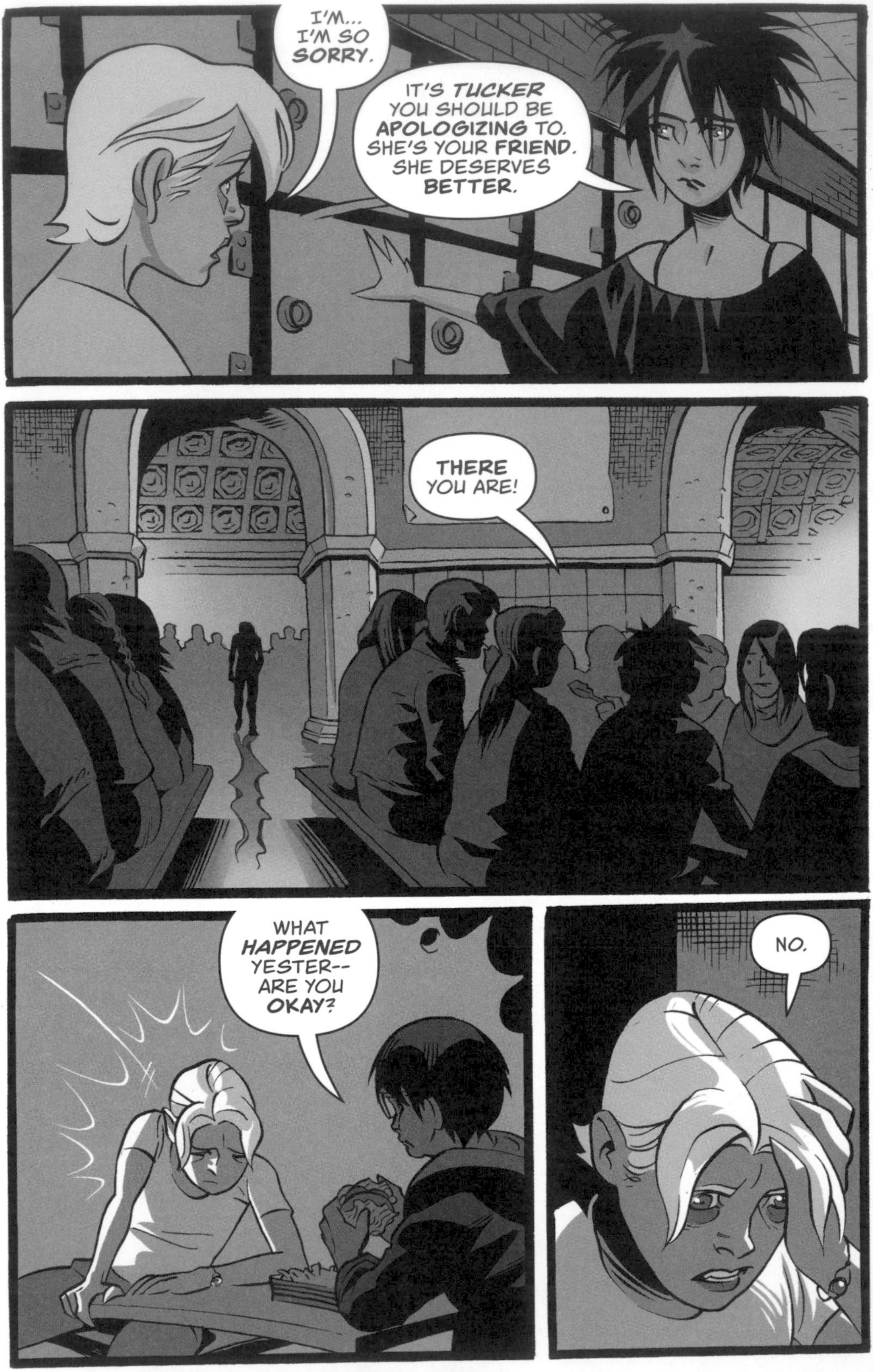
I'M... I'M SO SORRY.
IT'S TUCKER YOU SHOULD BE APOLOGIZING TO. SHE'S YOUR FRIEND. SHE DESERVES BETTER.
THERE YOU ARE!
WHAT HAPPENED YESTER-- ARE YOU OKAY?
NO.

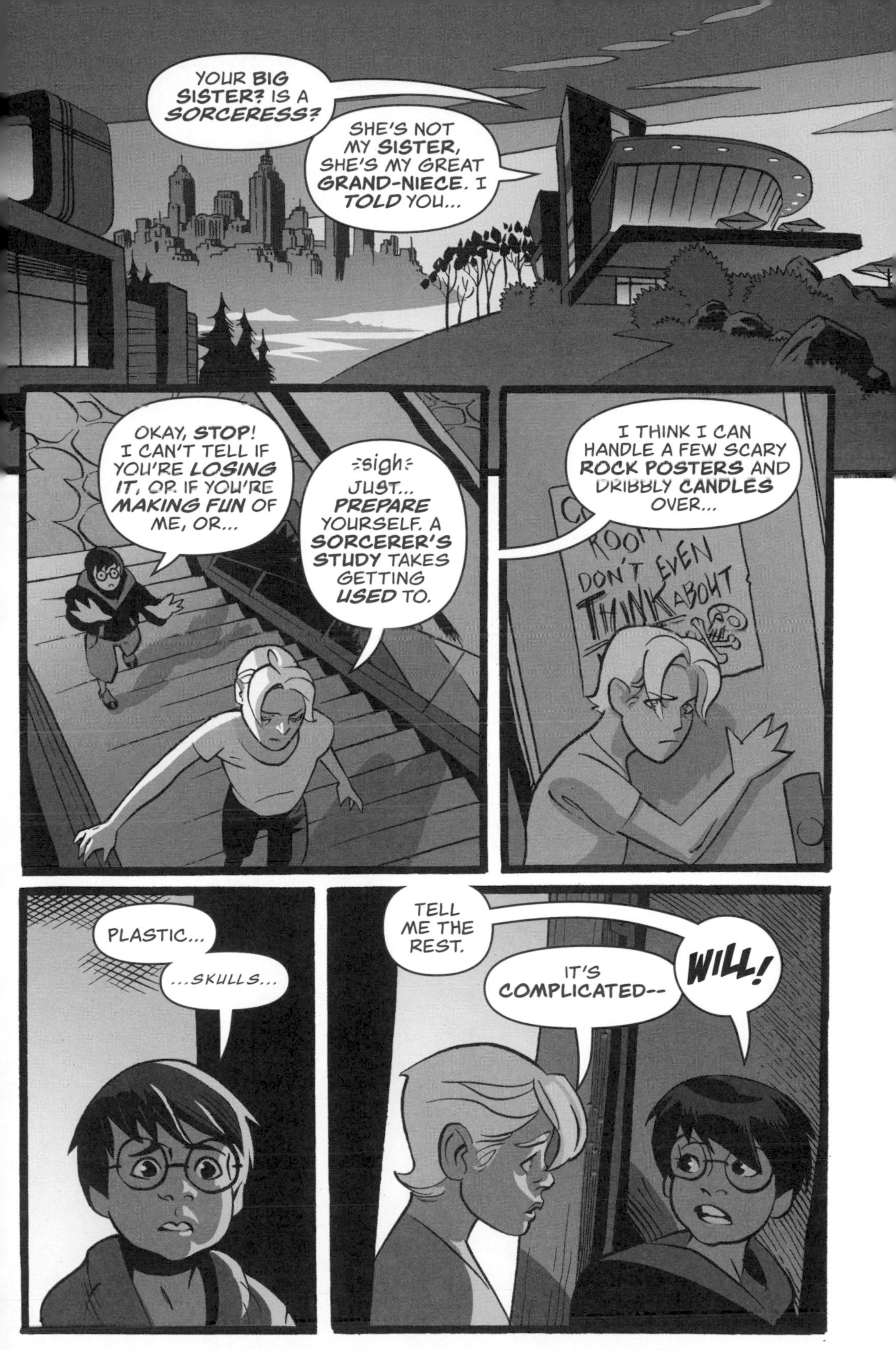
YOUR BIG SISTER? IS A SORCERESS?
SHE'S NOT MY SISTER, SHE'S MY GREAT GRAND-NIECE. I TOLD YOU...
OKAY, STOP! I CAN'T TELL IF YOU'RE LOSING IT, OR IF YOU'RE MAKING FUN OF ME, OR...
sigh
JUST... PREPARE YOURSELF. A SORCERER'S STUDY TAKES GETTING USED TO.
I THINK I CAN HANDLE A FEW SCARY ROCK POSTERS AND DRIBBLY CANDLES OVER...
DON'T EVEN THINK ABOUT
PLASTIC...
...SKULLS...
TELL ME THE REST.
IT'S COMPLICATED--
WILL!

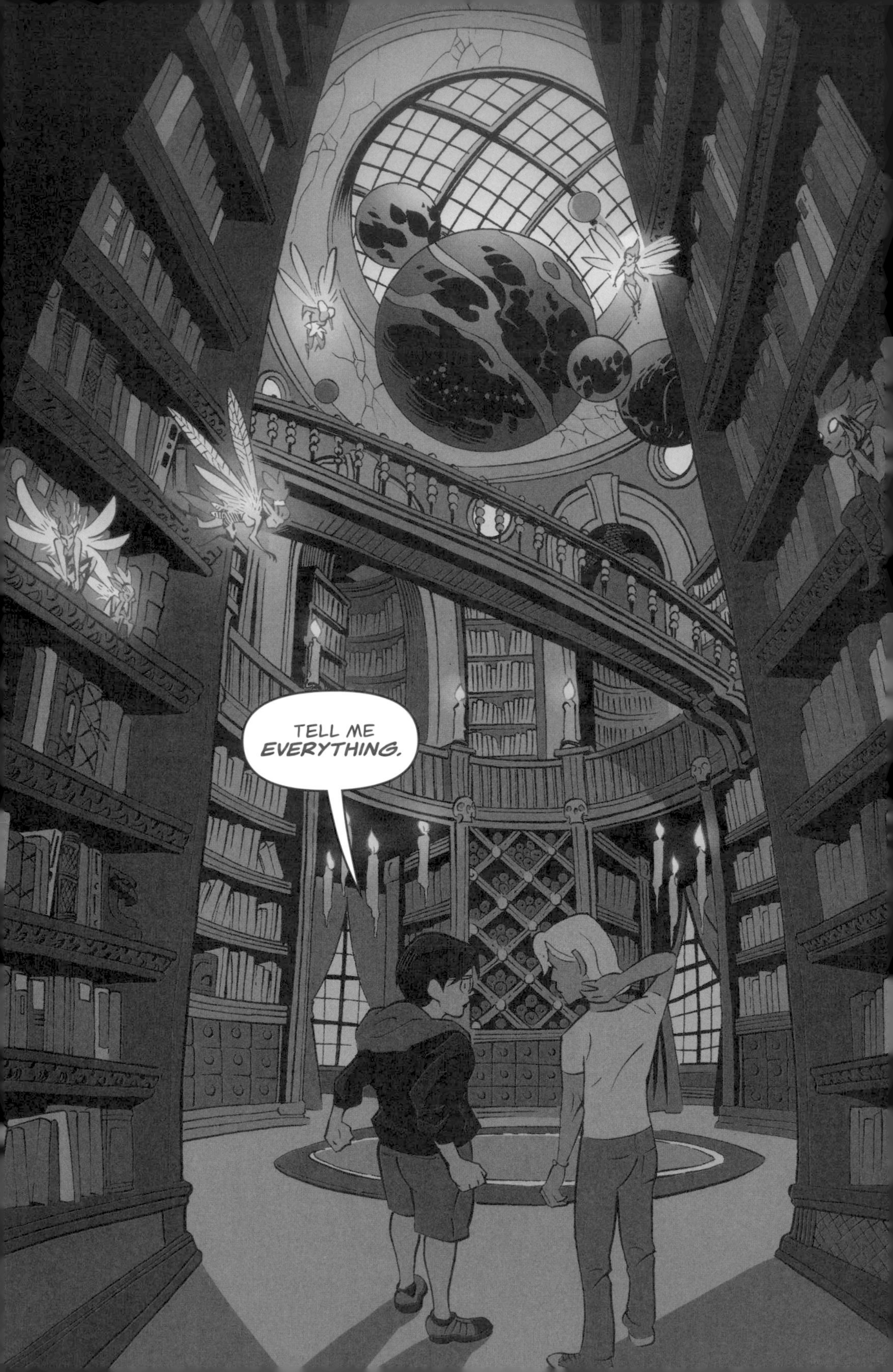
TELL ME *EVERYTHING.*

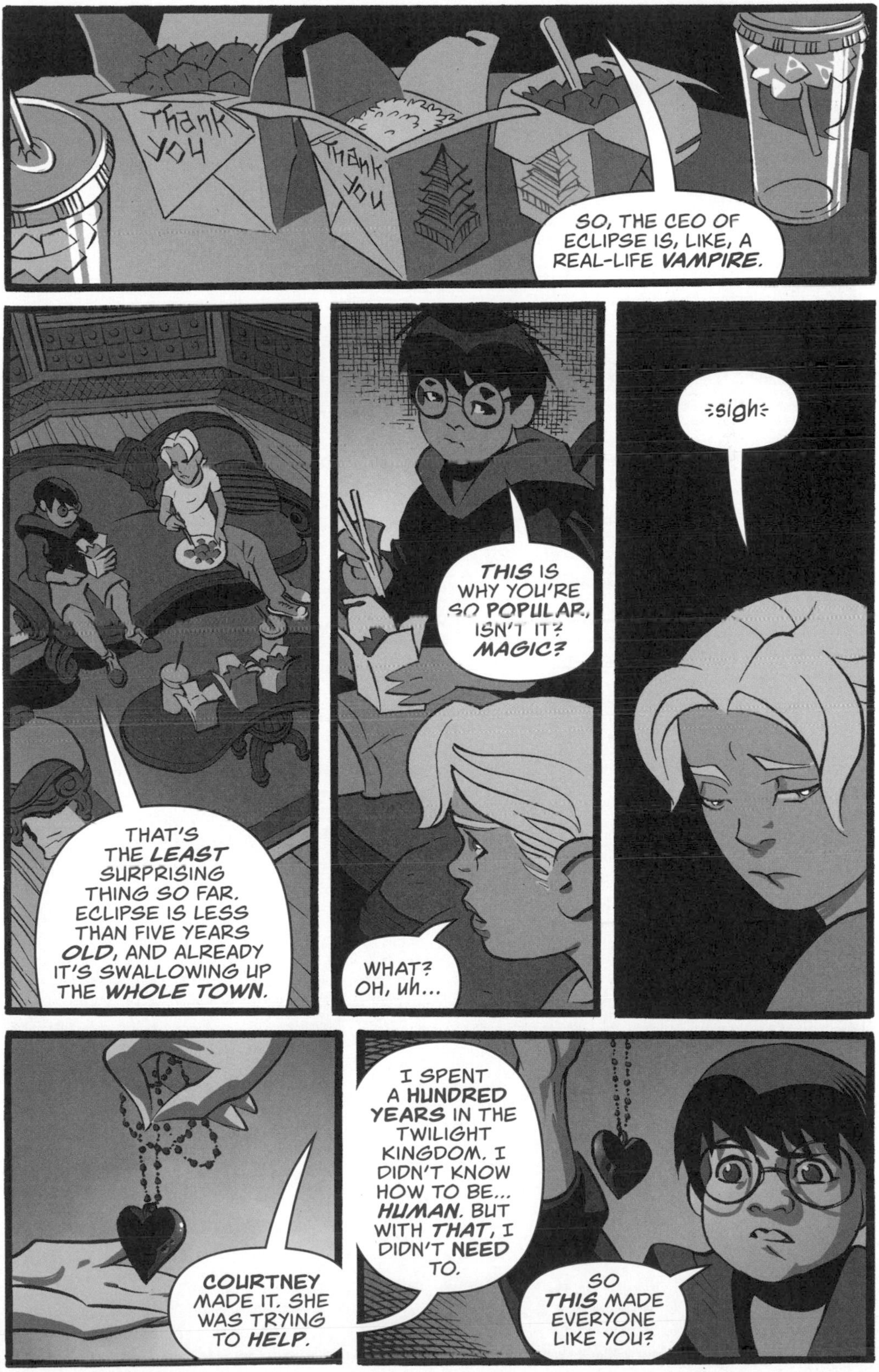
Thank You
Thank You
SO, THE CEO OF ECLIPSE IS, LIKE, A REAL-LIFE VAMPIRE.
THAT'S THE LEAST SURPRISING THING SO FAR. ECLIPSE IS LESS THAN FIVE YEARS OLD, AND ALREADY IT'S SWALLOWING UP THE WHOLE TOWN.
THIS IS WHY YOU'RE SO POPULAR, ISN'T IT? MAGIC?
WHAT? OH, uh...
sigh
COURTNEY MADE IT. SHE WAS TRYING TO HELP.
I SPENT A HUNDRED YEARS IN THE TWILIGHT KINGDOM. I DIDN'T KNOW HOW TO BE... HUMAN. BUT WITH THAT, I DIDN'T NEED TO.
SO THIS MADE EVERYONE LIKE YOU?

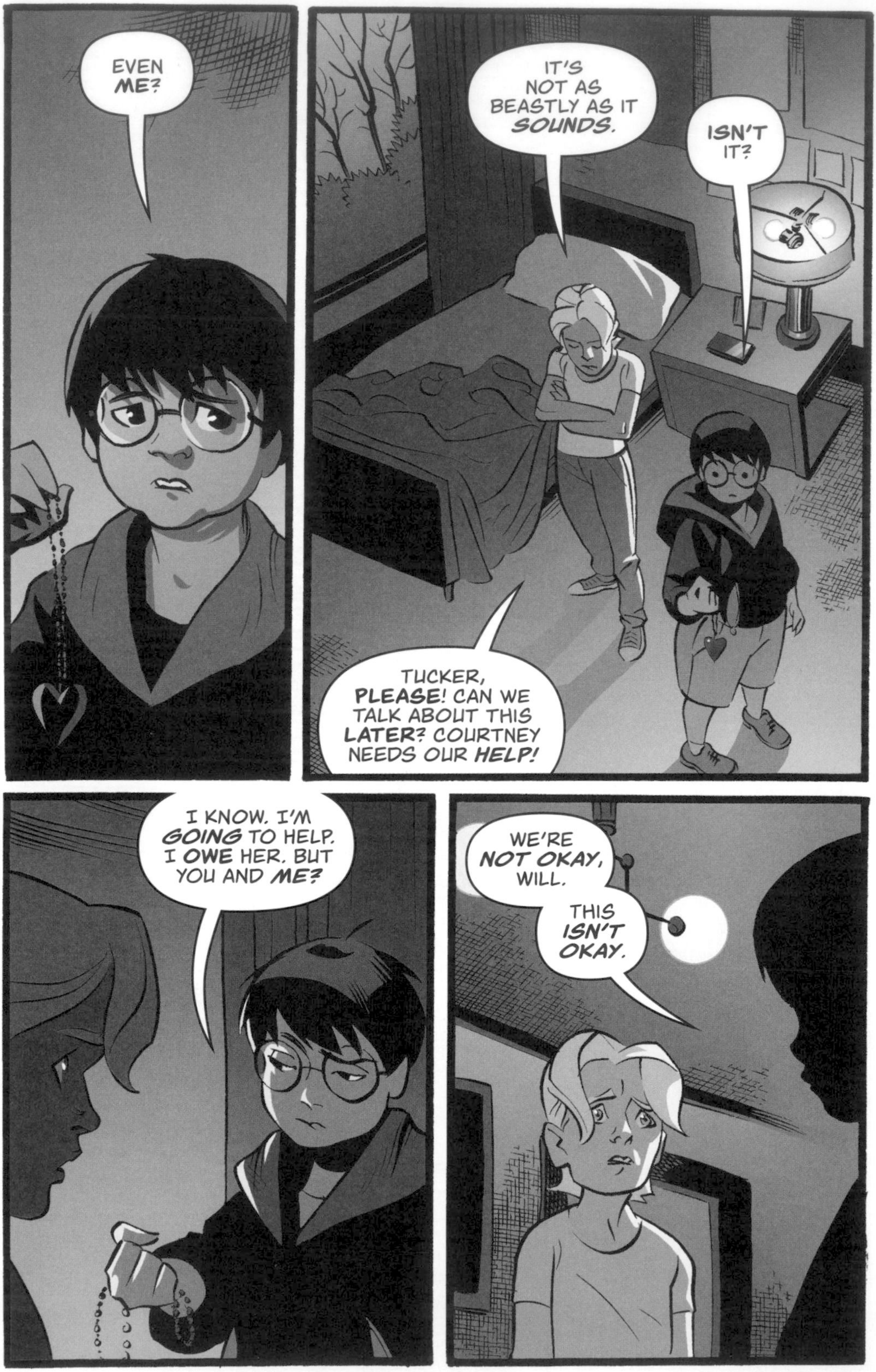
EVEN ME?
IT'S NOT AS BEASTLY AS IT SOUNDS.
ISN'T IT?
TUCKER, PLEASE! CAN WE TALK ABOUT THIS LATER? COURTNEY NEEDS OUR HELP!
I KNOW. I'M GOING TO HELP. I OWE HER. BUT YOU AND ME?
WE'RE NOT OKAY, WILL.
THIS ISN'T OKAY.

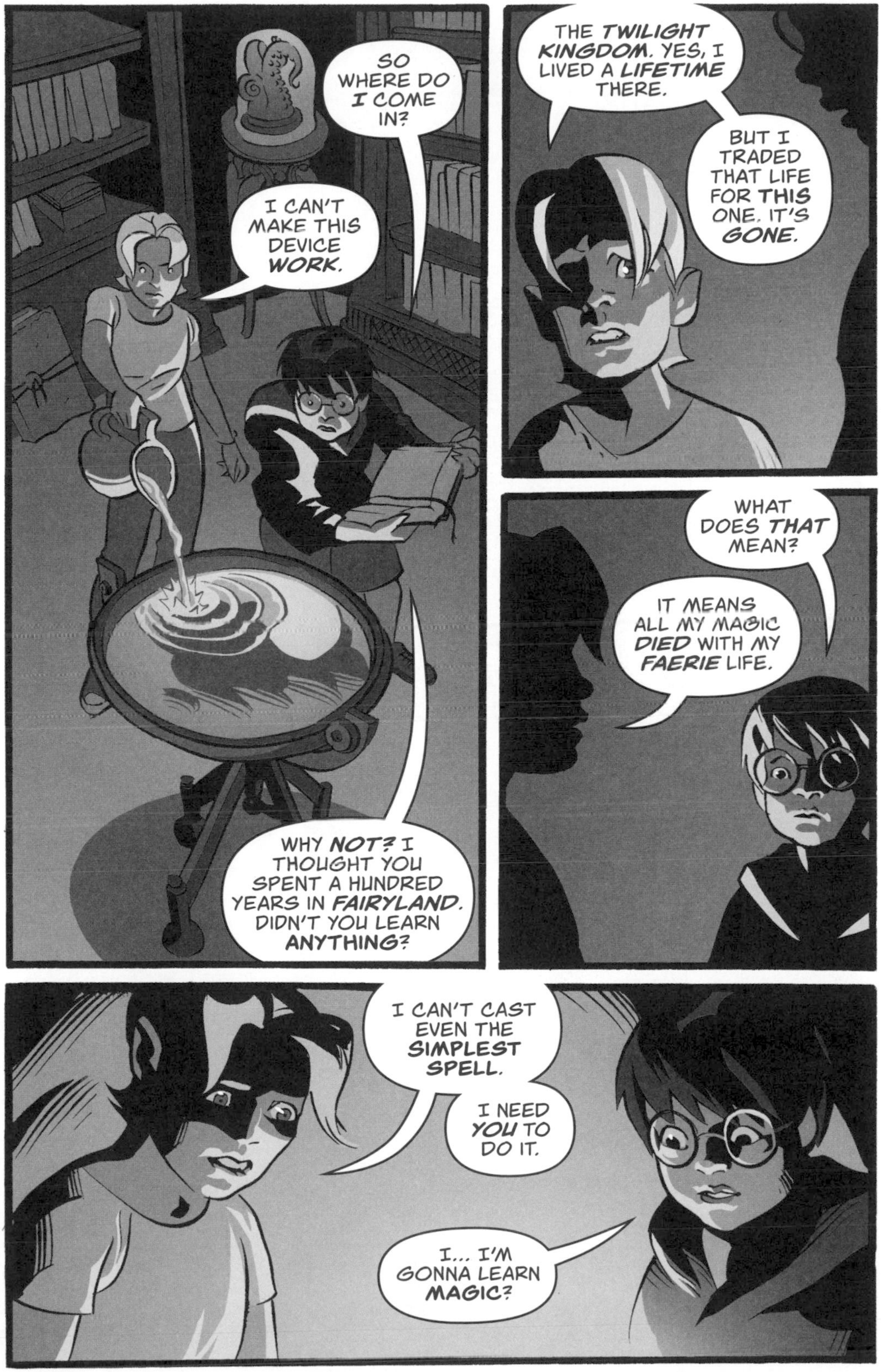
SO WHERE DO I COME IN?
I CAN'T MAKE THIS DEVICE WORK.
WHY NOT? I THOUGHT YOU SPENT A HUNDRED YEARS IN FAIRYLAND. DIDN'T YOU LEARN ANYTHING?
THE TWILIGHT KINGDOM. YES, I LIVED A LIFETIME THERE.
BUT I TRADED THAT LIFE FOR THIS ONE. IT'S GONE.
WHAT DOES THAT MEAN?
IT MEANS ALL MY MAGIC DIED WITH MY FAERIE LIFE.
I CAN'T CAST EVEN THE SIMPLEST SPELL.
I NEED YOU TO DO IT.
I... I'M GONNA LEARN MAGIC?

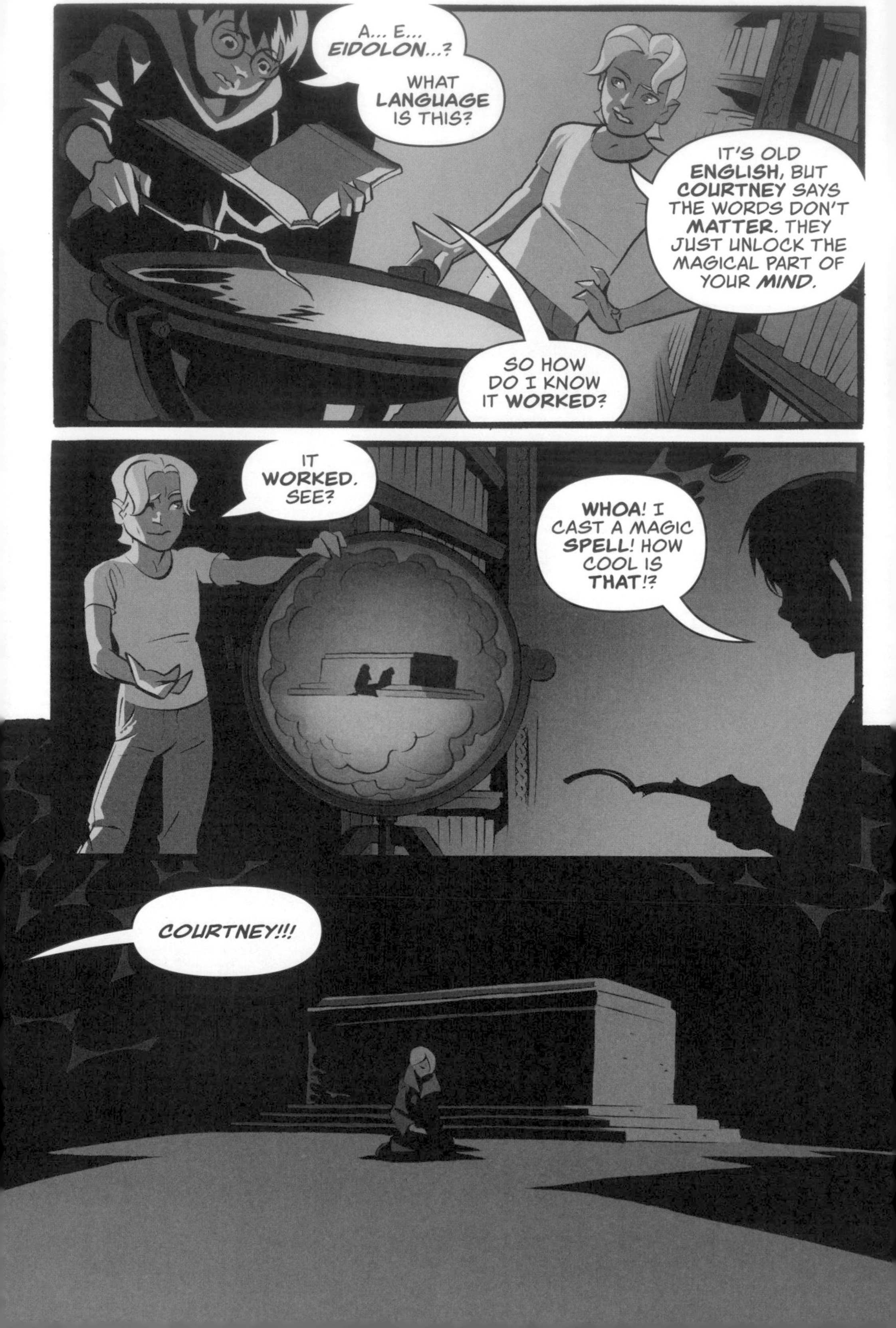
A... E... EIDOLON...?
WHAT LANGUAGE IS THIS?
IT'S OLD ENGLISH, BUT COURTNEY SAYS THE WORDS DON'T MATTER. THEY JUST UNLOCK THE MAGICAL PART OF YOUR MIND.
SO HOW DO I KNOW IT WORKED?
IT WORKED. SEE?
WHOA! I CAST A MAGIC SPELL! HOW COOL IS THAT!?
COURTNEY!!!

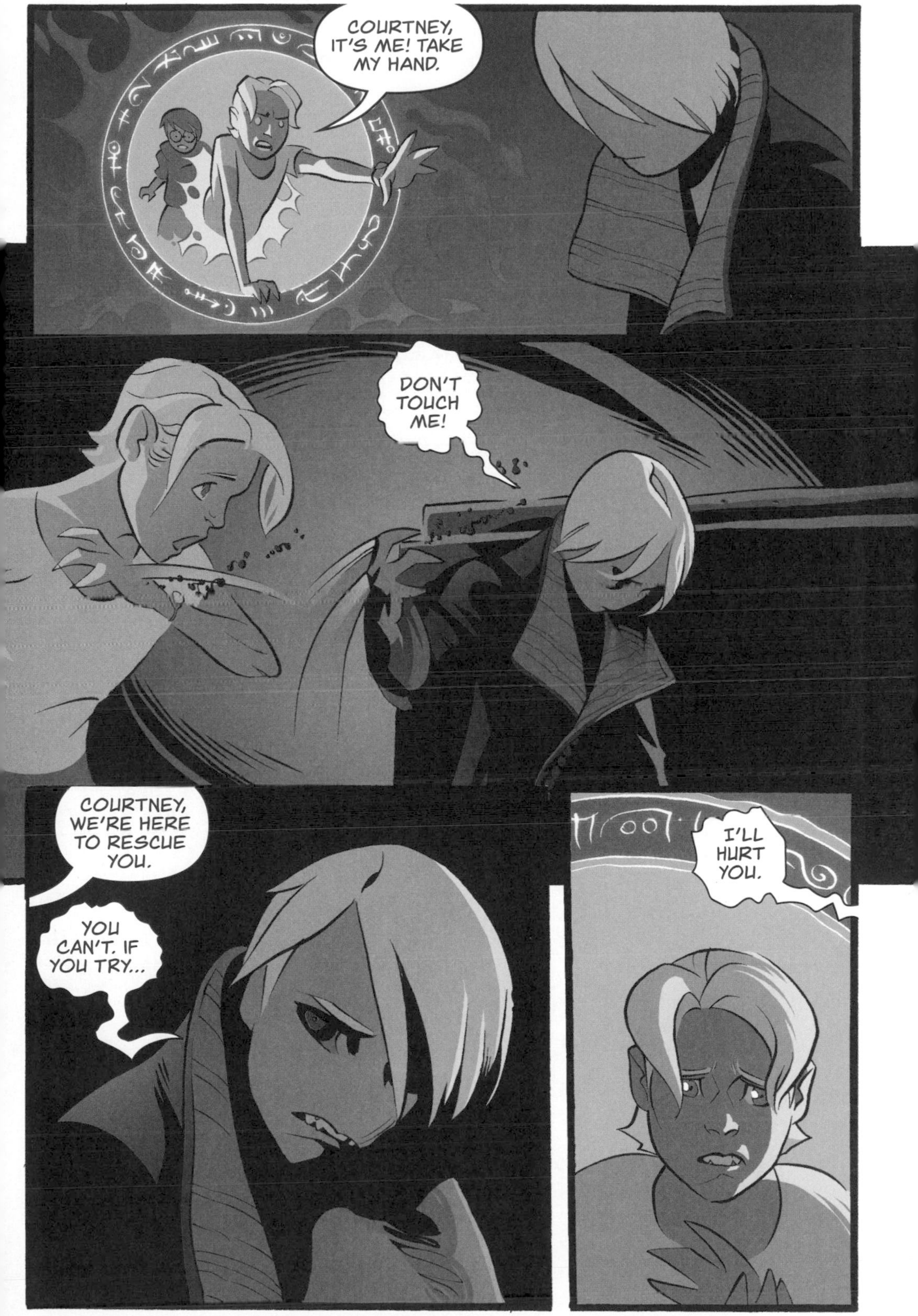
COURTNEY, IT'S ME! TAKE MY HAND.
DON'T TOUCH ME!
COURTNEY, WE'RE HERE TO RESCUE YOU.
YOU CAN'T. IF YOU TRY...
I'LL HURT YOU.

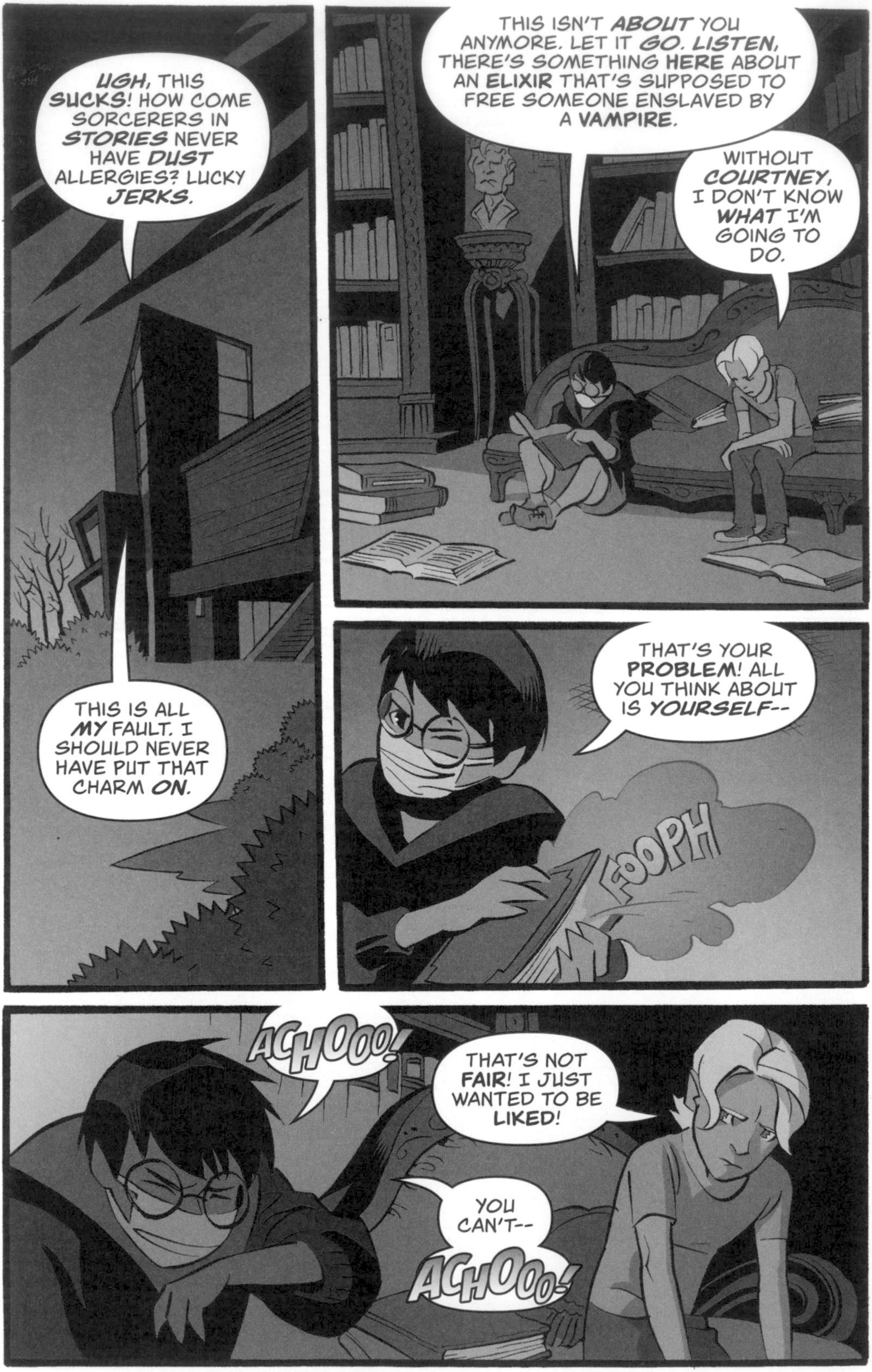
UGH, THIS SUCKS! HOW COME SORCERERS IN STORIES NEVER HAVE DUST ALLERGIES? LUCKY JERKS.
THIS IS ALL MY FAULT. I SHOULD NEVER HAVE PUT THAT CHARM ON.
THIS ISN'T ABOUT YOU ANYMORE. LET IT GO. LISTEN, THERE'S SOMETHING HERE ABOUT AN ELIXIR THAT'S SUPPOSED TO FREE SOMEONE ENSLAVED BY A VAMPIRE.
WITHOUT COURTNEY, I DON'T KNOW WHAT I'M GOING TO DO.
THAT'S YOUR PROBLEM! ALL YOU THINK ABOUT IS YOURSELF--
FOOPH
ACHOOO!
THAT'S NOT FAIR! I JUST WANTED TO BE LIKED!
YOU CAN'T--
ACHOOOO!

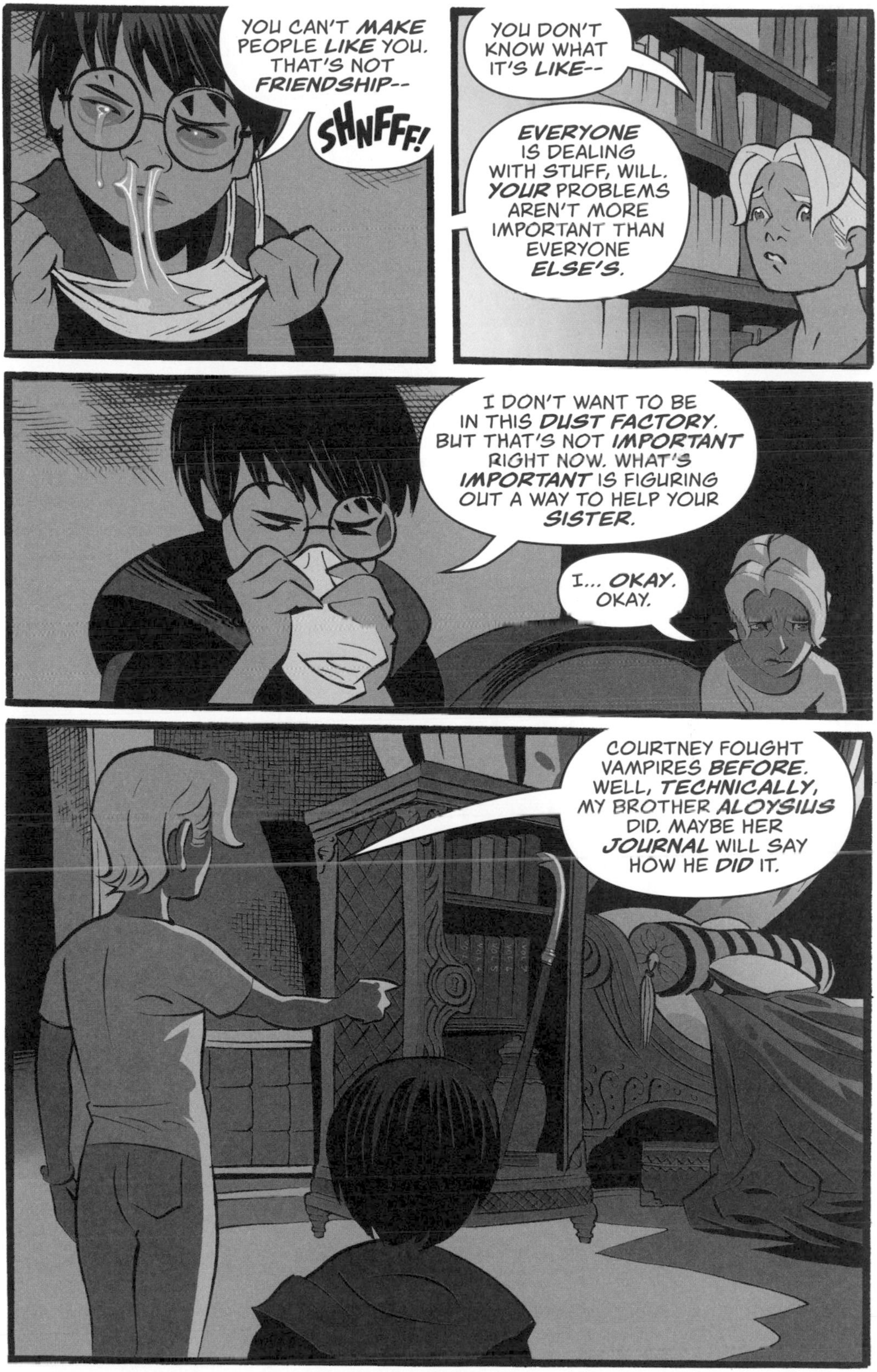

YOU CAN'T MAKE PEOPLE LIKE YOU. THAT'S NOT FRIENDSHIP--
SHNFFF!
YOU DON'T KNOW WHAT IT'S LIKE--
EVERYONE IS DEALING WITH STUFF, WILL. YOUR PROBLEMS AREN'T MORE IMPORTANT THAN EVERYONE ELSE'S.
I DON'T WANT TO BE IN THIS DUST FACTORY. BUT THAT'S NOT IMPORTANT RIGHT NOW. WHAT'S IMPORTANT IS FIGURING OUT A WAY TO HELP YOUR SISTER.
I... OKAY. OKAY.
COURTNEY FOUGHT VAMPIRES BEFORE. WELL, TECHNICALLY, MY BROTHER ALOYSIUS DID. MAYBE HER JOURNAL WILL SAY HOW HE DID IT.

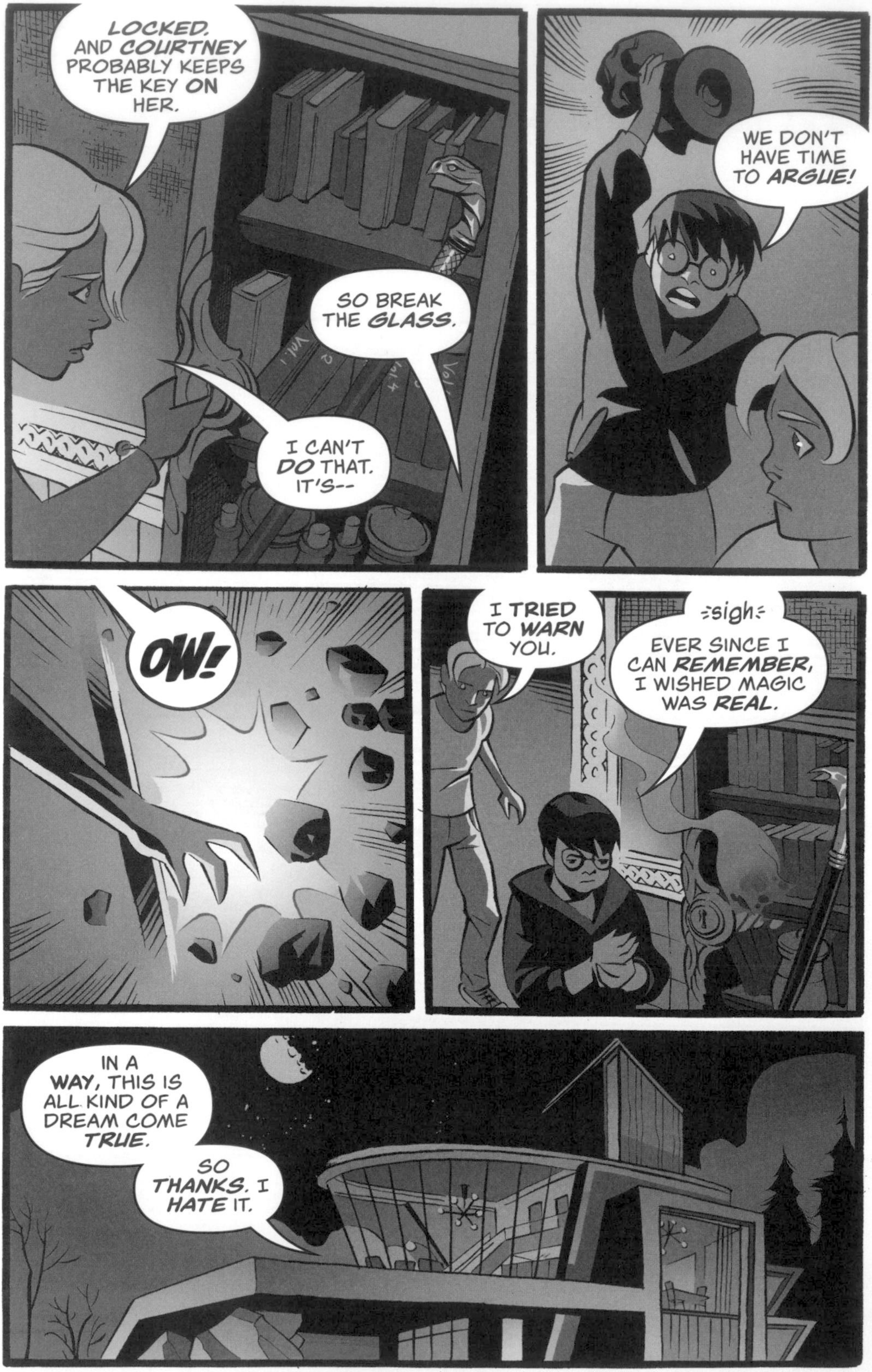
LOCKED. AND COURTNEY PROBABLY KEEPS THE KEY ON HER.
SO BREAK THE GLASS.
I CAN'T DO THAT. IT'S--
WE DON'T HAVE TIME TO ARGUE!
OW!
I TRIED TO WARN YOU.
sigh
EVER SINCE I CAN REMEMBER, I WISHED MAGIC WAS REAL.
IN A WAY, THIS IS ALL KIND OF A DREAM COME TRUE.
SO THANKS. I HATE IT.

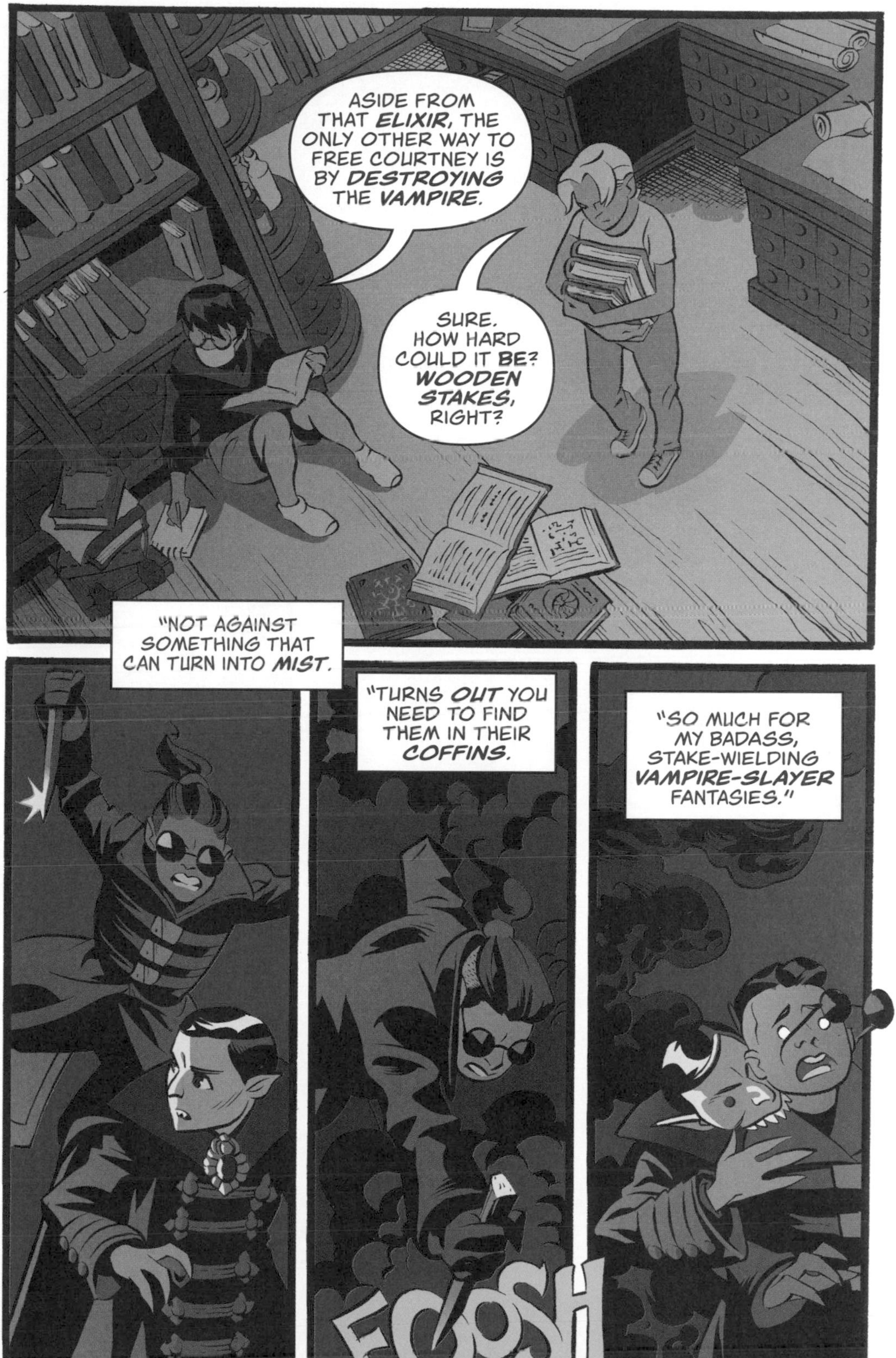
ASIDE FROM THAT ELIXIR, THE ONLY OTHER WAY TO FREE COURTNEY IS BY DESTROYING THE VAMPIRE.
SURE. HOW HARD COULD IT BE? WOODEN STAKES, RIGHT?
"NOT AGAINST SOMETHING THAT CAN TURN INTO MIST.
"TURNS OUT YOU NEED TO FIND THEM IN THEIR COFFINS.
"SO MUCH FOR MY BADASS, STAKE-WIELDING VAMPIRE-SLAYER FANTASIES."
FOOSH

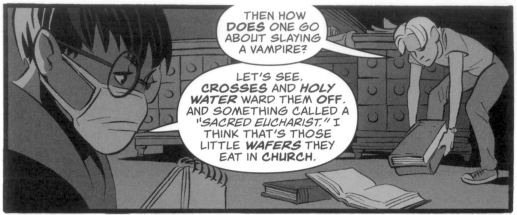

THEN HOW **DOES ONE GO** ABOUT SLAYING A VAMPIRE?

LET'S SEE. **CROSSES** AND **HOLY WATER** WARD THEM **OFF.** AND SOMETHING CALLED A *"SACRED EUCHARIST."* I THINK THAT'S THOSE LITTLE **WAFERS** THEY EAT IN **CHURCH.**

CHRISTIAN MAGIC IS... *WEIRD!*

DUDE, *ALL* MAGIC IS WEIRD. HEARD OF **APOTROPAIC** MAGIC?

THIS **TURKISH NAZAR** WAS IN THE DESK **DRAWER** WITH ALL THE **CROSSES** AND STUFF. I'VE SEEN 'EM IN **IMPORT SHOPS.** TURNS OUT THEY'RE SUPPOSED TO WARD OFF THE **EVIL EYE.**

WHAT'S **THAT** MEAN?

THEY KEEP VAMPIRES FROM **CHARMING** YOU, OR USING THEIR **VOICE** TO **CONTROL** YOU. IF I HAD ONE OF **THESE,** WE PROBABLY WOULDN'T BE IN THIS MESS.

VERY **FUNNY.** SO YOU'RE SAYING THE ONLY WAY TO GET **RID** OF THIS FELLOW IS TO FIND HIM IN HIS **COFFIN?**

EXCEPT *COURTNEY'S* GUARDING IT.

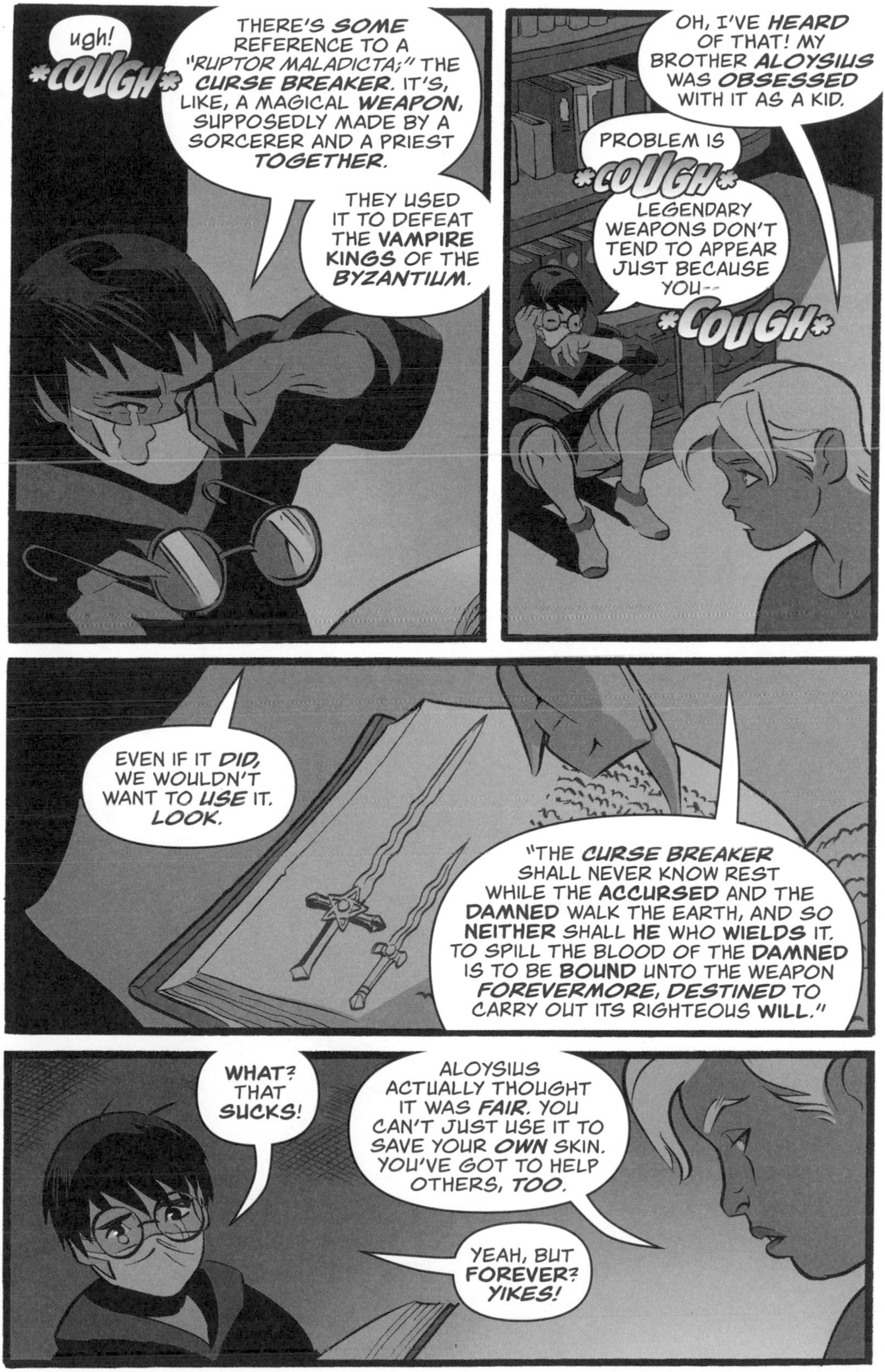
ugh!
COUGH
THERE'S SOME REFERENCE TO A "RUPTOR MALADICTA;" THE CURSE BREAKER. IT'S, LIKE, A MAGICAL WEAPON, SUPPOSEDLY MADE BY A SORCERER AND A PRIEST TOGETHER.
THEY USED IT TO DEFEAT THE VAMPIRE KINGS OF THE BYZANTIUM.
OH, I'VE HEARD OF THAT! MY BROTHER ALOYSIUS WAS OBSESSED WITH IT AS A KID.
PROBLEM IS
COUGH
LEGENDARY WEAPONS DON'T TEND TO APPEAR JUST BECAUSE YOU--
COUGH
EVEN IF IT DID, WE WOULDN'T WANT TO USE IT. LOOK.
"THE CURSE BREAKER SHALL NEVER KNOW REST WHILE THE ACCURSED AND THE DAMNED WALK THE EARTH, AND SO NEITHER SHALL HE WHO WIELDS IT. TO SPILL THE BLOOD OF THE DAMNED IS TO BE BOUND UNTO THE WEAPON FOREVERMORE, DESTINED TO CARRY OUT ITS RIGHTEOUS WILL."
WHAT? THAT SUCKS!
ALOYSIUS ACTUALLY THOUGHT IT WAS FAIR. YOU CAN'T JUST USE IT TO SAVE YOUR OWN SKIN. YOU'VE GOT TO HELP OTHERS, TOO.
YEAH, BUT FOREVER? YIKES!

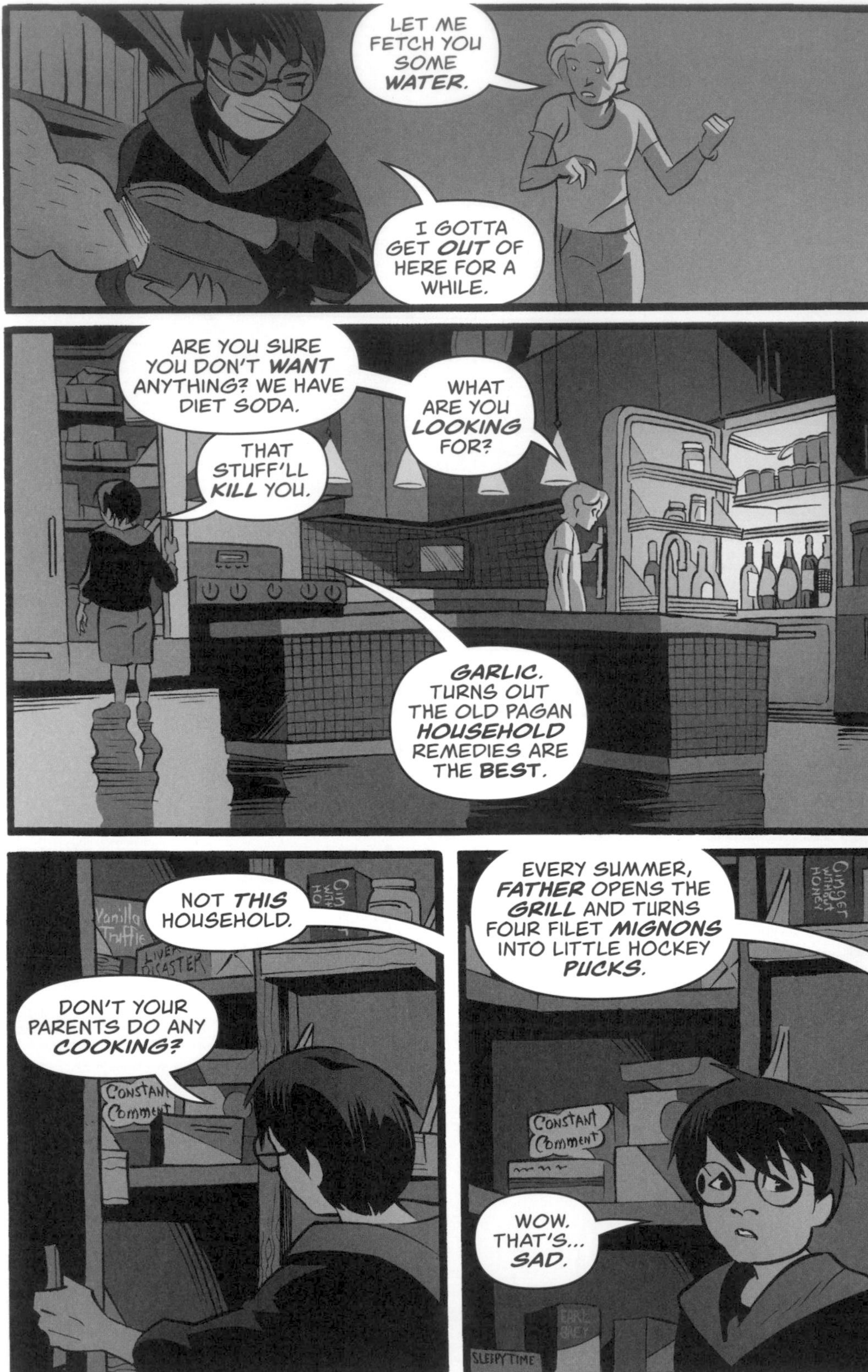
LET ME FETCH YOU SOME WATER.
I GOTTA GET OUT OF HERE FOR A WHILE.
ARE YOU SURE YOU DON'T WANT ANYTHING? WE HAVE DIET SODA.
THAT STUFF'LL KILL YOU.
WHAT ARE YOU LOOKING FOR?
GARLIC. TURNS OUT THE OLD PAGAN HOUSEHOLD REMEDIES ARE THE BEST.
Vanilla Truffle
NOT THIS HOUSEHOLD.
DON'T YOUR PARENTS DO ANY COOKING?
Constant Comment
EVERY SUMMER, FATHER OPENS THE GRILL AND TURNS FOUR FILET MIGNONS INTO LITTLE HOCKEY PUCKS.
Ginger without Honey
Constant Comment
WOW. THAT'S... SAD.
SLEEPYTIME

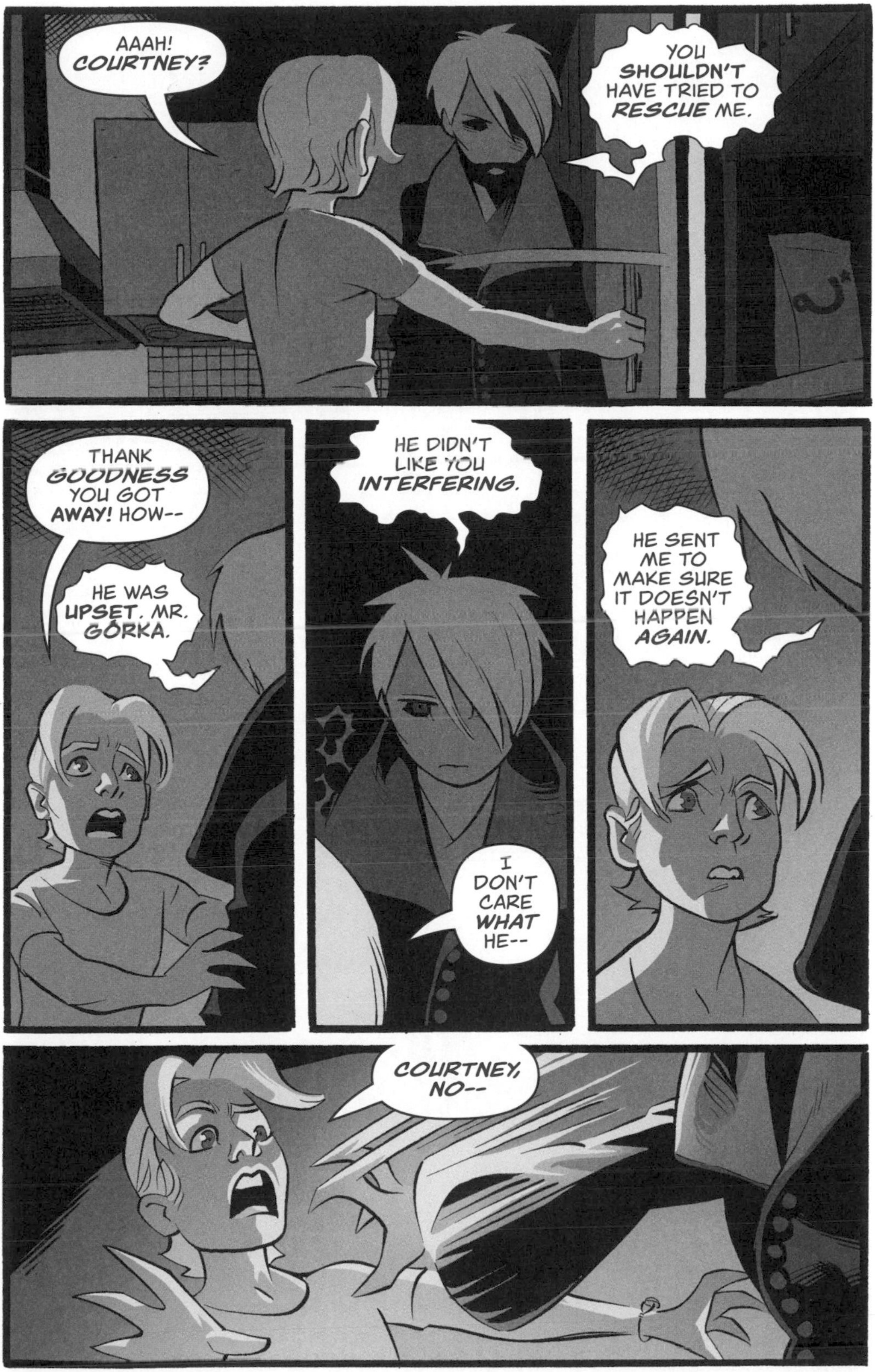
AAAH! COURTNEY?
YOU SHOULDN'T HAVE TRIED TO RESCUE ME.
THANK GOODNESS YOU GOT AWAY! HOW--
HE WAS UPSET. MR. GÓRKA.
HE DIDN'T LIKE YOU INTERFERING.
I DON'T CARE WHAT HE--
HE SENT ME TO MAKE SURE IT DOESN'T HAPPEN AGAIN.
COURTNEY, NO--

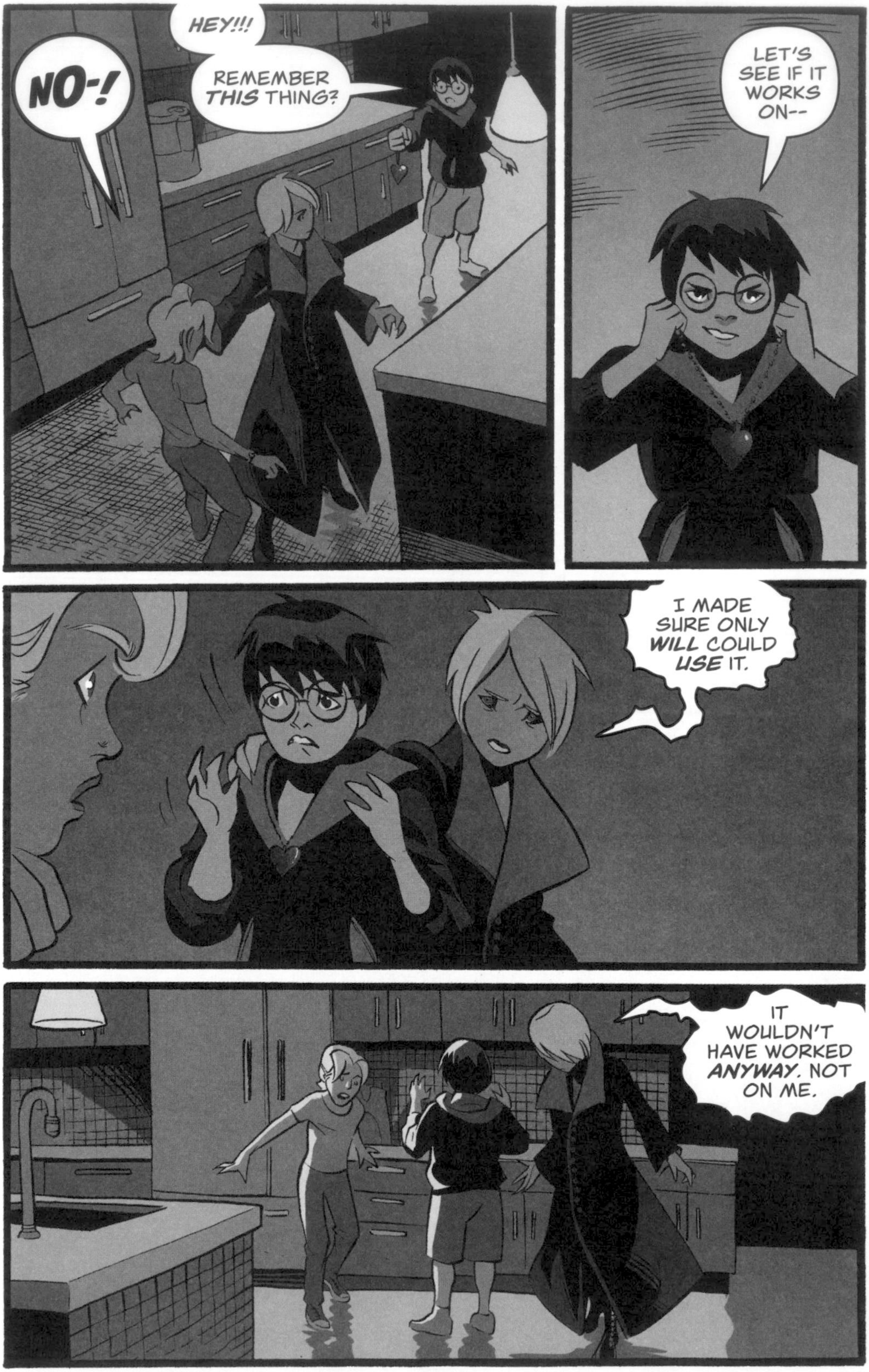

NO-!
HEY!!!
REMEMBER THIS THING?
LET'S SEE IF IT WORKS ON--
I MADE SURE ONLY WILL COULD USE IT.
IT WOULDN'T HAVE WORKED ANYWAY. NOT ON ME.

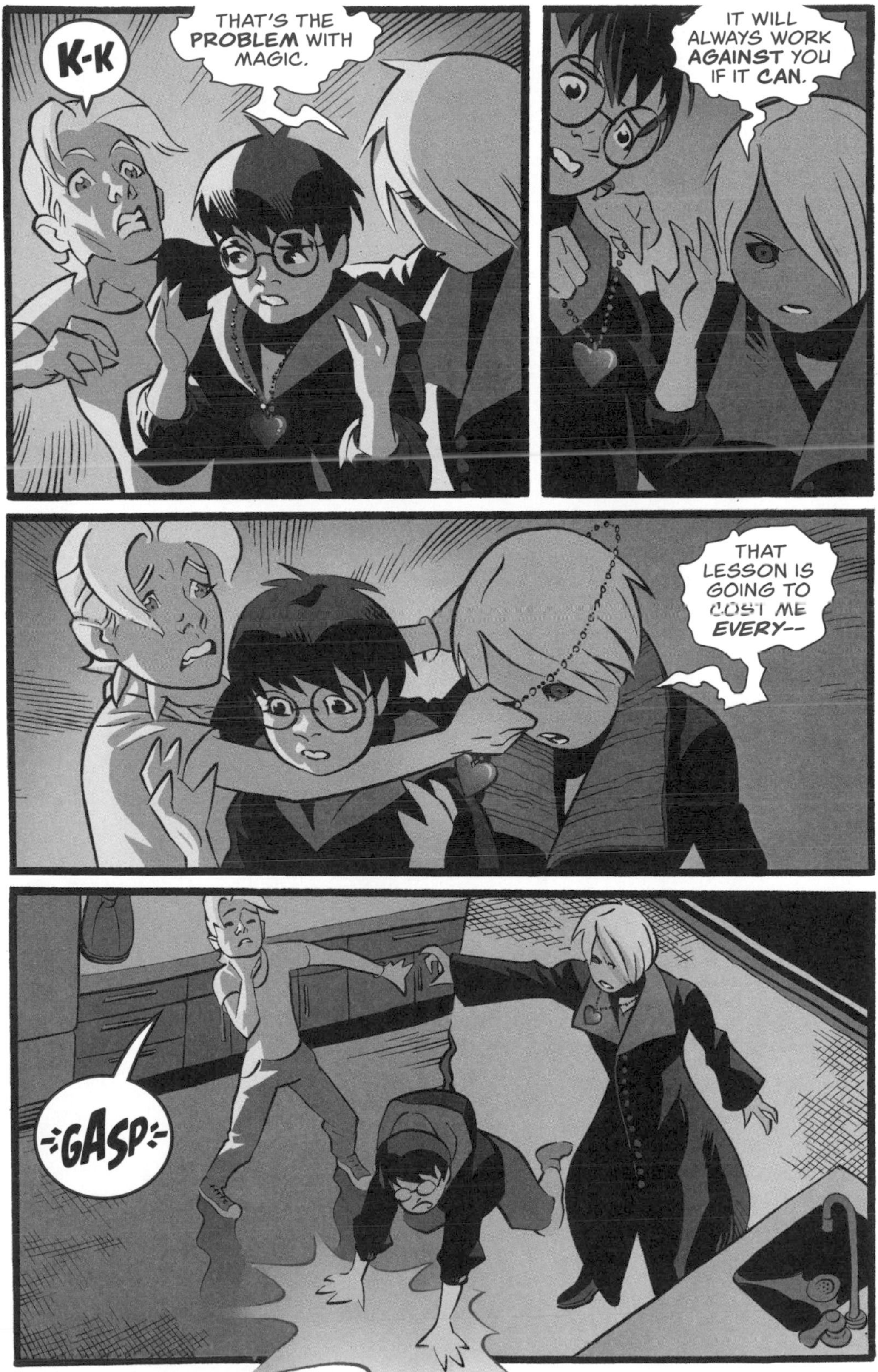
K-K
THAT'S THE PROBLEM WITH MAGIC.
IT WILL ALWAYS WORK AGAINST YOU IF IT CAN.
THAT LESSON IS GOING TO COST ME EVERY--
GASP

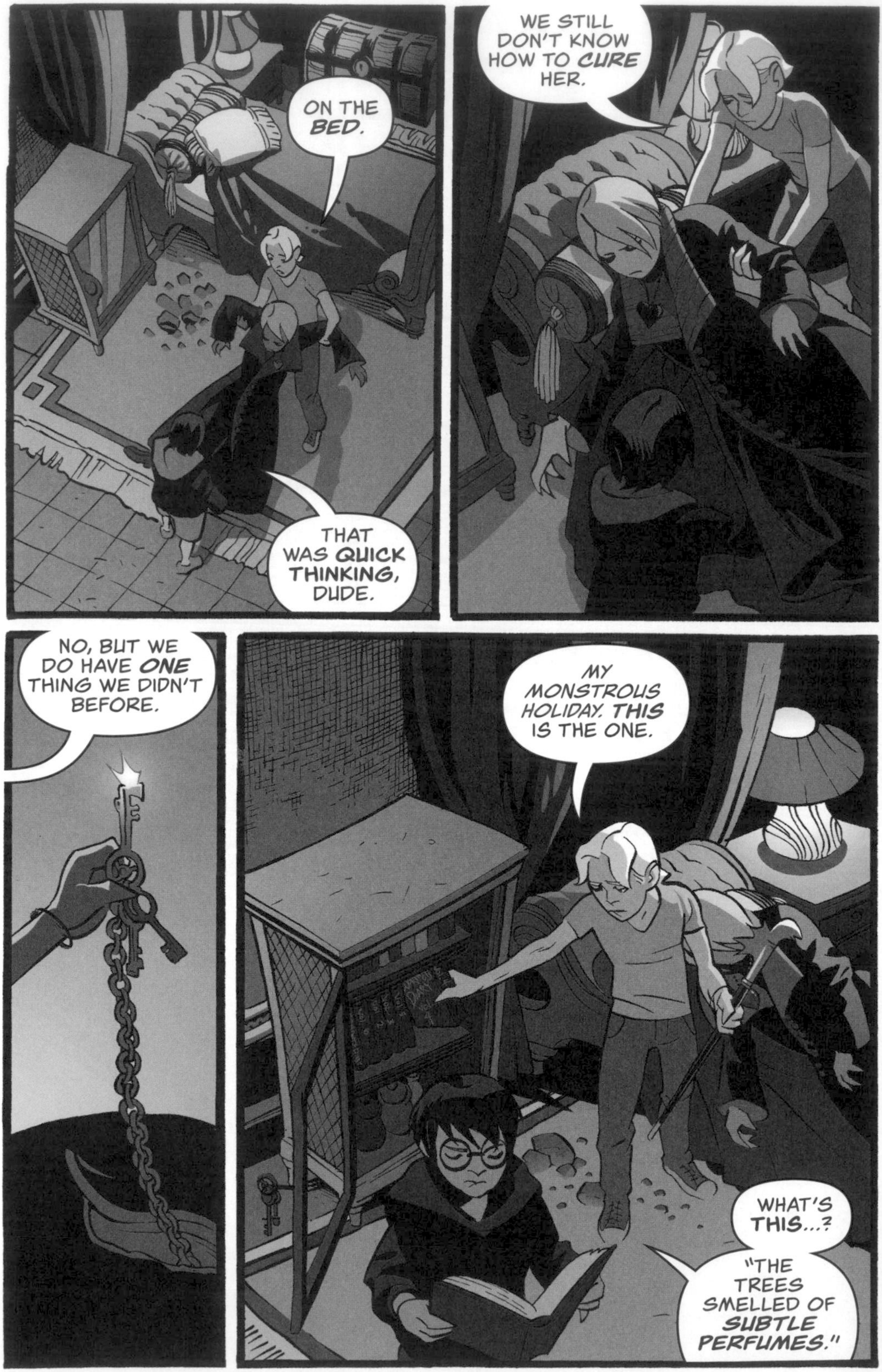

ON THE BED.
THAT WAS QUICK THINKING, DUDE.
WE STILL DON'T KNOW HOW TO CURE HER.
NO, BUT WE DO HAVE ONE THING WE DIDN'T BEFORE.
MY MONSTROUS HOLIDAY. THIS IS THE ONE.
WHAT'S THIS...?
"THE TREES SMELLED OF SUBTLE PERFUMES."

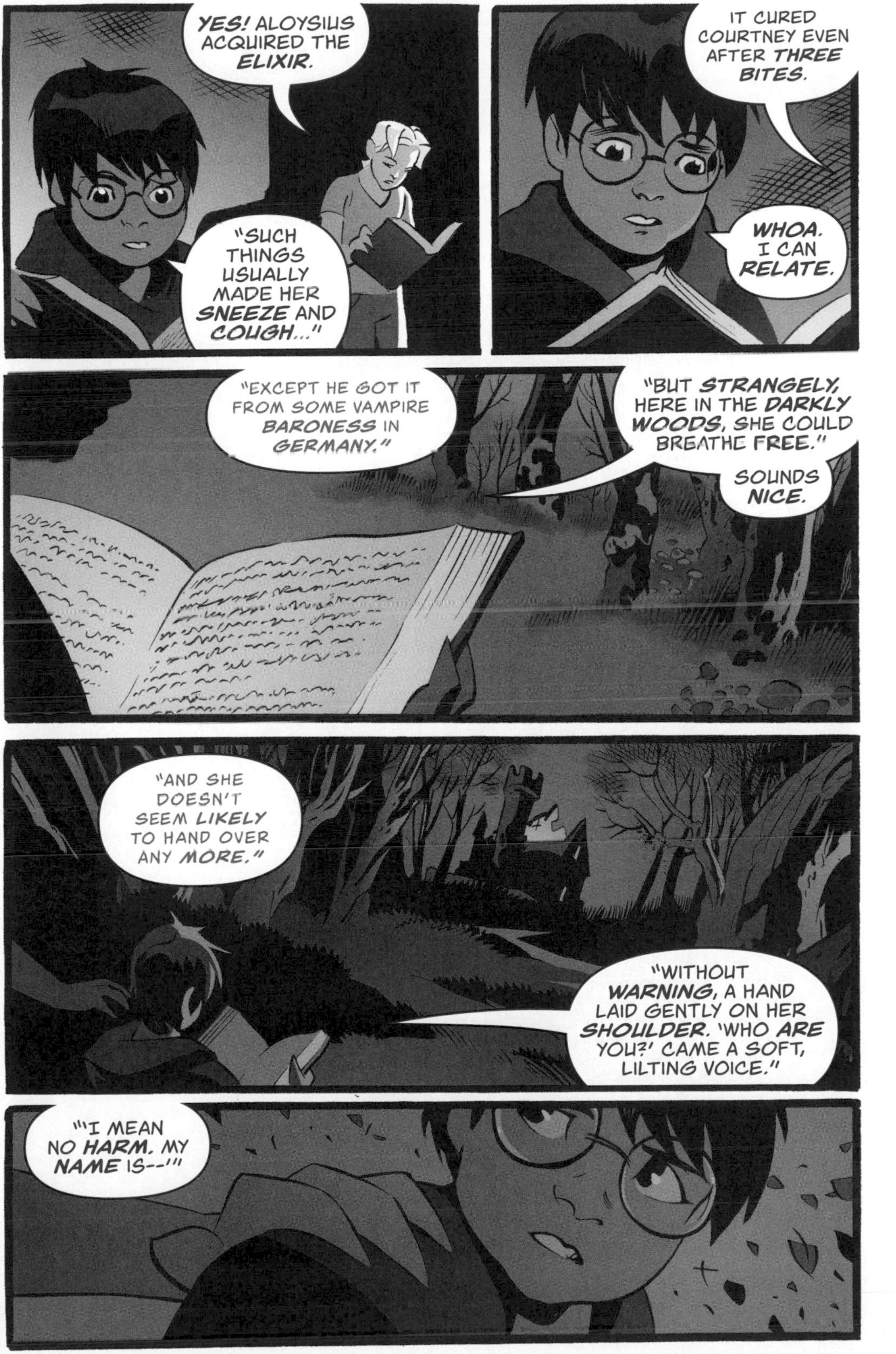
YES! ALOYSIUS ACQUIRED THE ELIXIR.
"SUCH THINGS USUALLY MADE HER SNEEZE AND COUGH..."
IT CURED COURTNEY EVEN AFTER THREE BITES.
WHOA. I CAN RELATE.
"EXCEPT HE GOT IT FROM SOME VAMPIRE BARONESS IN GERMANY."
"BUT STRANGELY, HERE IN THE DARKLY WOODS, SHE COULD BREATHE FREE."
SOUNDS NICE.
"AND SHE DOESN'T SEEM LIKELY TO HAND OVER ANY MORE."
"WITHOUT WARNING, A HAND LAID GENTLY ON HER SHOULDER. 'WHO ARE YOU?' CAME A SOFT, LILTING VOICE."
"'I MEAN NO HARM. MY NAME IS--'"

DON'T **LOOK** AT THAT!

WHAT? WHERE **AM...?**

WILL?

THAT BOOK BELONGED TO MY GREAT **GRANDMOTHER.** IF YOU READ YOUR **NAME** IN IT, YOU'D BE LOST IN THE STORY **FOREVER.**

IT'S MADE **HUNDREDS** OF PEOPLE DISAPPEAR.

IT... **WHAT?** ARE YOU **KIDDING ME!?**

DARKLY THROUGH the WOODS and other stories

THAT'S **AMAZING!**

YOU'VE GOT TO BE MORE **CAREFUL,** TUCKER!

THIS STUFF IS **DANGEROUS!**

DARKLY THROUGH the WOODS

I'M **BEING** CAREFUL.

NO, YOU'RE **NOT!** THAT MAD IDEA OF USING MY **CHARM?** YOU COULD HAVE BEEN **KILLED!**

=sigh= YOU THINK THIS IS SOME KIND OF **ADVENTURE** LIKE IN YOUR **BOOKS?**

LET ME **TELL** YOU SOMETHING ABOUT MAGICAL ADVENTURES.

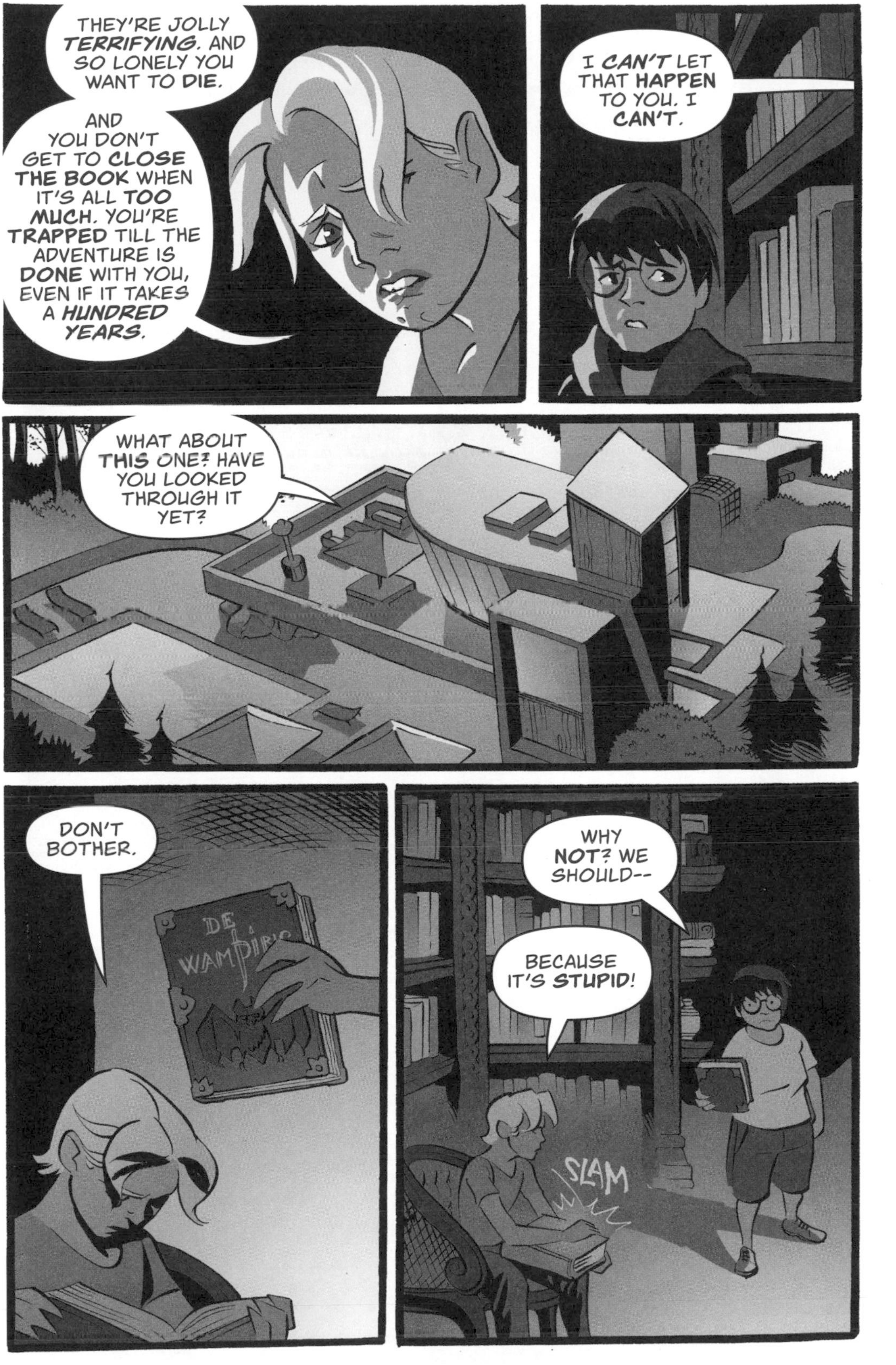
THEY'RE JOLLY TERRIFYING. AND SO LONELY YOU WANT TO DIE.
AND YOU DON'T GET TO CLOSE THE BOOK WHEN IT'S ALL TOO MUCH. YOU'RE TRAPPED TILL THE ADVENTURE IS DONE WITH YOU, EVEN IF IT TAKES A HUNDRED YEARS.
I CAN'T LET THAT HAPPEN TO YOU. I CAN'T.
WHAT ABOUT THIS ONE? HAVE YOU LOOKED THROUGH IT YET?
DON'T BOTHER.
DE WAMPIRIS
WHY NOT? WE SHOULD--
BECAUSE IT'S STUPID!
SLAM

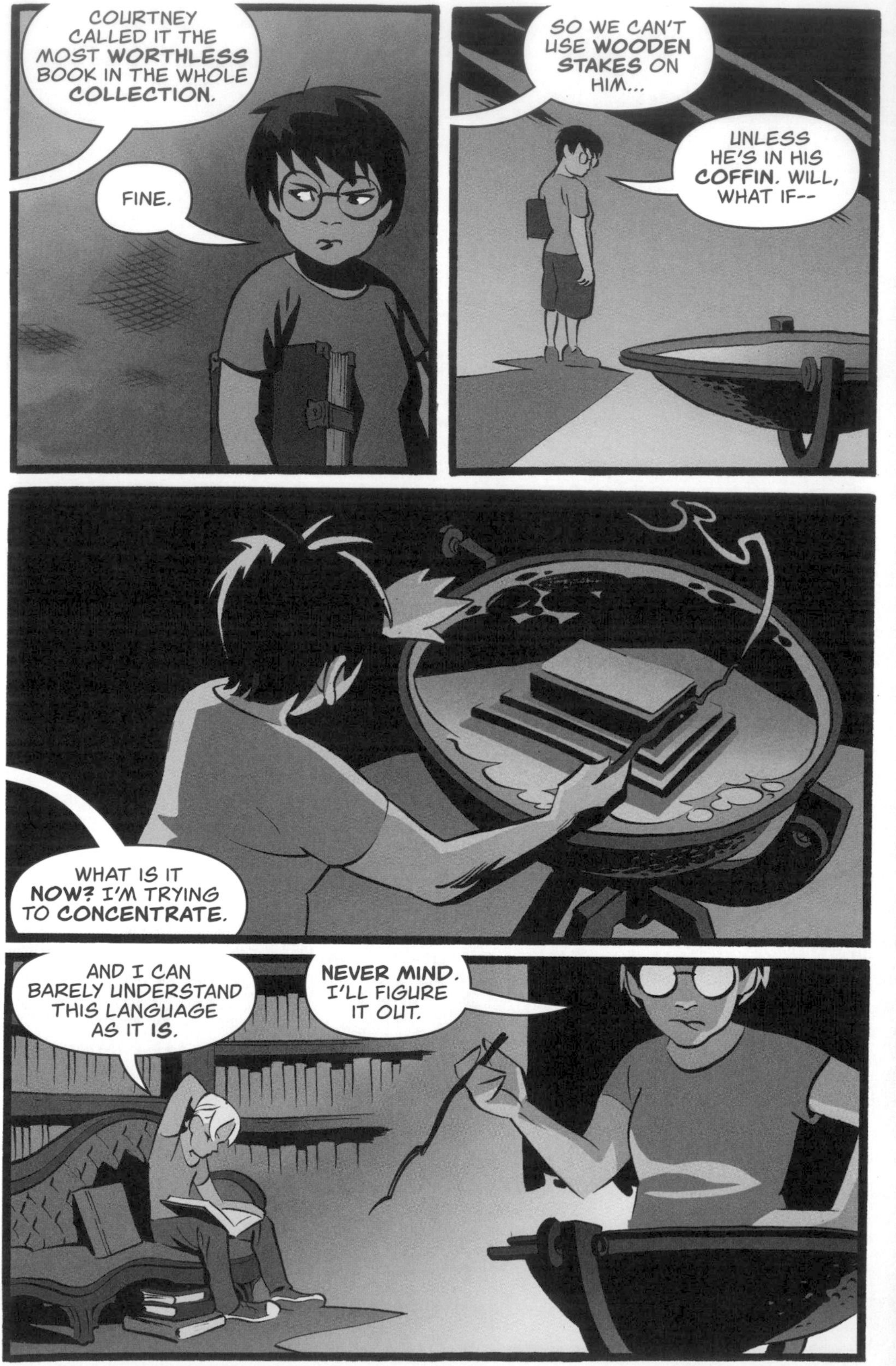
COURTNEY CALLED IT THE MOST WORTHLESS BOOK IN THE WHOLE COLLECTION.
FINE.
SO WE CAN'T USE WOODEN STAKES ON HIM...
UNLESS HE'S IN HIS COFFIN. WILL, WHAT IF--
WHAT IS IT NOW? I'M TRYING TO CONCENTRATE.
AND I CAN BARELY UNDERSTAND THIS LANGUAGE AS IT IS.
NEVER MIND. I'LL FIGURE IT OUT.

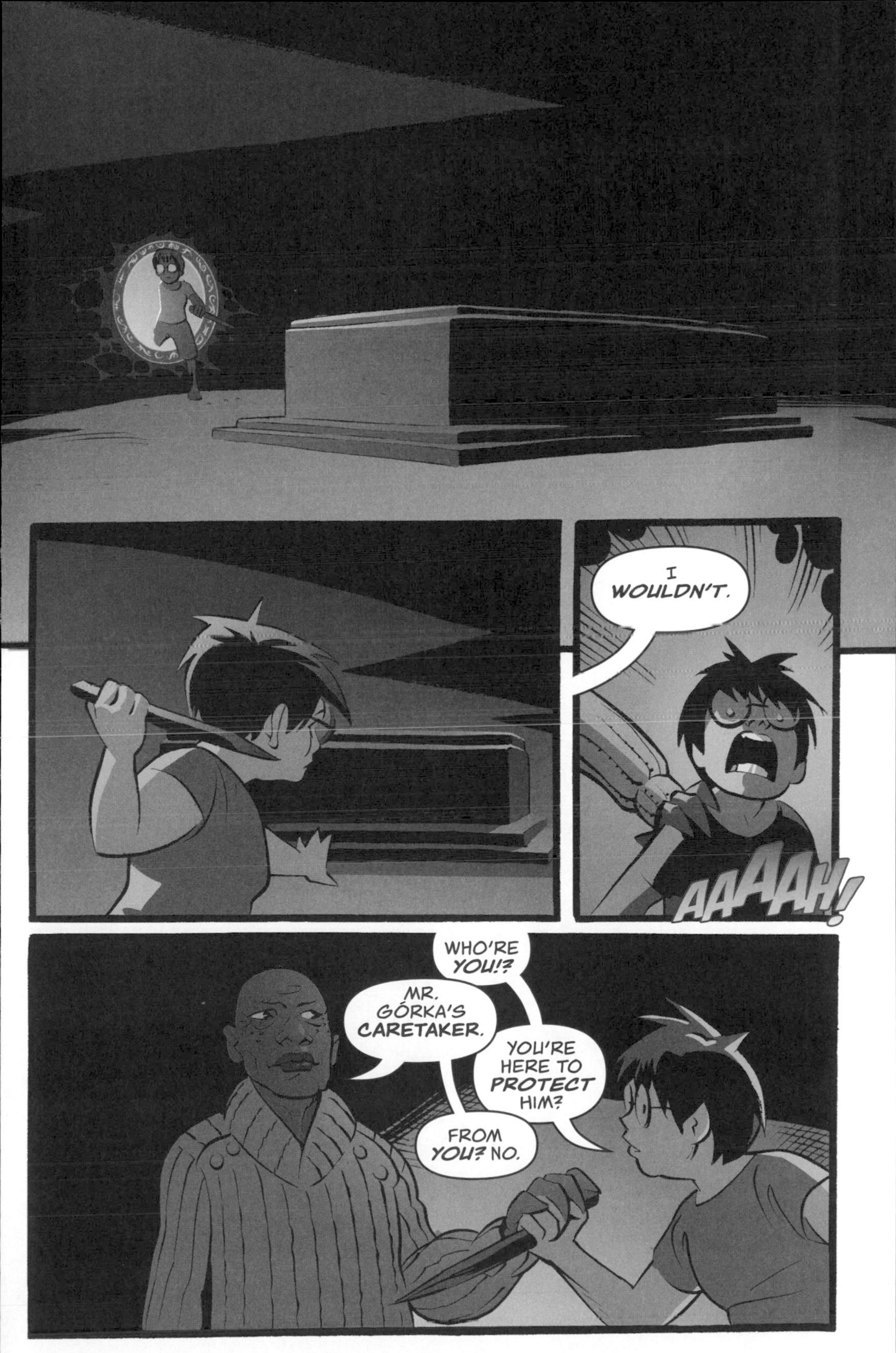
I WOULDN'T.
AAAAH!
WHO'RE YOU!?
MR. GÓRKA'S CARETAKER.
YOU'RE HERE TO PROTECT HIM?
FROM YOU? NO.

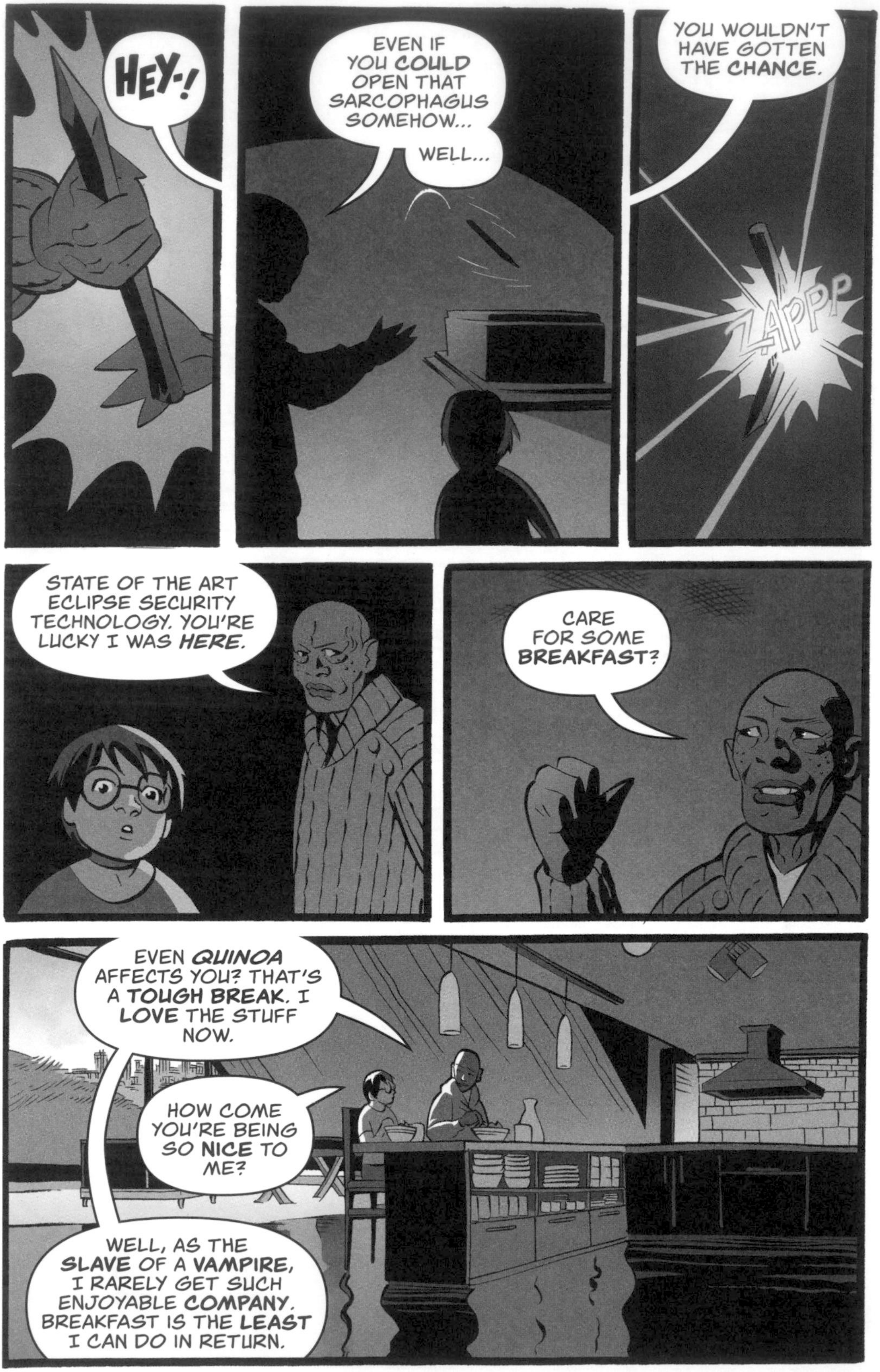
HEY-!
EVEN IF YOU COULD OPEN THAT SARCOPHAGUS SOMEHOW...
WELL...
YOU WOULDN'T HAVE GOTTEN THE CHANCE.
ZAPPP
STATE OF THE ART ECLIPSE SECURITY TECHNOLOGY. YOU'RE LUCKY I WAS HERE.
CARE FOR SOME BREAKFAST?
EVEN QUINOA AFFECTS YOU? THAT'S A TOUGH BREAK. I LOVE THE STUFF NOW.
HOW COME YOU'RE BEING SO NICE TO ME?
WELL, AS THE SLAVE OF A VAMPIRE, I RARELY GET SUCH ENJOYABLE COMPANY. BREAKFAST IS THE LEAST I CAN DO IN RETURN.

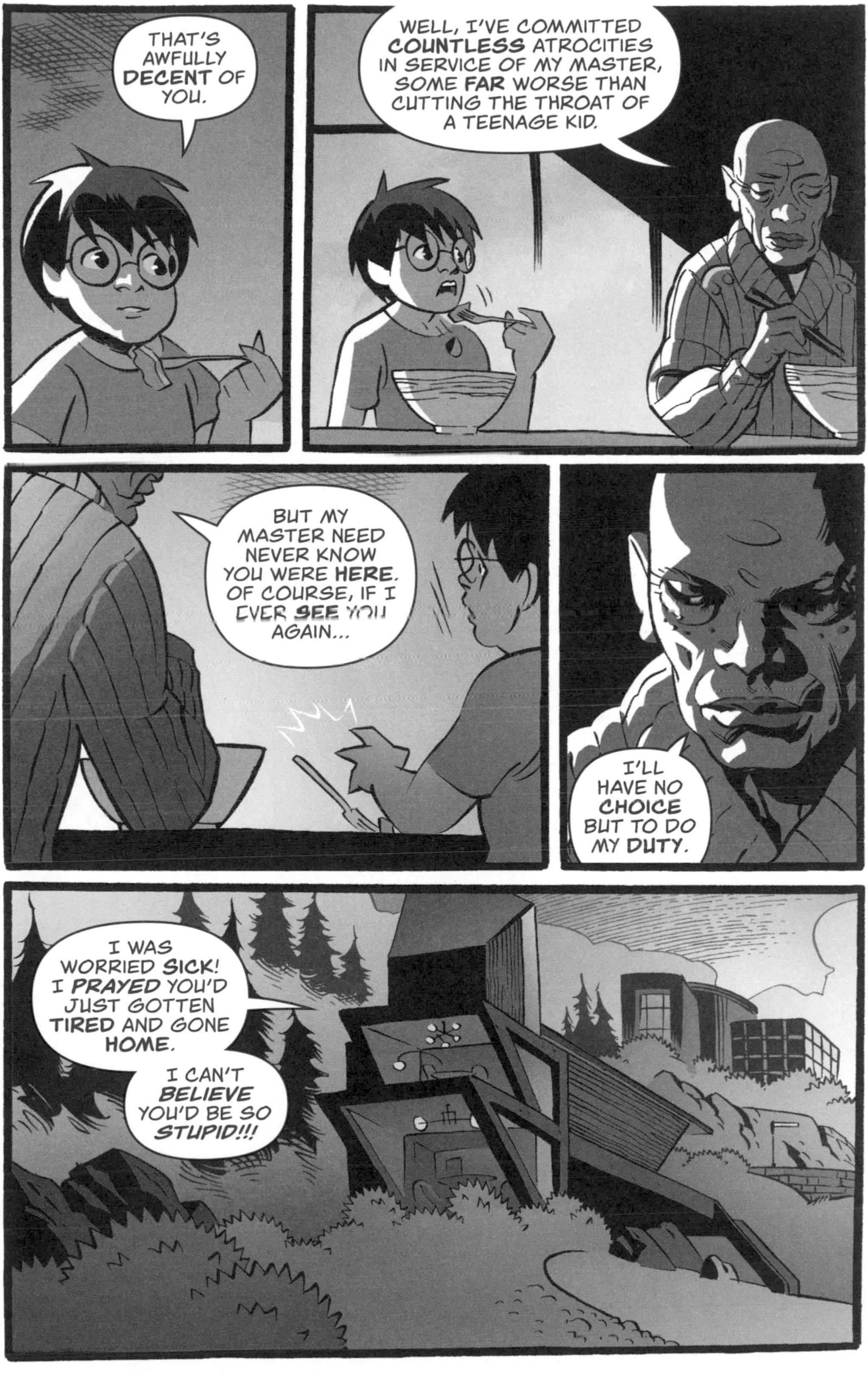
THAT'S AWFULLY DECENT OF YOU.
WELL, I'VE COMMITTED COUNTLESS ATROCITIES IN SERVICE OF MY MASTER, SOME FAR WORSE THAN CUTTING THE THROAT OF A TEENAGE KID.
BUT MY MASTER NEED NEVER KNOW YOU WERE HERE. OF COURSE, IF I EVER SEE YOU AGAIN...
I'LL HAVE NO CHOICE BUT TO DO MY DUTY.
I WAS WORRIED SICK! I PRAYED YOU'D JUST GOTTEN TIRED AND GONE HOME.
I CAN'T BELIEVE YOU'D BE SO STUPID!!!

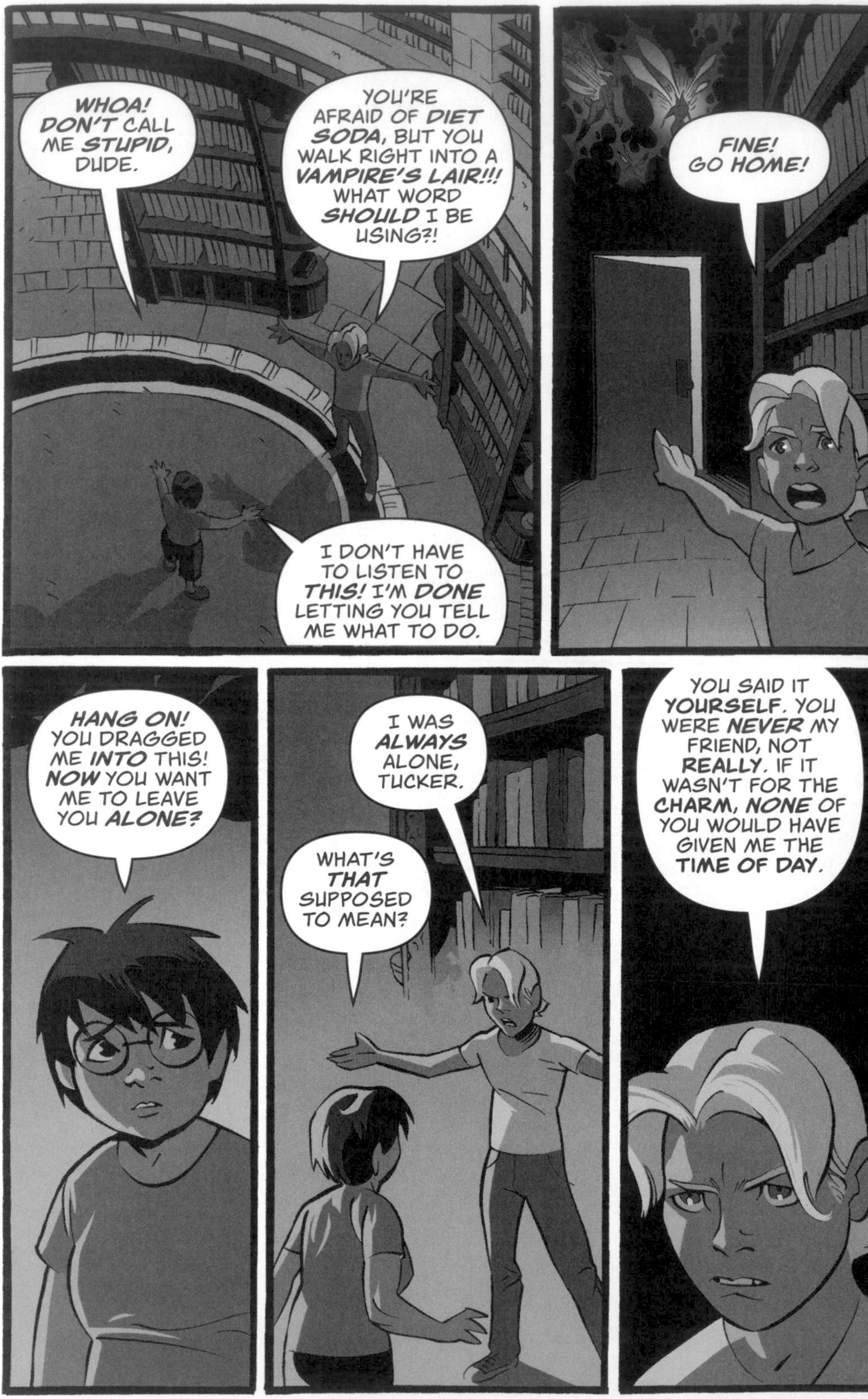
WHOA! DON'T CALL ME STUPID, DUDE.
YOU'RE AFRAID OF DIET SODA, BUT YOU WALK RIGHT INTO A VAMPIRE'S LAIR!!! WHAT WORD SHOULD I BE USING?!
I DON'T HAVE TO LISTEN TO THIS! I'M DONE LETTING YOU TELL ME WHAT TO DO.
FINE! GO HOME!
HANG ON! YOU DRAGGED ME INTO THIS! NOW YOU WANT ME TO LEAVE YOU ALONE?
I WAS ALWAYS ALONE, TUCKER.
WHAT'S THAT SUPPOSED TO MEAN?
YOU SAID IT YOURSELF. YOU WERE NEVER MY FRIEND, NOT REALLY. IF IT WASN'T FOR THE CHARM, NONE OF YOU WOULD HAVE GIVEN ME THE TIME OF DAY.

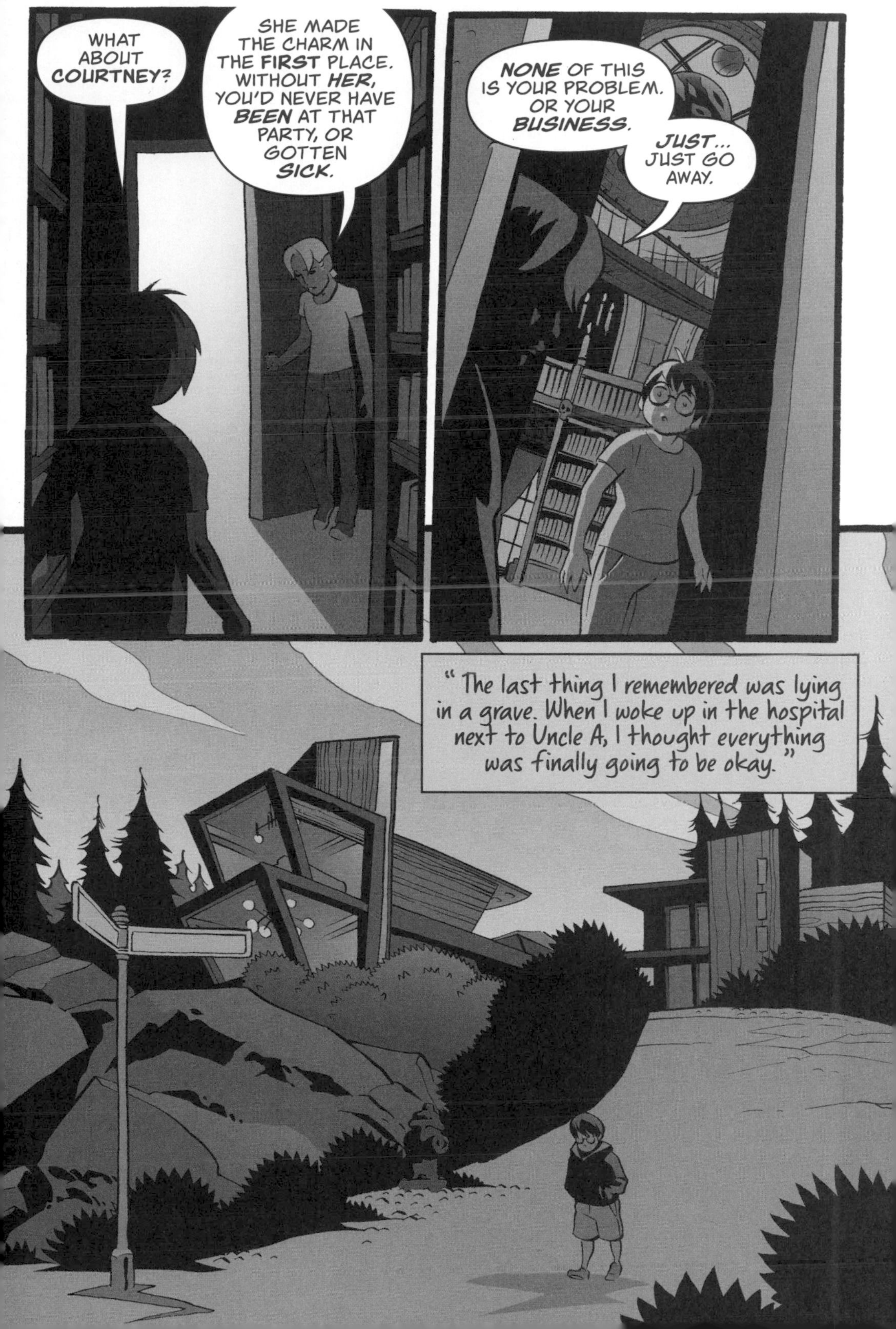
WHAT ABOUT COURTNEY?
SHE MADE THE CHARM IN THE FIRST PLACE. WITHOUT HER, YOU'D NEVER HAVE BEEN AT THAT PARTY, OR GOTTEN SICK.
NONE OF THIS IS YOUR PROBLEM. OR YOUR BUSINESS.
JUST... JUST GO AWAY.
"The last thing I remembered was lying in a grave. When I woke up in the hospital next to Uncle A, I thought everything was finally going to be okay."

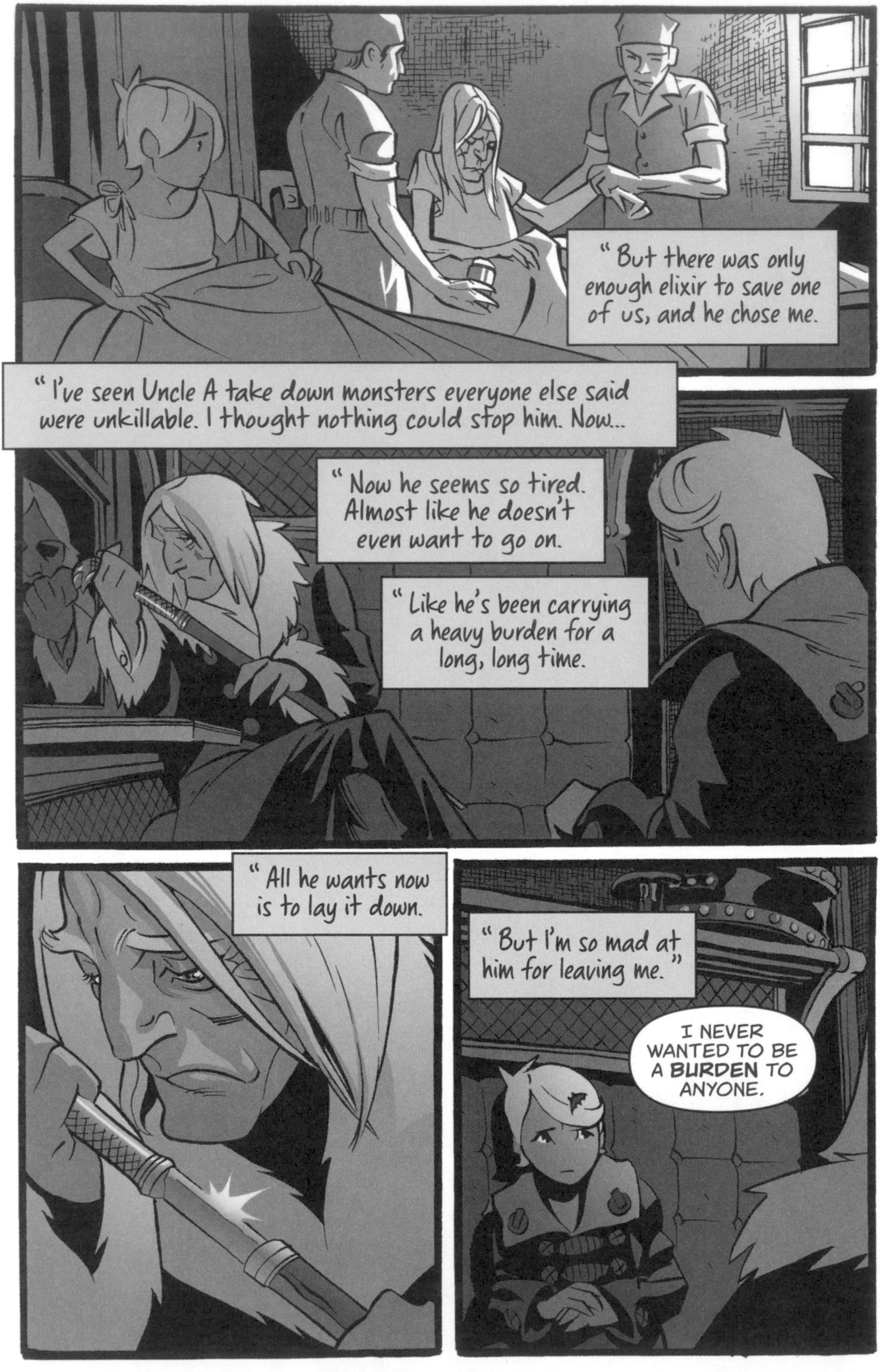
"But there was only enough elixir to save one of us, and he chose me.
"I've seen Uncle A take down monsters everyone else said were unkillable. I thought nothing could stop him. Now...
"Now he seems so tired. Almost like he doesn't even want to go on.
"Like he's been carrying a heavy burden for a long, long time.
"All he wants now is to lay it down.
"But I'm so mad at him for leaving me."
I NEVER WANTED TO BE A **BURDEN** TO ANYONE.

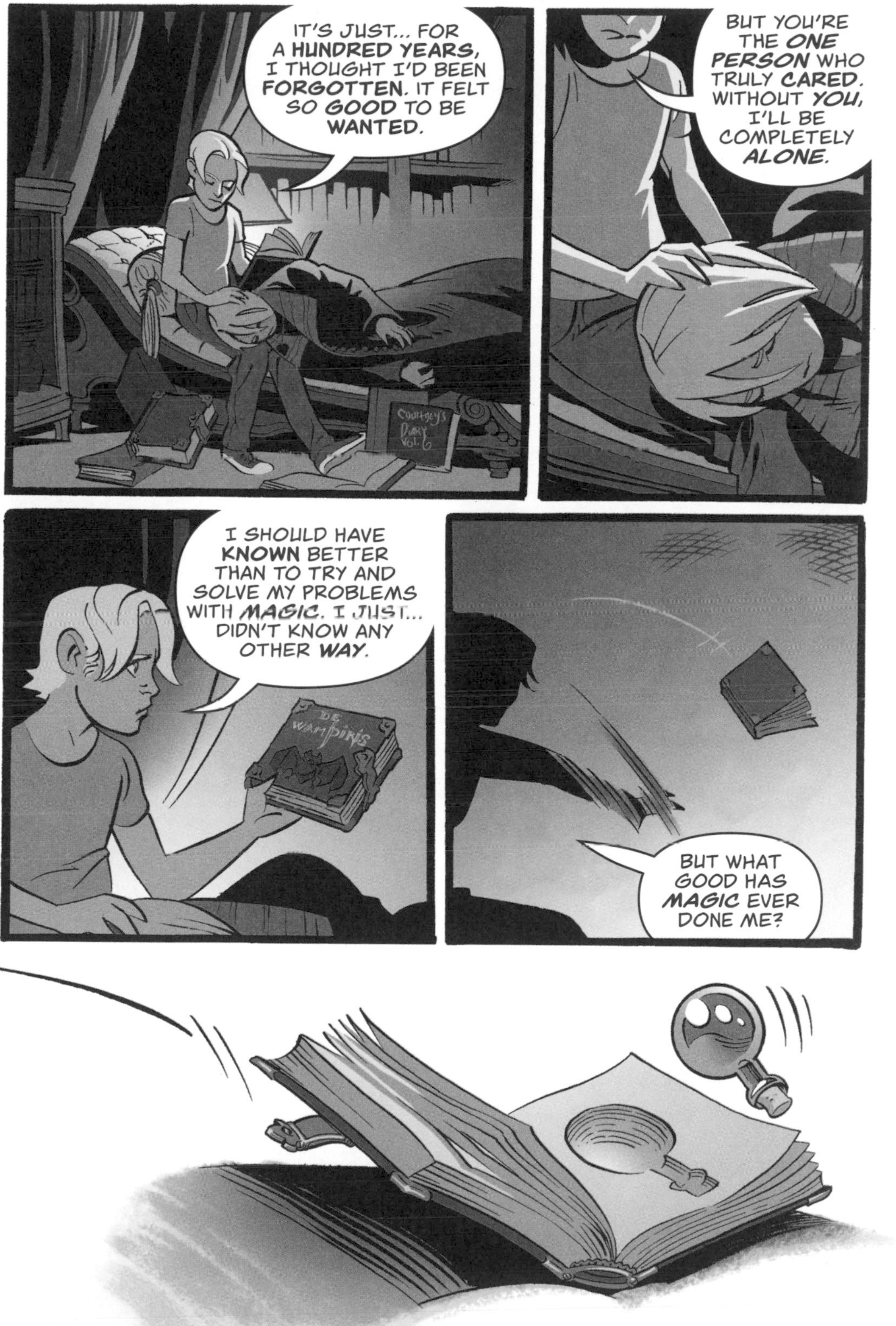
IT'S JUST... FOR A HUNDRED YEARS, I THOUGHT I'D BEEN FORGOTTEN. IT FELT SO GOOD TO BE WANTED.
Courtney's Diary Vol. 6
BUT YOU'RE THE ONE PERSON WHO TRULY CARED. WITHOUT YOU, I'LL BE COMPLETELY ALONE.
I SHOULD HAVE KNOWN BETTER THAN TO TRY AND SOLVE MY PROBLEMS WITH MAGIC. I JUST... DIDN'T KNOW ANY OTHER WAY.
De Vampiris
BUT WHAT GOOD HAS MAGIC EVER DONE ME?

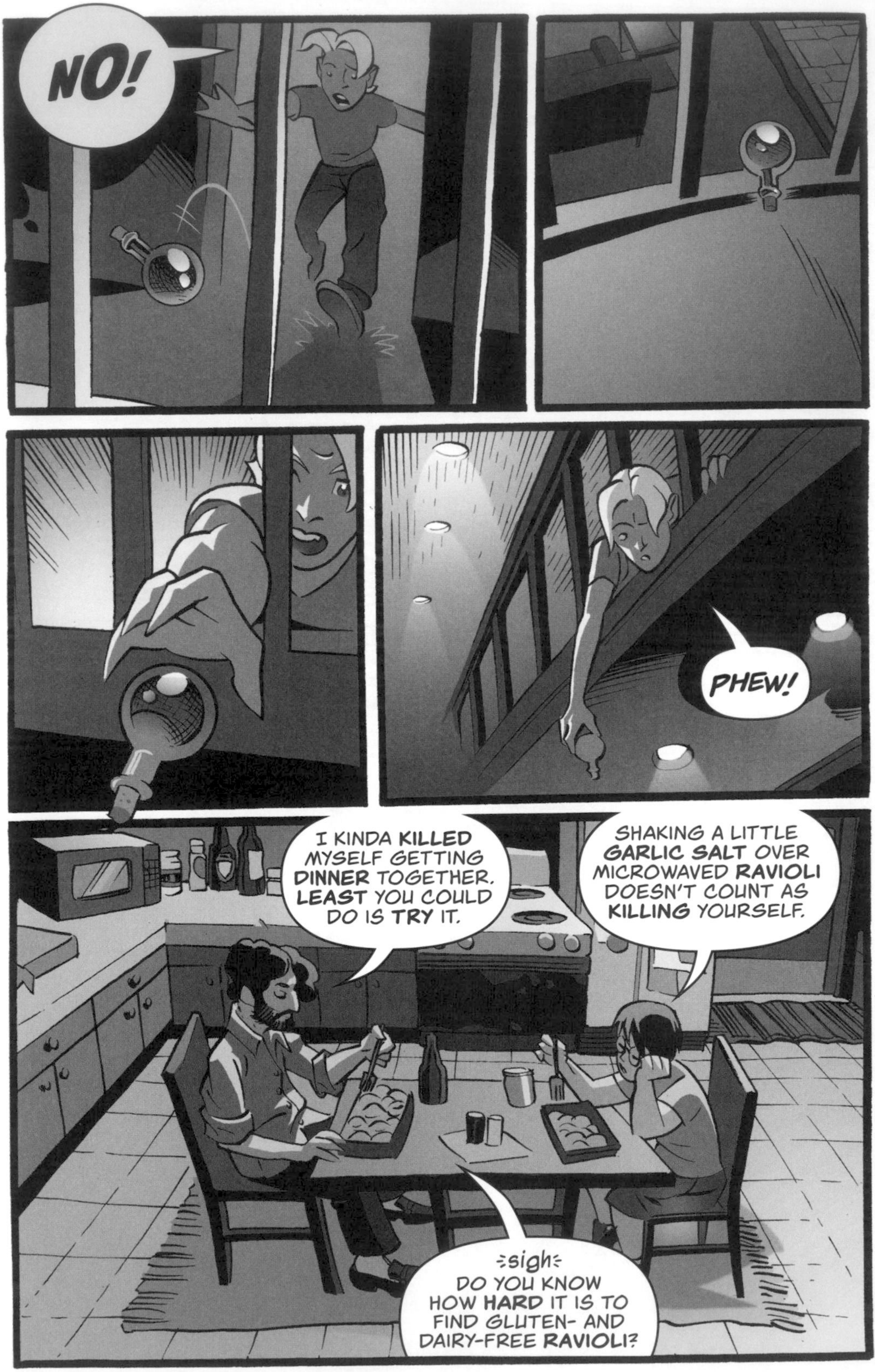
NO!
PHEW!
I KINDA KILLED MYSELF GETTING DINNER TOGETHER. LEAST YOU COULD DO IS TRY IT.
SHAKING A LITTLE GARLIC SALT OVER MICROWAVED RAVIOLI DOESN'T COUNT AS KILLING YOURSELF.
sigh
DO YOU KNOW HOW HARD IT IS TO FIND GLUTEN- AND DAIRY-FREE RAVIOLI?

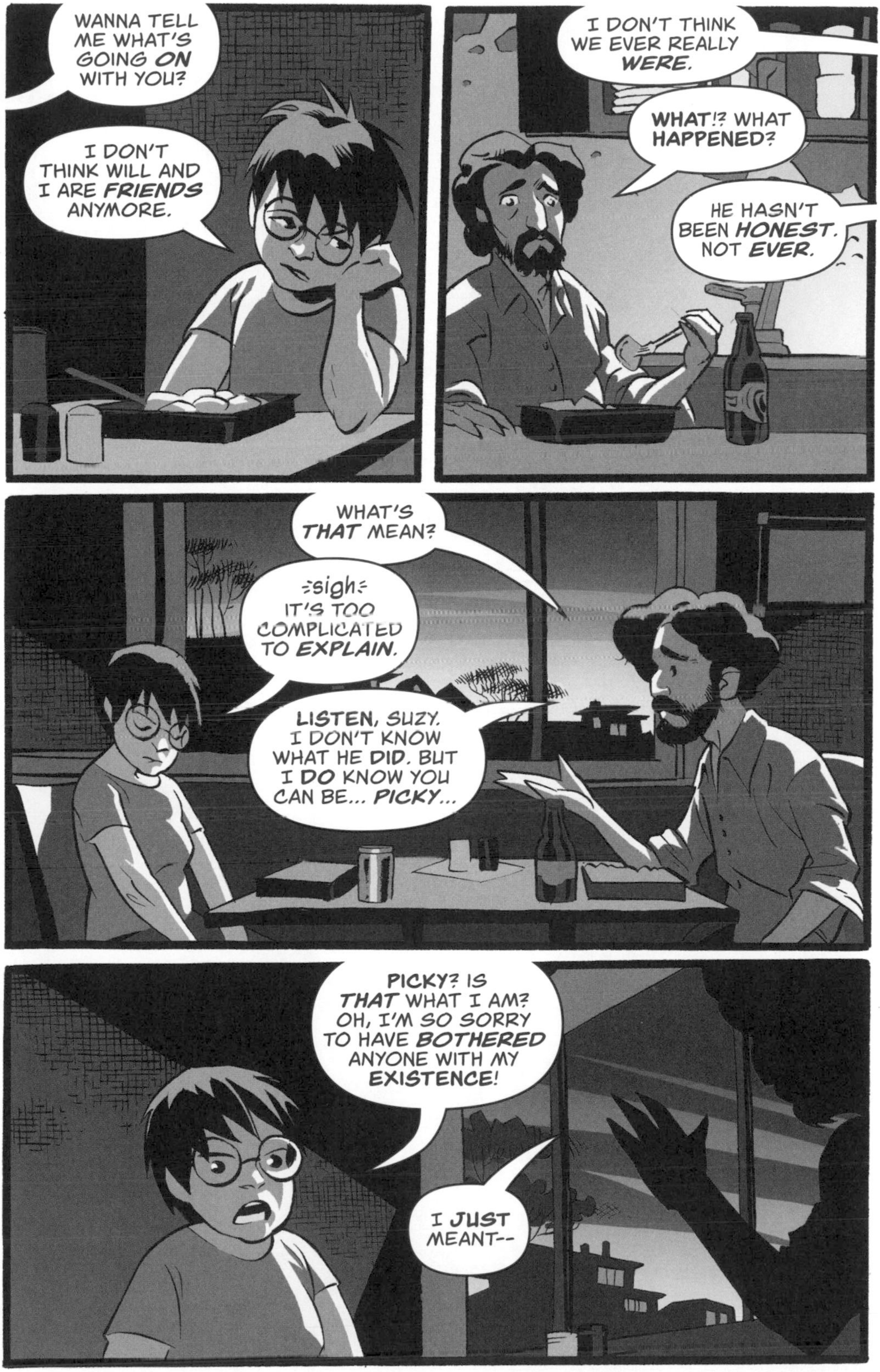
WANNA TELL ME WHAT'S GOING ON WITH YOU?
I DON'T THINK WILL AND I ARE FRIENDS ANYMORE.
I DON'T THINK WE EVER REALLY WERE.
WHAT!? WHAT HAPPENED?
HE HASN'T BEEN HONEST. NOT EVER.
WHAT'S THAT MEAN?
sigh
IT'S TOO COMPLICATED TO EXPLAIN.
LISTEN, SUZY. I DON'T KNOW WHAT HE DID. BUT I DO KNOW YOU CAN BE... PICKY...
PICKY? IS THAT WHAT I AM? OH, I'M SO SORRY TO HAVE BOTHERED ANYONE WITH MY EXISTENCE!
I JUST MEANT--

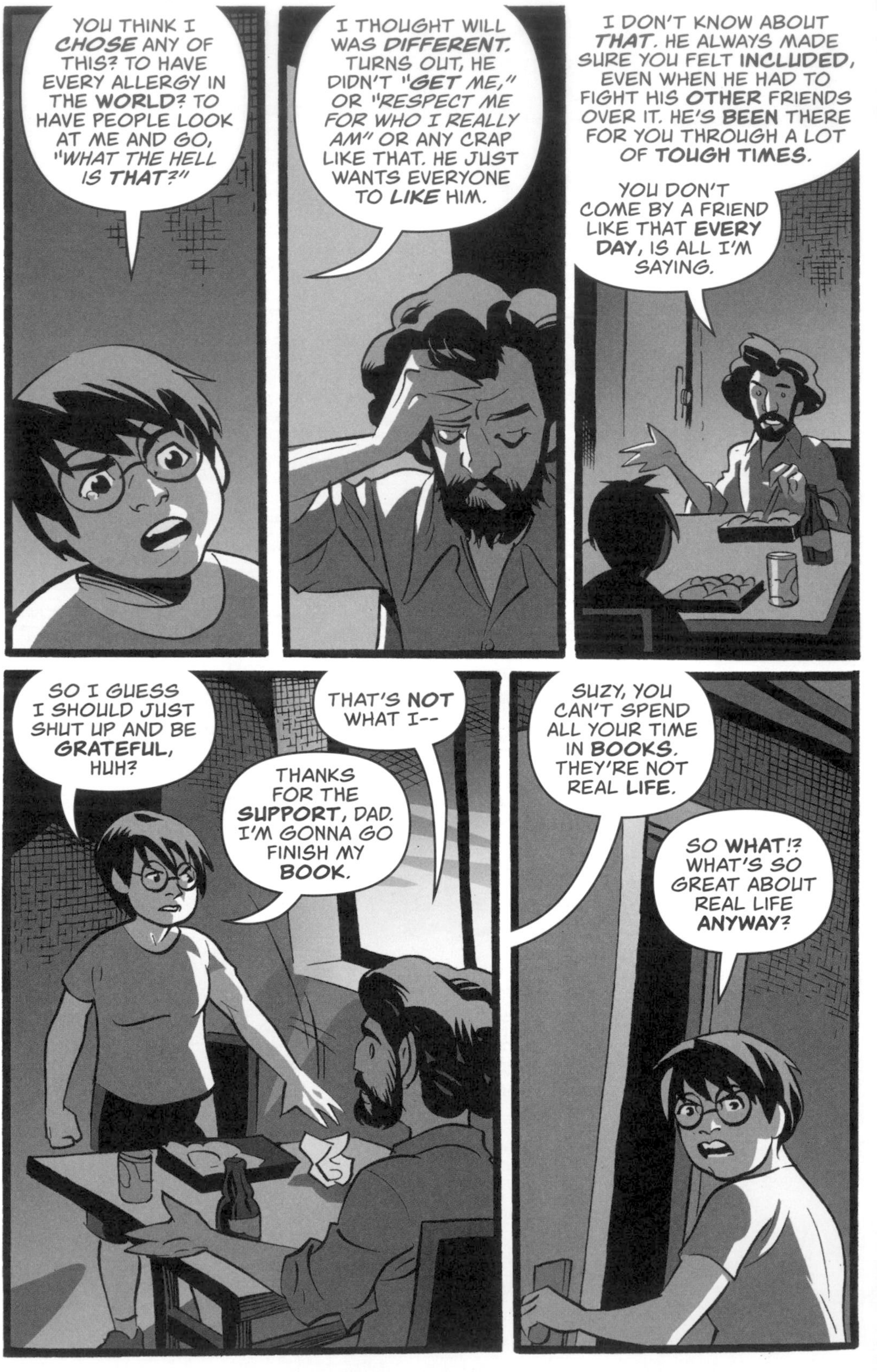
YOU THINK I CHOSE ANY OF THIS? TO HAVE EVERY ALLERGY IN THE WORLD? TO HAVE PEOPLE LOOK AT ME AND GO, "WHAT THE HELL IS THAT?"
I THOUGHT WILL WAS DIFFERENT. TURNS OUT, HE DIDN'T "GET ME," OR "RESPECT ME FOR WHO I REALLY AM" OR ANY CRAP LIKE THAT. HE JUST WANTS EVERYONE TO LIKE HIM.
I DON'T KNOW ABOUT THAT. HE ALWAYS MADE SURE YOU FELT INCLUDED, EVEN WHEN HE HAD TO FIGHT HIS OTHER FRIENDS OVER IT. HE'S BEEN THERE FOR YOU THROUGH A LOT OF TOUGH TIMES.
YOU DON'T COME BY A FRIEND LIKE THAT EVERY DAY, IS ALL I'M SAYING.
SO I GUESS I SHOULD JUST SHUT UP AND BE GRATEFUL, HUH?
THAT'S NOT WHAT I--
THANKS FOR THE SUPPORT, DAD. I'M GONNA GO FINISH MY BOOK.
SUZY, YOU CAN'T SPEND ALL YOUR TIME IN BOOKS. THEY'RE NOT REAL LIFE.
SO WHAT!? WHAT'S SO GREAT ABOUT REAL LIFE ANYWAY?

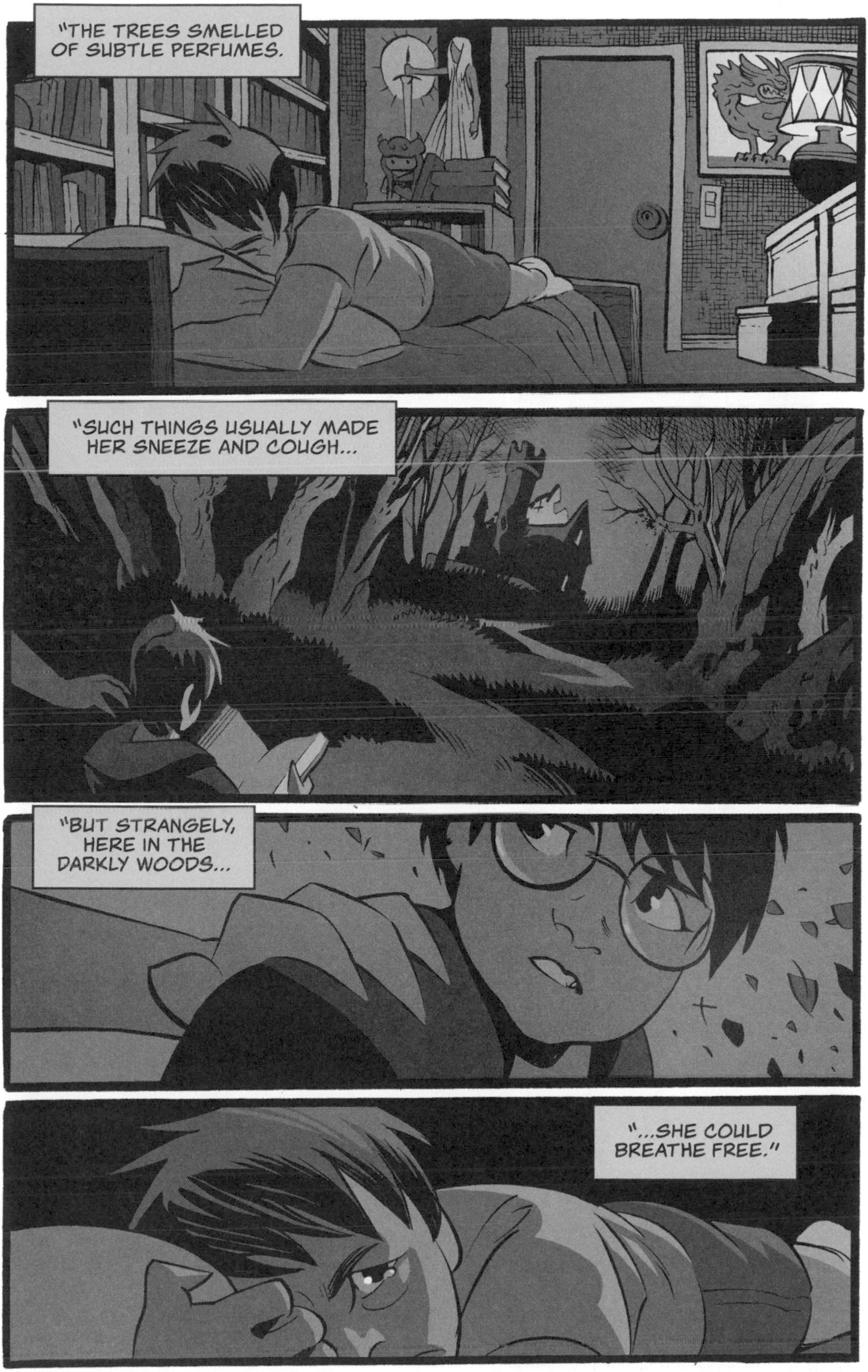
"THE TREES SMELLED OF SUBTLE PERFUMES.
"SUCH THINGS USUALLY MADE HER SNEEZE AND COUGH...
"BUT STRANGELY, HERE IN THE DARKLY WOODS...
"...SHE COULD BREATHE FREE."

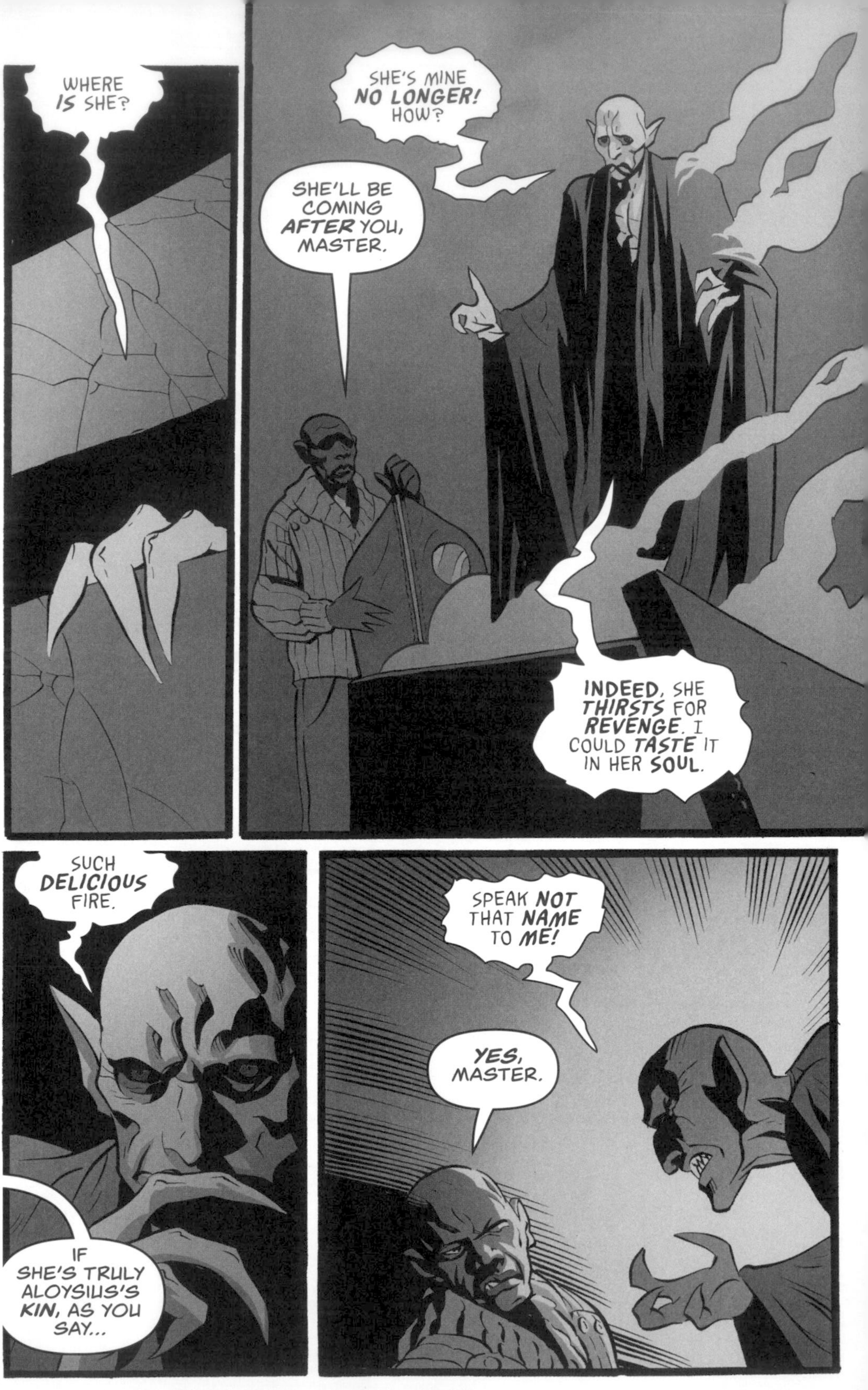
WHERE IS SHE?
SHE'S MINE NO LONGER! HOW?
SHE'LL BE COMING AFTER YOU, MASTER.
INDEED, SHE THIRSTS FOR REVENGE. I COULD TASTE IT IN HER SOUL.
SUCH DELICIOUS FIRE.
IF SHE'S TRULY ALOYSIUS'S KIN, AS YOU SAY...
SPEAK NOT THAT NAME TO ME!
YES, MASTER.

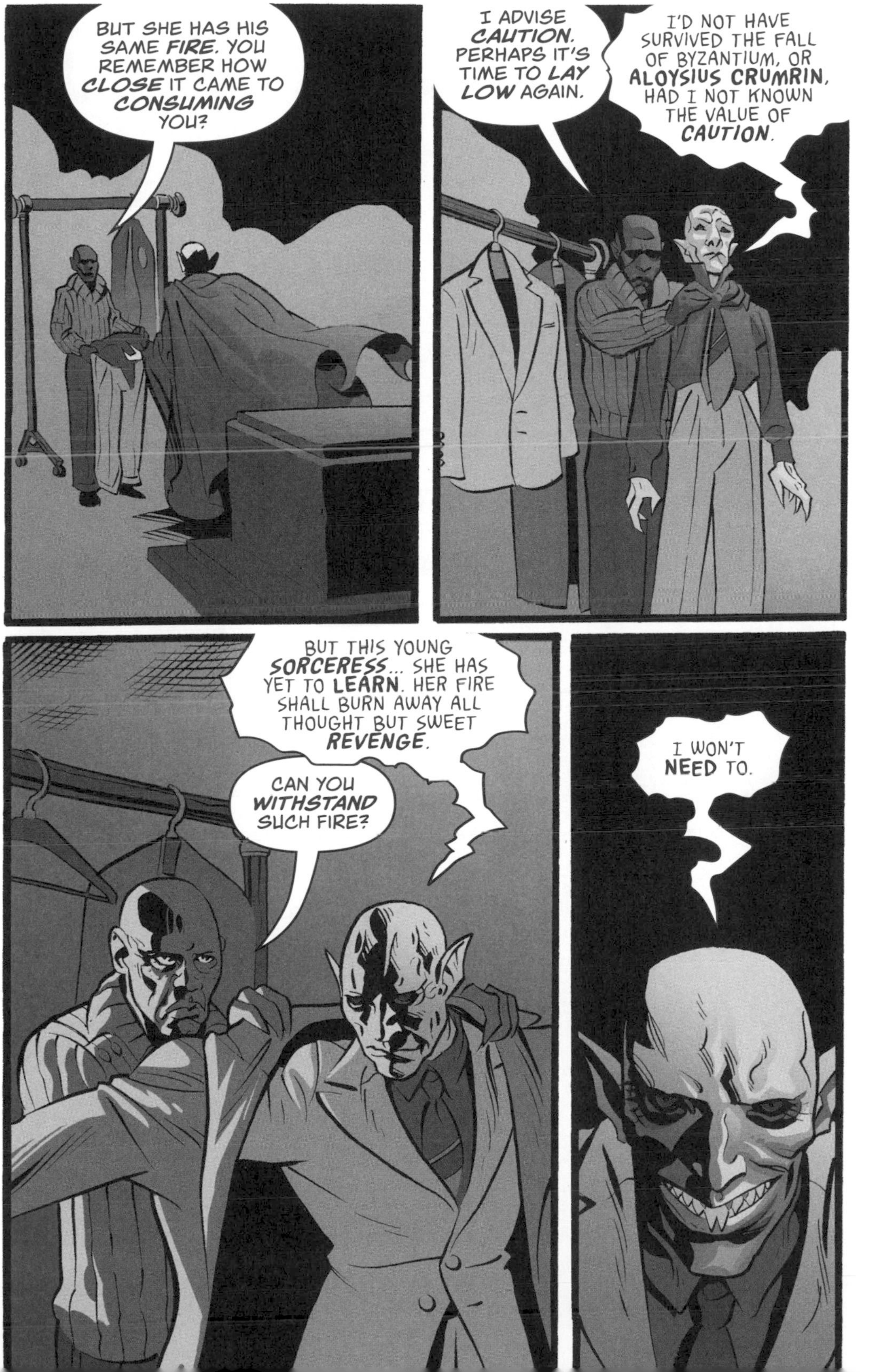
BUT SHE HAS HIS SAME FIRE. YOU REMEMBER HOW CLOSE IT CAME TO CONSUMING YOU?
I ADVISE CAUTION. PERHAPS IT'S TIME TO LAY LOW AGAIN.
I'D NOT HAVE SURVIVED THE FALL OF BYZANTIUM, OR ALOYSIUS CRUMRIN, HAD I NOT KNOWN THE VALUE OF CAUTION.
BUT THIS YOUNG SORCERESS... SHE HAS YET TO LEARN. HER FIRE SHALL BURN AWAY ALL THOUGHT BUT SWEET REVENGE.
CAN YOU WITHSTAND SUCH FIRE?
I WON'T NEED TO.

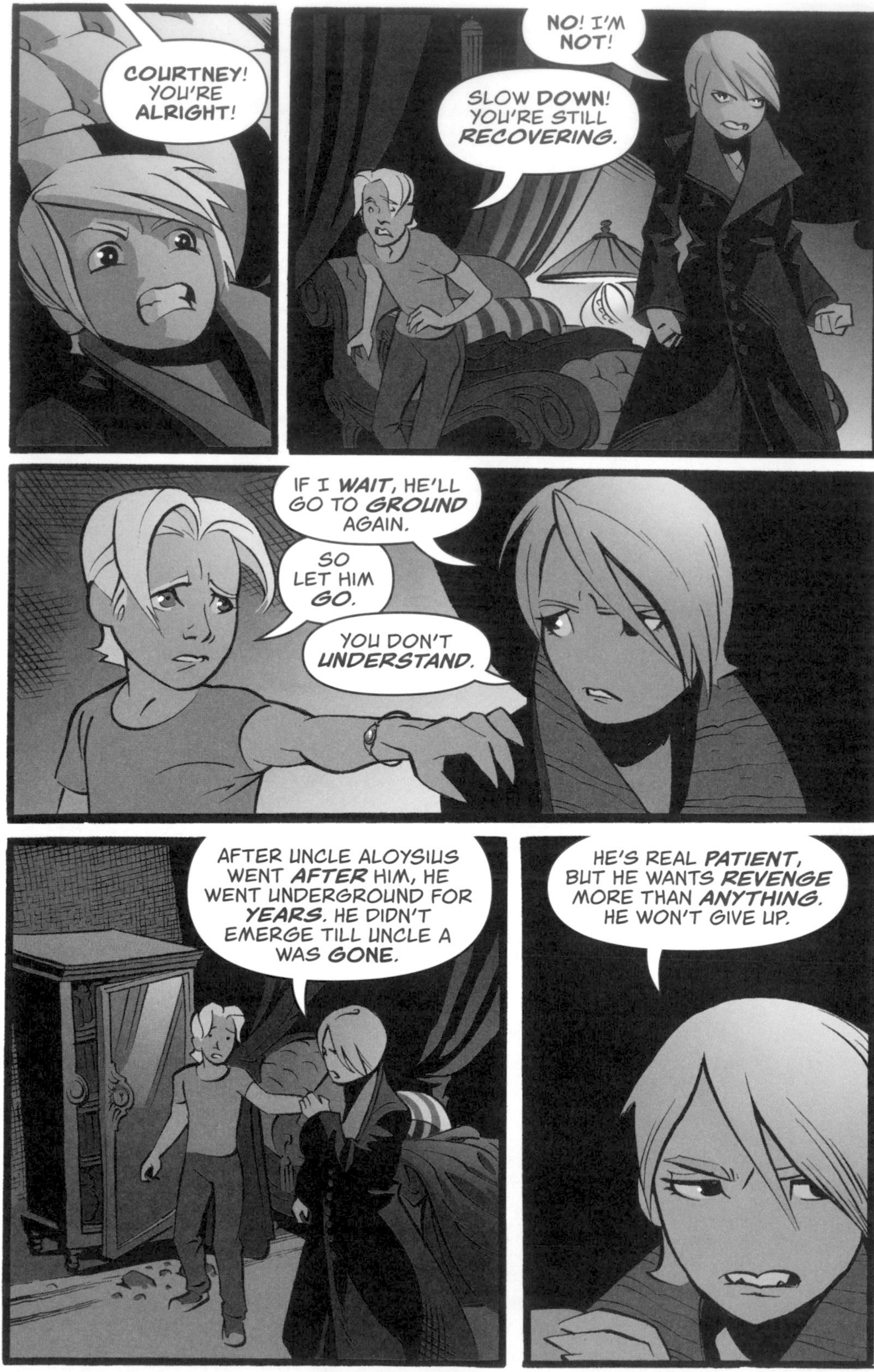
COURTNEY! YOU'RE ALRIGHT!
NO! I'M NOT!
SLOW DOWN! YOU'RE STILL RECOVERING.
IF I WAIT, HE'LL GO TO GROUND AGAIN.
SO LET HIM GO.
YOU DON'T UNDERSTAND.
AFTER UNCLE ALOYSIUS WENT AFTER HIM, HE WENT UNDERGROUND FOR YEARS. HE DIDN'T EMERGE TILL UNCLE A WAS GONE.
HE'S REAL PATIENT, BUT HE WANTS REVENGE MORE THAN ANYTHING. HE WON'T GIVE UP.

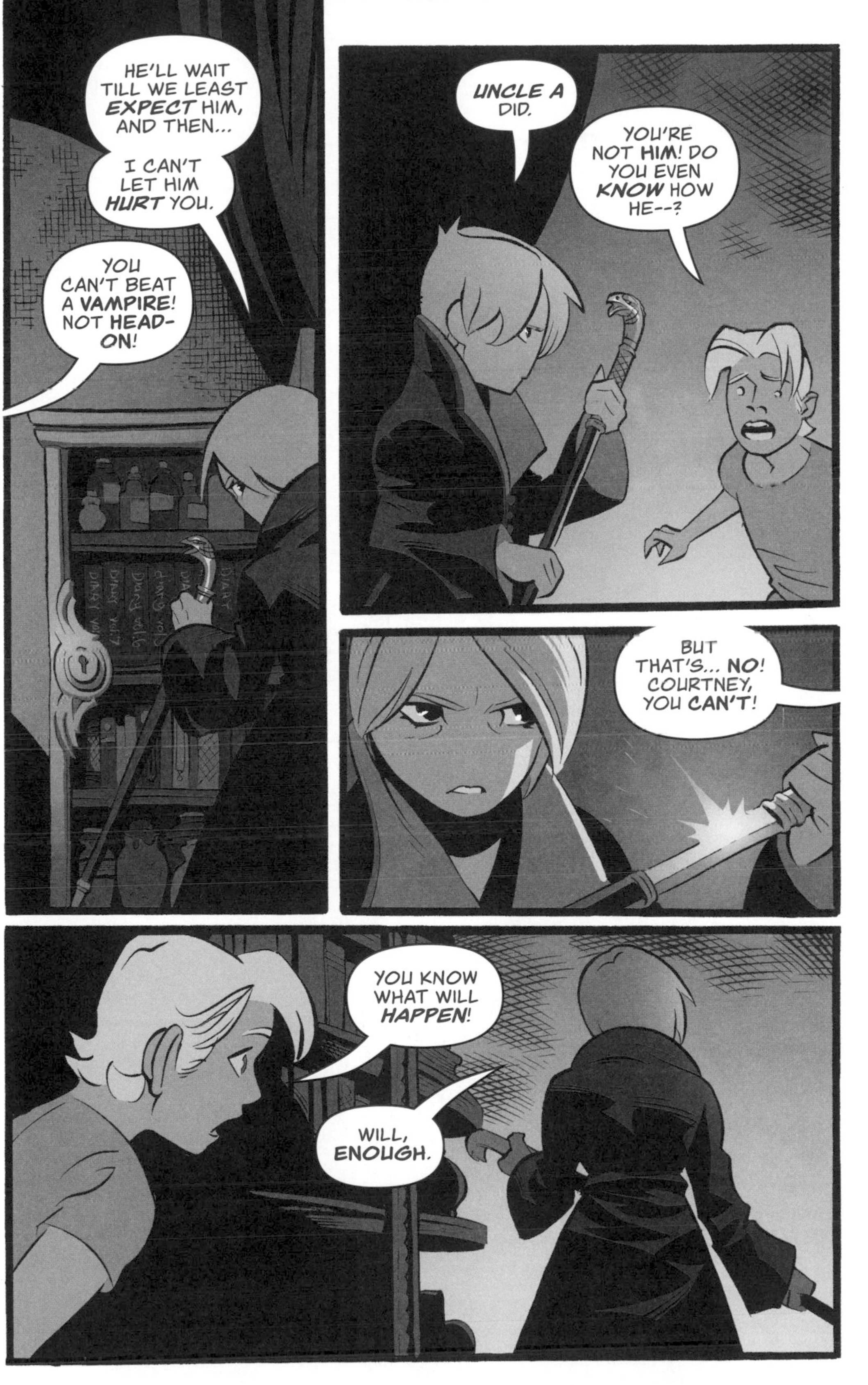

HE'LL WAIT TILL WE LEAST EXPECT HIM, AND THEN...
I CAN'T LET HIM HURT YOU.
YOU CAN'T BEAT A VAMPIRE! NOT HEAD-ON!
UNCLE A DID.
YOU'RE NOT HIM! DO YOU EVEN KNOW HOW HE--?
BUT THAT'S... NO! COURTNEY, YOU CAN'T!
YOU KNOW WHAT WILL HAPPEN!
WILL, ENOUGH.

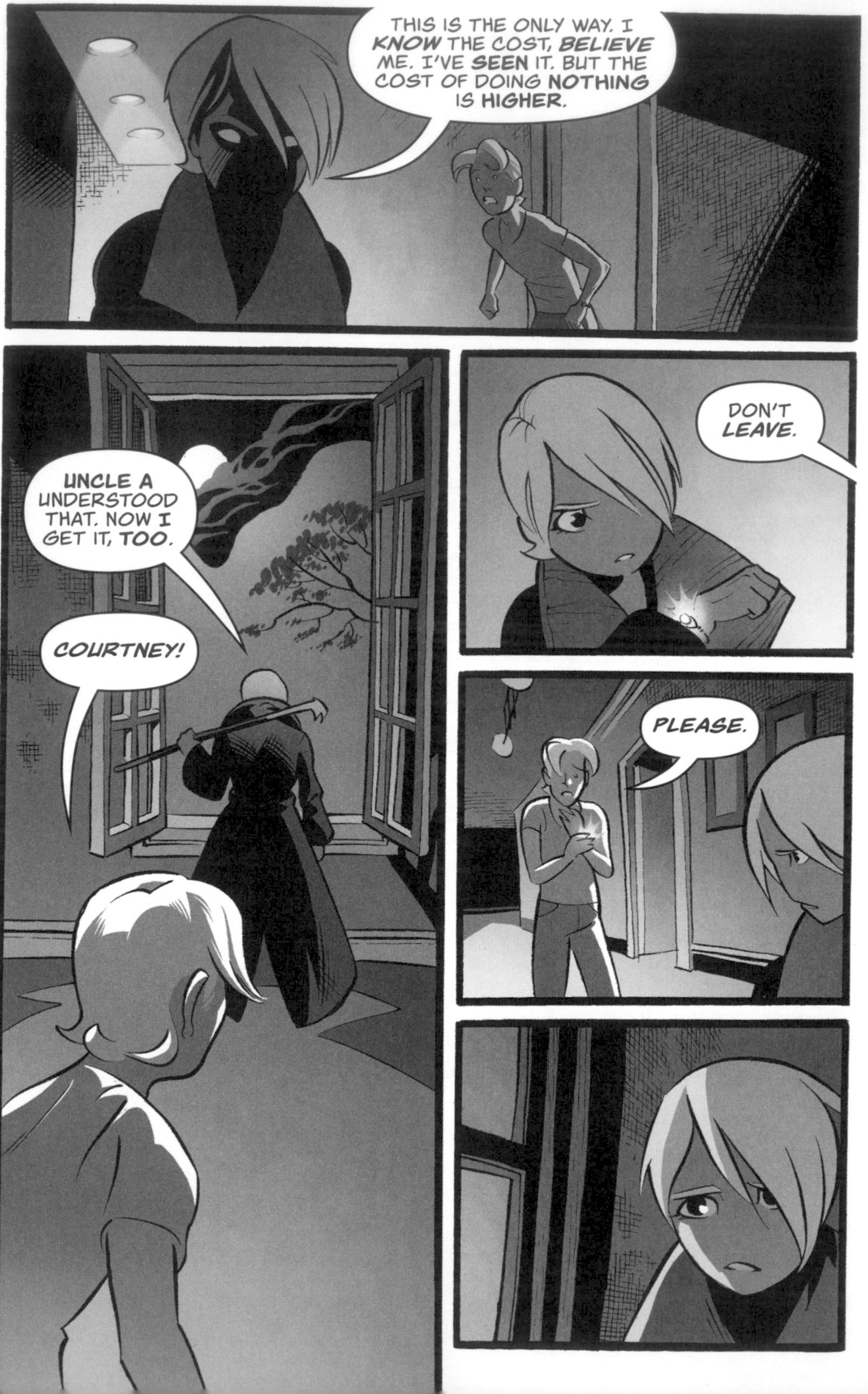
THIS IS THE ONLY WAY. I KNOW THE COST, BELIEVE ME. I'VE SEEN IT. BUT THE COST OF DOING NOTHING IS HIGHER.
UNCLE A UNDERSTOOD THAT. NOW I GET IT, TOO.
COURTNEY!
DON'T LEAVE.
PLEASE.

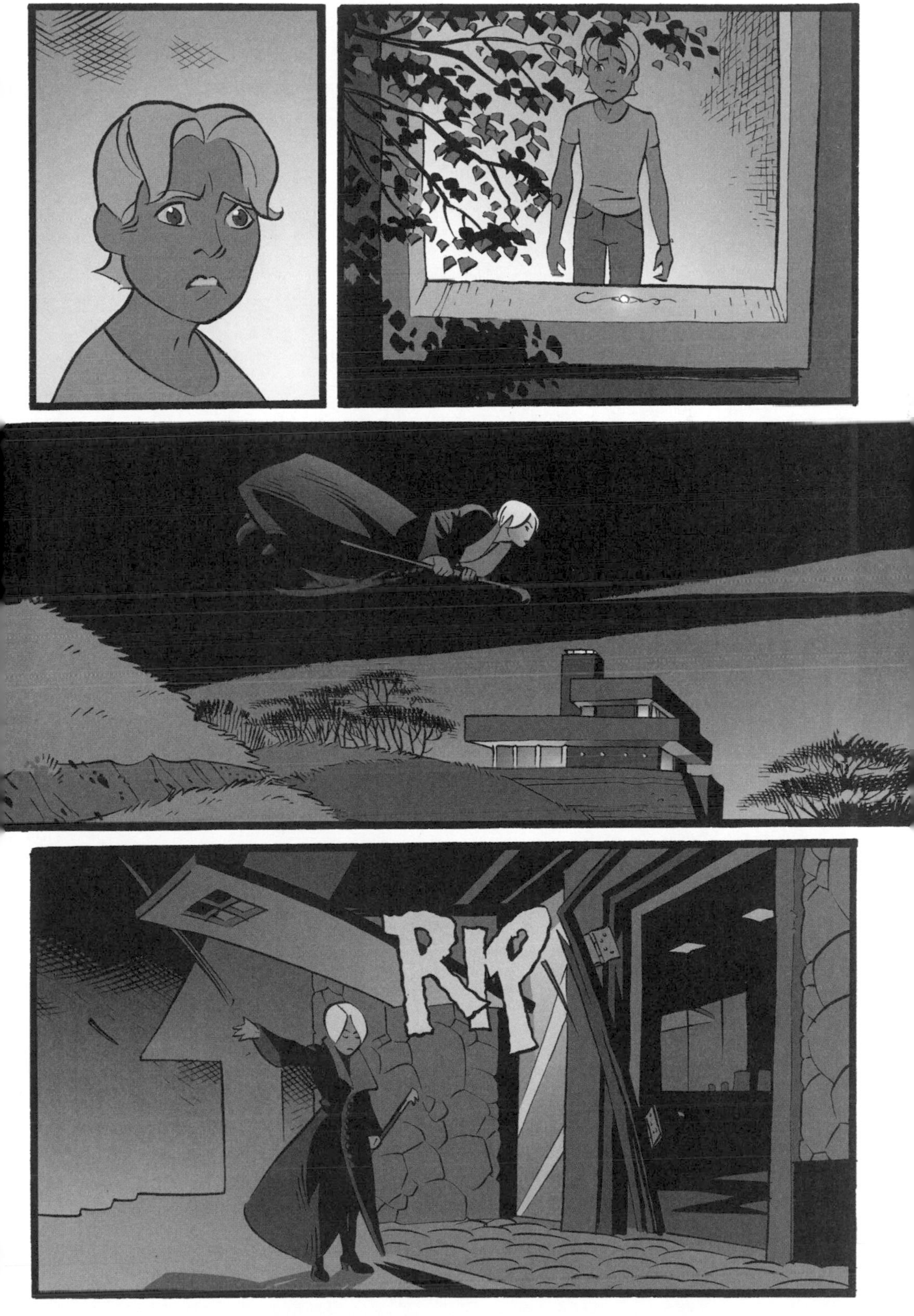
RIP

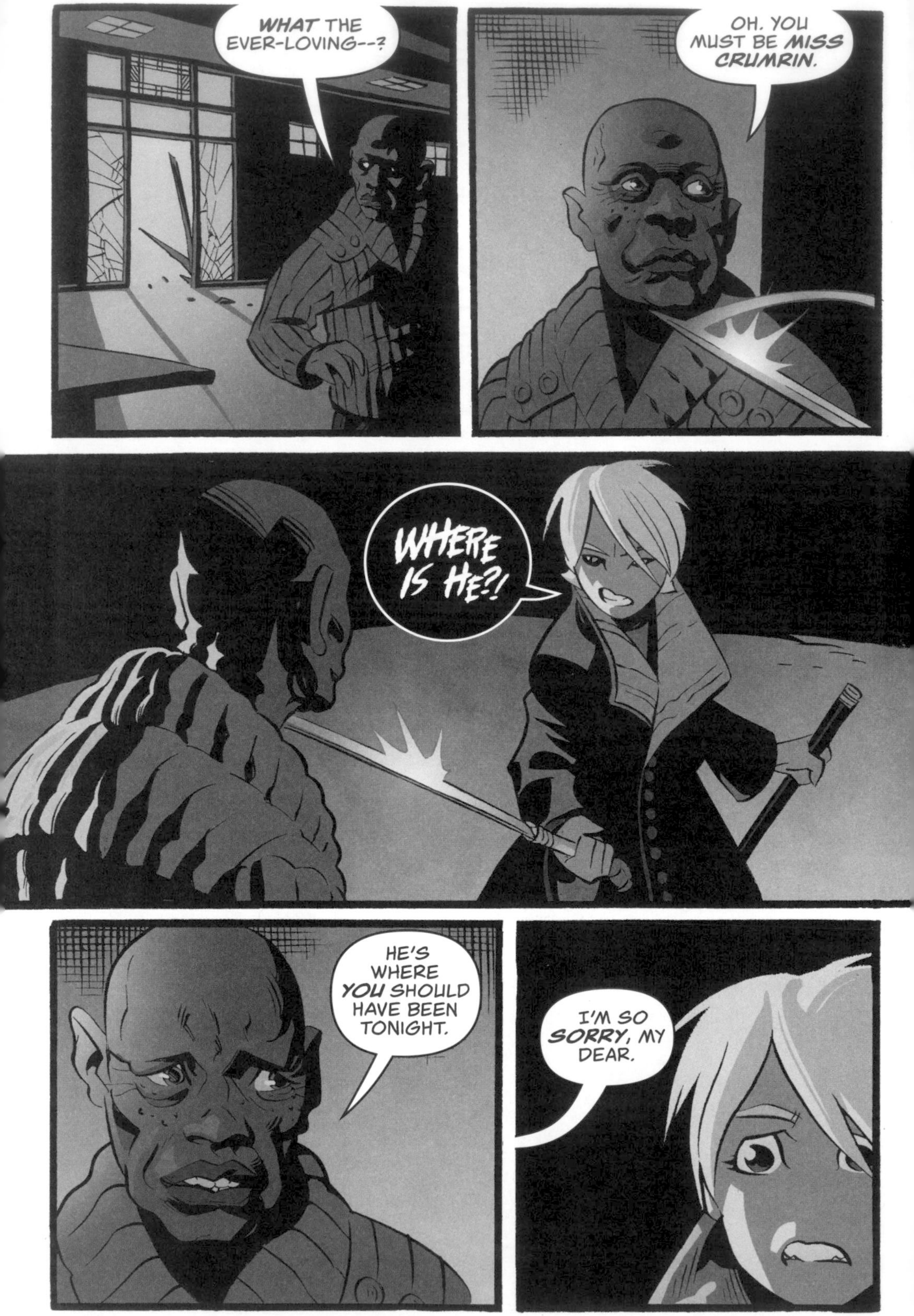
WHAT THE EVER-LOVING--?
OH. YOU MUST BE MISS CRUMRIN.
WHERE IS HE?!
HE'S WHERE YOU SHOULD HAVE BEEN TONIGHT.
I'M SO SORRY, MY DEAR.

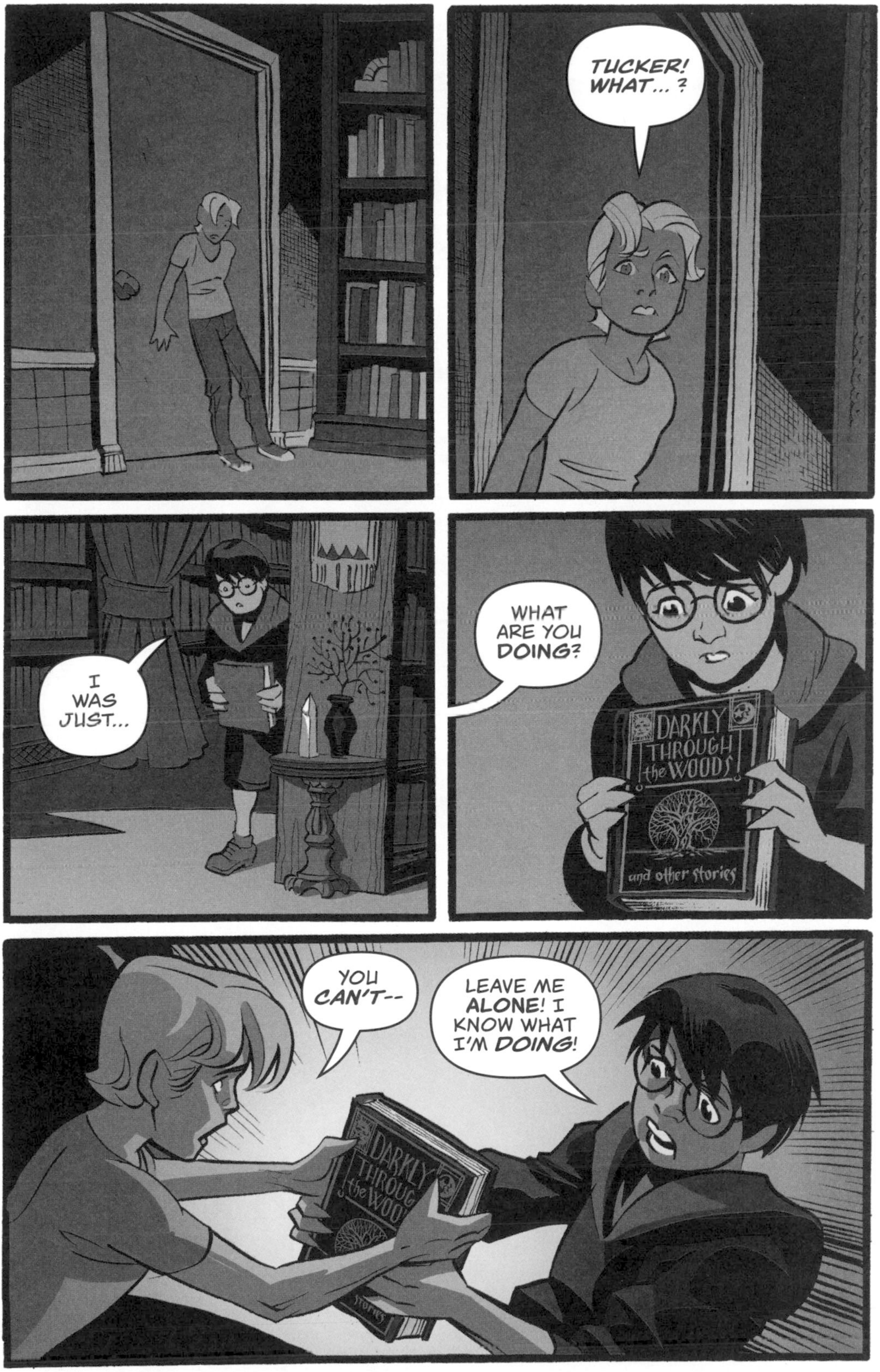

TUCKER! WHAT... ?
I WAS JUST...
WHAT ARE YOU DOING?
DARKLY THROUGH the WOODS and other stories
YOU CAN'T--
LEAVE ME ALONE! I KNOW WHAT I'M DOING!

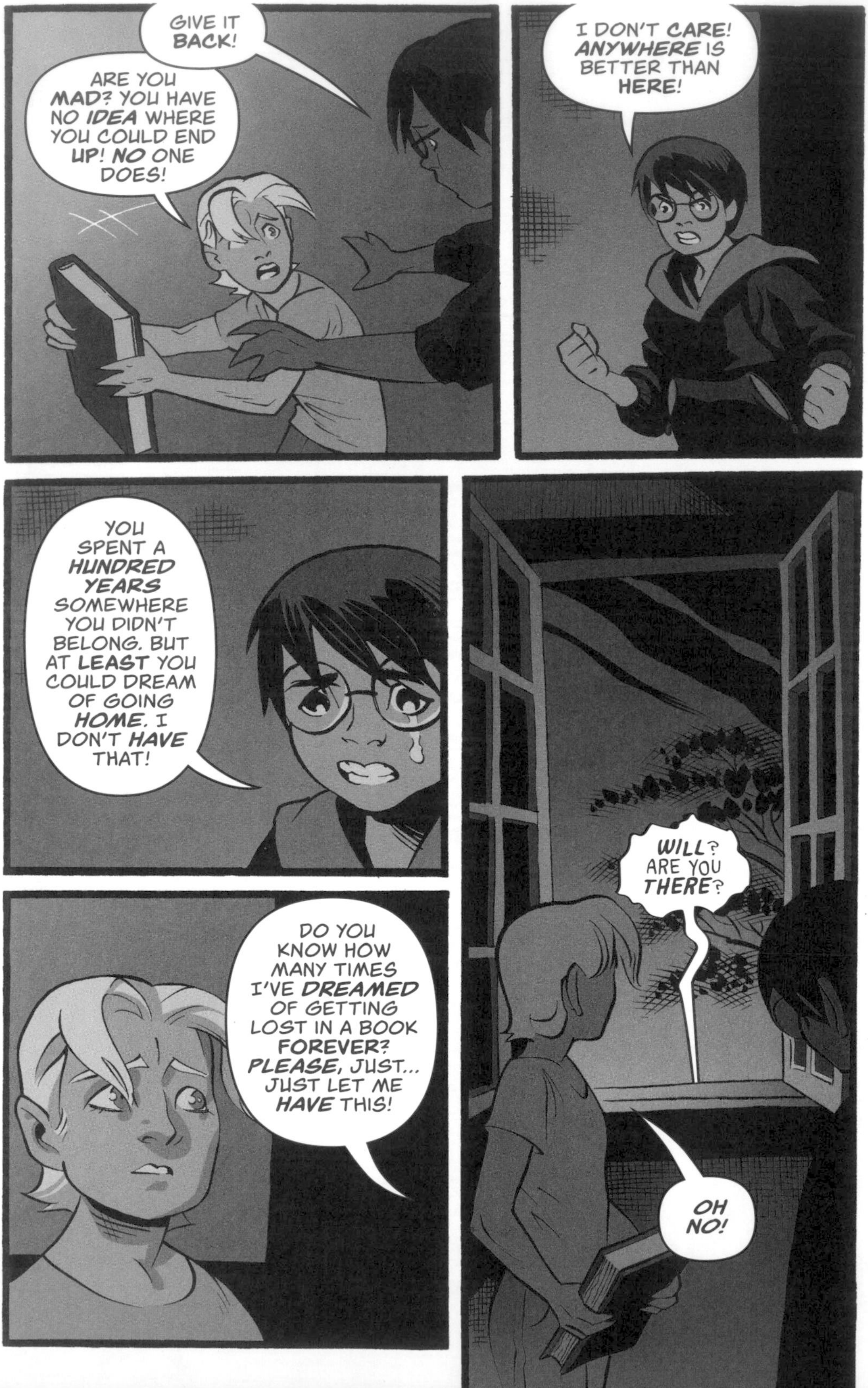
GIVE IT BACK!
ARE YOU MAD? YOU HAVE NO IDEA WHERE YOU COULD END UP! NO ONE DOES!
I DON'T CARE! ANYWHERE IS BETTER THAN HERE!
YOU SPENT A HUNDRED YEARS SOMEWHERE YOU DIDN'T BELONG. BUT AT LEAST YOU COULD DREAM OF GOING HOME. I DON'T HAVE THAT!
DO YOU KNOW HOW MANY TIMES I'VE DREAMED OF GETTING LOST IN A BOOK FOREVER? PLEASE, JUST... JUST LET ME HAVE THIS!
WILL? ARE YOU THERE?
OH NO!

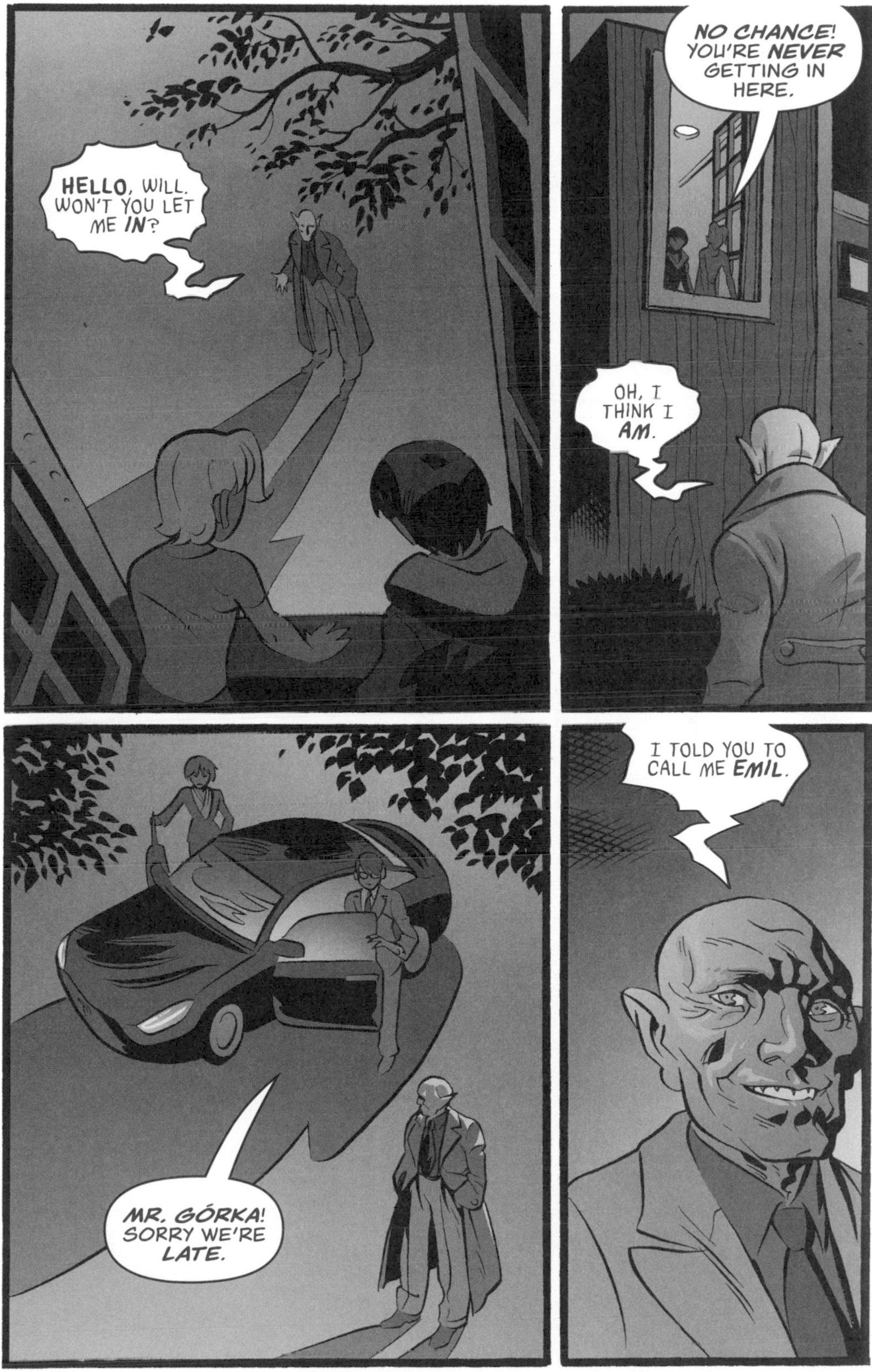
HELLO, WILL. WON'T YOU LET ME IN?
NO CHANCE! YOU'RE NEVER GETTING IN HERE.
OH, I THINK I AM.
MR. GÓRKA! SORRY WE'RE LATE.
I TOLD YOU TO CALL ME EMIL.

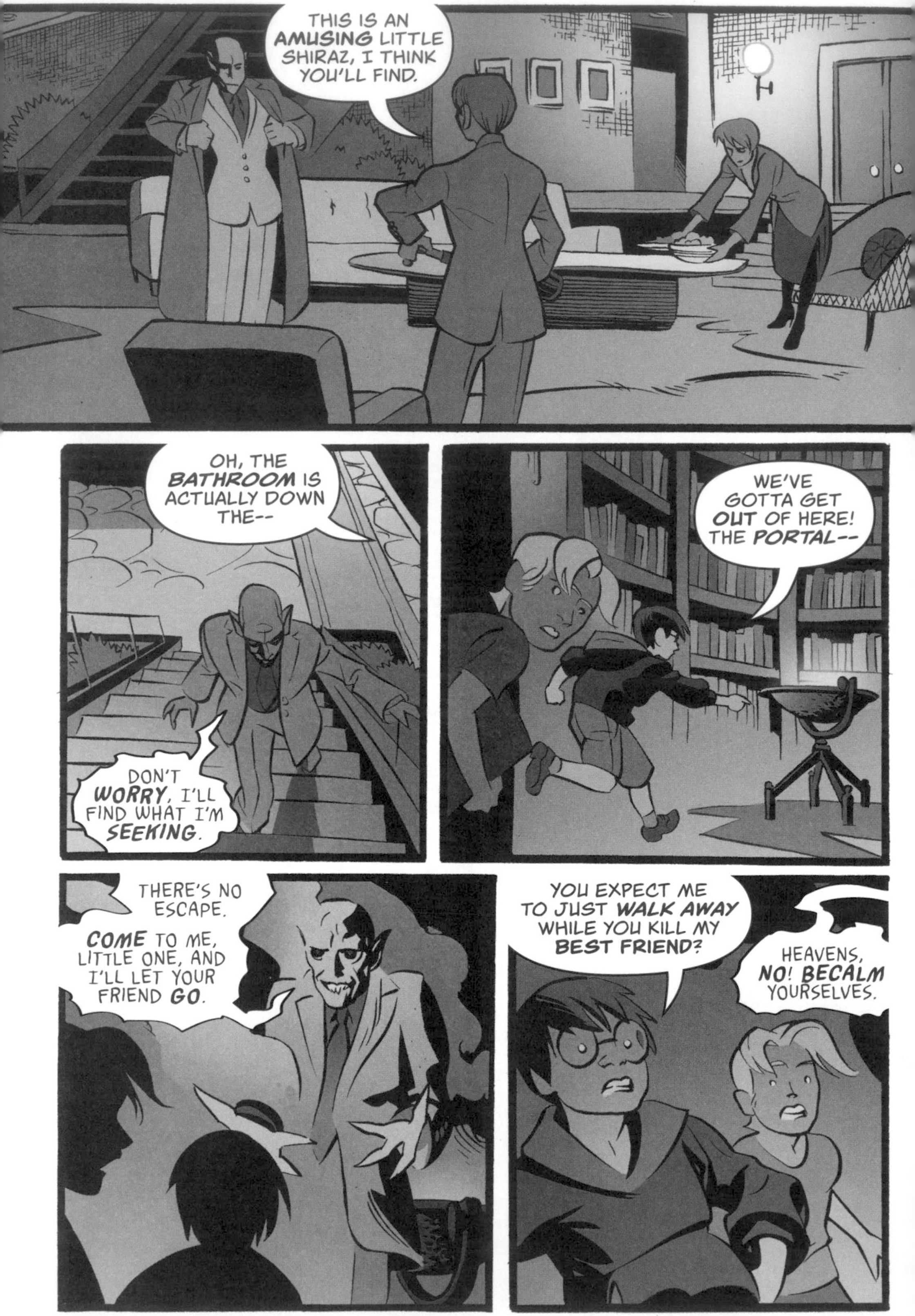
THIS IS AN AMUSING LITTLE SHIRAZ, I THINK YOU'LL FIND.
OH, THE BATHROOM IS ACTUALLY DOWN THE--
DON'T WORRY, I'LL FIND WHAT I'M SEEKING.
WE'VE GOTTA GET OUT OF HERE! THE PORTAL--
THERE'S NO ESCAPE.
COME TO ME, LITTLE ONE, AND I'LL LET YOUR FRIEND GO.
YOU EXPECT ME TO JUST WALK AWAY WHILE YOU KILL MY BEST FRIEND?
HEAVENS, NO! BECALM YOURSELVES.

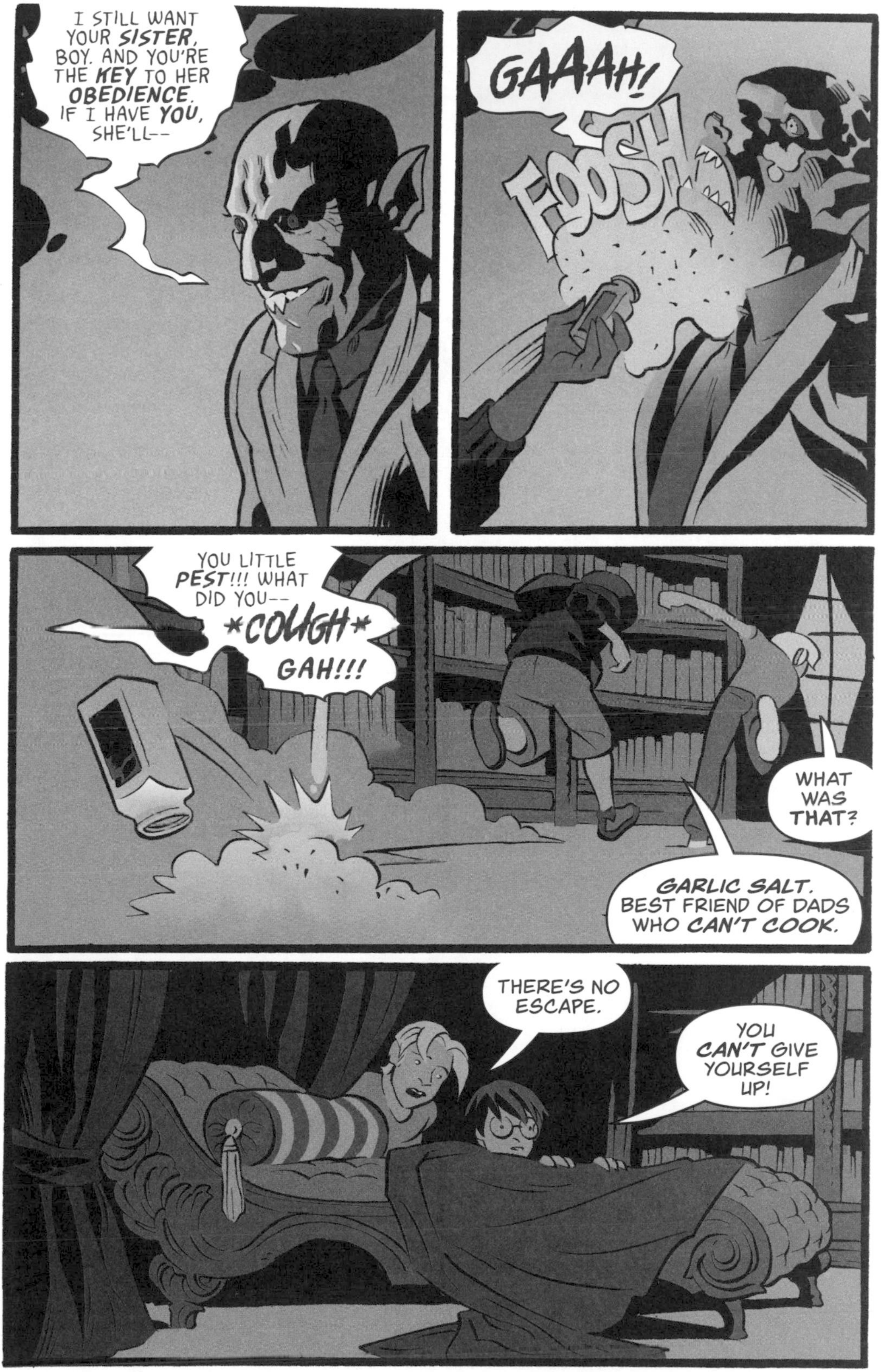
I STILL WANT YOUR SISTER, BOY. AND YOU'RE THE KEY TO HER OBEDIENCE. IF I HAVE YOU, SHE'LL--
GAAAH!
FOOSH!
YOU LITTLE PEST!!! WHAT DID YOU-- *COUGH* GAH!!!
WHAT WAS THAT?
GARLIC SALT. BEST FRIEND OF DADS WHO CAN'T COOK.
THERE'S NO ESCAPE.
YOU CAN'T GIVE YOURSELF UP!

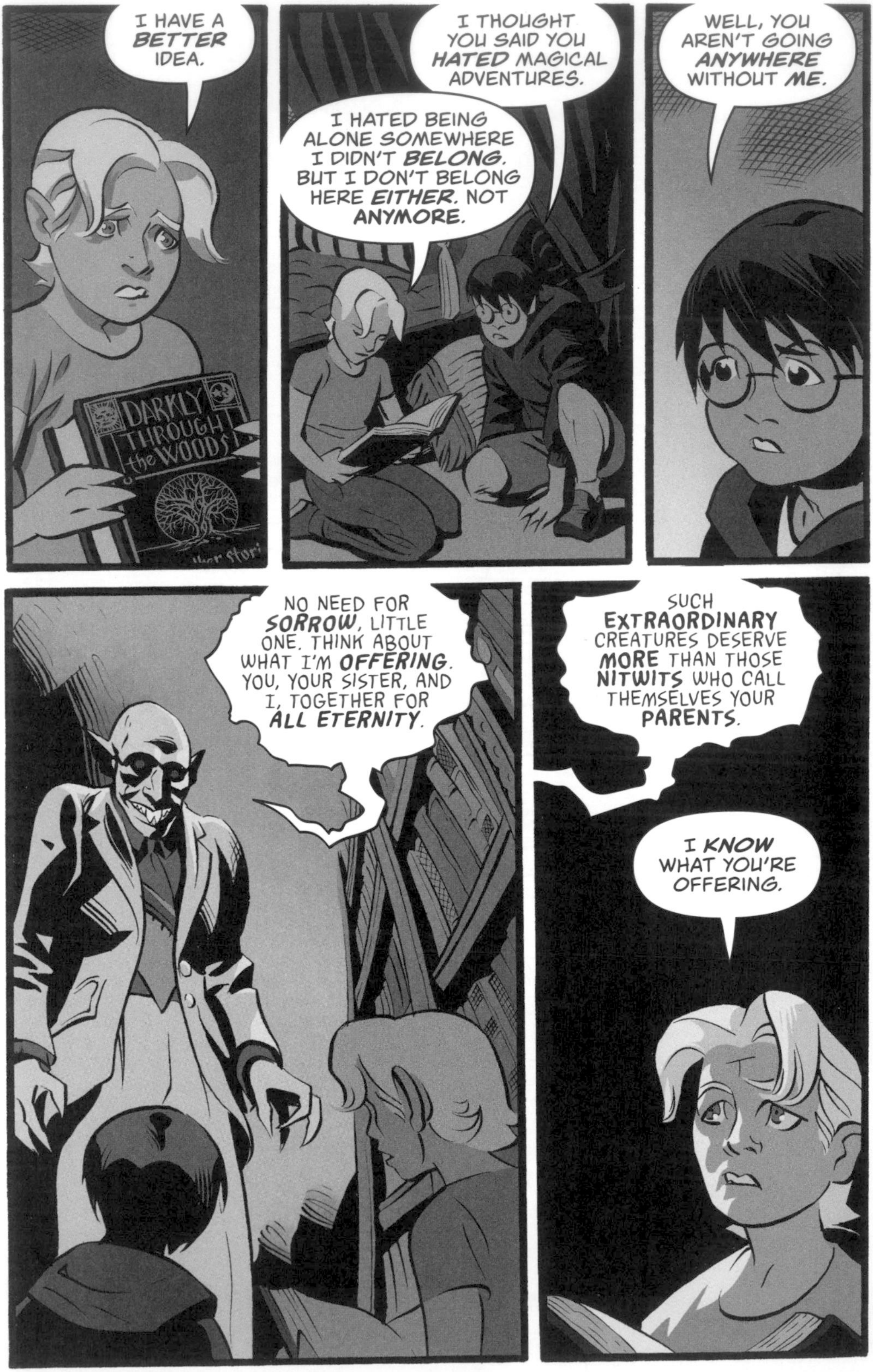
I HAVE A BETTER IDEA.
DARKLY THROUGH the WOODS
I THOUGHT YOU SAID YOU HATED MAGICAL ADVENTURES.
I HATED BEING ALONE SOMEWHERE I DIDN'T BELONG. BUT I DON'T BELONG HERE EITHER. NOT ANYMORE.
WELL, YOU AREN'T GOING ANYWHERE WITHOUT ME.
NO NEED FOR SORROW, LITTLE ONE. THINK ABOUT WHAT I'M OFFERING. YOU, YOUR SISTER, AND I, TOGETHER FOR ALL ETERNITY.
SUCH EXTRAORDINARY CREATURES DESERVE MORE THAN THOSE NITWITS WHO CALL THEMSELVES YOUR PARENTS.
I KNOW WHAT YOU'RE OFFERING.

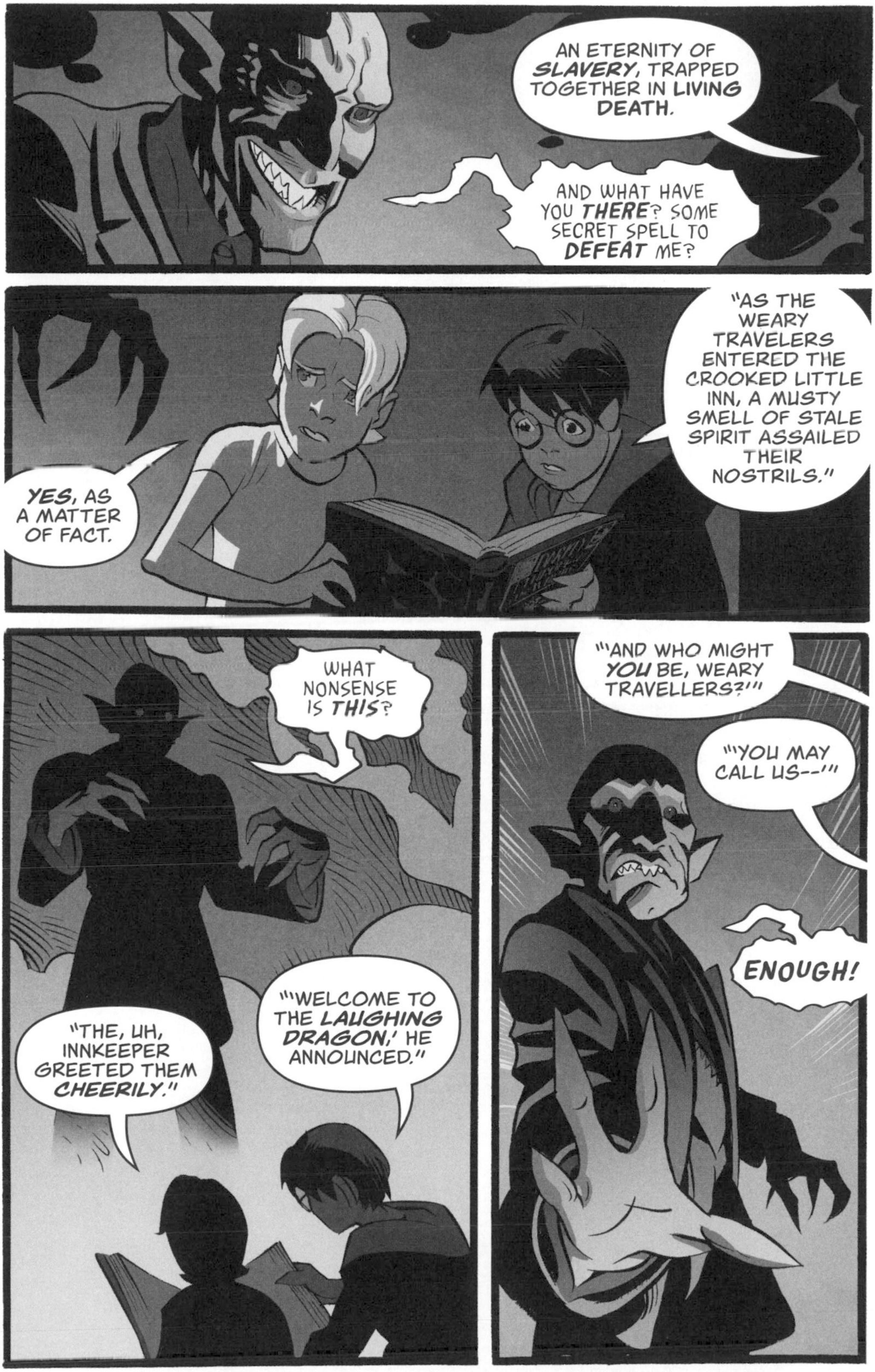
AN ETERNITY OF SLAVERY, TRAPPED TOGETHER IN LIVING DEATH.
AND WHAT HAVE YOU THERE? SOME SECRET SPELL TO DEFEAT ME?
YES, AS A MATTER OF FACT.
"AS THE WEARY TRAVELERS ENTERED THE CROOKED LITTLE INN, A MUSTY SMELL OF STALE SPIRIT ASSAILED THEIR NOSTRILS."
WHAT NONSENSE IS THIS?
"THE, UH, INNKEEPER GREETED THEM CHEERILY."
"'WELCOME TO THE LAUGHING DRAGON,' HE ANNOUNCED."
"'AND WHO MIGHT YOU BE, WEARY TRAVELLERS?'"
"'YOU MAY CALL US--'"
ENOUGH!

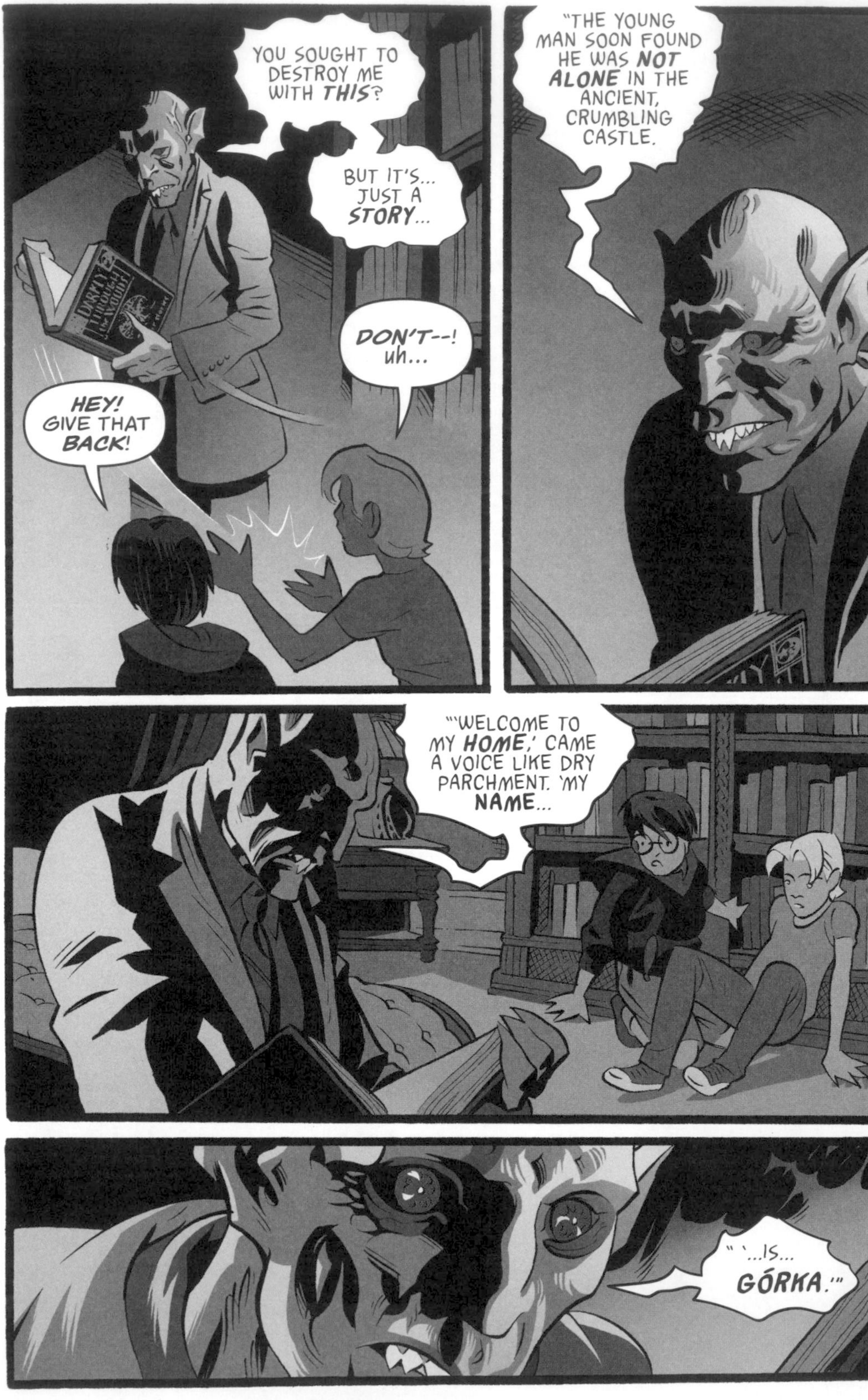
YOU SOUGHT TO DESTROY ME WITH THIS?
BUT IT'S... JUST A STORY...
DON'T--! uh...
HEY! GIVE THAT BACK!
"THE YOUNG MAN SOON FOUND HE WAS NOT ALONE IN THE ANCIENT, CRUMBLING CASTLE.
"'WELCOME TO MY HOME,' CAME A VOICE LIKE DRY PARCHMENT. 'MY NAME...
" '...IS... GÓRKA.'"

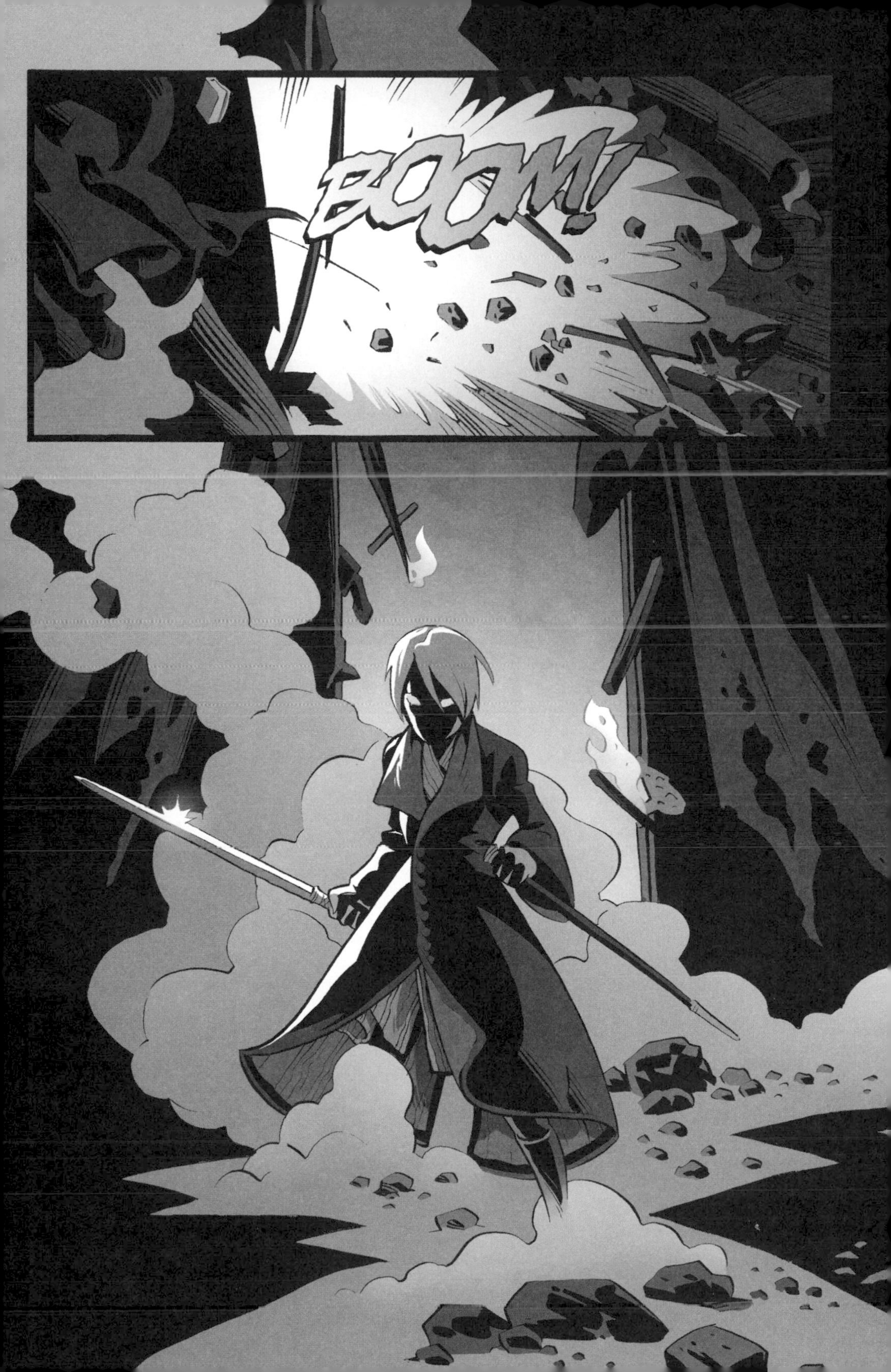
BOOM!

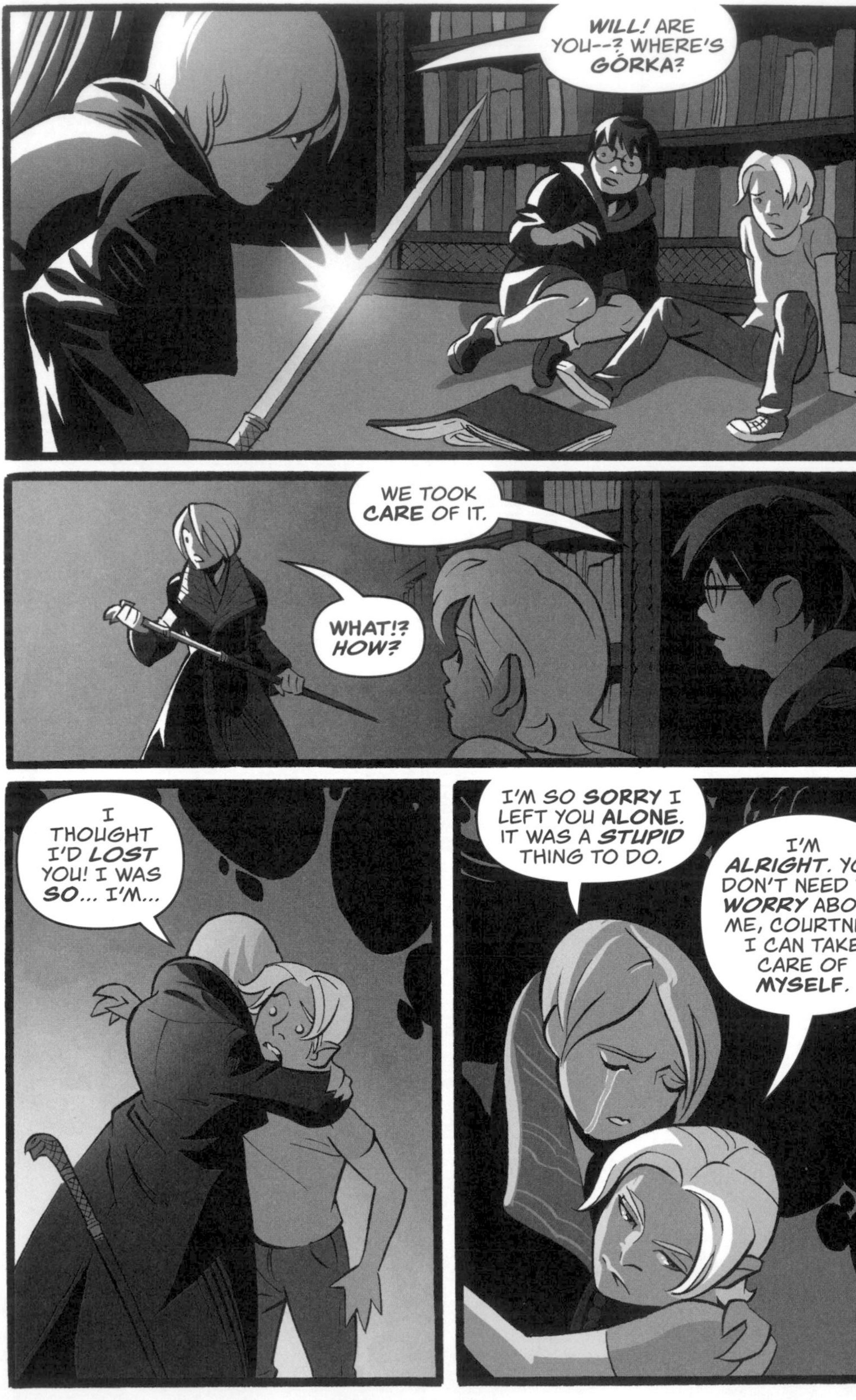
WILL! ARE YOU--? WHERE'S GORKA?
WE TOOK CARE OF IT.
WHAT!? HOW?
I THOUGHT I'D LOST YOU! I WAS SO... I'M...
I'M SO SORRY I LEFT YOU ALONE. IT WAS A STUPID THING TO DO.
I'M ALRIGHT. YOU DON'T NEED TO WORRY ABOUT ME, COURTNEY. I CAN TAKE CARE OF MYSELF.

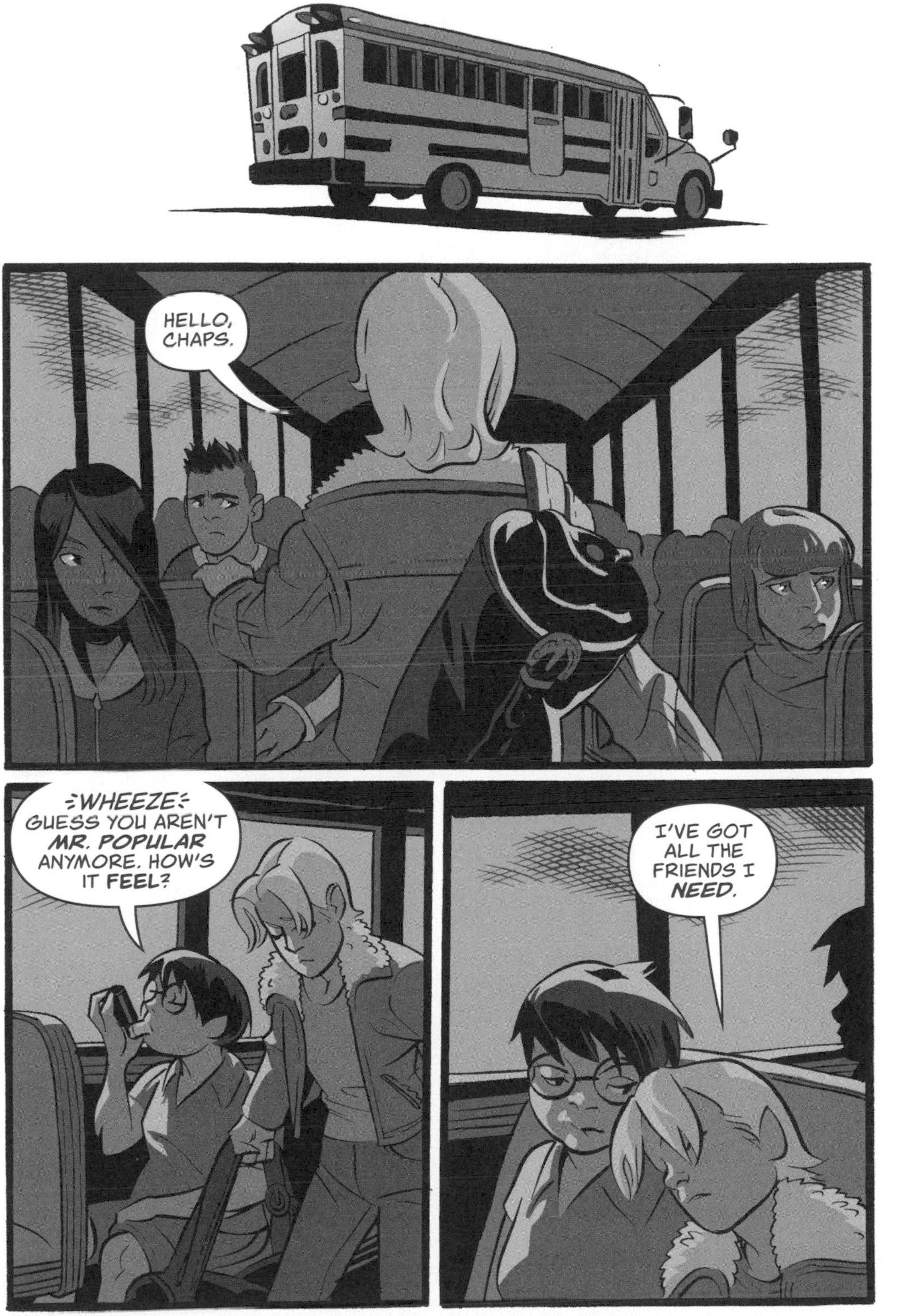
HELLO, CHAPS.
WHEEZE GUESS YOU AREN'T MR. POPULAR ANYMORE. HOW'S IT FEEL?
I'VE GOT ALL THE FRIENDS I NEED.

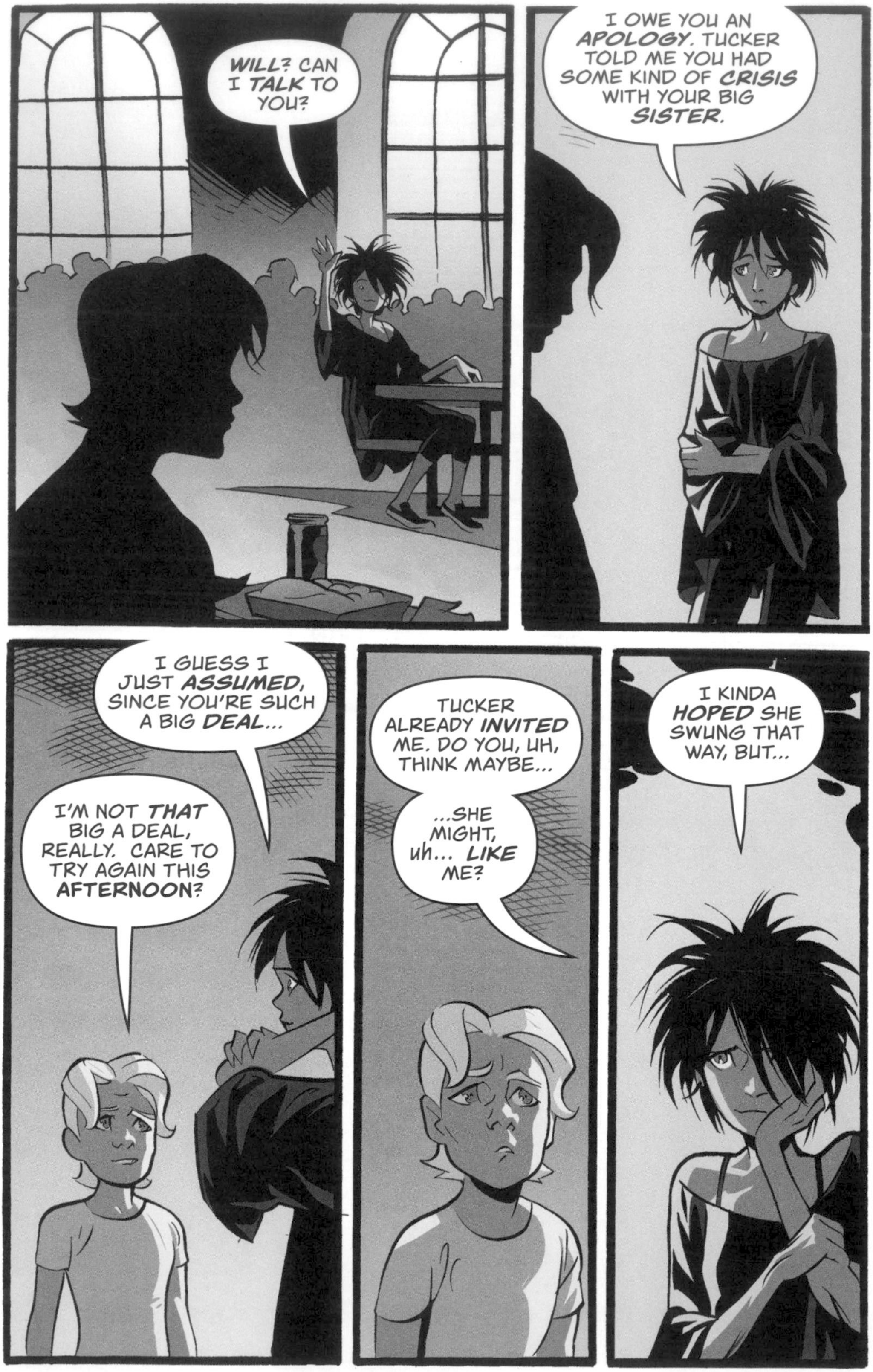
WILL? CAN I TALK TO YOU?
I OWE YOU AN APOLOGY. TUCKER TOLD ME YOU HAD SOME KIND OF CRISIS WITH YOUR BIG SISTER.
I GUESS I JUST ASSUMED, SINCE YOU'RE SUCH A BIG DEAL...
I'M NOT THAT BIG A DEAL, REALLY. CARE TO TRY AGAIN THIS AFTERNOON?
TUCKER ALREADY INVITED ME. DO YOU, UH, THINK MAYBE...
...SHE MIGHT, uh... LIKE ME?
I KINDA HOPED SHE SWUNG THAT WAY, BUT...

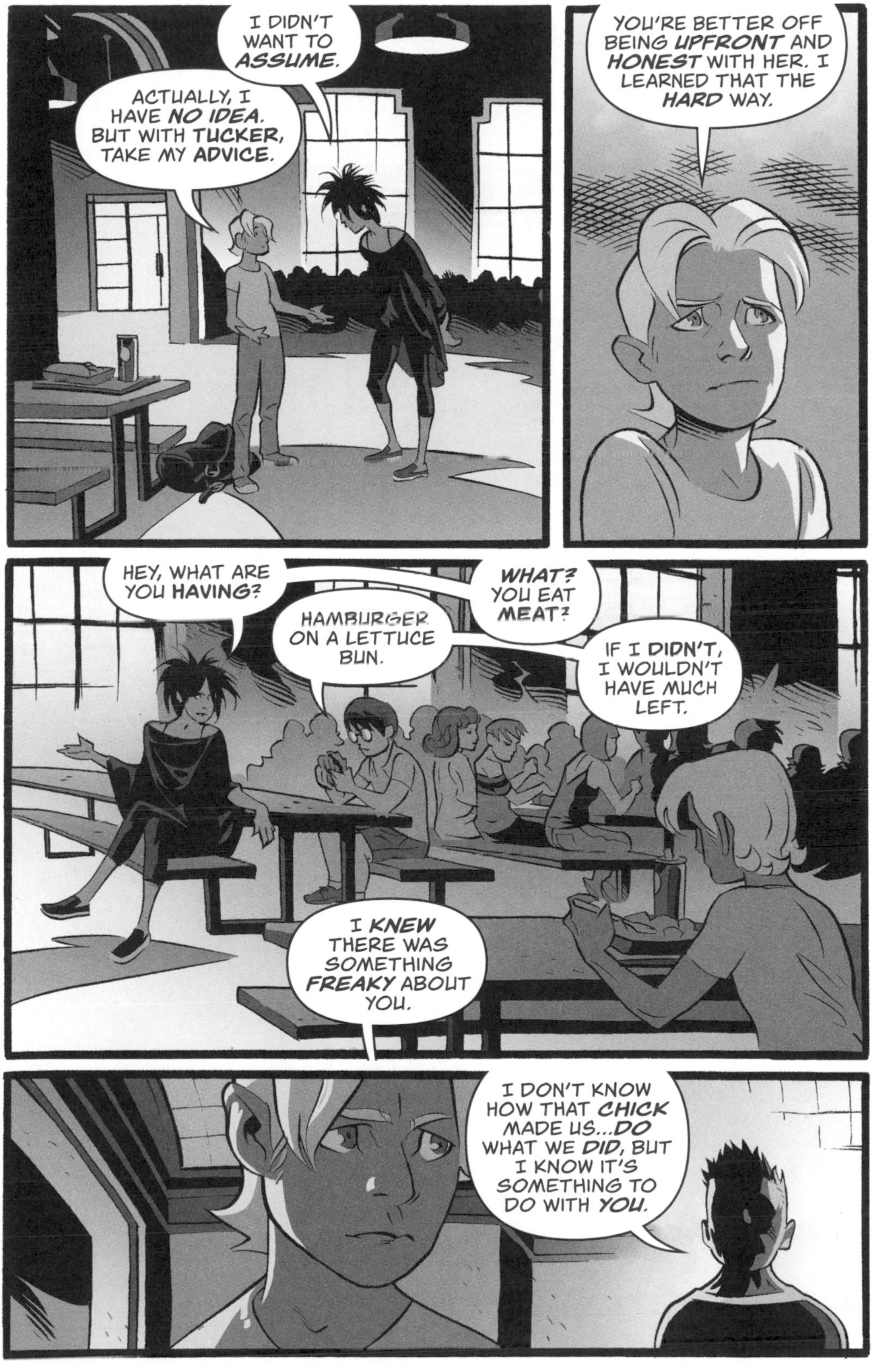
I DIDN'T WANT TO ASSUME.
ACTUALLY, I HAVE NO IDEA. BUT WITH TUCKER, TAKE MY ADVICE.
YOU'RE BETTER OFF BEING UPFRONT AND HONEST WITH HER. I LEARNED THAT THE HARD WAY.
HEY, WHAT ARE YOU HAVING?
HAMBURGER ON A LETTUCE BUN.
WHAT? YOU EAT MEAT?
IF I DIDN'T, I WOULDN'T HAVE MUCH LEFT.
I KNEW THERE WAS SOMETHING FREAKY ABOUT YOU.
I DON'T KNOW HOW THAT CHICK MADE US...DO WHAT WE DID, BUT I KNOW IT'S SOMETHING TO DO WITH YOU.

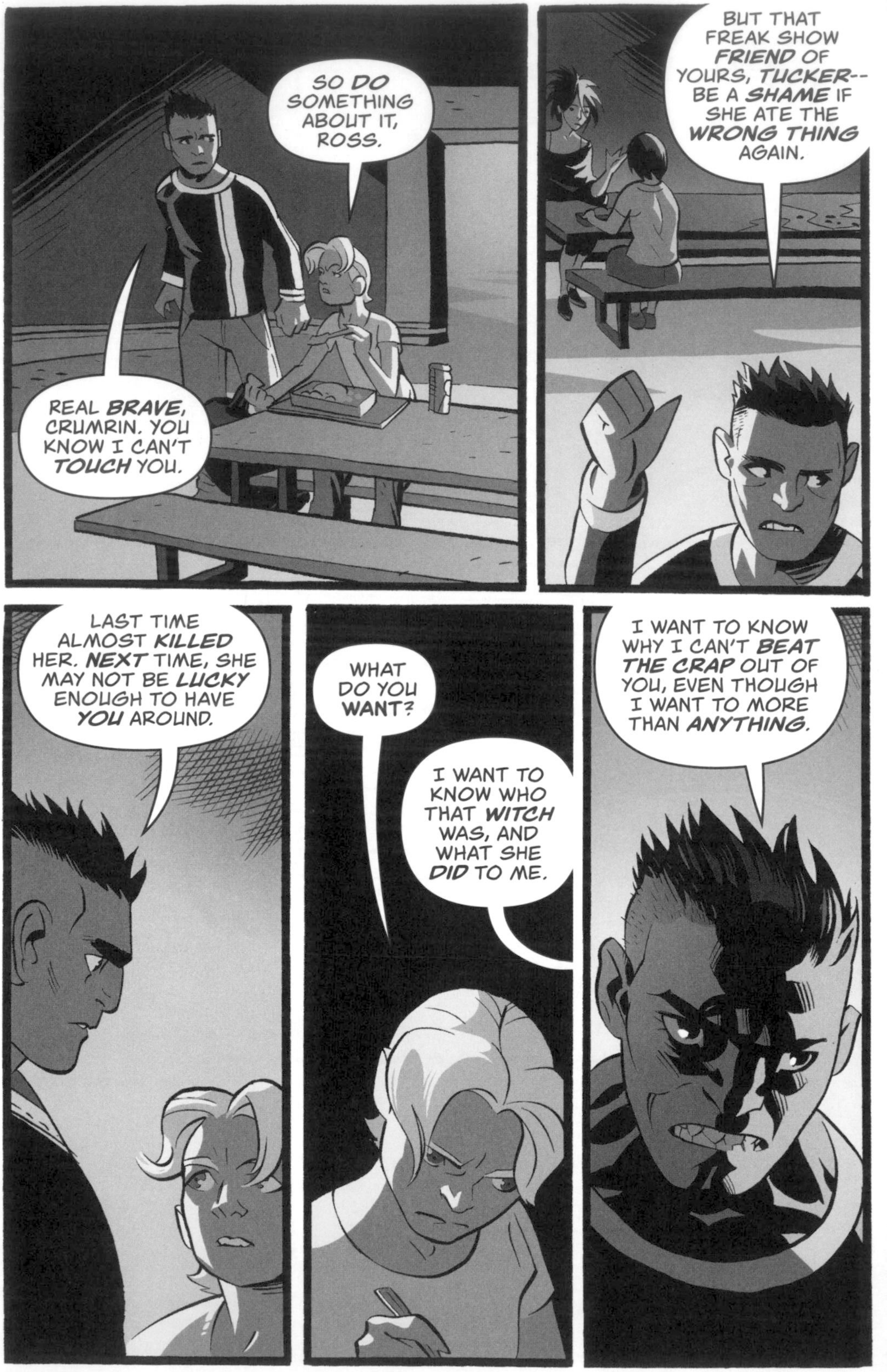
SO DO SOMETHING ABOUT IT, ROSS.
REAL BRAVE, CRUMRIN. YOU KNOW I CAN'T TOUCH YOU.
BUT THAT FREAK SHOW FRIEND OF YOURS, TUCKER-- BE A SHAME IF SHE ATE THE WRONG THING AGAIN.
LAST TIME ALMOST KILLED HER. NEXT TIME, SHE MAY NOT BE LUCKY ENOUGH TO HAVE YOU AROUND.
WHAT DO YOU WANT?
I WANT TO KNOW WHO THAT WITCH WAS, AND WHAT SHE DID TO ME.
I WANT TO KNOW WHY I CAN'T BEAT THE CRAP OUT OF YOU, EVEN THOUGH I WANT TO MORE THAN ANYTHING.

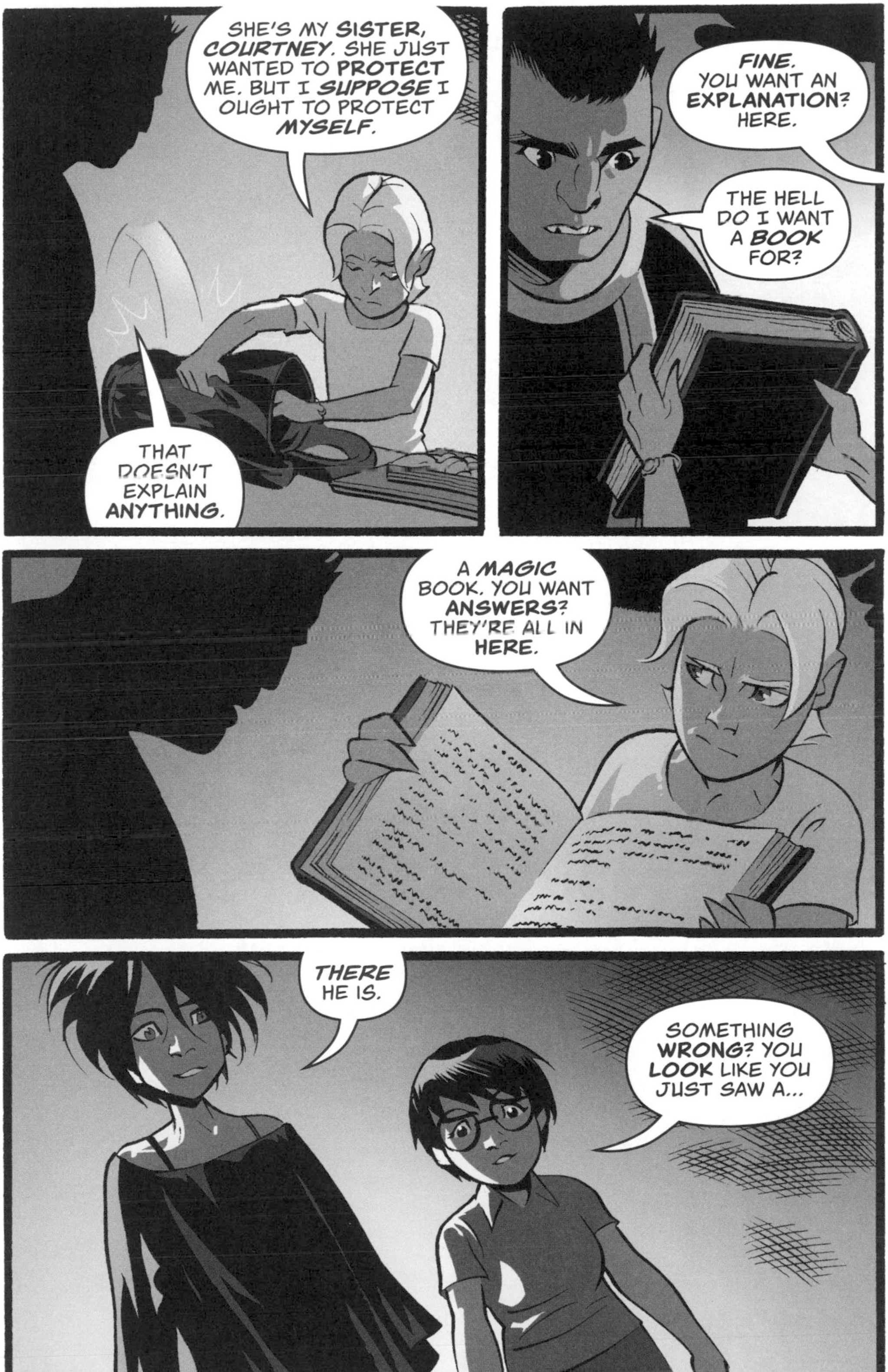
SHE'S MY SISTER, COURTNEY. SHE JUST WANTED TO PROTECT ME. BUT I SUPPOSE I OUGHT TO PROTECT MYSELF.
THAT DOESN'T EXPLAIN ANYTHING.
FINE. YOU WANT AN EXPLANATION? HERE.
THE HELL DO I WANT A BOOK FOR?
A MAGIC BOOK. YOU WANT ANSWERS? THEY'RE ALL IN HERE.
THERE HE IS.
SOMETHING WRONG? YOU LOOK LIKE YOU JUST SAW A...

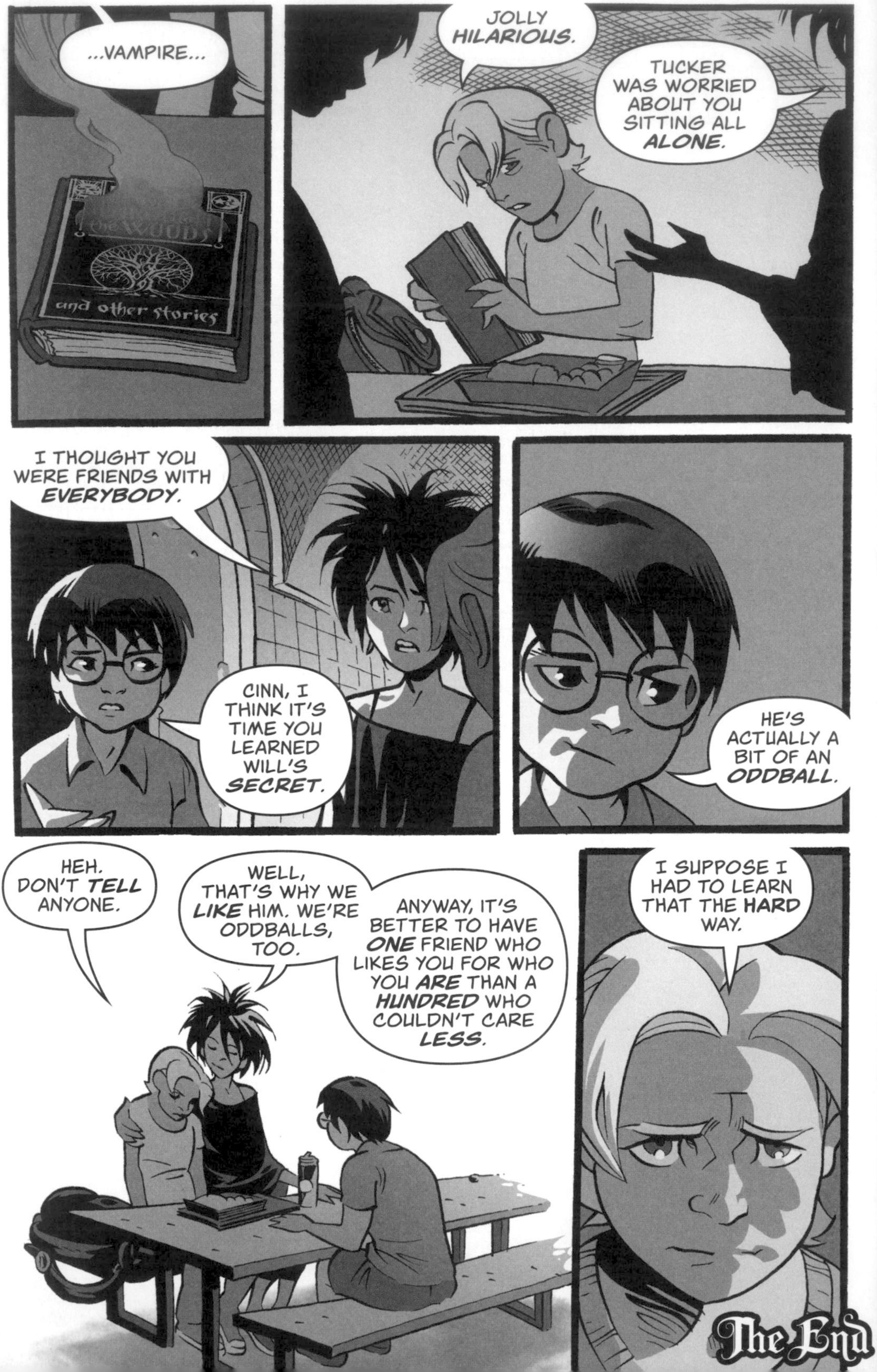
...VAMPIRE...
and other stories
JOLLY HILARIOUS.
TUCKER WAS WORRIED ABOUT YOU SITTING ALL ALONE.
I THOUGHT YOU WERE FRIENDS WITH EVERYBODY.
CINN, I THINK IT'S TIME YOU LEARNED WILL'S SECRET.
HE'S ACTUALLY A BIT OF AN ODDBALL.
HEH. DON'T TELL ANYONE.
WELL, THAT'S WHY WE LIKE HIM. WE'RE ODDBALLS, TOO.
ANYWAY, IT'S BETTER TO HAVE ONE FRIEND WHO LIKES YOU FOR WHO YOU ARE THAN A HUNDRED WHO COULDN'T CARE LESS.
I SUPPOSE I HAD TO LEARN THAT THE HARD WAY.
The End

VOLUME ONE

Sketchbook

Cinnamon:

This was an easy character to design. Dark as midnight and sweet as an unexpected kiss from a high school crush.

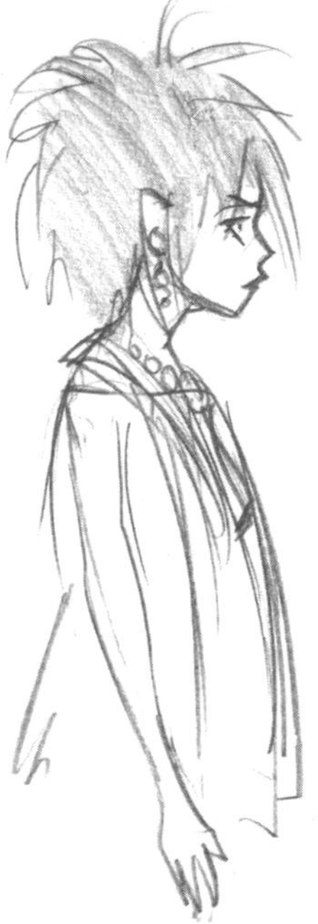

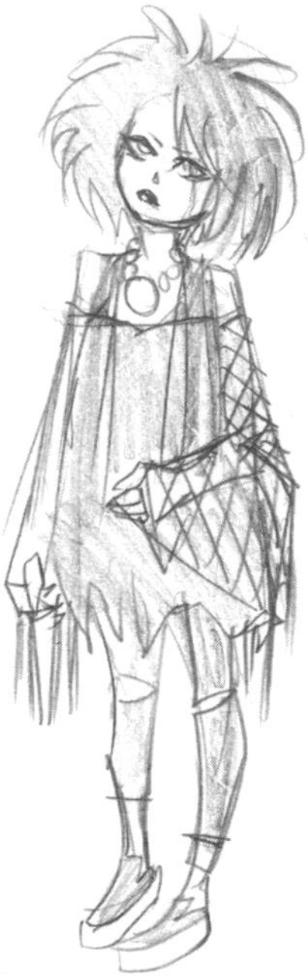

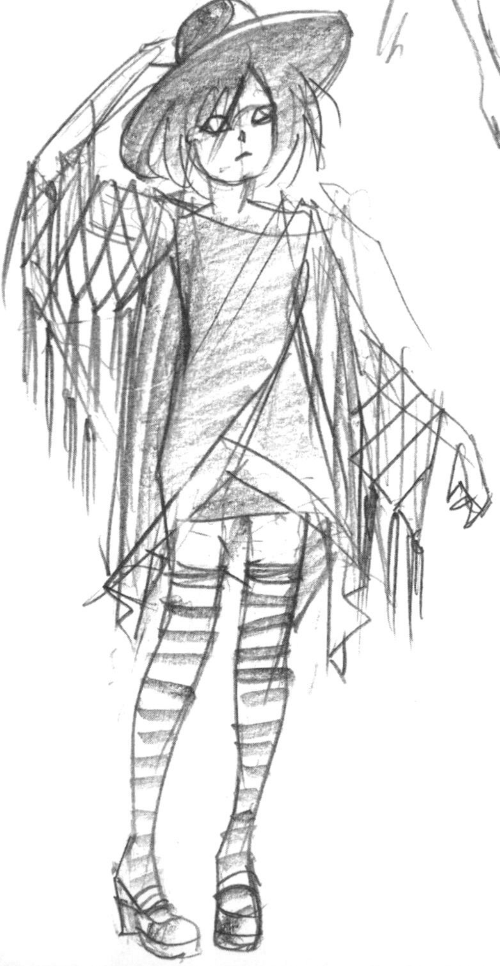

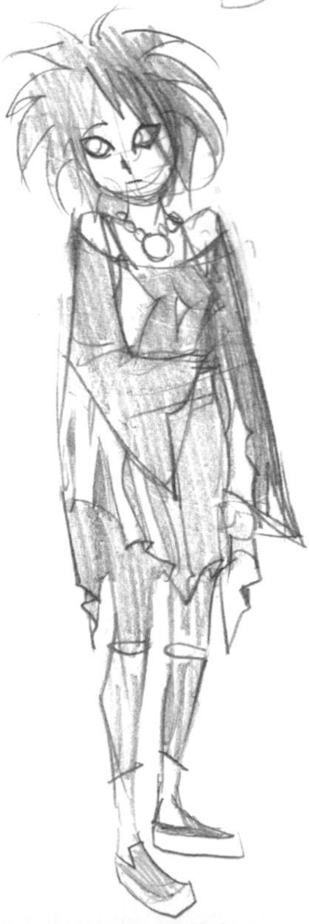

Tucker:

Originally a side character, Tucker grew in importance while my back was turned. I knew she needed a specific look, but not necessarily one that was too deliberate. Maybe one day she'll cultivate a style, like Cinnamon, but right now she's just figuring out how to be herself.

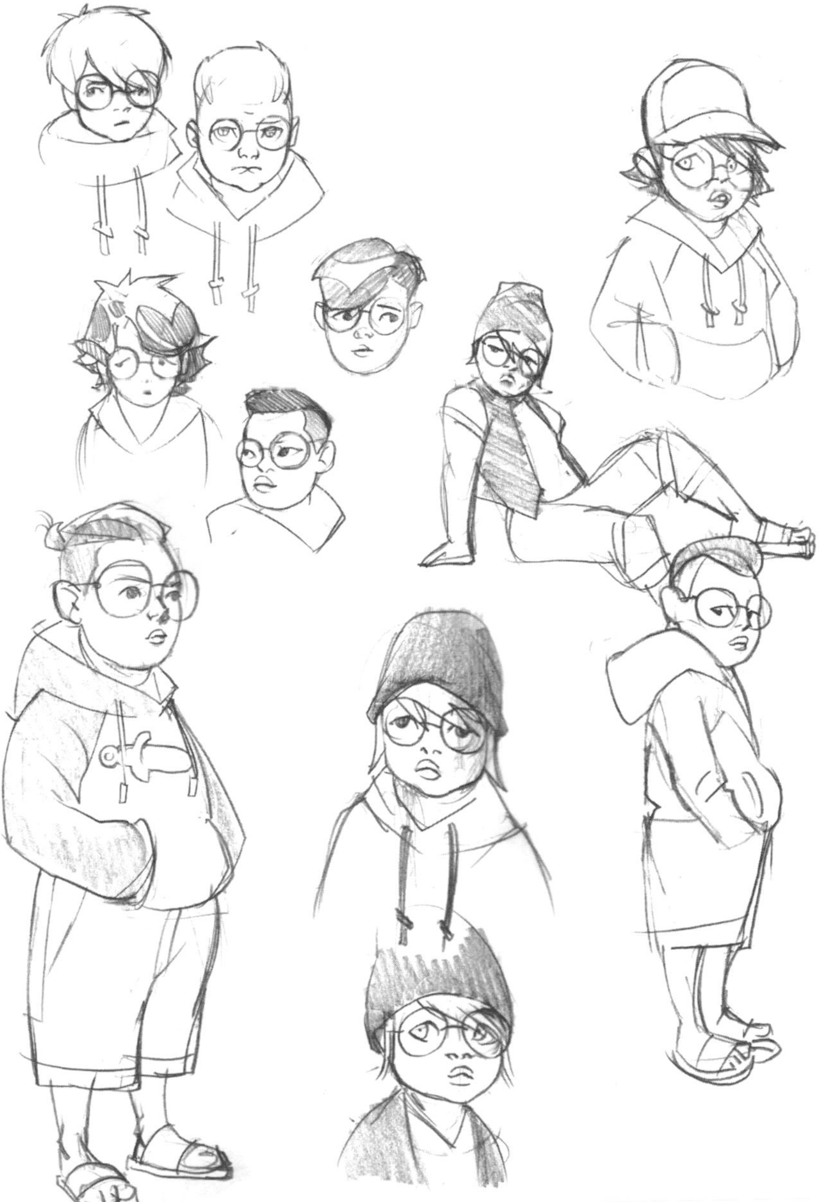

Amy, Joyce, & Johan:

I fear I made these two girls look far too interesting. To be honest, I forgot I'd done this sketch when it came to drawing the book. They'll look more like this in the next one. Maybe they need a mystery adventure, with the clueless boyfriend tagging along behind.

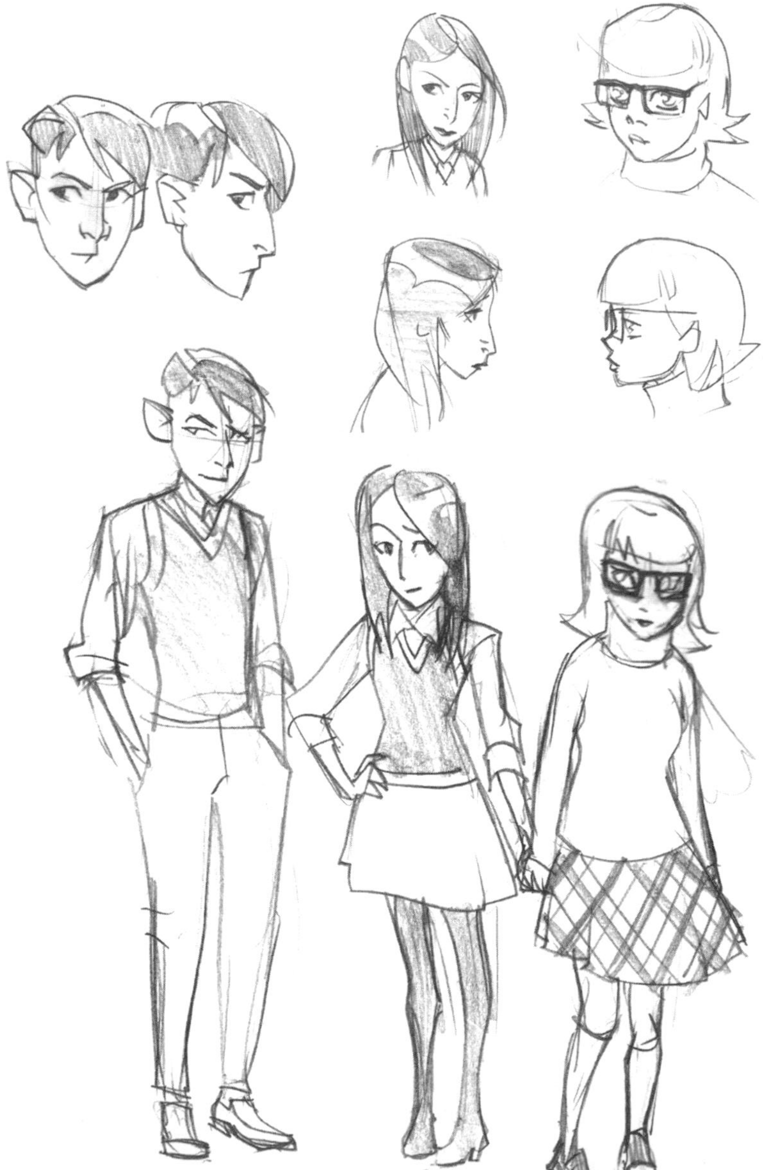

TED NAIFEH

Ted Naifeh first appeared in the independent comics scene in 1999 as the artist for Gloomcookie, co-created with Serena Valentino. After a successful run, Ted decided to strike out on his own, writing and drawing Courtney Crumrin and the Night Things, a spooky middle-grade series about a grumpy little girl and her adventures with her warlock uncle.

Nominated for an Eisner Award for Best Limited Series, Courtney Crumrin's success paved the way for Polly and the Pirates, about a prim and proper girl kidnapped by pirates convinced she was the daughter of their long-lost queen.

Over the next few years, Ted wrote four volumes of Courtney Crumrin, plus a spin off book about her uncle. He also co-created How Loathsome with Tristan Crane, and illustrated two volumes of Death Junior with screenwriter Gary Whitta. For best-selling author Holly Black, he illustrated The Good Neighbors, a three volume graphic novel series published by Scholastic.

Over the last decade, Ted wrote the sequel to Polly and the Pirates, illustrated by Spider-Gwen artist Robbi Rodriquez. To celebrate the tenth anniversary of Courtney Crumrin, he wrote and illustrated the final two volumes of the series. He followed that up with a new teen heroine, Princess Ugg, a barbarian girl going to princess finishing school.

Branching out into more experimental projects, Ted wrote and illustrated Night's Dominion, a genre mash-up of superheroes and fantasy. He also wrote Kriss, a dark hero's journey illustrated by Warren Wucinich, about a young heir to a fallen kingdom whose destiny to restore his birthright may be a fate worse than death.

Ted is currently writing Volume 2 of Kriss, and a new book for Abrams called Witch For Hire, about a problem-solving teen who's never seen without her pointy hat.

Ted lives in San Francisco, because he likes dreary weather.

Courtney Crumrin

By Ted Naifeh